SACRIFICE OF THE BADGE

● PART I - THE CALL

MATTHEW A CONE

Sacrifice of the Badge: The Call
Part I

This is a work of fiction. Names, characters, places, and incidents are either products of the author's imagination or are used fictitiously. Any resemblance to actual persons, living or dead, events, or locales is entirely coincidental.

ISBN: 979-8-9951709-4-5

First Edition
Printed in the United States of America

Published by Foresman Publications
foresmanpublications.com

Foreword

Life can often take someone on many twists and turns. Other times, it is a straight, narrow road that seems to go on forever.

For the LaDue family, it is a little of both. Donnie has served for over twenty years in Law Enforcement and Security. Carol has been an Emergency department nurse. Their worlds intersected, and their family grew to include a son, James.

They are far from ordinary; their life together changed, and the consequences were beyond anything they could have prepared for.

Hold on as you walk through their "Sacrifice of the badge."

Contents

1

The Weight of the Badge

Donnie sat alone in his recliner. There was a stillness that settled over him. He placed the reports on the small table next to him. He reached for his coffee cup. He paused as he looked at his hand. Staring, he saw scars along its top. His mind faded back to the times his hands had held people. People he didn't know. People he had been called to help with one problem or another. He thought of all the years he had spent helping others.

Over the years, Donnie had often considered ending his line of work. After more than twenty years, he had witnessed his share of pain and suffering in countless individuals. He had been called in to help people he didn't even know, sifting through humanity's garbage to find those he could save.

The military had taught him to suppress the feelings most humans carry, yet a spark of human compassion remained in him. Particularly when he witnessed children falling victim to adults, nothing he had seen over the years affected him more than seeing kids in pain. Hurt by those who had a responsibility to protect them.

Donnie spent most of his adult life serving the people around him in the military, law enforcement, or security work. He witnessed many things during those years of service. He knew he wouldn't be able to continue doing what he felt called to do forever.

It had cost him his marriage to the only woman he loved and caused him to miss a lot of time with his son. Donnie knew he had to serve; he had met Carol while working. He continued to regret losing her every day since the divorce.

It had been a few years since his son moved in with him. He and Carol had discussed it; they had agreed it would be best for James. They felt he needed his dad more often, not just on weekends.

It was nice to have James around and to finish his high school years with him. He had always been a great kid, athletic, an amazing student, and a great son. He was more like his mom than Donnie had noticed before. James graduated and went on to college.

James had kept quiet about what he was studying because he wasn't sure his father would approve. He felt that his father never seemed interested in his studies. However, after the divorce, James didn't realize that Donnie thought it best not to pry into his schoolwork.

Donnie had been concerned about pushing him away, just as he had with James' mom. He believed that telling her too much had been unwise and thought it best to let his son make his own choices, just as Donnie's dad had done for him.

One morning, while sitting at the kitchen table with his coffee, James again asked Donnie if they could talk. Donnie sensed it was important and inquired about the topic he wanted to discuss.

James told his father that, while growing up, he had known his dad worked in law enforcement and security. He shared that he had always been fascinated by the idea of following in his father's footsteps and wanted to start his career now that he was old enough. James showed his dad his grades from the last semester at junior college.

Donnie stopped, looked up, and asked him, “Have you spoken to your mom about this?"

He and James's mother were divorced years ago. They held differing views on his career choice. She never wanted to hear about the things he engaged in, yet she could never understand why he was so moody at times.

Carol never expressed her fears about his job. She knew he had to serve. Donnie never understood why she never wanted to know anything about his shift when he returned home. They never talked about it. He would ask Carol how her shift at the hospital had been; she would usually say it was okay and drop the subject. He never understood why and didn’t think to ask her, except that she said she didn’t want to know what happened during his work shifts.

Carol worked as an emergency department nurse when they met. One night, Donnie arrived with a ragged cut on his arm. As she checked his vitals, she asked him the usual questions.

He thought to himself, "She is a beautiful woman," and "she had a smile that lit up the room."

The doctor stitched up his cut and, as he was leaving the hospital, he found Carol and asked for her number. She looked at him for a minute and then told him, “It was 911.” They laughed, and he said, "OK, I understand." However, he also said he would return to ask again.

Over the next several months, Donnie visited the hospital and asked for Carol. They would talk for a few minutes when she wasn’t busy, and then he would leave. He would bring her coffee on occasion. She had mentioned several times that she didn’t date anyone in Emergency Services, including Security.

One night, he followed an ambulance to the hospital because a co-worker had been attacked and severely injured. As he entered, Carol shot him a look of anger and fear. He let her work, but waited for two reasons.

The first reason was that he wanted to talk to her and spend some time with her. The other reason was that he wanted to ask her why she had given him that look when he came in.

Donnie understood Carol's rule, but they had grown close over the past few months. He hoped he could change her mind.

After his coworker was stabilized and waiting to be taken to a room, Carol came out and found Donnie still there. She gave him a half-smile and walked towards the nurse's station to fill out her chart. He stepped towards her and said he was glad to see her. Her head was down as she was writing; she seemed busy. Knowing this, he started to walk away, but she looked up and said, "Sorry about that."

Carol, looked at him, and said, "This is why I have my rule about dating." Donnie responded that it would be okay. Carol explained that she had treated several emergency workers over the years. "How could this be okay? Every time she treated someone in a uniform, she now saw him," she said. Carol told Donnie she liked him, but it would never work out between them.

They stood looking at each other. Donnie could see Carol's determination to maintain the line she had drawn years ago, not to date anyone in Emergency Services.

Carol could see that he was a good man who wanted to get to know her better. They both felt a connection, but she was determined not to give in. Donnie, though respectful of Carol's rules, felt a pull toward her that he had never experienced with anyone before. She was an amazing woman, kind, sweet, yet feisty in a way that made him want to get to know her better.

Donnie felt the words slip out of his mouth, saying he liked her, too. They stood in silence for a few minutes. He told her he understood, muttering that he needed to check on his guy before turning to leave, feeling a bit dejected. Carol noticed his body language and playfully asked if he'd bring her a coffee later. He turned around, smiled, and said he would.

Donnie never gave up trying to win Carol's heart. He was a stubborn man. Carol was unlike the other women he had met over the years; she was quick-witted and could be sharp-tongued at times. He was falling for her and knew they should at least go on a date, but she steadfastly refused to date emergency workers because of the job's dangers.

Eventually, she said yes to a coffee date. A brief time later, they started dating. Carol told him she had given in because she felt sorry for him, and then they both laughed.

Carol, working in the ER, saw the results of fights and gunshot wounds. Fear and pain surrounded her, and she worried about him. His stubbornness could overshadow his caution, especially when children were involved. Carol knew Donnie's protective side all too well.

They realized they liked each other and understood that they were falling in love. After several months of dating and spending time together, they decided to get engaged. One of the agreements they made was never to discuss his work calls. She didn't want to live in fear of that knock on the door at 2 am. Carol was proud of Donnie and what he did; she didn't want to hear about it. She sometimes noticed bruises and scrapes on his hands, but never asked about them, already knowing the answers.

The wedding day arrived a year after their engagement. Carol and Donnie appeared to be the perfect couple for one another. They had planned for several months, and everything worked out beautifully. They had a small ceremony with mostly their close family and a few friends, most of whom were co-workers.

They celebrated into the night and then left for a weekend getaway, as that was all the time he could spare from his job. With summer coming, things would get hectic; they needed him at work. Although disappointed, Carol said she understood. She knew how things were; they had discussed how things could become. She also recognized how life with this man would unfold. One thing she found both impressive and annoying about Donnie was his commitment to his career. She felt similarly about her nursing career.

One night, a few years later, Donnie came home from working late, and Carol was already asleep, or so he thought. He changed out of his uniform and went to the kitchen for some food. When he turned on the light, he found an envelope addressed to him taped to the refrigerator door. He recognized Carol's handwriting on the envelope and opened it. Inside was a handwritten note from Carol that read, "I knew this day would come, and I wanted to tell you sooner, but I needed to be sure." He felt something else in the envelope, and when he pulled it out, it was a copy of a sonogram. He stood and stared at it for a few minutes.

He heard some movement behind him, and when he turned around, Carol was standing there, smiling at him, and asked, "What do you think, Dad?" For one of the first times in their marriage, he was speechless. All he could do was smile, look at Carol, and then back at the sonogram. Carol laughed and asked him again what he thought. He wrapped her in his arms and said he was terrified. But he was also excited.

During the first few years of James's life, Donnie and Carol devoted as much time as possible to him. Donnie even took time off when he fell ill. Carol and Donnie ensured that they didn't discuss any work-related matters in front of their son. They seemed to have a wonderful marriage and family, as far as everyone was concerned.

As the years passed, they stopped discussing work. Donnie became moody, and trivial things would upset him. Carol seemed determined to keep James away from a career in Law Enforcement or security, warning Donnie that if their son pursued those fields, she would never forgive him.

One night, after a rough day at work, Donnie made the mistake of telling her, in detail, what had happened that night. Carol begged him to stop, but years of unspoken feelings had built up inside him, and he spilled more than he should have. Carol told him she was done pretending she was okay with everything. She said she was going to move out and went to bed, slamming the door behind her.

Donnie sat in the recliner and pondered everything until he fell asleep that night. The weeks that followed were tense between them. They hardly spoke, and when they did, it was not like it used to be. Donnie knew they had had problems over their 11 years of marriage, but now it felt icy-cold. He started sleeping in the recliner to give her space, thinking this might blow over. However, his gut told him it wouldn't.

A few weeks later, he came home after another night shift, and the house was quieter than usual. He called out, but no one answered. He thought Carol and James were out somewhere. He went into the bedroom to change out of his uniform, and everything was in order. The room was always clean, and the bed was made. He opened the closet to hang up his uniform, and that is when Donnie noticed her clothes were gone. After changing, he made his way to the kitchen, where a note was waiting for him on the kitchen table. He picked it up with trepidation.

It read, "Donnie, I have stood by you all these years, knowing I would have a uniformed officer show up at the door one night and tell me you had been injured or worse. The reason I never wanted to hear about your work was that knock. If you think I don't love you, you should know I do. I dislike your career and the things you're involved in. I was glad when you left Law Enforcement. However, managing a security company that is so similar to law enforcement has only exacerbated the issue. I am moving with James, and we are moving into an apartment. I wish you the best, and I know you believe in what you are doing, but I don't anymore. I will not keep James from you, but I must be alone. What you told me about your job made me realize it was dangerous, but I never understood just how perilous it was. I can't sit and wait for that knock at our door any longer. I love you and always will, but I can no longer stay with you. Carol."

He sat there for a long time, rereading the note, knowing Carol didn't like what he did for work, but he thought she still supported him. He laid the letter on the table as he walked through the house. She was gone, having taken their son with her. She left the address of her new place next to the letter. He knew the area where she had moved, well. Donnie thought it was not a bad place to raise their son.

She wasn't wrong about the company. It was about the size of a small police department: 50 armed security officers who covered industrial and construction sites. There were also large apartment complexes and many other properties. The patrol staff covered even more locations around the clock. Officers worked in bars and retail stores, secured large venues and provided security for individuals, some in plainclothes and others in uniform. All of which he manages. The owner knew Donnie's background, yet he still placed him in an entry-level position. He worked his way up to management. He could honestly see her point.

Carol filed for divorce a few months after leaving. They didn't fight over anything, so it was a smooth transition for their son. They decided that Donnie should stay in the house where he had been living alone since she moved out. Neither Carol nor Donnie remarried.

A few years later, James returned to live with his father. Donnie and Carol decided it would be best for him to stay there for a while. James was always busy with school and work. When he asked to hear about his dad's job, he would respond, "Maybe another time." He didn't want a repeat of the situation with Carol.

James was proud of his dad and everything he did for people, and he had always wanted to hear about his dad's experiences. He had asked his dad a few times over the years to tell him some stories.

James returned to live with Donnie during his junior year of high school. He secured a job at a large retailer and maintained his grades. He was an amazing kid overall. He had always believed his son was smarter than he was, and he knew his son would excel in college.

After high school, James went to the local college. Even as he worked, Donnie knew he would always prioritize school. Unbeknownst to him at the time, James was taking Criminology classes. He was studying to begin a career in law enforcement. He had earned honors in all his classes.

One afternoon, Donnie spoke with James and said, "I know you've asked me to tell you about my career, son, but I've always hesitated to share most of the things I've seen and done over the years. Your mom never wanted to hear about them, so I kept them from you all."

"Dad," James started nervously, "there is something I need to tell you." His dad could tell he was hesitant to say what he was about to say. He continued, "I applied for an open position with the Sheriff's Department. I remember hearing you and Mom talk once about your years in law enforcement, and I want to follow in your footsteps."

His mind raced as James spoke. He looked at his grown son, but could only see a 10-year-old kid with messy hair. The thought of him wearing a badge made Donnie feel both proud and fearful. He had assumed his son would choose something other than joining law enforcement.

After taking a few minutes to absorb what James just told him, he asked, "Have you spoken to your mom about this decision?" He said he would, when the time was right. Donnie told him there may never be a right time.

He recalled what Carol had said and what she had written in the letter years ago, when she left, taking James with her.

Donnie decided it was time to discuss some aspects of law enforcement. "James," he began, but paused, trying to find the right words to use, "there have been some dangerous situations I went through. I was lucky to have survived some experiences. Other things I tried hard to forget, but they remained in my mind, as if they were still fresh in my memory. I have had trouble sleeping on some nights because the memories show up in my dreams."

He continued, "Now that you are older and want to follow in my footsteps, I need you to hear about those things, to help you make an informed decision. I owe you that, and with the way things are now, you will face worse situations from the start of your career, situations that took me years to face and overcome. Are you ready to hear about them?"

He responded, "I am ready, Dad." His eyes held a look of amazement as he gazed at his dad; he thought he knew what his dad did, but had never heard him speak about it like this before. James believed he was finally ready to hear about things. At least, Donnie hoped he was.

Sitting at the kitchen table with him, Donnie watched James as he had looked at many people before, searching for any signs of whether he was listening. He observed James's body language to gauge his reaction to everything. Knowing that some of the stories he was about to tell would sound unbelievable, they were real and deserved to be shared. His mother never wanted to know, and he was unsure whether she would want him to tell James. But James was old enough to hear about what Donnie had been through; some things were too funny not to share. Some stories might shock him, but James was a tough kid and would understand what was about to be revealed.

The talk would have to wait until they had more time. Donnie needed to leave for work, and so did James.

2

The Oath of the Badge

Donnie had a couple of days off. Although he was still on call, he was relaxing in the recliner, reviewing some paperwork, when James came home from work. Upon seeing his dad, James entered and asked if he wanted to share a story.

He put the paperwork down and looked at James, smiling as he thought about his son's excitement in hearing the stories. He wondered when his little son had become a man and why he had missed it.

Donnie got up and poured himself another cup of coffee, asking James if he wanted one as well. James replied that he did. Donnie poured one for James and returned to the living room.

Donnie had been reflecting on what Carol had shared with him years ago about his career choice. Although it was never an argument between them, there had been a long silence about Donnie's decisions.

James was a blend of both Carol and him. He had a fire inside him that Donnie could see. He wanted to serve the public. Both Carol and Donnie shared this desire, but they had taken different paths to achieve it. Carol chose the healing path; he chose to serve and protect.

Donnie had always known that Carol was more worried about him encountering a situation he couldn't get himself out of one day. She didn't want a knock at the door at 2 am notifying her that he was in the hospital fighting for his life. He was willing to do whatever it took to ensure others were safe, always mindful of the necessity to return home every night to his little family. However, he was also prepared to do what needed to be done.

Carol once told Donnie that she knew he was willing to take all the risks to keep others safe, and that scared her. She had always loved him, but being married to him stressed her out because of the chance that it might not work out. Over time, that stress became an increasingly heavy burden. Society had changed so much; she saw it every day at the hospital. Working in the emergency room, she observed the results of those changes. She also noticed how people reacted to uniforms, whether worn by law enforcement or security personnel. The lack of trust had grown over the years.

Donnie had always known that, even though they loved each other deeply, their worlds sometimes felt miles apart. She was a natural healer and wanted him to be safe; Donnie wanted everyone else to be safe. Carol had struggled to balance the love she had for him with the fear of losing him.

Donnie looked at James as he handed him his coffee; a childlike wonder shimmered in his eyes. He felt a thrill at the prospect of embarking on this new path he wanted to explore. He embodied both Carol's desire to heal and his wish to keep others safe. This combination could benefit law enforcement, but he would soon realize that the life he was choosing would change him.

As he sat down again, he saw James looking at him while sipping the coffee. Donnie wasn't sure how to start the conversation with him. Most people entering law enforcement or security work want to hear every heroic story they can. Usually, he would share those. Yet, this is his son, and he felt he needed to convey the good, the bad, and the ugly of choosing this career path. It isn't all just riding in to save the day; there is so much more to it.

After taking a sip of the hot coffee and setting the cup down, he began by reciting the following:

"I, Donald James LaDue, do solemnly swear that I will support and defend the Constitution of the United States against all enemies, foreign and domestic; that I will bear true faith and allegiance to the same; and that I will obey the orders of the President of the United States and the Constitution of the United States." Donnie finished reciting and sat in silence for a few minutes.

He watched James as he recited the oath he had always taken so seriously. He knew that when he spoke those words, they meant something to him. They had changed him. He was just like his son when he took the oath for the first time: ready to take on the world and defend others, never fully understanding what that truly meant, but felt he needed to.

Donnie continued speaking. "I took that oath twice in my life. Once for the Military and once for Law Enforcement. An Oath that has no expiration date to me and millions of others. The same oath you will take.

It is a serious oath, one that requires men and women to lay their lives on the line for people they don't even know but are willing to do so because they believe it is the right thing to do," Donnie told him.

"I took it as a young man," he started again. "With eyes wide open, I was ready to do my part to help this country and the people stay safe. I got scared at times, but I knew many wouldn't do what we were doing" Donnie paused.

Continuing, "I hope that makes sense to you, son. After over two decades of working within the criminal justice system, the things that have happened will seem unreal to most; yet, knowing it firsthand, it has been a reality every day of my life."

Donnie paused to look at James and see if he was following his dad's advice. He wanted James to fully understand what he was getting into. James lowered his cup to his left leg and sat quietly, listening.

He continued, "I have been involved in responding to calls for service for so long that it takes something unusual to shock me. I used to wonder how someone could do what they did, but now it just makes some twisted sense to me," he said.

He continued, "there have been good, bad, and ugly things that I have seen or had to deal with in the time I have been the one people called to help them. Someone who had to make decisions based on what I saw in front of me, and then write it out so the attorneys can fight it out, and a judge or jury will judge them or me."

Donnie began with the reality of things before he could tell stories about what he had seen and experienced. He told James that there was a lot of paperwork involved, and even though James was a great writer, it felt like writing school papers; it was simply a matter of presenting the facts of what happened. There was nothing creative about it, and the sheer volume of paperwork became a burden. Additionally, public opinion on the Department's or company's mandates has become more significant, and considerable involvement in this work is evident.

He continued, “Have I ever stepped over the line before? Some would say I have, but I don’t think so. If I did, it was necessary. There are times when the rules don’t apply to a particular situation. And you choose how to deal with the situation in the moment. Others are looking at you to keep them safe. Emotions are running high, and fear plays a significant role in everything happening. Life decisions are sometimes made in a split second, and there is no going back once they are made. Mistakes are made, but we hope we have learned from them. Don’t let your ego get in the way. Remember, son, there is always an opportunity to gain experience, to help us do things better, quicker, and safer.”

Donnie paused, reflecting on his years in Law Enforcement and Security. Donnie sat and thought about the things he had seen. Continuing to speak, “there is always a learning curve, especially now with so many phones out there watching everything you do. The News usually shows only a few seconds of the situation to fit its narrative. And it seems the one in the uniform is always wrong.”

He looked at James and asked him if he understood. James took a drink of his coffee before responding. “Dad, you know I've watched you my whole life, and just today I realized you and I are more alike than I thought. I can hear the heart you have for others, but I also hear the fear in your voice. Is that because I want to follow in your footsteps, or is it something else?” James asked.

Donnie knew the answer to that question. While he was concerned about James entering Law Enforcement, he also recognized that his son was a lot like him. It reminded Donnie of the day he came home and told his parents he had enlisted in the Military.

Donnie could see it. Even now. Their family had been in the military for generations. He felt the call and decided it was time for him to join. At

18 years old, he thought it was time to do what so many others had done before him: defend against all "enemies, foreign and domestic." He told his dad about his decision.

Donnie's dad sat him down for a conversation. His dad knew he couldn't back out of his enlistment, he wanted to share his military experiences with him. Determined, he didn't listen to his dad, as he was always stubborn; his dad knew that too. Donnie saw his father looking at him, and what his father said still lingers in his mind today.

"Donnie," his father had started, "Please be aware that, although I would prefer you not to go, I will support you during your time of service. All I ask is that you talk to your mother and tell her you love her every day until you leave. Then, every time you speak to her while you are away, you tell her you love her. Will you do that for her and yourself?" Donnie had agreed, even though he was confused at the time.

Donnie's father went on to discuss more before he concluded the conversation. Donnie's mom could be heard in the other room. He remembered the fear he felt about telling his mom he had joined the military, but he stood and went to tell her, to remind her of his love for her.

Donnie's mind turned back to James' question. Donnie knew he needed to answer James's question, but he was also unsure how to respond. He wanted to take some time to think about his answer. James had a knack for putting his dad on the spot with his questions, and this one was particularly significant.

Did he fear losing his son? Yes, but he also recognized the risk of losing him just by driving to work. He wanted to express his fear in a way that conveyed support rather than judgment. He recognized the importance of having someone to talk to about their daily experiences, which helped law enforcement officers decompress. They needed not only colleagues but also family members who would listen. Donnie thought as they sat together.

He could tell James was waiting for his dad to answer him. He started with, "There you go again, asking your questions like you have since you were a little kid." He paused and saw a smile on James' face. He began again, "Son, it's not so much fear as it is apprehension about the prospect. You have both your mom's healing nature and my desire to defend the defenseless. I believe those will clash as time and the job begin to merge. You are not a weak person, so please keep that in mind."

"I was never able to speak to your mom about most of what I'm about to tell you, so I had a hard time getting past some of it. Some things are still with me today. But I will always respect your need for privacy to work through things. Please know that I am here to listen and offer support. I will not judge your experiences and will only provide advice when you ask," Donnie said. Donnie paused for a moment.

Donnie said he wanted to share something with James. His father had once told him, before he went into the military, "James, let me share some words. I remember your grandpa telling me after I told him I had enlisted in the military. He said this to me: "I know there is a desire to serve and a need to protect others. It is who you have always been. I want you to understand that there will come a day, if you see combat, you will watch other young men die, and it might even be you. Please be assured that although I would prefer you not to go, I will support you throughout your service." As Donnie finished, he fell silent.

He paused to watch his son. James sat silently, aware that he was thinking about everything he had just heard. Donnie had a little more to tell him. "Son," he continued, "your grandpa had more to say to me that day. The mothers, fathers, sweethearts, wives, or husbands of military personnel and Law Enforcement also sacrifice when their loved ones join the military or enter law enforcement. For the mothers and fathers, it is their child who is gone, and they fear their child will never come back to them. Sweethearts, wives, or husbands fear the one they may lose is the one they love."

Donnie continued, "Of all the things I ever heard your grandpa say or try to teach me, the last part stuck with me the most," he told James. "Life for many a family during war and here at home was never the same after a funeral. Lying a child beneath the ground is the one thing a parent never wants to experience. We as warriors don't think of that in the middle of a fight; we do what we have been trained to do."

"Have you discussed your decision to pursue a career in law enforcement with your mom?" Donnie asked.

"I know it is time you understood why your mom and I split," he told James. He explained how they met and what Carol had communicated to him from the beginning. Donnie had never thrown away the letter Carol wrote to him as she left with their son. He pulled it out and handed it to James to read.

As James opened the letter, he looked up at his dad for a second before reading what his mom had written. As James read the words, his mind went back to the move. The words, written by his mom, caused pain in his heart. But as he read the letter, he understood things a bit more.

James remembered their move and had felt confused about how it happened. As a kid, he accepted his parents' actions, but he always had questions about why things happened.

James finished reading the letter. He finally understood why neither of his parents dated nor remarried. He looked up from the letter and studied his dad's face. For the first time in his life, he saw genuine sadness on his father's face. His dad's beard was gray now. As James grew up, he noticed his dad's facial hair turning from brown and red to gray, and in that moment, he also recognized his own age. There were lines on his forehead and around his eyes.

"Dad," James started, and his voice was now a bit strained. "Mom never told me why you guys split. It was rough on her. I heard her crying at night, even though she never knew I had. It was all because of the possibility of you getting hurt or killed, and someone knocking on our door?"

He looked at his son, saw the look on his face, and said, "Have you told your mom yet?" Pointing at the letter in his hand, he continued, "That letter was the reason why I asked you that question. The fear your mom had about me will be a thousand times greater with you. You owe her that." As Donnie finished, he saw that his son realized he needed to tell his mom.

James looked at his dad and said his mom still asks about him every time they are together. James understood better why she did. He told his dad that he now understood both of them better. They still had love for each other, yet the fear had kept her away.

"I will talk with her today about my decision. Today seems like the right time," James said, looking back at the letter and then at his dad again.

As he sat there, silence filled the room for a few minutes between them. James knew his dad had a way of encouraging him while also advising him on various matters they discussed. He understood that his dad was concerned and wanted to know his thoughts. Now he understood why.

Donnie broke the silence between them. He told James, "It will be easier on her if you tell her before some background investigator calls her or she opens a letter from the department asking about her only son." James nodded at that.

Donnie knew Carol would never yell at James about his decision, but she would again live with her fear from the years they had been a family. He also understood that she would call him about it, which would lead to a lengthy conversation. He realized Carol would not like it and would ask him how hard he had tried to talk James out of it. Silence fell on the room again.

James contemplated how to approach his mom with the information she needed to hear. He never wanted to disappoint either of his parents, knowing they loved him and supported all his decisions. He wondered if she would support this one.

They sat and sipped their coffee for a while. Donnie got up, poured a refill, and brought it back to James. The silence gave them both time to think.

Donnie sat contemplating how the phone call with Carol would unfold after she learned about what James wanted to do. He understood her concern and fear that James would follow in his footsteps by choosing a career in law enforcement.

Across the room, James was trying to rehearse what he would say to his mom. He wondered how she would react, whether she would be angry at him, at his dad, or both.

James knew his mom was proud of everything he had accomplished growing up and only wanted a bright future for him. He could feel a knot growing in his stomach as he thought about the conversation he needed to have with her.

As the two of them sat thinking their thoughts, they sipped their coffee. And the silence covered them.

3

The Reality of the Badge

Breaking the silence in the room, Donnie told James he would share more of his experiences. James smiled, aware it was going to be a long night.

Donnie started by going back years. He began with, "I grew up watching Cop shows on television and thinking that it was amazing how they could solve every crime they faced within an hour. They were so professional that everyone listened. How could they catch the villain and put them behind bars? None of it seemed to affect them personally; they always seemed superhuman." James looked like that ten-year-old again, eagerly anticipating the stories his dad would tell him.

"As a child, that was what I wanted to be. My friends wanted to be sports heroes or space heroes. I wanted to be a crime-fighting hero. It seemed to me that I could help people by wearing a uniform and a badge, driving around in a car with lights and a siren, and racing to help someone in need. That I could save the day!" That made James laugh: imagining his dad in a cape made it even funnier.

"James," he said, "In the beginning, that was what it felt like. But over time, I realized I could only apply a Band-Aid to society's broader problems. Victims of crime want you to solve everything, just like the TV shows do. Most didn't understand that real life was not TV."

Donnie continued, "Had I become numb to it all? Yes, I had. However, I will share with you highlights of the good, the bad, and the ugly of my experiences. Life is stranger than fiction, and what happens out there is real. They might make you laugh or cause you to gasp; others may give you nightmares or shock you with how ugly one person can be to another."

Donnie began by saying, "I started my career working in private security in the small town where I grew up in California. It was a farming town with large dairy farms surrounding us. The farmers could grow anything. We were a mixed group of people, and people got along when I was growing up."

He continued explaining, "As Private security, we worked at stores, weddings, and large events. This story takes place at a large dance."

"It was one of the first events I worked after starting with the security company. I was in my early twenties, about twenty-two. There were seven security employees among a few thousand people. I was positioned close to the stage area, my back against the wall. I was armed with a single pair of cuffs and nothing else. We had no radios and no way to call for help if anything went wrong. But I was just cocky enough to think I could manage anything, especially since I had received only about an hour of training."

James could see that his dad was remembering the whole thing. Donnie continued with a smile. "The event was going well. People dancing and drinking, everyone looked like they were having a fun time. Then it happened. A fight broke out."

Donnie looked as if he were reliving it as he spoke to James. His hands pointed out the scene to James. "There was a woman I saw who walked up to a table with a group of about eight people sitting there. The woman appeared to be yelling at someone at the table. I couldn't hear anything because of the loud Mariachi music playing. I watched what was happening, trying to make sense of it." Donnie paused.

"The woman's arms were moving as if she were flying away, but then she leaned forward and punched a guy at the table in the face. She then grabbed the woman next to him, pulled her up by her hair, and took her away from the table. Next thing I knew, they were fighting." Donnie said.

Donnie looked at James. "Son, when you think everything is okay, and people are okay, in that second, you will need to snap back into reality, because things can turn in a heartbeat. Always be ready for anything and everything. Never become complacent while working. I have always hated it when the news claimed it was a routine traffic stop. There's never anything routine."

Again, he continued, "I tried to get the attention of the other security, but no one came to help. I had to do something. I started moving towards the fight, then realized that a group of men were fighting as well as a couple more women."

Donnie paused, looked at James. He continued. "Slipping and sliding on the wet concrete floor, I tried to get to them. However, they began moving towards the stage, where the band was still playing. I looked up and saw the keyboard player's face. Being on the front corner of the stage, his mouth was wide open, and his eyes looked like they were even wider open. He looked shocked and scared. But he kept playing on the keyboard. Then I looked back at the group; they were still fighting, and a couple more women had joined the men. I kept trying to get to them. Glancing back up at the keyboard player, I saw that he was stepping back from the fight, still stretching his arms out in front of him and keeping up his playing on the keyboard. I remember smiling at what he was doing." Donnie told James.

He saw the look on James' face, Donnie continued, "The keyboard player had moved so far from his keyboard that he was stretching to continue playing the song. Think of someone lying on the floor and stretching their fingers to the ends to play the keyboard. That is what was happening."

He paused and allowed his son to ponder the scene he had just described. He knew James was reflecting on what he had just shared. He could sense that James was arranging everyone in their respective places. A smile was beginning to form on James's face.

He continued, "As I got closer to the group fighting, they just stopped and started dancing. The fight was over almost as fast as it started. The woman who started it all walked away with a handful of hair as a trophy. The poor keyboard player finally moved back towards the keyboard; he looked relieved, smiling again." Donnie said.

James put his hand up towards his dad. "Wait, they just stopped fighting and started dancing? So, they were only play-fighting?" he asked.

"They had been fighting, throwing punches at each other. The original woman and the one she had grabbed by the hair were fighting," he assured his son, "it was a real fight." Donnie paused again, letting it all sink in as James thought about the whole thing.

"Finally, a couple more security personnel arrived where I was. I was laughing when they reached me, yet they looked at me as if I were crazy. When I explained to them what had happened and what the keyboard player had done, they both stared at me." Donnie paused, looked at his son, and smiled at the shocked expression on his face.

"It was all so funny; the fight abruptly stopped, and they started dancing. Everything the keyboard player did was to stay safe, but he didn't stop playing. The whole thing was amusing, but the other security team members didn't think so," Donnie said with a chuckle.

Donnie saw a smile on James's face. He waited for him to react to what he just told him. Donnie knew he was envisioning the whole scenario in his mind, just as he had since he was a little guy.

James looked at the floor for a moment, then returned his gaze to his dad and started laughing. Amid his laughter, he asked why the other Security didn't find it funny. James remarked that it was hilarious and asked whether it was true. This made Donnie chuckle as he replied, "Yes, son, it's true."

He moved on to another story. He began to explain that weddings are significant occasions for the bride and groom, as well as for their families and friends. Receptions typically include a feast, dedications, and dancing. The last thing anyone wants to do is ruin it for the bride, or so one would think.

Donnie began again, "As a Security employee, I would work at weddings from time to time. One of the wedding receptions I worked at didn't end well for one guy." Donnie told him.

As Donnie began to speak, James leaned toward his father. One thing he knew was that if his dad was talking, it was essential to listen. His dad didn't talk much; when he did, there was something about the way he spoke to others. Always calm, he never lost his temper, even when others did; his dad remained quiet.

James couldn't remember ever seeing his dad angry. He knew there had to be times when he did, but not in front of him. It was as if he would hide his emotions, only to release them later. James once asked his dad if he ever got angry; his dad replied that he did, but had learned to control it. He went even further and told him that an explosion wouldn't resolve or correct the issue.

It was also the way Donnie told a story that made people stop and listen. The pauses he used enhanced the timing of his words, emphasizing his points, almost like a punchline to the topic. It always drew James and his friends into the story or subject. He thought his dad would have made a great teacher if he had ever had the opportunity.

His dad could tell that James was lost in his thoughts, so he paused until he returned to the present moment. When he did, he continued.

Donnie began, "I was working with another Security employee, and we were posted outside checking the invitations of everyone. During the reception, a man approached us and said we were needed inside because of a problem. When we asked what was needed, he said we needed to come inside and see for ourselves. When we entered the interior door, a guy was lying on the floor in a pool of blood, not moving." Pausing to ensure James understood what he was telling him, then continued.

"After we checked on him, they all said they would take him home. He was the groom's cousin and got a little too handsy with the bride. The groom stepped up and hit him. He dropped like a rag and hit his head. Someone brought a towel to wrap his head up as they dragged him out. A couple of the older women quickly cleaned up the mess. After everyone had settled down, the party started again, and our shift was over. As we were leaving, the groom and bride came out and apologized to us on behalf of their family member. I have always wondered if he was ever allowed at family gatherings again."

James was nodding as his dad spoke. After a couple of minutes, he said, "I would not want to be the person who ruined a wedding for a bride. She would never forget or forgive that person." Donnie smiled and nodded.

Throughout the years, he had seen various things. Some things stuck with him, while others became so commonplace that he attended to what needed to be done and moved on.

Learning that some people couldn't manage their alcohol and created issues for themselves and others. Others were never happy, no matter their situation. Some hate cops and security personnel, who may want to fight. It doesn't matter what you said; they believed they would win until they didn't.

Donnie learned that the calmer he stayed, the more confused those around him became. His refusal to reveal his feelings, with a blank look on his face, made them second-guess what they were planning to do. If they couldn't read his facial expressions, they weren't sure if he was angry or scared.

No matter what they were saying. Whether they made threats or not, either against him, a significant other, or kids, as long as his face remained blank, most walked away. Those who hadn't learned that he didn't back down often learned the hard way. Donnie had tried to avoid physical altercations, but he would defend himself or others if necessary. James knew his dad preferred not to fight.

"James, do you remember hearing about how I met your mom?" James said he did, recalling the ER visit his dad made when he met his mom. Donnie continued, "The cut I got happened in a bar. We were called to a fight; four guys were fighting when we arrived. We separated two of them and cuffed them. The other two were still fighting, and one grabbed a broken bottle and swung at the other guy as I reached for him, and I got cut. He hit the ground moments later."

"I went to the hospital after the medics had arrived and cleared me to drive," he said. The medics knew he didn't want to ride with them. They had responded to a couple of other things and checked him out before.

"When I arrived at the ER, I made sure to clear and secure my weapon. I took off my work belt and left it in the vehicle. As I entered, a beautiful nurse looked up, saw the blood-soaked wrap around my arm, and came towards me quickly. That was all it took, just one look at your mom. She took me to an exam room and called in the doctor. I am not sure she even noticed much about me other than the bloody wrap, but I noticed her." Donnie told James.

James smiled at his dad while he reminisced about that first meeting. He could tell his dad enjoyed the memory. His voice changed as he spoke, almost in a hushed tone, recalling that special moment. James could sense that his dad still loved his mom.

Donnie looked up at James and could see the smile on his son's face. Donnie took a sip of coffee to pause in that memory. He continued, "After the doctor stitched me up, I had to ask for your mom's number. I will never forget her response: "My number is 911," and she laughed at me. I burst out laughing too and said, "Okay, but I'll be back. I asked her if she drank coffee, and she said she did. I went right then and found a coffee shop open and bought her a coffee and brought it to her."

"Son," he continued, "it took months before she would even agree to meet me for a cup of coffee. She had a rule even then: she never dated anyone who worked in Law Enforcement, Security, or emergency services. I just knew she was the one for me. It took forever for her to say yes to marrying me, but it was worth it because you came along a few years later, and I am glad you are my son."

Donnie glanced at the clock and decided it was time to call it a night. He told James there was more to share, but they needed some sleep. He asked James if they could talk again tomorrow, and James agreed. Donnie got up and headed to bed.

James sat on the couch, reflecting on his dad. He knew there were things he might never share with him, and he was concerned about his decision to pursue a career in law enforcement. Regardless of how his dad felt, James understood he was drawn to serving and protecting.

James thought about how he would tell his mom. He knew she would be worried, but hoped she would understand. "Have you told your mom?" kept coming to his mind. He sat there trying to rehearse what he would say to her.

4

The Cost of the Badge

When James came home from work, he asked his dad if he had more stories to share. His dad chuckled and said the stories from the other night were just a teaser; the real tales were coming.

James had stopped on his way home to buy them some food. James set the food on the table and asked if his dad was hungry. The response was yes, and his dad said he didn't realize what time it was until he heard James come in.

After sitting down to eat, Donnie decided to share a few things he needed to tell James.

"Son," Donnie said, "please understand I wasn't saying I don't have my moments of anger and express them when the need arises. I am human, just like everyone else, and have those times when I cannot keep my anger from spilling out into the world. But I try to keep it in as much as I can." He paused to watch his son's reaction.

James looked at his dad and realized he was still just as strong as he had always thought. He also recognized there was much more to his dad than he had ever known. He wondered why his dad had never shared these things before. James understood that his dad had never had an easy life, and all those years working in Law Enforcement and Security had taken more from him than they had given.

As they finished their food, James remembered the outings they had taken when his dad seemed to look around all the time instead of at him while he spoke, even though his dad had told him to look at him during conversations. His father looked around whenever they entered a room, and watched certain people even from across the room. Even in restaurants, his dad always chose a corner table or booth, sitting with his back against a solid wall and watching everyone who entered. He even made James go around a group in public, even though there was a faster way to get back to the car. James understood why his dad didn't trust many people. All of this shaped his dad into who he is now.

James made coffee for them, cleaned up as they talked. There was something about his dad that he couldn't figure out, as if his dad had something on his mind today. He looked at his dad and knew something was bothering him. Donnie smiled at his son. James recognized that smile; it was a bit forced, but it was meant to put him at ease. He sensed that something this evening would not be easy for his dad to say.

James had always felt pride in his dad. He had watched him age and couldn't understand the forced smiles when he was little, thinking his dad was just unhappy with the family. After the divorce, his dad seemed to withdraw from social activities more, preferring work to life. This had always confused James, but he was beginning to see his dad in a different light as his dad shared stories from his work life. He could better understand why his dad was the way he remembered him during his childhood.

Donnie never hid his love for his son. He always made a point of telling James how proud he was of him. Donnie had kept the details of his work experiences from James to protect him and had always hoped his son would choose a different career path.

To a young person, chasing bad guys and helping other people might sound great, but the reality of the work was entirely different. Though rewarding, it also took a toll on those involved. Each law enforcement officer dealt with the stresses of the job differently, but for many, it led to struggles at home with their families, just as it did for Donnie and Carol. He understood this firsthand when he shared a harrowing work experience with Carol. That night marked the end of their marriage; even though Carol still loved Donnie, she could no longer stand by and fear the knock on the door.

These are things Donnie knew he needed to explain to James. That was part of the reason he never remarried. He didn't want to subject another person to the life he had chosen. Some might say he was selfish for putting his career before his marriage. Donnie and Carol agreed it was who he was, and nothing, not even Carol, could change that.

"When your mom left, I realized I was not going to bring anyone else into the world I lived in. No one else would be able to survive living with me the way your mom did for so long."

"James," he continued, "I am going to tell you what caused her to leave. What I am going to say will help you understand what happened."

"Dad, are you sure? I have never questioned why she left. I know you both still love each other." What he had just told James left him confused. Why was he discussing their separation and divorce with him now?

"I can remember the night like it was yesterday," he started. "I was paired up with another officer that night, and we got a call from one of the local hotels we were assigned to patrol, and that call changed my life."

Donnie looked at James's face and could tell he was a bit confused, but wanted to hear the stories he was finally telling him. His voice dropped slightly as he began again.

"The desk clerk called to tell us she heard gunshots coming from one of the rooms. There was yelling from some guy she couldn't understand. I could tell she was scared." He could hear her trembling, tight voice straining to get the words out.

I asked her if she had called the police yet. She said she hadn't yet, because they were to call our number first. I said OK and asked for the room number. I told her we were only about three blocks from the hotel and would be there in a couple of minutes. I asked her to leave a maintenance key for us on the counter. I also told her to go to the back office and lock the door for her safety. Once she told me she was, I told her to hang up and to call the police, and we were almost there." Donnie paused after this, taking a drink of his coffee, which he had in front of him on the table.

James sat still and listened, observing his father's expressions change as he spoke. It seemed his dad was reliving everything as he told him the story.

Donnie continued, "Once we arrived, we both drew our weapons, unsure of what we would find. We entered from different doors for safety. I waved at the camera, so the clerk knew we were inside. Looking around, we made our way to the room we were told was where the sounds came from."

Again, it seemed to James that his dad's memories made him relive every second. His dad even looked around and pointed as he spoke. James knew his dad wasn't aware of what he was physically doing. What made him pause was how this affected his dad as he told the story, as if he were there again.

"We checked the rooms on either side of the one room," he continued, "to make sure people were OK. Still, we had no idea what waited behind the door." Pausing as his mind recalled the scene from that day, he continued, "There was a family in one of the rooms, so we had them leave and go to the lobby while we stood by, making sure they were gone before we knocked on the door."

"James," he said, "because there is never a way to know what is behind those doors, you always need to be careful. While I stood on the left side of the door, my partner stood on the right. I knocked on the door and waited."

Donnie seemed nervous to James as he recalled what Donnie had told him. He could tell this was one of the more painful memories his dad had hidden from him. It affected James deeply as his dad continued to tell the story, because it had such a profound impact on his father.

"I knocked a little harder on the door and announced who we were, telling whoever was inside to open it so we could talk. We heard movement and yelling from somewhere in the room. I knocked again, urging them to open the door. We exchanged glances, realizing we needed to go inside to make sure everything was okay. As my partner began to insert the key into the lock, we heard a male voice yelling that if we came in, he would kill us too."

As Donnie spoke, James saw him slightly shake his head from left to right. He understood his dad and recognized that he was standing right there in the hallway as he recounted the incident. It felt like this was his report of the event, detailed yet concise.

James recalled what one of his Criminology instructors had said in report writing class, "Write your reports, speaking of what the responsible did, but with just the facts of what you saw, what you heard, and what you did. That is all you need, because some attorney would read it and do everything they could to blame you for doing your job." James finally understood that now. He also knew something was coming that would shock anyone who didn't realize what people involved in Law Enforcement or High-end Security had to experience. He knew his dad well and understood that if his dad was telling him about this, there was a purpose, and he needed to listen.

"Kill us too," Donnie repeated. "That could mean someone was dead or dying inside the room." We looked at each other and nodded in unison. We were going to enter the room anyway. Donnie put his hand up, as if telling the other officer to wait. "I called out to the one talking inside; I told him we needed to come in and check on everyone, and asked him to open the door."

"We had to get into the room," Donnie said, as if he were again trying to convince himself. It was the right decision for them. "Using the pass key, we heard it unlock. I pushed to open the door, but it halted about a third of the way as it swung open. I leaned in to help it open further, but it stopped. As I entered the room, I could smell the gunpowder. Looking around, I heard a door slam to my right, behind the door. I stopped, waiting to feel a push against the door from the other side. Nothing happened, so I slowly moved into the room. That is when I saw them. Two males were lying on the floor, bleeding from their heads. It looked like they had been shot. We now knew there was at least one male with a gun somewhere in the room."

"There was a door to my right, possibly a bathroom. I heard someone screaming in that room. I moved to the far side of the room as my partner entered. Motioning toward the closed door, we conducted a quick visual search, and no one else was seen. We moved towards the closed door. Again, moving to either side of the door, my partner knocked. The one who had yelled started screaming and shot at the door. One round shattered the door."

Looking at James, he was trying to read his face. There was nothing he could decipher, yet there was also a look of concern more than fear. Donnie thought he might say something at this point; his son was sitting and listening to all this as if he had been there before. It was like watching a movie. "We were able to get the door open, but when we did, the male inside started screaming at us. I saw the gun in his right hand and grabbed his hand. My partner entered, grabbed him, and held him as I got the gun away from him, letting it hit the floor with a loud thud. That is when the male began fighting with us. We were finally able to get him handcuffed." He paused for a minute, then continued telling the story. "I asked my partner if he had the guy secured, and he told me he did. I made my way to the males lying on the floor. I checked them both for a pulse. One, I could not find a pulse, but the other one had a faint one." Again, Donnie stopped and just stared straight ahead. "I looked him over and saw lots of blood; there was still blood seeping out of the wound in his head, and I began to apply pressure to the wound." He had stopped at this point; it looked like he was listening to something.

"That is when Law Enforcement showed up. I was holding the victim in my lap, applying pressure to his wound, and telling them I could not find a pulse on the other guy. My partner said he had one in cuffs in the bathroom, but he was becoming combative again. I sat there like that until the paramedics arrived. I can remember looking up at them and then at the other guy."

James could tell there was pain in his dad's words; it was as if he were reliving the experience as he told the story. He sat there, transfixed by his dad, hanging on every word.

Donnie continued, "Sitting there, the medics said they would take it from there. I held onto the guy until one of the paramedics had him in their hands. I slid back so they could work on him. Finally getting up, I looked around and saw all the people in the room." He shook his head as if he couldn't believe what he had been through that night.

"I looked at my partner; he appeared shaken up, and I suppose we both were at that moment." His dad seemed, to James, as if he was there in that room, even though they were sitting at the kitchen table. "I heard the medics say they needed to get the guy onto a gurney and transport him right away. I heard one of the law enforcement officers tell me to follow, and they would meet me at the hospital."

"Law enforcement had the shooter and were prepared to take him to one of their cars. I remember telling them I had gotten the gun out of his hand and had not touched it since it hit the floor. All they said was OK. They told me my partner needed to stay behind to give a witness statement. He told me he was good with that, and they also called the detectives to respond. As I was leaving, more law enforcement were arriving."

Donnie paused and looked at James. He knew, from his dad's facial expression, that the memory of all this had come alive for him, even though he hadn't realized it while talking about it. James noticed his dad was staring at his hands, as if still checking for blood on them.

He continued, "I didn't realize I was covered in blood until I got to the hospital, and your mom came running up to me to make sure I was OK. The guy was already in a room and being worked on by a crew. The paramedics had told your mom I had been there and was on my way in to see her. What they failed to tell her was that I was OK. I remember your mom asking me if I was OK; I said I was, but wanted to check on the guy. Of course, your mom cleaned me off while I was there, at least my arms, neck, and face. I'm sure she was checking to make sure I was OK."

"No one told her the details of what happened, and I started to, but she stopped me and said she wanted me in a room so a doctor could check me. I almost said no, but she insisted. So, I went to a room. The other nurse pulled off my shirt and T-shirt so the doctor could examine me. As I mentioned, I was fine and looked at your mom and said I was fine."

He looked at his son and said, "James, we could have been shot, but I made sure your mom never found that out. She looked scared enough, and all the ER staff knew we were married and thankfully never said anything to her like that either."

"After getting checked out, and when our statements were taken, and our reports were completed, I was finally able to head home. I didn't realize how hard it all hit me until I was in the driveway at home. Your mom's car was already in the driveway. When I went inside, I headed to the shower to wash everything off. When I was done, she was sitting on the couch sipping tea; a cup was waiting for me, too. We sat there for a while in silence."

James could hear the trepidation in his dad's voice. He had never seen his dad like this before. The impact of the incident was still visible on his face as he recounted the story. He was waiting for his dad to finish; he knew it would be hard on both of them to relive that night. But his dad was determined to share it with him.

"James, as we sat there, I had a million thoughts running through my mind. I was beginning to shake. The two victims were maybe 20, I think, but they were young either way. I felt a wave of emotion I had never experienced before, one that made me blurt out everything that had happened: from the initial call to holding the one guy in my lap, holding his head." Donnie finished.

Donnie paused. James noticed how it was affecting his dad. He was reliving the entire incident and the conversation with Carol once more. James had never seen his dad behave this way. He always seemed so strong and rigid, never really showing any emotion in his presence.

"Your mom asked me to stop telling her," he continued. "I remember hearing her say that, but I couldn't help myself; I just kept speaking. She finally raised her voice at me and stood up. She looked at me with tears running down her face. For the first time in all the years I have known her, she appeared scared."

James noticed that his dad's voice sounded shaky, as if all the emotions he felt at that moment were resurfacing again.

"James, I have always loved your mom and her strength, but that night, telling her what happened and what we did struck her as if she had been hit by a train. That night, everything changed between us. She decided she could no longer wait for that knock on the door, saying I had been injured or worse. She told me she was going to leave and take you with her," Donnie explained.

"Dad," James started, "I understand so much more now why you guys broke up. Mom never told me why she left, but now I know it was because of her love for you. As painful as that was for you to tell me and as painful as it was to know I could have lost you that night, I am glad you told me what happened."

"Have you spoken to your mom yet, son?" he asked. "Your mom loves you more than life itself, and it will cause her to go through a series of emotions when she knows what you want to do. Honor her by being open and honest with her. Don't let this information come from someone else."

All James could do at that moment was nod in agreement. Everything his dad had just said, along with watching his reaction, made him think deeply. He was sure he wanted to join law enforcement; it was something he felt he needed to do. However, he was nervous about telling his mom and sharing any of this with her. Nevertheless, he knew his dad was right, and he did need to tell to her.

"James, I felt I needed to tell you why we split. Your mom stood by me for years, supporting me through this lifestyle. When you came along, we shared more responsibilities, knowing there was a lifetime ahead to watch you grow into adulthood and start your life as you chose. She wanted both of us to share that with you; the thought of raising you alone became a reality for your mom that night. It had always been a possibility, but that night she truly understood it could be a reality."

He looked at his son, who thankfully resembled his mother. His face, minus a bit of stubble, mirrored hers. For years, their friends would jokingly ask who James' father was, since he looked like her. After the divorce, he kept to himself, went to work, and came home. He would have James on weekends, and they would do activities together, which helped strengthen their bond. When he moved back in, the house was rejuvenated, and Donnie was grateful to have James there. But now, with him applying to the Sheriff's Department, he knew he had to explain everything about the job to James.

In the middle of his thoughts, the phone rang. It was work, and Donnie needed to attend to an incident. He said he would be there as soon as he could and hung up. He had hoped they could spend more time discussing what he had just shared with James, but now it would have to wait.

James looked at his dad and asked, “Something serious?” His dad said he wasn’t sure yet, but if James wanted to hear about it and he was allowed to, he'd tell him when he got home. James nodded, as if to say, "Okay." “Son, are you alright?” his dad asked. “I think I am. I want to think through everything you told me, Dad, you know how I get,” he responded. “I know that was a lot to dump on you, son; I am sorry for that,” he said to him. James interrupted his dad, saying he would be fine, and told him to get going, too.

As Donnie left, he kept remembering that night. He headed into work to address the issue he had been called about. He also thought about James, who had sat quietly through everything he had revealed to him.

5

The Understanding of the Badge

James and Donnie had been working different shifts since their conversation. It wasn't a conversation; it was Donnie explaining to James what had happened the night Carol decided to leave him. He hoped James had not been scared off from his Law Enforcement career because of what he had said. He also hoped his son had not judged his mom for her actions.

Donnie knew Carol and recognized that she loved their son more than anyone else in the world. He understood that she had acted in accordance with what she believed was right for everyone at the time. It had taken a toll on all of them, yet they had managed to survive.

So many times, over the years, Donnie had seen families torn apart by fear, violence, and substance abuse. They were broken people, some still living in the same building, but it was no longer a home. Donnie was glad that Carol never kept James from him, and they still talked almost daily.

Donnie had so much more to share with James about his years in law enforcement and high-end security: stories he knew would make him smile or frown. Tales stranger than a Hollywood movie. Over the years, he had encountered people, situations, and experiences that had changed him; yet much of what he had seen encompassed both the best and the worst of life.

He also knew that Carol was still afraid of losing him to his job, not in the sense of being a workaholic but in the context of potential violence. She never wanted to face James with the message that his dad was gone.

Donnie was home for a few days of rest after working long hours and covering open shifts due to call-offs or other reasons. It was just part of being the boss of a large security company. They had a large staff of young people, and he knew they needed time off to spend with their loved ones. He had always been willing to do whatever was necessary to ensure the company and its clients received the best possible service, including men and women facing challenges he had never encountered during his over two decades of service. Some thought he might be too old to do the job now, but they saw him handle things effectively.

For some reason, he was thinking about that, and it made him smile. People had underestimated him for years, more so now as the gray in his beard had taken over. But he also knew he couldn't go on forever.

He was deep in thought when he heard the door open and looked up to see James come in. He looked tired but also happy to see his dad. Donnie told him coffee was ready if he wanted some. James smiled, nodded, and went into the kitchen to get a cup. He then returned to the living room and sat on the sofa.

They sat in silence for a few minutes until James broke the silence by looking up and seeing his dad sitting there, sipping his coffee.

"Dad," he began, "the other night when you told me about the night of the shooting, what were you wanting me to understand?"

Donnie looked at him and said, "I wanted you to understand why your mom left and what caused her to leave. I never meant to hurt her and still wish I hadn't told her."

James sat there for a few minutes and finally told his dad about the past few days. "I went and saw Mom and told her about my application for the Sheriff's Department. I never knew how much you two are alike. She sat there, listening to everything I told her and to why I felt the pull to serve people. The only thing she said was she knew already." He smiled at his dad. "I asked her if you had told her, and she said no. I asked her how she knew. She told me I was your son and that it is what the men in this family do." He looked at his dad again. "She asked me if I had spoken to you about it yet. I told her I had, and you had told me to talk to her before the background investigators called her. Then she smiled and told me she was proud of me. Dad, she seemed to be pleased that I have chosen to follow in your footsteps," James finished as he looked at his dad.

Donnie wasn't sure what to say, but he also knew he was her son and would do everything he could to ensure his safety. "Thank you for talking to her about it. I know it meant a lot to her that you did," he said to James. He nodded to his dad.

There was a bit of silence, and James began, "The other night, when you were talking about the night you and Mom had the talk that led to her leaving, it was eye-opening for me. I could tell you were reliving the whole thing again as you talked to me about it. I could also see how it affected you. I had never seen you like that before. It seemed it really affected you and still does now." Donnie started to speak, but James raised his hand to stop him. "Not knowing the complete circumstances of everything you saw and went through other than the things you told me, I have a few questions about it. Are you okay with answering them? And anything you don't want to answer, please tell me." James stopped to let his dad answer.

Donnie was still in shock that James had done the same thing to him that he had done for years, and he smiled at that. But he told him he would answer everything.

"Why did you smile at me just now?" James asked. "It was what you did with your hand; you put it up, knowing I was about to say something," James responded. "First, why did you go into the room?" he asked.

"It was what I was supposed to do; I was the senior officer, and there had been a shooting inside, and we needed to check for life. The shooter was still somewhere in the room, and he needed to be disarmed and held for Law enforcement." Donnie replied. "Would you have shot him if he had pointed his gun at you?" James asked. "Yes." He responded.

"Okay, second question, what were you thinking when you went into the room?" James asked. "Son, there had been a shooting, an unknown number of victims or shooters; we had to know the numbers. If anyone was still alive, we needed to get to them."

"Next question, when the shooter shot through the door of the bathroom, were you sure he wouldn't shoot you too as you entered the bathroom?" "There was no way of knowing. Training kicked in, and I didn't even think about it." He told James, "You sound more like an attorney," then he smiled at his son.

James wore a serious expression, aware that he had been contemplating the questions he wanted to ask.

"You and your partner seem to know each other pretty well. How long did it take for the two of you to reach that point?" James asked

He realized James was asking because he knew he would one day face the same situation. "He and I had worked together for years, but it took about six months for us to get to the point where we just knew what to do. If I took the lead, he was to back me, and if he took the lead, I was to back him. Son, the more time you spend with another officer or officers, the better you learn to read each other; there are no words needed."

James sat quietly for a few minutes, pondering what his dad had told him. He realized he had much to learn, but also wanted to absorb as much knowledge as possible from his dad.

"Mom never told me why you guys split up. I never knew why, but I realize now that she loved you so much; she didn't want to bury you one day because of the job."

"And she feels the same way about you, too, son," Donnie said. Looking at his son, he knew he was thinking of anything else he wanted to know. "I have worked with people I could never trust to have my back. Others I would still trust my life with," he told him.

"As a rookie, you will need to earn the respect of the senior Officers. Then the other officers. Achieving this goal requires time and effort. There are some deputies still around who know me; they will take you under their wing in the beginning." Donnie could tell his son was imagining a situation similar to the one he had described the other night. He also knew that, given the current state of affairs, his son would need to learn quickly or quit.

The drug trade is pervasive these days; gangs are running the streets, and there is less law enforcement to manage the demands. Adding in the animosity towards uniforms will make for a steep learning curve for James. However, Donnie knew his son and was confident he would make it through everything.

"James, is there anything else you want to ask me about what I told you the other night?" "I can't think of anything at the moment, but I reserve the right to recall the witness at a later time." They both laughed at that.

The humor helped them both, and they spent the rest of the evening discussing other topics. They were both trying hard not to remember the conversation from the other night. James got up from the couch a bit later and told his dad he needed to shower and get some sleep. He wished him goodnight and headed to the back of the house.

Donnie thought about calling Carol, but, looking at the time, realized it was too late to reach her. He wanted to discuss James and his plans and find out if she was truly okay with his choice. He sensed that she wasn't.

Donnie got up, took the coffee cups into the kitchen, and headed to bed as well. It had been a long week. Work had been difficult, and he was now ready for a few days off.

6

The Preparation of the Badge

James was gone when Donnie woke up. He had prepared coffee for both of them before he left. Donnie poured a cup of coffee and went into the living room. Sitting in his recliner, he took a sip of the coffee. Seeing the paperwork he had to complete, he reached for it and began working on it.

While he was working on the paperwork, he kept thinking about calling Carol to discuss James. He was worried that she was concealing her true feelings about James's decisions.

With the coffee gone, he got up to pour another cup. As he headed back to his recliner, the phone rang. Looking at the caller ID, he saw it was Carol.

"Morning," he said when he answered. "Morning, how are things?" Carol asked and followed up with, "I wanted to call you this morning and talk about James."

"Things are okay, and a funny thing is, I was going to call you last night about that, but it was too late. I'm glad you called," Donnie said, and "James said you are okay with his decision, and that doesn't sound like you. Are you okay with him joining the Sheriff's department?"

"Donnie," Carol started, "I am better with everything these days. I have realized he is your son, too, and that he shares your drive to serve and keep people safe. I'm not overly excited about it, but he's an adult. My fears of losing you cost us our marriage, and I should have been more supportive of you, just as you've always been for me. James told me you spoke to him about us and mentioned some of what you have encountered. I am glad you did."

Carol sounded a little lost about everything with James. Donnie felt bad, and she still blamed herself for the end of their marriage. Donnie never knew she blamed herself for the divorce. James had told him the other night that he remembered hearing her crying after they moved.

Donnie heard her begin speaking again, "Donnie, I am worried he will get hurt, the same as I have always worried about it happening to you. But I have finally realized that my job can be just as dangerous. With all the violence from gangs, the drug usage, it has become more dangerous for our medical staff, so much so that we now have armed security In the building." Carol paused for a minute. "I had heard something about that," Donnie said.

She continued, "I had recommended your company to the hospital when they were looking for a company, but they decided to hire their own. I would have preferred your company there; I remember how you trained your employees. These people are not like the ones that work for you."

Donnie heard Carol's voice; she seemed sad. "Thank you for thinking of us for the job. We would have provided the security we know how to do. Our people are well-trained and certified in everything they do."

Carol told him she remembered the company and the training manual he had written for it. "Will you do me a favor, please?" she asked. "Train our son before those idiots ruin him?" That made Donnie smile for a second. "I will," he told her.

Carol thanked him, mentioned that she needed to get to work, and added that she was glad they had talked that morning. Donnie agreed and wished her a good day.

Setting the phone down, Donnie sat and reflected on the conversation he had just had with Carol. This was one of the times she sounded different; it seemed like she had changed to him. She sounded concerned but also understanding of James's decision to enter law enforcement. He realized she knew his company was, at least to her, a good one. He smiled, remembering her discussion of the training manual he had written years ago. It had changed and been adjusted since, but he was proud of it. It took a long time to win the owners' approval. He also remembered having her read it before he submitted it. He had always valued her opinion and input on the things they discussed.

Sitting in the quiet of the living room, his mind drifted back to when James was young, running around the house, his laughter echoing and his smile lighting up any room.

Now, at twenty-one years old, he aspires to be a Deputy, embarking on a career in a field he has been a part of for so long. Donnie wondered what it would cost James and if he could handle all the garbage he was going to face. Dealing with death, violence, and hate would take a toll and change him, or would he be able to get through it all? Donnie knew it had changed him and cost him so much. There are days he wonders if it has all been worth it. He knew his son was strong, but he asked if it would create issues for James as well. He remembered some of the things he had faced and the scars he still bore. Everything combined caused Donnie to think of Carol again. They met when he was working, so he had her and James to be thankful for above all else. They alone made it all worth it.

Donnie turned back to the paperwork he needed to complete. The paperwork for the Operations Manager never seemed to end. He was reviewing incident reports written by employees.

Within the past two weeks, they have reported twelve fights and twenty-one detainments for offenses ranging from shoplifting to domestic violence. There were ten fights and two incidents of graffiti on the buildings.

The patrol logs found thirty-five unlocked doors during that time, four people sleeping in cars, and nine individuals passed out from drinking, either on the ground or in their vehicles. Patrol also discovered two separate couples having sex in a car outside bars. It's never a dull moment for the employees. Donnie was about to rotate onto patrol for the next six weeks, a role he undertakes twice a year, where he rides with the staff and assists with additional training. Since the company has 24-hour patrol vehicles, the patrol will be split between the two. He needs to work with three employees, and it's their evaluation time.

There were rotations for all employees across the company, allowing them to learn every job the organization required. He always believed that well-trained staff allowed them to operate more effectively, and thankfully, the owners agreed. There were always two employees per patrol vehicle for safety reasons.

Over the years, he observed changes in the individuals they interacted with. The people had become more violent and aggressive toward employees, necessitating a different training approach. The three-week training course and subsequent Field Training Officer (FTO) time with each employee proved beneficial. The staff changed somewhat during that time, with most being younger and less experienced than in previous years. It was like a rookie deputy or beat cop situation: they learned, or they left.

Law enforcement or high-end security wasn't for everyone. Turnover was down to about 10 percent, while the average was higher elsewhere. He would call in new employees after a serious incident to talk with them. He always smiled as they entered his office; they were always nervous, as if they thought they were in trouble. One of the supervisors once told him it was funny to watch the employees when Donnie came onto a property; they would almost snap to attention.

Donnie remembered the transition from the military to his first law enforcement job. It was a transition for him. Initially, it had been difficult;

the hours were a change. He worked seven 10-hour shifts, followed by three days off, which often amounted to just one day, as he slept during the first day off and needed to rest before his shifts started for the next 10-day run. At that time, he didn't mind because he was single and not in a relationship. He spent all his time trying to learn everything he needed to know. It was tough, but he was determined to be the best until he realized he would never stop learning. Once he recognized this, it became an opportunity to learn every day, and he began actively seeking out those learning experiences.

He discovered that life, whether at work or home, was a lifelong learning opportunity. Even over the past two decades, he never stopped learning something new every day. Some of the people he had worked with never understood this, and it has cost them. As he reflected on this, he realized that Carol had told him the same thing many times: if we don't seek out learning opportunities, we may miss the chance to learn. He hoped James would understand that as well.

Donnie looked up, realizing he had been working for several hours and needed to eat something. As he stood up to go into the kitchen, he heard the front door open. He called out to see who it was, and James replied that it was him. Donnie told James he was about to make something to eat and asked if he was hungry. James said he had eaten, but came into the kitchen anyway.

James told him that he had been gathering paperwork for the Sheriff's department to initiate a background check. Donnie asked if he had been offered the job. James smiled and said he had been asked to get everything ready, and they would call him when it was time to submit. Donnie knew they were close to offering him the job, but chose not to mention anything to James. This meant they wanted to find out who he was and inquire about everyone he knew, including his family, friends, exes, co-workers, clergy, schoolteachers, and bosses. Every name he wrote down would be contacted to ask about him. Typically, they check back ten years and dig deep. The initial screening phase of the hiring process excludes many applicants. They also check the medical and criminal history of everyone. No one is ever immaculate, and if someone claims to be, the department usually investigates the applicant more thoroughly.

Donnie's company also conducts its own background checks on each applicant. Like law enforcement, the company's nature leads it to examine everything about everyone. This process is performed by an external company that is compensated to uncover all relevant information. It is completed by the end of the three-week training process. Because of their certification process for each employee, they ensure nothing is hidden. His company requires everyone to comply.

James could tell his dad was deep in thought, so he asked him about what he was thinking. Donnie smiled as he turned around, knowing James knew him well. "I was thinking of the background checks Law Enforcement does, and everything involved in them," he said to him.

"Son, most members of Law Enforcement have been the ones who did plenty of growing up but never got caught. That is why so many are good at finding things." He looked at him for a minute, and James' face flushed a little. He knew his son wasn't a saint, but now he understood that James had done some of the things kids often do. Donnie kept looking at him. After a few minutes, Donnie smiled and returned to making his food.

James stammered, "How do you know everything? I have never figured out how you do." Donnie broke into laughter at that. "I just do son," Donnie said.

Sitting at the table with his sandwich, James joined him. They were very much alike but thankfully different. James asked if he had more stories. He said he had shared the last two with a couple of friends, who laughed at them. However, he kept the one about the shooting to himself; that felt like it was just for family.

As Donnie asked James what his plans were for the night, he told his dad he was staying home. "Maybe we should talk about some of the stories I have to share with you, if you'd like to hear them," Donnie said. James said he wanted to hear more and got up to make fresh coffee.

Donnie asked James if he wanted to move to the living room. James said it would be more comfortable. He told his dad he would bring him coffee when it was done.

Donnie walked to the recliner and sat down. As he reviewed the paperwork he had been working on, he organized it and set it aside for the time being. While waiting for James, his mind wandered back in time for a few minutes. Lost in thought, James handed his dad a cup of coffee and sat on the sofa. The coffee always smelled good to Donnie, and he realized he had not had much of it the day before, but it tasted good today.

7

The Mindset of the Badge

They sat and sipped coffee before he spoke to James. "Son, when I started in my early days of security, there were people who still liked us, but it has changed almost to hate. We get called want-to-be cops, rent-a-cops, and, of course, that guy in the movies who was a mall security guard. That is why the company has such an extensive training program."

"Mom told me you wrote that," James said. Donnie smiled and said he had. "Did she tell you she wants me to train you, too?" James shook his head as if to say no, started to speak, but stopped. "It has helped our company and benefited the organization in several ways since we began the training, allowing us to remove those who cannot perform the work early on. At least our men and women are more professional than many of the law enforcement officers I meet these days. Something about the system they are being forced to follow has changed them."

James looked at his dad. "So that is why Mom wants you to train me?" He asked Donnie. "Son, she wants you to be better prepared to manage things as a Deputy Sheriff and quickly earn the respect of the older officers," he told him.

"How worried are you both about me getting into Law Enforcement? Please tell the truth, Dad," James asked. "Son, your mom understands things better now, but to say she isn't concerned, I would be lying to you. As for me, I respect your decision to join, and I believe you will do an amazing job. As my only son, I am still worried about how society will react when you arrive at a call. They are not like they used to be when people wore badges. All I ask is for you to do what I have always done," Donnie paused. This made James look straight at his dad as Donnie continued, "I call it working scenarios through your mind. It is a way to train your brain to react almost immediately to any situation. In other words, think about if someone does this, I can do that. Switch up to other ones, and that way you can train your brain to know already what to do in about 95 percent of situations you will encounter.

"Also, build up your strengths quickly, and your weaknesses will follow. For example, when you played, you would, over time, develop a sense of what the other person was going to do so that you could react to it quicker. Somewhat like being a defensive driver. Does that make sense, son?" Donnie asked.

James smiled and nodded to his dad. "You sound like one of my instructors," James quipped. "He would tell us that in defensive tactics. As I watched some of the other students, they seemed to struggle more with that. I did okay, but I know there's a lot more for me to learn," James finished. "Every day is a learning opportunity for anyone, but especially for the Emergency Services people. I still learn something every day on the job; some things are not great, but some things have helped me throughout the years," Donnie concluded.

"Now, on to some stories I think you might find interesting. But I also need another cup of coffee first," Donnie said with a smile, handing James his cup to refill.

Over time, the first company I worked for began experiencing financial difficulties, and I had a couple of bounced checks. I became concerned about having money for rent, gas, and food. I started searching for another company to work for. Still new to security, with about six months of experience at the time, I joined another company and initially worked in bars and businesses. After about four months, they asked me if I wanted to drive around and check properties for them. I told the boss I did, and they then had me driving around town, checking on various properties, or responding to issues on those properties."

Donnie continued, "Being the only one doing the Patrols, I learned quickly what to look for and began to learn how to deal with people when they called for someone to stop and help them. The only training I received was to learn about the properties, drive through them during the day, and become familiar with them. They provided me with the managers' names and phone numbers, as well as a phone to use for work."

"That explains a lot to me, Dad," James said, "and why you are so adamant about making sure people get trained."

"I made some mistakes along the way, but I learned from them," Donnie said to James.

Donnie continued, "One night, I was driving through an apartment complex. I was supposed to check the pool area after a certain time to ensure no one was in the pool. That night, there was a couple in the pool. They were partly in the Jacuzzi, having removed all their clothes. The male was sitting on the side of it with his legs in the water, while the female was in the water, leaning face-first between his legs."

"As I applied my brakes, making a screeching sound, I thought they would know I was there; they did not hear me. I stepped out of the car and slammed the door, but still nothing. I walked to the gate, opened it, and let it slam; still, no response from them. I stopped on the opposite side of the pool and turned on my three-cell Mag flashlight, aiming it directly at them; yet again, there was no response from either of them. I called out multiple times, and finally, the male looked at the flashlight and slid into the Jacuzzi. I told them they needed to leave." Donnie said with a smile. James giggled at that.

"Both got out of the water. The male was hunched down, putting his pants back on. However, the woman stepped out and turned towards me, fully nude and smiling, and slowly put her clothes back on, making sure I saw everything. When they were clothed again, I asked them what apartment they lived in; they said they were guests. As I waited for them to leave the property, they each entered separate vehicles and left." When Donnie finished, James had to ask his dad about the woman, "Was she good-looking?" James asked. "She was okay, but not someone I would want to get to know better. Ask your mom, "I am picky."

"I continued to work the night patrol route and didn't run into much, just an occasionally parked car on a property or an open door. Looking back, I realize I wasn't even armed; we just had a flashlight, a pair of cuffs, and some pepper spray. That was it."

James stopped Donnie and asked him why he was not armed. Donnie responded, "We never were armed when I started; just flashlights and cuffs, mainly."

Donnie continued, "About a month later, I received several calls from tenants in the same complex. They were complaining about a loud party in an upstairs apartment. When I got to the complex, I could hear music coming from the apartment across the street. I went to the apartment and knocked several times before a male came to the door." He looked like he had been drinking, and I could smell it as well."

I explained why I was there and asked him to lower the music. He became cocky with me and asked if I knew who his dad was; I told him no. He had someone turn the music down, and then he explained to me who his father was. He was the son of a Deputy District Attorney in the local office, and his dad was going to get me fired. I thanked him for turning the music down, and that was all I needed. As I was leaving, he yelled out for me to never come back and immediately turned the music back up. That was one of the times I got angry, son. "I wanted to turn around, break down the door, and yank the guy out of the apartment," Donnie said.

"When I reached my car, I called the local Police Department for help. When the officer arrived, I explained why I was there and who the renter said his dad was. He smiled and said the renter had been an ongoing problem."

I accompanied him to make contact, and the music was shut off immediately. The officer then asked for ID from everyone else. A second officer arrived to assist the first officer. There were five underage teenage girls in the apartment, and the renter was twenty-one. The second officer took the names of the teenage girls, and they arrested the twenty-one-year-old renter, who was reminding the officers of who his dad was. He was charged with contributing. The teenagers' parents were called.

"A couple of days later, I was called by the renter's dad and asked to come to his office at the District Attorney's office. When I arrived, he asked me why I called the Police on his son. I explained why and asked how he knew the District Attorney by name. I even suggested he call the D.A. in so I could say hello." The look on his face was priceless, like a deer in the headlights." Both Donnie and James laughed at that.

Donnie began again, "When the D.A. came into the room, he asked me how I was, and why I was in the office. I explained why and who had called me in. He turned to the dad, who was a Deputy District Attorney. He said he looked forward to reviewing the file and would be assigning the case to another Deputy District Attorney for prosecution. He turned to me, said it was great seeing me, and left. The dad said Thank you for coming in, and I could go."

"All my life in the town I grew up in, I dealt with the 'rich kids." I came from a modest family. I did not hold people at bay because of my parents' money; I worked for everything I had," Donnie said.

"As I grew up, I began to make 'friends' with those people. The kids' parents bragged about their wealth. Most of those parents were decent people, while some were not. However, it was helpful to have someone I could call for assistance. During this time, I also learned to speak a couple of more languages besides English. These languages proved useful as I bounced around to other jobs during that period."

When Donnie finished, he looked at James. James sat there in silence for a few minutes. James asked, "What made the attorney think to call you in to his actual office?"

"Because he was part of the higher-paid group in town, I later found out, he had done this before. He thought he could protect his son from charges, just as he had several times before. He didn't know I knew his boss." Donnie told James.

Donnie stated to James, "From what I was told, he left the D.A.'s office a few months later and went into private practice. Knowing the D.A., he made it very clear the kid's dad was no longer needed or wanted at his office."

Donnie concluded, "Most of my time working with the security company was boring; nothing ever happened when I was on duty. They soon shut the doors, so I had to find something else to do."

He added, "One of the things I learned in my early years was that there needed to be more training for anyone working in security. Interviewing and hiring people from help-wanted ads doesn't necessarily mean they are qualified, ready, or capable of doing the job. Without training and background checks, a company cannot determine the qualifications of its potential hires. I have had some amazing applicants who have felonies on their records. They cannot work for the company because of that. But the only way to know is a background check and the training."

"Anyway, let me get down from my pulpit, felt like I was a preacher just then," Donnie said with a smile. "Amen, Dad!" James yelled.

They both laughed at that. It had been a while since Donnie had thought about the things he did when he was starting. He remembered them, but only the things that stood out in those early years. He was glad he had been involved early on, but also lamented never having received proper training to do the job.

Training is essential for performing the job correctly. Being taught to recognize and handle various situations and to deal with people is necessary for both Law Enforcement and any security role.

Donnie told James, "I found a job in loss prevention for a large national chain store. We had our moments there. Most of the time, it was watching the cameras or walking around the store. I do remember the boss; he was such an idiot. The town I'm from was farm-based, and he wanted us to dress professionally, meaning slacks and a shirt. We stuck out. We were supposed to look like customers, but we looked more like the rest of the employees. I was often asked to help someone with something. He finally let us wear jeans and a shirt instead." Saying that, he started to shake his head back and forth like he was disgusted by the thought. James looked at his dad and knew it meant his dad wasn't happy about the situation.

"The store had cameras that we would monitor, and in a few areas, there were two-way mirrors overlooking the sales floor. You had to climb up there to look through them." James understood what he was talking about because Donnie always waved to the cameras when he was in a store.

"One day, while sitting in the perch, as I liked to call it, I saw a man using his arm to scoop large amounts of kids' clothes into a large bag. He cleared whole shelves as he went. I radioed my office and stepped onto the floor. As I watched him do this, I followed him to the front door. He had one 30-gallon bag full in each hand. As he exited the store, I called out for him to stop, and he turned around. I told him he needed to come back into the store with me." He just looked at me for what seemed like several minutes." Donnie paused for breath.

Then he continued, "he tossed the two bags of clothes at my feet and started to run. I chased him as far as the street line, as I was not allowed to cross the street. It was while I was watching him run through traffic that I remembered hitting a side mirror with my shoulder on a pickup truck we had passed. I called the Police. When they arrived, I gave them the description of the man. The Officer said he might know who it was." He looked at the replay on the cameras and said, "Yes, he knew who it was."

Later, they arrested the man for attempting to steal. I was shown a line-up of six pictures and pointed to his picture. The Officer then told me that the guy usually carries a gun in his waistband, and I had been lucky not to have been shot."

"I was called into court to testify against the man. He was staring at me the whole time. As his attorney questioned me, I found myself looking at the man each time I answered. The man finally stopped staring and looked straight ahead. The man was convicted of theft and other charges." Donnie concluded, looking at James for any reaction. James had been sitting there, listening, not interjecting anything.

James, that was the first time I had testified in court," Donnie told him.

"Dad, as you tell your stories, just like when I was a kid, you seem to make everything come alive to me. I may be partial to your stories, but the way you speak about them, they are amazing and crazy." Donnie smiled at James. "Why do you say that?"

"I was seeing the guy, watching you watching him, then you chase him. And all of this without back-up or a weapon. You once told me most people have either a flight or fight mechanism in each, but you have no flight mechanism anymore, sounds like you never did." James was shaking his head as he spoke.

"It isn't anything I speak much about to other people. I have trained many young officers, mainly in High-end security, but they have all under-estimated me and my abilities. I am in no way a superhuman, but I do the job the way it is to be done. If anyone in Law Enforcement or security is going to engage someone physically, they need to go all in or don't even try. When people hesitate, they get hurt. All or nothing." Donnie said.

James was looking at him, impressed by his dad and understanding better why his mom worried about him. He was what people called old school, someone who had learned how to do a job and had always done it the way most people his age would be afraid to. He also understood why training was so necessary to his father. It keeps people safe.

Donnie began again, "There was another time when an employee was suspected of embezzling money from this store. As we watched the cameras, I noticed her lift her foot, and it appeared that she had placed something in her boot. She was called back to the office, and $100 was found in her boot. Her cash till was counted, and it was found to be $100 short. She was fired on the spot. The boss had me escort her to the door and watch until she got in the car and left. She promised to pay the money back right away but never did."

"It has always amazed me how people think they can get away with things when there are so many cameras around recording all the time." They will lie to your face until they are shown the camera footage that plainly shows they did what they are being accused of," Donnie concluded.

James was learning more about his dad and all the things he had seen and done. Many people have parents who have just skipped by in life and never experienced the ups and downs of how people act, yet they want to judge those, like his dad, who do the things others won't.

"On another day," Donnie started, "a man came into the store with a backpack on. He was seen browsing around the men's jeans section. As I watched him, he put five pairs of jeans in his backpack. I approached him while he was kneeling on the floor and placed my hand on his shoulder. I guess I scared him so badly that he passed gas that curled my nose hairs. He was escorted to the Office, and the Police were called. When they looked in his backpack, they also found burglary tools."

"Working with retail loss prevention, there are many people who try to get away with theft. Many get caught, most don't. It was a learning experience for me. It has helped me in later years find things others never looked for."

Donnie looked at his son and could tell he was absorbing the words and trying to picture everything in his mind. Donnie had these stories in his mind for so many years and had shared them with the trainees he had taught and mentored. He also knew the stories would only get crazier as he told them to James. The things he saw had an impact on him, not always for the better.

In a thoughtful tone, Donnie explained, "There are times I look back on these years and wonder. Those were good training years, even though none of the businesses provided me with training. It was a learn-as-you-go approach for me, which, at times, could make things difficult because I made many mistakes. I learned from those mistakes and vowed to myself that I would not make them again, even though I made the same mistakes several more times, just not as big a mistake each time. Trial and error, I suppose you could say. That is why I believe in early training and ongoing training for everyone".

"One more story, there was a woman I was watching one day," Donnie began, "she was walking around but kept looking over her shoulder towards the central register, she picked out some children's clothes and I watched her place them in a bin, a short distance from the register. She then went shopping some more, selecting a couple of other items. She paid for them, walked back to where she had left the other items, slipped them into her bag, and started to walk out. When I stopped her at the door, I asked her to look in the bag and the receipt. She refused and started walking towards her car. I followed her to the car and told her she needed to come with me. She started to refuse, and our other Loss Prevention person came out to where we were. We escorted her back to our office and showed her the video we had of her stealing. We called the Police, and when they arrived, they asked her for her Identification. She claimed she had none. The officer told her she would have to be arrested at that time because they had no way to identify her. She stood up and pulled her Driver's License out of her front right pocket. The Officer issued her a ticket for the theft, and we escorted her out of the store".

As he spoke, James' eyes were wide open, and he had leaned forward. He was following every word spoken, nodding here and there. Donnie had never seen him so interested in anything as he is now.

When Donnie was finished, he asked James what he thought of that. Sitting there for a minute, and then he smiled at his dad. "People are stupid, aren't they?" James started to laugh at what his dad had told him.

"Son, people aren't necessarily stupid; they just don't think they will get caught, and when they do, they try to lie their way out of the trouble they are now in." That made him stop laughing. He had never thought of it that way. After all the years his dad had worked in Law Enforcement and High-end security, he thought people were not stupid for the things they tried to get away with. So, he asked him, "What are you telling me is you don't think people are stupid?"

"They act stupid, but they aren't all stupid," Donnie said. "Some will act like they are better than other people, some will belittle and try to ridicule people, because they have no real power over anyone. They believe they are entitled to something in life. They will use and abuse weaker people until they can't anymore."

"When they get caught in a situation, they blame and accuse others for the trouble they are in. They will blame anyone and everyone, but they often believe they are a victim." Donnie continued, "They aren't stupid; they manipulate and blame because they got away with things by blaming someone else. You will increasingly encounter this as you start handling calls in Law Enforcement. It can be socio-economic, racial, gender, or gender identification, or wrong place, wrong time, targeting because of any of those, or because it is simply something they want or they are owed it, and the list goes on. Does that make any sense to you?"

"To me, Dad," James started, "It is all stupid and wrong. Why would they blame someone else for their choice? That doesn't make sense to me at all. You're telling me that they'll blame the one in uniform for their own choice to do something that'll put them in a situation with the Law and the courts? Sounds more like a three-year-old making an excuse for what they did." James sat there after he finished speaking, just shaking his head.

"Welcome to the life, son. It has become worse over the years. Many people have never been taught to take responsibility for their actions. Family and society have protected many for most of their lives. Things like, my child wouldn't do that, and you, the person in uniform, are making it all up. Remember some of your classmates in school? Remember how they would get away with everything they did with an excuse? Those are many of the people you will have to deal with," Donnie concluded.

"I had not thought about it that way. Many people come to mind when I think of school. This is going to be interesting for sure. There are some I will gladly hold accountable for their actions," James said.

"Stop right there, you cannot target anyone. It often becomes a conflict of interest; it is both illegal and immoral to do so. If you arrest someone due to past issues, an attorney will investigate, and the case may be dismissed. You will be brought up on charges for it and could face disciplinary action, including losing your job. It happens sometimes, but you should remember to call for assistance in those situations. Always keep it clean and clear, okay, son?" Donnie looked at James when he finished to ensure he understood.

James sat there for a bit, thinking about what his dad had said. He was reflecting on his school years and wondering how people could get away with certain things. He knew that if he had tried, it would have ended badly for him with both of his parents.

To help him understand, he asked, "When I was growing up, I thought I would get in more trouble from you and mom, is that true or did I just make that up in my mind?"

Donnie looked James in the eyes and asked what he thought would happen if he were like so many other students. He thought his parents were harder on him than other parents.

James sat for a few minutes and thought about it, and told his dad, "Not that you two were harder on me, but I also knew you both taught me to respect myself and others. I was to be someone others could look to for help when it was needed, and not back down if things escalated to the point of a fight. I also remember you telling me, Dad, that I should never start a fight unless someone were being attacked, but should stand between the aggressor and the one getting bullied or messed with. But being harder on me, I don't think so, but I also never wanted to disappoint mom or you either."

Donnie smiled. He knew his son, and he knew he would be honest with him, at least mostly. Especially now that he had gotten older. James was a good son, and his dad was proud of the man he had become in the past few years.

James told his dad he was hungry and asked if he wanted to make something to eat. Donnie told him he wanted to take them out to eat. They both got ready and decided to go to a restaurant across town. Donnie asked James if he wanted to call his mom to see if she would like to eat with them, as it was his treat tonight. James called his mom, but it went to voicemail. After leaving a message, they finished getting ready and left for the restaurant. Carol called him back, asked where they were going to eat, and said she would meet them there. James turned to Donnie, who was driving, and told him that Mom was meeting them. He then asked his dad why he wanted her to have dinner with them.

James had not seen his dad smile in a long time. "I thought it would be nice to have a family dinner for once," he stammered. It reminded James of the time he asked a girl for his first prom in High School. James laughed at his dad and looked at him. "Dad, James said, I know you pretty well, but I have not seen you look like that ever." Knock it off, it's just a meal shared with family, son," Donnie quipped.

8

The Trial of the Badge

After a couple of years working in security, Donnie returned to school and completed his college coursework. Then, he started applying for Law Enforcement positions.

In his mid-twenties, he applied for a position with the police department in a neighboring town. After approximately six months and the completion of the background investigation, he was hired.

Donnie attended the Police Academy. At the academy, he realized that he had found his career path. With all he had seen and experienced in a short time in security, Donnie wanted to learn more and move forward in his new career. He felt excited but had some trepidation about everything. However, he believed he could handle anything he encountered with the training he was receiving.

Like so many young rookie Law Enforcement officers, he soon realized that the academy was not real life. The events on the streets differed from those at the training center. In training, everyone was compliant; they didn't want to struggle or resist. The instructors made sure of that. The slow-motion practice did not represent real life. He quickly learned that people don't like handcuffs put on their wrists. Sometimes, when cuffing, the cuffs cannot be locked in place due to the person's demeanor. That there were women who fought harder than some men. Donnie learned fast;

he was not prepared for all of that. But he continued, adapting to everything he knew. He listened to his Field Training Officers and absorbed their directions, so it all became second nature to him. He learned to rehearse scenarios in his mind until they became second nature. If this happened, he could do A, B, or C, resolving it more quickly and safely for everyone.

Donnie learned that he needed to always look around himself and the other officer he was working with. They had to protect each other during all the calls they got involved in. He learned to trust someone else with his life.

After the F.T.O. finished his additional training, Donnie was able to work alone, with backup close by in case anything happened that he could not handle alone. The department ensured that dispatchers would check on every officer on a call to verify their status, specifically to confirm they were Code-4, meaning they were okay.

Donnie learned the Law Enforcement phonetic alphabet, similar to the military phonetic alphabet, but also understood the differences. He learned the laws and, fortunately, had a "cheat sheet" of the most frequently used sections for quick reference. He realized that most Law Enforcement officers began to speak differently. Instead of saying something like, we had a male who committed an Assault and Battery, it became we had a male suspect commit a 240-242. A drunk driver became a deuce.

He learned to use terms like WMA (White Male Adult) and HMA (Hispanic Male Adult). Females were WFA or HFA. Everything was shortened but descriptive when broadcast over the radio. Everyone had a call number; his was R-49. They would call Robert-49, 11-10. Which meant he, R-49, was receiving a call for service.

It was a different culture for him, but he adapted quickly. It soon became second nature to him, and the conversations with other Officers were always in "code speak." Donnie realized that all professions had their own language, but Law Enforcement was sometimes unique and sounded strange to outsiders. He also discovered that this was intentional. His life took on a rhythm he had not expected. Responding to calls was soon something he looked forward to. He began to handle them without having to ask a senior Officer for assistance. He entered his comfort zone.

It happens to everyone somewhere between 18 months and two years into their Law Enforcement career. This is usually when something occurs to shake up the Officer and bring them back to the reality of the job. Law Enforcement is a rewarding career, yet it can be hazardous at times.

Donnie's came when he was called to a domestic violence call, a 273.5 (a). "Robert-49, 11-10," came over the radio. "Go ahead, dispatch. Respond to this 2275 Hemlock for a 273.5 in progress."

He had dealt with other calls like this, but this one was different in the extent of brutality. Most of the time, it was just the couple yelling and throwing things at each other. On this call, he learned people can be cruel and brutal. When he arrived, his Sergeant was already on scene. When he entered the residence, a male was sitting on the couch in handcuffs. There were scratches on his face and arms. What appeared to be blood on one side of his mouth, as if he had been punched.

He was motioned to an adjacent room by his Sergeant. When he entered the room, a female was sitting on the floor. She was only wearing a T-shirt and panties. Donnie looked at her and could see blood on her face and forehead; her hair looked like it was a bird's nest. She had bruises forming on her face and arms. He saw a hole behind her in the wall, like someone had punched it. As he looked around the room, it looked like there had been a struggle. Things were knocked off the dresser's top, and the bedding was thrown against the wall.

The woman was crying and rocking back and forth. Donnie spoke with her and started asking questions. She told him she had been in bed asleep when the male, her boyfriend, had come back drunk. He yelled at her to get up, but she refused. According to her, that was when the male threw the bedding against the wall and grabbed her by her hair and pulled her out of the bed.

She went on to say he told her to fix him something to eat, but she said there wasn't anything to eat. It was at this point that he shoved her against the wall so hard that her head went through the sheetrock and broke it. He then slapped her and punched her several times in the face. She told Donnie she tried to fight back, but he grabbed her and threw her down onto the floor and started kicking her legs, back, and butt. She told him he had kicked her so hard she had feces in her panties and showed him it was still in her underwear she had on.

At the sight of the woman and what she had told him, Donnie became enraged and turned towards the male. His Sergeant stopped him, told him to go back to the office, and wait for him there. It took a few seconds to register, and the Sergeant repeated the order. There was another officer on scene, so Donnie left and headed to the office.

As he waited, Donnie thought he would be suspended and placed on leave, pending an investigation. However, when the Sergeant arrived about an hour later, they sat down and discussed the situation. The Sergeant understood, but he also reminded Donnie of his sworn duty to everybody. He was not a vigilante on the streets to end crime, but a law enforcement officer who had taken an oath. That oath was the line they could not cross. Donnie had calmed down by the time the Sergeant arrived at the office. Donnie had also had time to think. The Sergeant admitted he had felt the same thing, but also knew the line could not be crossed. He gave Donnie a look over and knew he was responding to instinct. He had gotten to know Donnie well and knew he cared deeply for other people.

The Sergeant told Donnie that there would be no written report about the situation and made him promise to remember the Oath he had taken. But he also warned him not to let it happen again, or he would have to file an internal report. Donnie realized this was his only chance to continue working in Law Enforcement. He agreed to remember his Oath and to watch how he reacted to situations in the future.

His Sergeant looked at him and said something he will never forget, "We, you and I, were taught to protect women and children at all costs. We were given the responsibility of treating them with respect. In this job, we will encounter situations like tonight, which will test us as human beings and seriously challenge our humanity. There will be other times when we will only see the worst in others. How we react to the worst situations determines the course of our lives and those we encounter and deal with daily." He continued, "We see people who have suffered the worst by those they oftentimes love the most. When it is a stranger, we can somehow justify it. When it's a family or a spouse or a dating situation, it doesn't make sense."

While Donnie was sitting in the recliner and thinking back on his time in Law Enforcement, James came in and asked how he was doing. Donnie looked up at James and said he was thinking about his years in Law Enforcement.

James asked his dad if he wanted to talk about it, and Donnie said he did. "Do you want some coffee?" James asked his dad. "That would be good," Donnie replied.

After James got everything ready, brought his dad the coffee, and sat down, he looked at his dad. "When I came in a bit ago, you seemed to be thinking about something. Is everything okay, Dad?" He asked.

"It is, sorry about that, I was just thinking of the early years of my Law Enforcement career. I was thinking about the training; it has evolved over the years, but remains largely the same. The main thing I remembered was how unprepared I was after leaving the academy for the actual job. Life is different than the training center. Sure, you get the basics, but not much more. There is a lot more to understand about the job." Donnie paused to take a drink of his coffee.

"Until you encounter everything, you will not be prepared for everything. I also remembered my first bad domestic experience. How I was unprepared to see a woman beaten, bruised, and bleeding, sitting on the floor and feeling the need to show me the feces she still had in her underwear, after being kicked so hard, she crapped her pants from it." Donnie just shook his head at that.

James' eyes widened at that; he realized that there were things that still deeply affected his dad, even after the considerable time he had spent in Law Enforcement and security work.

"Anyway," Donnie began, "I started applying for my first cop job about 2 years into my security work. I got hired and went to the academy. My first Field Training Officer was a peculiar individual who had only one good working eye. He was also the department's evidence officer. He insisted everything we found got turned into evidence, including open cans of beer." He used to say, "You never know what an attorney will ask for, so always be prepared."

"He would put duct tape on each open can to stop the smell from seeping out. After 90 days, he would discard everything that had not been requested. It all seemed a bit too much to me." Donnie was smiling at the thought. The FTO was a tall guy with a big belly, wore glasses, and seemed to have had the worst case of Dandruff Donnie had ever seen. His dark blue uniform shirt's shoulders were always covered with it.

James stopped his dad after his father made the statement. "You had a one-eyed FTO who was also the evidence officer?" "Why did he keep every can of beer?" James asked, then added, "His dandruff was that bad?"

Donnie started to laugh at the questions his son asked him. "He was one-eyed and had horrible dandruff. Funny thing is, he was almost bald too, so I have no idea how he had so much dandruff." James laughed at the image of the FTO with an eye patch and made a pirate noise. Donnie laughed with his son over all that.

"When I first started at the Department, I was riding with one of my Sergeants. During my first shift, we got a call about shots being fired behind a downtown bar. My Sergeant pulled up in front of an adjacent building. And we were positioned along a wall. The other responding officer pulled into the alley behind the bar, and he drew his gun. I could hear him yell at the subject. A couple of seconds later, he radioed that the male subject was running on the south side of the building towards us. A couple of minutes later, he ran across the street in front of us, and we started to chase him into a vacant field. My sergeant took the lead, and I was to his left as cover. I saw the male had his hands in his hoodie pockets." Donnie told James.

After a pause, he continued, "While we were chasing him, he turned around and attempted to get his left hand out of the hoodie pocket. We didn't know if he still had the gun, so I aimed at him as he fought to get his hand out of his pocket. When he did, it was empty. He turned again and kept running. With us chasing him, he turned around again, this time it was his right hand. He fought to get that hand from the right pocket. As he fought, I felt myself slowly pulling on the trigger of my gun. After a few seconds like this, he managed to get his hand out of his pocket. His hand was balled up, as if he had something in it, then he opened it. When I saw that, I released the pressure on the trigger. We didn't know it at the time, but he had dropped the little gun behind the dumpster he was hiding behind when our officer entered the alley."

"He continued to run from us until he tripped over a low garden fence in the dark. I still had my gun drawn because of the adrenaline pumping through me. My Sergeant told me to holster it and cuff the male." Donnie said.

"After we got him to his feet and started walking him back towards the Patrol vehicle, the other Officer radioed that he had recovered the gun. He told us he was coming around to the front of the bar with it. When he got out of his unit, he showed us the gun. It was a small .380 caliber and had a 9mm round stuck in the slide area. The lead tip was stuck into the barrel of the .380, with the casing portion angled down towards the lead tip. There was no way for the gun to be fired at that point. Had he fired it, the lead bullet could have caused the barrel to explode instead; if not, the bullet would have been stuck in the barrel. He didn't know much about guns."

It seemed to James that his dad was standing there looking at the gun again and wondering just how crazy it was. "He tried to jam the larger bullet into the gun," James said. "That doesn't make a lot of sense to me. He thought it would work, I suppose." James sat there, trying to figure out the mechanics of the whole thing, but all he could do was shake his head in disbelief.

"It was obvious to us that he didn't understand the difference between gun calibers, as if he could simply interchange a larger caliber into any gun," Donnie said with a smile.

"The one thing I have always wondered about that night is what he was going to use the gun for. I mean, he was behind this bar, with a loaded gun. Was it for someone? Was he going to try to rob the place? We never did find out because he never told us." Donnie looked at him when we said this, and James could tell it still bothered his dad.

"The not knowing still bugs you, doesn't it?" James asked Donnie. "It does because I have always wanted to know what he was going to do with the gun".

"My first night on the job, I almost shot someone. This is part of what I was saying about how the academy doesn't completely prepare anyone for every situation Law Enforcement encounters. I have wanted to speak to the instructors to ask why they don't prepare the cadets for everything. The other thing they don't do is engage in a form of combat or movement practice when it comes to shooting. If they move away from the static targets, objects that don't move, you are always stationary when qualifying on the range. They need to teach movement, setting, and shooting; it would be better for every officer who graduates and enters their career." Donnie said to James.

James looked at his dad and knew he was right. He can shoot a target well, but if he had to move, position himself, and then shoot, it would be more challenging. He wanted to practice movement. He knew of an instructor who used a style called the President or "El Presidente". It was a move-and-shoot type of course, after you needed to run between 10 and 20 yards to the first target. Then you zig-zag between targets, getting closer to each cover position, all the while being timed.

"My department's range Master would set up the move and shoot course. But he would add things like throwing ping-pong and golf balls, a loudspeaker, siren sounds, and poking us with a stick. I learned more from him and how to control myself in a shooting situation than I did at the 4-week course about shooting, in the academy's range practice of standing and shooting only." Donnie realized he was "preaching" to James, but felt it needed to be said to his son.

"The reason why so many shots are fired in most incidents is that combat techniques or tactics are never taught. At least my academy didn't." Donnie paused for a minute.

"Even though a majority of the public understands that Law Enforcement members see the sidearm as just another tool to be used last. Less lethal is taught more and more these days and teaching the recruits to use a gun as a last resort and only if a life or more is in danger. Unfortunately, some still see Law Enforcement as old west gun fighters with a bad attitude". Concluded Donnie.

James was looking at his dad as he spoke. He was caught up in the words, just like he had as a young kid. Now that he was entering Law Enforcement, he knew he had a lot to learn. It might be more complicated than he first thought, but he also knew he could overcome everything the academy would put him through. He also had a profound admiration for his dad. Realizing he wasn't perfect, but also stronger than he had realized growing up, James remembered thinking his dad was larger than life as he was growing up. Now he saw a man who had experienced more than he ever knew and still seemed willing to sacrifice to make sure others were safe.

"Dad", he started, "do you regret any of the choices you have made. I mean, with everything you have been put through during your years of wearing a badge, you have had people's lives in your hands at times. I am realizing the weight beneath the badge you have worn, and I am about to place one on my uniform".

James looked down at his cup of coffee and thought about it all. There could come a time when he, too, would face the same situations his dad had faced. He felt a heaviness flood over him as the reality finally dawned on him.

"Son, please understand, I would gladly do it all over again. It has not always been easy, but it has always been worth it. When you can help someone, they pay the bill that this life charges you. When you save a kid or a woman from abuse, it gives you the strength to face another day. It has always had ups and downs. It can cause many to question their life choices. Then you end your shift and come home to your family. They become the reason why you get up every day and do it all over again," Donnie explained. "The only thing I would change is losing your mom," he added.

They sat in silence for a few minutes, lost in thought, both contemplating this kind of life. One was starting his, and the other was nearing the end of his call to service.

"I remember when it would rain in town, the water would puddle up on several intersections," Donnie started. "Everyone in town knew it but never seemed to think they would be the one to get stuck in the water driving. One time, there was heavy rain, and the usual corners were flooded. One driver attempted to drive through the water. It didn't end well. When I received the call and arrived, the man was sitting on the hood of his car, yelling and cursing. He told me he was going to be late for work now and demanded I help him get his car out of the water." Donnie was smiling at the thought.

"I told him I needed to call for a tow truck because they could pull him out. He didn't like that and again demanded I pull him out with my unit. I told him again that I needed to call for a tow truck. He then jumped off his car into the water. The water came up to his knees as he started to walk towards me, angry that I wasn't "willing" to help him. By the time he got to me, the struggle of walking in the water had calmed him down. He apologized to me and asked if he could wait with me for the tow truck. I said it was okay. We waited for about 20 minutes for the tow truck to get there." He paused and then continued, "The driver told me he knew he would get stuck but had been running late, even driving slow through the water, and he stalled. I just nodded and said I understood. There was no point in telling him I thought he had acted stupidly, and that the towing company would now bill him, and he would need to get his vehicle repaired and cleaned. Or that he should have gone the additional 3 blocks to get around the water. I wanted to but decided I wouldn't".

By the time Donnie ended the story. He and James were laughing about it. Donnie said he could still see that the guy wanted to act angry, but the struggle to walk in the water made it difficult to keep it up. He told James that within a couple of hours, the intersection would be back to normal again. James started laughing again as Donnie chuckled.

Donnie had seen a lot over his more than 2 decades in law enforcement and high-end security. He had dealt with just about everything imaginable. Some situations were life-threatening; most were not. However, everything he had experienced left a lasting impression on his mind. Some had left a mark on his body, like the scar on his right arm from a cut he got breaking up a bar-fight. Every time he saw it, he remembered the night he met Carol. A chance encounter that changed his life.

Some of the things have made him laugh, while others have scared him. But all of them have helped him become who he is today.

James was looking at his dad and realized he was lost in thought. He let him remember, then he asked, "Dad, more memories coming to mind?" Donnie looked at his son and smiled, saying, "Yes, and most are good ones."

"Son, there are so many good and bad memories. Some have had a lasting impression on me. Add in the people I have worked with or encountered along the way, some good and some bad". Donnie looked at James to see if he understood what he was trying to tell him.

"Dad, it makes sense. I haven't experienced the things you have, but I get it. I've been there too, in sports, school, and work already."

"One night, while I was working, I heard Robert-49, 11-10. I responded, Robert-49. The dispatcher instructed me to respond to a traffic collision just north of town. Little did I know what I was about to get into." Donnie lowered his voice for a minute. "When I was attempting to get to the scene, I had to pull to the side of the road due to stopped traffic. I got out, advised our dispatcher and the other officers responding that traffic had stopped, and that I was on foot. Both lanes on one side of the interstate were filled with vehicles. I ran to the bridge, and as I got there, I saw 5 vehicles all over it. People were out of their vehicles, and I saw a vehicle axle in the middle of the lanes." Donnie stopped and saw James's expression change.

"I radioed what I found to the other officers. I could hear sirens, and the Sheriff's deputies arrived at the scene. Highway Patrol was also responding. I advised the dispatcher that we needed medical personnel to respond, as several were complaining of injuries. Because it was a Highway, the Highway Patrol needed to be on the scene for reports and such. I found 2 witnesses who had seen everything happen right in front of them. I took their names and started talking to everyone else. Got their information and which vehicle they came from." Donnie shook his head and said, "It was a mess."

"I had people on one side of the bridge so that HP, Highway Patrol, could find everyone. A couple of people had broken bones, mostly just small cuts, and bruising was seen. One vehicle had originally carried 4 people, 2 of them little kids. They were screaming, and the axle belonged to their car. I waited for everyone to arrive, organizing them and keeping them apart. HP arrived about 10 minutes later and started taking statements after checking with me. I told them I had called for medical to respond. Our volunteer firefighters arrived and started treating people. At that point, I contacted my Sergeant, and we devised a plan to divert traffic around the accident area. Since it was a bridge, we needed to turn them back into town to get around the area".

James was leaning towards his dad, listening to every word. And he realized that he could face a situation like that one day. He realized he could learn from these stories, not just by listening to them.

"The ambulances showed up from two different towns that had hospitals and were directed by the Firefighters as to who needed the most attention. All these people were doing a great job. HP called for several tow trucks because all the damaged cars were in such a state that they needed to be towed, especially the one with the missing axle. At first, no one could figure out why the axle had fallen off until one of the Highway Patrol officers took a closer look. The thing fell off the car. The brackets holding it on were rusted through. The profanity from that officer made me laugh!"

"Now", Donnie continued, "while I was on the bridge, the backed-up traffic was slowly moving and being redirected. My Sergeant pulled his vehicle over and got out, helping them get started. An off-duty Deputy from a large Law Enforcement agency pulled up to speak to him. He said he was traveling back home, and while he was waiting to get going again, 3 guys in the vehicle beside him were seen drinking and making vulgar comments towards his wife. The Deputy had decided not to take any action at that time, but wanted to advise my Sergeant of the situation. He radioed the vehicle's make, model, and license plate to our dispatcher. As soon as he had, one of our local deputies said he had them in front of him and was pulling them over. A Highway Patrol officer pulled in behind the deputy. The 3 males were arrested. One had an outstanding warrant as well."

James just shook his head at that. He asked his dad, "What were they thinking? Why would anyone be stopped at an accident scene and drink alcohol"? Donnie just shrugged his shoulders at James.

"The out-of-town Deputy thanked our Sergeant and asked if he would tell the other officers the same, got back into his vehicle, and drove away. There are times when Law Enforcement and emergency responders can work together swiftly and effectively. That was one of those times".

"After almost three hours, we were able to clear the road, and traffic flow started up again," Donnie said.

"Dad, is that normal for accidents to take that long to clean up? It sounds like it was handled almost like a military drill. All the different agencies were working together to resolve the situation, and it still took that long".

"There are steps to cleaning up vehicle accidents that require the department to do certain things. In this case, the first part is to triage the victims and get statements. They all had to be identified and questioned, then sent to one of the hospitals. Five vehicles are being removed. Typically, there is gas and oil on the road that needs to be covered, usually with sand. And then we needed to make sure there weren't any sharp metal pieces left behind or glass, to cut through tires, causing another wreck or blocking a lane of traffic". Donnie then asked James, "Does that make sense, son"?

Donnie continued, "On top of all that, there is the waiting for ambulances and towing companies to send the necessary equipment to clear everything up, so the road can be opened again. Seven tow trucks and five ambulances were used in that accident, along with local fire personnel.

That's a lot of organizing to get everything completed. That isn't always the case, though".

"I had no idea it took all that for an accident scene to get cleared. There is more to it than just moving the vehicles out of the way. Sounds time-consuming for everyone. Guess I won't be so frustrated the next time I'm stuck at a vehicle accident," James sounded confused, but also as if he understood what his dad had just told him.

Donnie continued, "There are times when it's as simple as moving a vehicle out of the way, such as a simple fendor bender. There was not much damage to either vehicle. At other times, such as the accident involving multiple vehicles and the resulting mess, it took longer. There is never a hard and fast calculation to do for time spent on any accident."

As an example, we received a call one night about who had jumped a tall curb and hit a brick and rod iron fence. When we arrived, the car was high-centered on the fence. When we arrived, there was only one guy next to the vehicle. As soon as I was close to him, I could smell alcohol on his breath. I asked the man if he had been drinking, and he swore he had not, because it was against his faith to do so. When my partner looked in the vehicle, he saw a half-full bottle of Brandy. Of course, the man said it wasn't his, but the breathalyzer showed otherwise. He was twice the legal limit. I then told him he needed to turn around because he was under arrest, but he decided to fight with me. He took a swing at me, missing me, but my partner was on him quickly, and we were able to get him cuffed. One of our other officers arrived as we were putting him into the vehicle. The tow truck took almost an hour to arrive and get the vehicle, and about another 40 minutes to get the vehicle untangled from the fence." Donnie stopped for a sip of coffee.

James was confused. He asked his dad, "The vehicle had jumped over an almost 12-inch curb and ended up going halfway through a brick and wrought iron fence? How is that even possible?" James also asked why it took so long to get the vehicle off the fence.

Donnie reminded James that the vehicle was halfway through the fence, which could mean a fuel line was broken, the transmission was damaged, or the radiator was punctured. "The tow truck driver was trying not to damage the car even more. And the property owner, who had called us, said he didn't want the fence damaged any further, so he decided to take his time."

James is realizing that the duties he will be asked to do will involve a wide range of responsibilities. Anything is possible in Law Enforcement. Everything will become routine, and it will be different every day. Listening to his dad's stories, he is realizing the possibilities that lie ahead.

James asked his dad, "Every day you were in Law Enforcement, it sounds like it was never routine and always something new to face. How did you keep up with everything?"

"There were days when you had to find something. We did everything from issuing tickets to responding to calls. We also did preliminary investigations of all crimes. So, we could always find something. Sitting on a corner using a radar gun, looking for things that didn't belong. All became part of the day-to-day. Assisting other agencies when they called. Follow-up on crimes committed earlier". Donnie said.

"One night, as an example, my partner and I were driving up our main street in town and noticed a couple of kids moving around in the backseat of the car in front of us. We followed the car for about a block, and we saw one of them standing in the back seat. We decided to pull the car over. When we approached the car, we noticed a problem. There were two women in the front seats, but it was the backseat that caught our attention. As we were talking through the front windows, we kept seeing little faces pop up. We asked the women to exit the vehicle and then asked them to call the kids out of the vehicle as well." Donnie paused for a few seconds as a smile started to form.

"It was like watching a clown car at a circus, the kids kept popping out. These two women had nine little kids hiding in the back of the car, and it was just a two-door! The passenger was holding a baby in her arms. We cited the driver, had her lock up the vehicle, and made them walk the next three blocks to her house. We had been driving about 20 miles an hour, but it was still hazardous for the kids. As they were leaving, it looked like baby ducks following their mom." Donnie was shaking his head as he spoke, remembering the whole thing.

Donnie could tell James was thinking through what he had just heard. He was processing as a smile formed on his face, too. Slightly tilting his head, he looked up and began to speak. "There were a total of ten kids in that car and the two women. Yet all you guys did was issue the driver a ticket and make them walk. Why not call the family services to report them for endangering the kids? Why not arrest them for that?" "Dad," he continued, "I would have arrested at least the driver for child endangerment. Even driving slowly doesn't mean the kids can't get hurt in an accident. I don't agree with what you two did in this case". James was upset as he spoke, and Donnie could hear it in his son's voice. He also knew what was happening that night.

"James, we made our decision based on what the family needed to do at that time. When Law Enforcement officers allow personal feelings to get in the way, they create situations that never needed to happen. In this case, those kids didn't need strangers to grab them and tear their world apart. Yes, the two women put them in needless danger, but the kids would have been the real victims. We decided to keep them all together," Donnie told him.

James looked at his dad; he was still upset about what they had done the night before. He is much like his parents in that he feels compelled to protect children from harm. For that reason, James didn't understand. He told his dad, "I understand your reasoning, but I still don't agree that kids should be put in danger, hurt, or abused in any way. It goes against what you and Mom taught me."

"It took us 20 minutes of weighing out all the possible scenarios to come up with that. We didn't decide lightly, and to the best of my knowledge, they never drove that many kids around again. It served the purpose". Donnie said to James.

Donnie realized James was still frustrated with the story and needed a break. Donnie told James he needed to get some paperwork done and asked if he would be good at picking up the conversation later. James nodded and said, "Yeah, I need to calm down." He got up and went to the back of the house. Donnie turned back to his paperwork, which he had been working on before they started talking, and realized they had been talking for a couple of hours already.

9

The Mark of the Badge

Donnie was deep into the paperwork he had to do when James entered the kitchen again. It had been several hours since he had left for the back of the house. "Dad, I want to apologize to you for my anger earlier. I was wrong."

Donnie looked up at him and said, "Thank you," and then told his son, "No need to apologize, you are who your mom and I raised. You have a heart for those who cannot defend themselves, and always have. I appreciate your candor and willingness to express it. I am not lecturing you with what I am about to say; however, based on my experience, I would advise caution in Law Enforcement. It is a trigger, something I call a hot button; we all have one or more. I have trained many people over the years, and it always comes out and can affect the job", Donnie said to James.

"Noted," James said with a smile. He had always known his dad was a fair man when it came to dealing with him and the few things he had gotten into. He had always supported James and encouraged him to explore the answers to the questions he had posed before. James had learned more from doing that than he had learned in other ways. Always the one to do research and never take things at face value, he had always wanted to know what was beneath the surface. It has helped him cut through the nonsense around him and find the buried truth behind words and actions. Although several of his teachers in school didn't like that, they later came to admire his tenacity.

Donnie was smiling at James. He knew his son was more mature than most people his age. He had been called an old soul by a few people over the years, and his dad is finally coming to understand that he might be one himself. He was an educated man, and the child he had raised was now a man. Donnie felt a lump rise in his throat as he thought of how proud he was of his son. Carol and he talked often about who he was becoming and how proud they both were of him. "Thankfully, we didn't screw him up," Carol had said once to Donnie. He had to agree with her. They had done well together, raising him.

"Are you ready to hear about some more stories yet"? He asked James. "I am hungry and think we need to eat first," James responded. Donnie looked at the wall clock and realized it was about time to eat. James asked what he wanted for dinner as it was his turn to cook. Donnie told him he wasn't very hungry, but the sandwiches sounded good tonight. "Your usual Ham and cheese with mustard and mayo, topped with lettuce and tomato"? Donnie agreed, saying that would be perfect. James got everything out, made one for his dad and two for himself, grabbed a bag of chips and a couple of soft drinks, and headed to the table to sit down.

As they ate, they continued with small talk. James asked questions about the paperwork he had been working on, and Donnie inquired about his work. They brought up people they knew, and Donnie asked about James' friends and what they thought about him joining the Sheriff's department. James said he had only told a couple of people, but they thought he would be a good fit.

James cleaned up as he worked, and Donnie started another story. "We got a call one time for a wreck under our train track underpass. A semi with a full box trailer behind it had turned over. As I approached the scene, I saw the tractor lying on its side. I couldn't see the driver anywhere. I pulled up and jumped the barrier to look into the cab as a responding deputy, coming in with lights and siren on, almost hit my vehicle from behind. He swerved just in time to avoid hitting my vehicle. I then got back into my vehicle and moved it to the other end of the accident scene, as two lanes were blocked and we now needed to redirect traffic. I radioed our dispatch center and asked for a large towing truck. The semi was a local trucker hauling for a local agricultural business."

James had turned around and was looking at his dad. "Wait, the deputy almost rear-ended your Police cruiser?" "Yeah, he was responding at a high speed, and I hadn't turned my emergency lights on because I was in a hurry," he told James.

"Anyway, this was about 6 am, and I was supposed to be off shift at 8 am. I asked the dispatcher to contact the business owner and see if the business owner had heard from the driver. After she called the business owner, she advised me that he had not. We were directing traffic, and a couple of other Officers arrived to help. When the tow truck arrived, he was unable to lift the loaded trailer. Now we needed to get some of their workers to empty the trailer." James saw his dad's face, and he looked frustrated. The memory wasn't a happy one for him. "We waited for the workers, almost an hour and a half, and we had five workers with forklifts show up and start to empty the trailer. It finally took another 3 hours for the trailer to get back on its wheels. Then another semi-truck had to move it. Almost 5 hours later, I headed back to the Office to write my report. Unlike any other job, you cannot leave when your shift is over. The OT was good, but it was a long 15-hour shift by the time I was able to leave, and then the 35-minute drive home".

James looked confused for a minute, then asked, "There was no one else to take your place at the time?" "There was, but because I was first on the scene, I had to stay with the scene. We had a policy that the first Officer, unless transporting someone, had to stay at the scene until it was cleared.

And we never found the driver of the Semi, which was another reason I stayed. He fled the accident and didn't report it either," Donnie said.

"We had traffic lights on the interstate that divided the town. In winter, dense fog often caused whiteouts, as a river lay just north of town. We had a lot of accidents at those lights before the state finally decided to remove them and build a bridge over the highway. It could be dangerous to cross in dense fog. I remember coming to work one morning, and there was already a 5-car pile-up near those lights".

Donnie continued, "I was paired up with a partner one night, we had pulled over a guy for suspected drunk driving, performing the FSTs, or Field Sobriety tests, on him. While we were doing so, we heard a loud crash that sounded like it came from the interstate at the lights. We looked at each other, and I remember asking him, At the lights? He said Yeah. I said we need to respond; he told me we will wait for a call. About 2 minutes later, the 11-10 came over the radio." Donnie stopped for a minute, as if lost in thought of that night; James could see it on his face.

"As we responded to the call, I remember getting to the lights. We did have our siren and emergency lights on at the time. He paused to check traffic, and I saw what looked like a small car facing the wrong way on the north side of the lights. As we got closer, I saw two adult males and a kid running around the car, screaming. When we got out of the vehicle, there were two women in the backseat with their heads down. We had to check them for a pulse. He radioed that we had two fatalities and three additional victims. He advised the dispatcher to respond with the fire department, ambulance, and Highway Patrol. As I was trying to get the attention of the two males, I could hear sirens in the distance". Donnie paused and had a drink of coffee before continuing. "As the volunteer firefighters responded, I remember being asked to help get the 2 males and the kid off the highway area and to the shoulder of the road. As they sat down, I could see cuts on the scalp of one of the males. I told the firefighter what I saw. As he was cleaning the wound, it looked like teeth marks on the man's head. Apparently, from one of the women in the backseat".

As more interagency officers arrived, we had them start directing traffic and lay out a flare pattern to divert traffic to one lane. The Highway Patrol arrived and took over the scene, as it was on the highway, and their job was to handle it. Our Sergeant showed up as well. We gave all the flares we had in our vehicles to the deputies setting the flare pattern south of the accident. I asked a trucker if he had a C/B radio in his truck. He said he did, and I asked him if he could have other northbound truckers help us slow traffic as it approached. He agreed, and that helped. The fog was dense that night." Donnie looked like it was one of those vivid memories he had. James asked him if he was all right, and he said he was; it was just all coming back to him. Then he smiled for a minute.

"James, there was a Highway Patrol officer with a long 45-minute flare, directing the traffic through the accident area. These two people were trying to see what had happened, barely moving. The Officer tried to move them, but they were determined to see what was going on. He lost his patience with them, and I can still remember him throwing his lit flare at the driver's side of the windshield, which hit with a thud. The driver then looked up, saw the flare, and decided she needed to speed up and get through the scene. The Highway Patrolman put his hand up and retrieved the flare that had fallen off the woman's car, and once he picked it up, he started waving people through the scene; they complied after that." Donnie was chuckling as he finished telling James about that. James just shook his head and chuckled along with his dad.

"I remember overhearing the Highway Patrol officer and my Sergeant talking about the other vehicle, and they had a possible identification of the type of vehicle it could have been. They thought it had to be a semi-truck because of the damage to the car, and there were no other signs of grille pieces, bumper, or headlight glass on the ground. It was at that moment that I remembered seeing a large, folded blue tarp by the traffic light base where we had taken the three males. I pointed it out to them and told them I could see what looked like a flatbed semi-trailer with its taillights on, about a quarter mile north of the lights. The Highway Patrol asked me to contact the driver and get his license and his driver's logbook. As I approached him, I saw him putting on his hearing aids as he stepped down out of the cab of his truck. I told him he needed to stay in the truck, but I needed his License and driver's logbook. He handed them to me, and I went back to hand them over."

Donnie looked at James for a minute, then started speaking again, "The truck driver looked to be late fifties or early sixties." After pausing, Donnie began again, "That area had speed restrictions and lane controls for the semis, to help prevent these accidents from happening. The Trucker should have been going only 35 miles an hour and in the outside lane. According to the HP accident investigator, the truck was traveling at fifty-five miles per hour and was in the inside lane. That was the only way the car could have been pushed to where it stopped, according to his investigation. The driver was arrested and charged with two counts of vehicular manslaughter as well as the traffic violations."

"After the arrest and the vehicles were removed, the Fire Department made sure the roadway was clear of debris, and we were all finally able to clear the scene. The fog had made it dangerous for everyone, including the vehicles entering the area and the emergency workers. When something like this happens, everyone needs to be cautious. It doesn't always happen, but they should. Donnie finished and sat there silently for a few minutes.

James could tell the stories his dad was telling him were bringing up memories. Some are bringing up some painful memories for him. He can see it on his face and hear it in his voice. James understood his dad better with each story; he was gaining a clearer sense of why his dad did things the way he did and why he had been so careful when James was a kid. "Dad, are these memories causing you any hurt or pain?" James asked, then followed up, "It seems like there are times you are right back there as you are telling me about your experiences."

Donnie looked at James for a couple of minutes before he said, "The memories are what they are. They happened, and some I haven't thought of in a while. Some are a bit difficult to recall due to the circumstances, but they did happen. I cannot change them, but if they can help prepare you for what you will encounter, I will share them. Incidents like that accident, where people died, are tough for everyone to look back on."

They sat there in silence for a bit, each of them drinking the coffee in front of them. There wasn't much to say as each person processed what had been said. Donnie was recalling the entire accident scene and what had been said. He could feel the cold of the fog and rubbed his arms. James was going through everything his dad had told him. He knew his dad was still reliving the incident. He knew his dad never let anything go that he went through; the reason was so he could learn from everything. His dad had said that several times over the years. Even when James was playing sports, his dad would "debrief" him afterward to help him reflect on what had happened and prepare for next time. James has found himself doing the same thing over the years, and it has helped him.

Donnie cleared his throat and started to tell another story. "One night, my partner and I were patrolling the stretch of the interstate we could and observed an old station wagon turn onto the interstate, and the driver had overcorrected as he entered the lane in front of us. I was driving, so I decided to follow it. As I pulled up a little closer, I saw it weaving in the lane. I flipped on my overhead lights to advise the driver to pull over for a traffic stop. The vehicle started to speed up. We had been driving at the speed limit of fifty-five, but now the driver was trying to speed away. My partner grabbed the radio mic and advised our dispatcher of the situation. When I looked down at my speedometer, it read 80 miles per hour, and it was climbing. The next time I looked down, we were going 100 miles an hour. Then the driver slammed on his brakes. I did the same; we quickly dropped back down to 70, then they sped up again to almost 100 miles an hour. I was pacing them. My partner was relaying everything to our dispatcher. We pursued the vehicle for about 3 miles to an off-ramp. They took it and hit the edge of the off-ramp, coming to a stop. We stepped out of the vehicle, and I grabbed the radio mic as he switched it to the loudspeaker. Guns out, I ordered the driver out of the vehicle and to back towards me with his arms raised. As the driver moved back towards me, my partner moved towards the vehicle and looked through it." Pausing for a second, Donnie smiled. James had leaned forward in his chair. He continued, "I had him drop to his knees, cross his feet, and place his hands behind his head. I approached him and cuffed him. Standing behind him, I called out to my partner, asking if he was Code 4 and if he was OK. He said he was, then reached into the back seat and pulled out a rifle. He checked it and said it was loaded. He cleared it and brought it to our vehicle, placing it on the hood. As I patted down the driver, I could smell alcohol on his breath. As I found items in his pockets, I placed them on the hood of the patrol car. I asked him for his name, but he refused to tell me, claiming he was a member of the Coast Guard and that I had no right to arrest him. I placed the driver in the back seat. My partner checked more of the car that was visible and found nothing. We advised our dispatcher we were code 4 and had one 10-15".

Donnie paused, and as he took a drink of coffee, James had to ask, "As you're telling this story, there's no emotion in your voice. Were you scared?" Donnie smiled at James and said, "Would it have changed the situation? I was on a high from the pursuit; everything else was just what needed to be done. I wasn't thinking of the weapon found in the vehicle, the driver was driving drunk, and there could have been a whole lot more to deal with if he had crashed or hit another vehicle. Luckily for all of us, he took that off-ramp instead, and the highway was surprisingly clear. So, no, I wasn't scared, son."

"We decided to leave his parents' vehicle where he stopped it. No damage was visible to it. We headed to our station house to do the preliminary paperwork. The whole time, he kept telling us he was a member of the Coast Guard, and we could not arrest him. He also insisted we call his Commander. This was early on a Sunday morning, around 0130 am. After attempting to complete the paperwork, we decided to contact his Commander when he refused to provide any information. Keep in mind that we are on the West Coast, while the base is on the East Coast, resulting in a four-hour time difference. It was 0600 in Virginia that Sunday morning, and we made the call. He started acting smug as my partner talked to his Commander. Then he handed the phone to an 18-year-old young man who was about to have his entire world flipped upside down. As he and the Commander spoke, his smile vanished, and he began to look defeated, as if he had been punched in the gut. At first, it was a conversation on his part that quickly turned to nothing but "yes, sir" and "no, sir." After a couple of minutes, he handed the phone back to my partner. His hand was shaking, and he lowered his head. The Commander spoke with my partner for a couple of minutes and then hung up the phone."

Donnie stopped speaking and smiled from ear to ear, while James' eyes widened in shock, his mouth agape. Shaking his head, he just stared at his dad in disbelief. Not wanting to interrupt but wanting to hear the rest of this story, he just sat there waiting.

Donnie continued, "After the phone call, we got all the info we needed. He was over the legal limit, so we booked him for drunk driving, evading, and high speeds at the local jail. He was placed on a military hold as well, per the base commander. My partner waited until we were leaving the booking area to tell me what the Commander said to him." Donnie was chuckling now. He had to pause to control his laughter. After the pause, he continued, “My partner said the base Commander would be sending two MPs to pick the guy up, but they would be driving from Virginia to our local jail. It could take up to 5 days for them to arrive, as they were told to be careful and take their time. Stop and find lodging as needed so they are well-rested to drive. They would then drive him back to Virginia and address their affairs. After which he would return the guy, via bus, to our county jail.” James couldn’t help himself; he laughed, knowing the guy was in deep trouble. Donnie put his hand up and said, “There’s more. After about 6 months we received a call from the base Commander telling us he drove the guy to the bus station, he had been court-martialed and even so, if he did not receive a call from our local jail in 5 days, then he would personally come out, find the guy and send him to the military prison to complete his sentence for them.

When the guy got back, he went straight to jail, notified his Commander of his arrival, and then went through our county court system. He received another 6-month sentence, a suspended license, and a $5,000 fine. His life was ruined by a decision to drink with his friends and drive.”

James sat in silence, absorbing everything he had just heard. While James sat there, Donnie got up and poured some more coffee. Brought the cups back and set them before James.

His son was looking at the freshly filled coffee cup, rubbing the rim with his index finger. James was thinking about the stories his dad told him, knowing they could be his own in a few years. As a Deputy Sheriff, he would encounter similar situations. As he was immersed in his thoughts, he realized his dad had been through a lot, and it could have changed him. “Dad, how much have the years you have been involved in Law Enforcement and security changed you? Have you become a different person after the years you have dealt with things like you are telling me?” James asked.

“Son, you can ask some tough questions sometimes. But I will try to explain it to you. I was a lot like you when I started this adventure. I wasn’t ready for many of the things I was going to see. I thought I was, but the job revealed something different. That first night in Law Enforcement made me understand that this wasn't going to be easy. I learned to make decisions in a split second. And to be willing to take a life to save a life, if needed. When I saw that woman sitting in her underwear and learned that he had kicked her so hard she had soiled herself, it taught me that people can hurt others without thinking about it. I grew up in a loving family and had never seen hate that bad before." Donnie paused before he continued to answer James's question. He knew James needed to hear about the changes he had made, but there were also subtle changes that had occurred over time.

"There are pieces of me that I have lost, and they have been replaced with a view of the world and others that is different. I have always felt the drive to keep people safe. To put myself between them and harm. But it will cost the warrior in each of us as we fight the battles we face every day. It can make us each stronger, but it can also weaken us." James nodded his head as his dad spoke.

"It is hard to describe how this life changes you. You begin to trust strangers less, looking for a motive or a threat; you start to harden to the situations you get into, and you're less shocked by the things people do to each other. There is a way you enter a room, scanning everyone and looking for that one who may be a problem. You watch body language, pay attention to the clothing, and learn to find the five words of truth in a 3-paragraph statement by someone. All of this takes a toll, and you are always watching, thinking through even simple encounters with others. I find myself talking to strangers in line, asking whether they are having a good or bad day. Making a mental note of vehicles, including their make, model, and license plates, will become a habit you look forward to. You will become vigilant in every part of your life; everything is noted in your mind," Donnie finished, looking at James.

"Dad, I have always noticed that when you enter a room, you sit with your back to the wall, in a place where you have full visual control of the doors and windows. You have always been observant; I know you also listen in on nearby conversations. I didn't know some of the other things. Have you always been that way?"

"No, I wasn't, and it has become so second nature to me that I don't even know I'm doing it. It was training and learning to do it; now it is, and will always be, a part of me. Do you remember your two friends coming home from combat, and you telling me they now look up at rooftops? That will always be with them, thanks to their training, and it was what enabled them to stay alive and come home. It bugged your mom at first, but she learned to accept that I am this way now. I would watch her do her job at the hospital and remember thinking to myself, 'It all came naturally to her." Donnie concluded.

James sat there, thinking through what his dad had told him, and wondered how long it would be before he was just like him, doing those things because of training and learning the way to survive as a law enforcement officer. But he also gained a better understanding of why his dad does what he does. He remembered how strange it was to him that his dad could never stop looking around the room, no matter where he was, whether in a restaurant or a store. Driving with him was a whole different story. He remembered how his dad kept glancing at the other cars; he had thought it was because he was trying not to get hit, but it was deeper than that. It was beginning to make sense to James now.

"That makes a lot more sense to me now. I remember talking to you as a kid, seeing you looking around the room at everyone, guiding me through the crowd; it was all confusing. As I grew older, I became angry, even though I followed your directions, thinking you were just being overly protective. But now I see why," James said, asking Donnie, "So that is the future I can look forward to?" "As long as you work in Law Enforcement and even after you leave, it will be who you will become," he told James.

"Son, I need to get some paperwork finished and head into the office for a bit. Can we pick this up later?" he asked.

James said it was OK, he had a few things to do as well. Finishing his coffee, he asked his dad if he was done for now. Donnie turned up his coffee and drank the rest, then handed his cup to his son. James rinsed them and set them aside for later.

As Donnie was reaching for his paperwork, James told his dad he would see him later and headed out. Donnie then got to work, checking everything he needed to before heading into the office.

10

The Defense of the Badge

While Donnie was working on the last few pages of the report he needed to look over, the phone rang. Absent-mindedly, he looked at the phone, thinking it was the office administrative assistant, but it turned out to be Carol instead. With a smile on his face, he answered the phone.

"Well, hello," Donnie responded. "Hi, am I interrupting anything"? Carol asked. "Nothing that can't wait," he said jokingly. Carol laughed, remembering him always taking her call unless he was in a situation at work, "I have been thinking about the dinner we all had the other night and how enjoyable it was to spend time with you two. I was wondering if we can do it again soon, this time my treat", Carol asked hopefully. "That sounds great. James isn't home right now, and I have a few things to deal with at the office, but yes, let's plan something. When are your nights off over the next couple of weeks?" he asked. "I still have Tuesday through Thursday off each week", Carol responded. "What night do you prefer"? Donnie asked Carol. "Should we leave it up to James to decide? I am open to any of those evenings," Carol said. "Sounds good, want me to ask him or do you want to, then just tell me when and I will be there," Donnie inquired. "I can ask him, and we will set the time and place," Carol said, sounding hopeful. Donnie could hear a smile in her voice as she spoke to him. He had a smile on his face as he spoke. "I will let you get back to what you were doing, probably paperwork for the office, Carol said jokingly, even though she knew that was what he was doing. "You always could remember my schedule, couldn't you?" Donnie teased. "We are all people of habit," she shot back. They said goodbye and hung up the phone. Donnie finished his paperwork, smiling the whole time. When he finished, he headed to the office.

Still smiling, he entered the office, but his smile quickly faded as he heard someone talking from the other office. There had been another attack as he was driving into work on one of their Security officers, Charles Rush. He rushed to the office and was met by the administrative assistant, Susan. She hung up the phone and looked at Donnie. "I was just calling your cell. It isn't good, Donnie. He is on his way to the hospital right now," Donnie was told. He immediately began asking who and where the officer had been, and whether someone was already on site to cover the location. Where did he need to go? Donnie had to make calls to get everything taken care of, but he decided he needed to go to the hospital and told Susan who she needed to call. He told her where he was headed as he neared the door, and she said she would call with updates. He said, "Thank you and he grabbed the doorknob and turned it.

He raced to his car, and as he sat in the seat, the phone rang. As Donnie started the vehicle, he said hello to his boss, sharing what he knew and where he was headed. The boss told him to keep him informed and hung up. As he drove to the hospital, Donnie's mind was racing to sort things out. How did this happen? What was the cause? Was it random or targeted? What was his officer doing? Where was he standing? The things he needed to know were the number of suspects, their appearance, and whether the cameras in the storage facility captured clear images of them. He had entered his mode of thought as he struggled to determine whether the officer was okay. What was law enforcement doing? Everything was racing through his head as he made his way to the hospital.

When Donnie arrived at the hospital, he was met by security. The doctors knew he would be there. The security guard walked him to the waiting room and asked him to wait. For some reason, Donnie noticed that one of the hospital security officers stayed in the room. He was wondering why he was. Donnie asked, "Is there a reason you are still here"? The officer looked nervous at the question. He stood and stared at him for a minute. "We were asked to stay by the Doctor," he responded. Now, Donnie was more agitated by that statement. "Why would the doctor tell you that"? Donnie asked, his voice straining to hide his growing anger. He saw the young officer speak into his extender mic attached to his radio. A few minutes later, a senior Security officer arrived, talked to the other officer, and approached Donnie. "Sir, the attack was a bad one. We know who you are and what your reputation is, as does the doctor. So, he asked us to wait with you until they can come and speak with you." Now, Donnie was getting angrier with every word. He started to say something, but stopped when he heard a familiar voice. "Donnie, the doctor is making sure Charles is okay," Carol said as she walked in. She told the hospital security that they could leave and that she would sit with him. "How bad is he, Carol?" Donnie asked. "He took several severe hits to the upper body and head. He is not completely conscious now. He has a severe concussion and at least two stab wounds, but they are not life-threatening. Mainly on his arms, like the night we met," Carol said, trying to smile at him, but knowing him, she could see the anger growing.

"When can I see him? What else are you not telling me?" Donnie questioned her. "Law Enforcement has not arrived yet, so it could be a while. Donnie, he is in good hands; the Doctor will take care of him." Carol responded. "I need to let his wife, Stacy, know how he is; she still doesn't know," Carol heard the strain in his voice. She reached her hand to hold his. He looked at her and said, "He is James's age." Donnie said. "He will be alright, Hun". Give the doctors a little more time, okay"? Carol asked. "I trust you. I also need to call his wife", Donnie responded. "Let me call her, if that is alright with you"? Carol asked. Donnie handed his phone to her, gave her the name, and sat trying to clear his head. Charles is James's age, and Stacy just told him a few days ago that they are going to be parents. Donnie stared at the wall as Carol spoke to Stacy. She has always been so strong, he thought to himself. She has a caring, loving side to everyone. She knows how to word things; she told her she would meet her at the emergency room entrance and that Donnie was already there. She also reassured her that her husband would be alright.

Carol handed Donnie back his phone. He was looking at her the way he used to look at her. She saw his eyes and saw the awe he had for her. She felt the same way for him. "Stacy is on her way with her mom," Carol told him. "Thank you for doing that, Hun. You always could word things just right and make everyone feel at ease, even at times like this", Donnie told her. Carol said she was going to wait by the door, and as she reached out and squeezed his shoulder before leaving the room, she felt a sense of relief.

Donnie called his boss and told him what he knew. He then called the office and spoke with Susan, who briefed him on the phone. They had someone at the storage unit, and they were covered. The manager said he had a good view of the three guys who had attacked him and would give the company a copy of the photos. He instructed her to obtain them and hand them over to the patrol officers, but only to report any sightings to Law enforcement. He also told her to tell them to contact him if they saw any of them. Susan knew what that meant and told him she would pass on the information to their patrol staff.

Donnie was deep in thought about the situation. He was also thinking about James and what it would have been like if it had been him. Since Charles and James were the same age, Donnie wondered how Carol would react. She was always good at hiding her fear in public, but he knew she was concerned that this incident had brought reality to them both. It could have been James.

Donnie heard a radio and looked up to see a Police officer enter the waiting room and walk towards him. He knew the officer. He told Donnie they had photos of the assailants; they were known to the Police Department. As best they can tell, it was a random attack, and he was not the intended target. More of a wrong place, wrong time situation. From what he saw on the video, his officer was close to taking two of the three down when he was struck in the back of the head by an object. He didn't go down right away, and looked like one of them got a broken nose in the incident. He reassured Donnie that they would ensure all three were arrested. Then he sat next to Donnie and asked him if he was okay. Donnie looked at him for a minute and asked, "What do you think?" The officer let out a sigh and said he had to ask; the lieutenant told him to. They all knew Donnie was protective of the officers who worked for him. The Lieutenant also knows James is the same age as the Officer who got attacked. He wanted reassurance that Donnie wasn't planning to have a "talk" with the attackers. Donnie had a reputation with the local Law Enforcement officers.

"Donnie, we need to handle everything with this. We will locate them and ensure they are arrested. We have the video, and we know what happened, so please let us handle it. Your young officer needs to heal so he can testify in court. We will need to talk with him to see what he remembers." "I am aware of everything you need to do. Just do it before I need to." Donnie responded. The officer, knowing him, knew he meant every word of it.

He reassured Donnie that they were looking for them, were getting arrest warrants, and would be canvassing the area. "That is part of the problem with Law Enforcement; you must get everything organized, go through political channels to get things done. My patrol staff is already out there looking and has been advised to contact your department if they find them. They will allow you to arrest them," Donnie quipped. The Police Officer knew the tone of his voice and how Donnie worked. "I just wanted to let you know what we are doing to catch them", the officer said. "Thanks for the update. Have you tried talking to my officer yet"? Donnie asked. "We have two detectives trying to now, but what I am hearing, through my earpiece, is the doctor is not allowing it yet", he said to Donnie. "I knew that already, he took a tough hit to the head, it could have killed him", Donnie spouted. "Are we done? I have more calls to make," Donnie said. "Yeah, for now", the officer responded, got up, and left the room.

Donnie knew he would soon get a call from the lieutenant and would hear the same song and dance again. But right now, he needed to ensure that Charles would recover with minimal damage to his brain. As he was thinking through all of this, he saw Carol and Charles's wife walking in, followed by her mom.

Donnie stood up to greet her, and she ran into his arms as a daughter would. Carol smiled to see Donnie being so caring to Stacy. She knew he was just a teddy bear when it came to things like this. As Stacy was sobbing, Donnie tried to explain to her that the Doctors were still checking him over and they would let her know soon how he was. He said the Police were here too, but needed to wait to talk to him. He looked at Carol as if asking her to help. Carol walked over and asked her if she wanted some coffee, water, or a soda. Stacy said she wanted some water. Carol left to get it and some tissues for herself. Within a couple of minutes, Carol came back and sat on the other side of Stacy. Carol reached over and took her hand, telling her that the Doctor checking her husband was one of the best ER doctors she had worked with. He is very thorough and will make sure Charles is taken care of. Carol introduced herself to Stacy and her mom. She told her she knew Donnie was doing everything he could to help catch the person or persons responsible, but right now, everyone was taking care of her husband.

Donnie admired Carol for stepping up to help him with all this. His mind was calculating everything. She knew he needed to process everything and get everyone where they needed to be. Then Stacy lay her head on Carol's shoulder, and Carol hugged her. Carol looked over at Donnie. He saw a look in her eyes he knew all too well. She was watching him to see what he would do.

He heard a commotion in the hallway and looked up to see the doctor enter, followed by the two detectives. The doctor told them to wait, and they both looked at Donnie; he knew one of them. He saw the younger one look puzzled, so the senior detective said they would wait outside. He turned and looked at Donnie as he left.

The Doctor approached the four of them, who were sitting, and began to speak to Stacy. He explained that her husband had a concussion, and they were working on the protocols for that. He has a few cuts on his arms that required stitches, and they were taken care of. They were getting ready to move him into a room, so she could go and see him. He also explained he was in and out of consciousness. He said he is a strong man, and that will help him in the next few days as he recovers. He looked at Carol and Donnie and told them he needed to get back to his patient. Donnie followed him out to talk to him more and to speak to the detectives. Carol stayed with Stacy and her mom.

Donnie asked the doctor just how bad it was. The doctor told Donnie that a few inches lower, and his neck would have been broken by the blow he took. "He is a fighter, thankfully", the doctor said. Donnie nodded and said, "Thank you. He then went to find the detectives. They were outside the ER entrance. "Look, he will need a couple of days before you can talk to him". They looked at Donnie. The younger one asked who he was, and the senior detective told him. "Donnie, you know how the job is, and we are only here to get a statement if he can give us one", he said to him. "You need to give him time to unscramble his thoughts", Donnie responded. He added, "For the record, I told my guys to call you if they see them anywhere. "Donnie, I know you well. We worked together years ago. I also know how you are. Let us find them, please", the detective said. "As I said, I told my people to call you if they see them and tell the Lieutenant I said hello". The senior detective laughed at that; he was familiar with the history of those two. The younger detective looked confused. "We will check in on him later", the detective said and turned to walk away with the younger detective following.

Donnie turned and walked back inside. Carol and Stacy were still in the waiting room. Carol told Donnie that a nurse had said they would move him into the room shortly, and she would come and get them when he was settled in. Donnie nodded, and he said to Carol, "Thank you for helping." She smiled and said, "Any time." Stacy raised her head and asked how they had come to know each other so well. This caused them both to laugh, and Donnie asked if Carol wanted to tell her. Carol smiled and said they were married. Stacy smiled and said they made a great couple, and now she understood.

Donnie and Carol looked at each other for a minute. The nurse came in and said her husband was settled in and she would take them to the room. As she stood, Stacy hugged Donnie, thanking him for taking care of her husband. She had heard a lot about him and was glad he was his boss. Carol told Stacy that Donnie thought of the employees more like family, and she agreed that he was one of a kind. As she spoke, she smiled at Donnie.

The four of them followed the nurse to the elevator, and once inside, she told Stacy to brace for what she was about to see. As the elevator doors opened, they stepped out and headed to Charles' room. When they entered, Stacy let out a gasp. Charles' face was swollen and bruised; his head was wrapped up after they stitched him up. She could see the bruising on his hands and the bandages on his arms. She started to weep, and Carol leaned over to her, reminding her to be strong for Charles. She nodded her head as Carol spoke to her.

Stacy went to Charles's bedside and spoke to him. He opened the eye that wasn't swollen. He smiled at Stacy. He knew who she was and apologized for the scare he'd caused her. Stacy reached over and held his hand, telling him he needed to heal and that nothing he did was wrong. Stacy had tears rolling down her face as she stood by him. Stacy told him she was proud of him. Charles faded in and out of consciousness.

Carol turned to Stacy's mom and said it was a great sign that he knew Stacy. It means there is probably no permanent brain damage. Stacy's mom looked at Carol and asked, "How did you know that?" Carol told her she was an RN and had worked in the ER her entire nursing career. Carol went on to say that that was how she met Donnie.

Stacy told her mom she wanted to stay with Charles and would probably spend the night at the hospital so she could be near him. Her mom agreed that it would be a good thing. Carol told Stacy that she needed to go on shift in a couple of hours, but would check on Charles throughout the night. Stacy's mom walked over to Stacy and hugged her. She reached over to Charles' hand and gently squeezed it. She told Stacy to call her if she needed anything and to provide updates on Charles. As she turned to leave, Carol noticed tears in her eyes and followed her out of the room.

Carol walked with her and apologized for not having introduced herself earlier. "I am Carol," she said. Stacy's mom looked at her and told her, "I am Teri." Teri then asked the question she had been wanting to ask, "Is Charles going to heal completely? They are expecting their first baby, and I love Charles like a son." Carol looked at Teri, "I think he has a bit of healing to get through, but his recognizing Stacy was a great sign that he will. With concussions, it can be difficult to tell early on, but he is also a fighter. It will be tough at the beginning, but the love they share will also help him heal. Donnie will be there the whole time for both, helping them get through it, too." "You and your husband have been through this before?" Carol smiled, wondering if she should tell her they were divorced, but she didn't. "I know how Donnie feels towards the young people he is in charge of. I am a nurse, so I guess you could say yes, we have been through this before." Teri realized her son-in-law was in good hands. She saw how they dealt with him and her daughter. She felt at ease for the first time since learning about Charles's injury. "I need to get going. I am going to stop by later with some clothes for Stacy. Hope to see you again, Carol. Thank you both". Teri turned and walked towards the Hospital entrance, her head held high. Carol could see her reach up and probably wipe a tear away now and again. There is a tough woman, Carol thought to herself. She turned around and re-entered Charles' room. She saw Donnie next to the bed, leaning over and speaking to Charles.

Donnie had been receiving texts from his patrol staff about where they were and where they were looking for the assailants. He told them to keep looking. Every time Donnie got a text, Carol would look at him. He just told her it was work. He also told Charles he just needed to focus on getting better. Reminded him that he had a baby on the way and a fantastic lady by his side. He told him he would handle things for him, and he didn't need to worry.

Carol knew what that meant, but didn't say anything to Stacy. It was nearing the time for her to start her shift. She asked Donnie if he wanted to walk her to the ER. He agreed, and they both told Stacy they would be back throughout the night to check on both of them. Stacy forced a smile as she wiped away a tear and told them, "Thank you for being there; it would mean a lot to Charles."

They left the room and entered the elevator. As the door shut, Carol turned to Donnie. "What are your plans to handle this situation? I know you very well, mister, so tell me," Carol said in a stern, almost demanding voice. Donnie smiled and said, "Our patrol staff has photos of each of the three; they are helping look for them and have been told to contact Law Enforcement if they see them." Carol looked at Donnie. She knew there was more, "and?" she asked. "I told them to let me know if they found them so that I could talk with them first." Donnie knew not to lie to her. He couldn't tell if he tried. Carol always could see right through him. She looked at him for a minute, then said, "Good, I was hoping you would. Those three need to understand they can't get away with this. I was thinking of James this whole time and what we would do if something like that happened to him." It shocked Donnie to hear her say that. He realized she had come a long way from when they were married. She has a fight in her, a protective mama bear side he was seeing for the first time. He was glad; he knew she was tough but was only now realizing how tough she was. "I will make sure they understand, Hun," Donnie replied.

On impulse, he put his arm over her shoulder, drew her close, and kissed her forehead. When he realized what he had done, he started to step back, but she wrapped her arms around him and squeezed him. "Thank you," she said, "I have missed those forehead kisses you used to give me." Looking at each other, they smiled. Donnie told me he missed giving them to her. Their embrace was brief, but they were both smiling as the elevator doors opened to the ER. Carol heard her name being called by another nurse. She told Donnie she needed to go, then turned toward the voice.

Donnie walked out of the Hospital and went to his car. He had a company vehicle equipped with a scanner, a radio to reach his Patrol and the rest of the staff. Once inside, he radioed his Patrol supervisor on shift. David-22, he said. "Go ahead, David-3." David-22: Give me a 10-21, which meant he should call Donnie. "10-4" was the response.

Less than a minute later, the phone rang. Donnie picked it up and began asking questions about the search for the three assailants. Michael, his supervisor, relayed everything to Donnie. He had assigned the patrol staff to various sections of the area. All the Patrol staff were out early and would work through the night to find the 3. "Michael, remember to contact me when you find and can confirm you have any of them. They have probably separated by now; remember always to use caution. They attacked one of our own, and we take care of our own," Donnie said. "Yes, sir," Michael responded.

"How is Charles, by the way?" Michael asked. "Better than expected, his wife is with him. The doctors and staff will be checking on him throughout the night. The next 48 hours will reveal how quickly he recovers and what the lasting effects of the attack might be. I told Charles he needs to focus on healing and let us handle the issue," Donnie stated. "And we will, Donnie," Michael responded. "Yes, we will," Donnie said. He told him he needed to call the owner about Charles and to keep looking. Hanging up, Donnie took a deep breath and then dialed the phone.

"I am leaving the hospital and heading to the office. Charles is better than expected; his wife is there with him now. I will check in on them later," Donnie told his boss. "Donnie, I know you. What do you have going on? There is a fire in your voice I recognize. That is the same as when you were a cop." "I told the patrol officers to keep a lookout for the 3; they have pictures of them, but to call Law enforcement if they see them", Donnie responded. "What else do you want done?" His boss asked him. "Better yet, don't tell me, it is better I don't know. I would not want to be those guys when you do find them." Donnie, just be careful", his boss told him. "I always am, but this is family, too. I need to call Susan; I'd better let you go," Donnie said. His Boss said Alright, keep him updated on Charles. He told him he would.

Donnie then called Susan and asked how things were going at the office. Susan told him things were OK and asked about Charles. He told her what the doctors had said about Stacy being with him and that he would check on him later. Susan asked Donnie if he had any information on the whereabouts of the three assailants. He said not yet, but everyone was still looking. Donnie told her I would join the search for the assailants. "Donnie, be careful, please", Susan admonished him. "Always am," Donnie quipped. "I just needed to say it," Susan responded. "Susan, thank you for the reminder," Donnie said.

David-22, David-3, Go ahead David-3. What's your 10-20? Where are you, Michael? That's what it meant. I am on 5th Street south of Meadow. Give me a location. Where can we meet up? That is what he is asking. David-3, we can 10-25 at 5th and Magnolia in the parking lot. 10-4, he understood, in route to that 10-20, I am headed to that location. Donnie headed to the parking lot to meet with Michael. Donnie knew he would tell him he needed to stay out of the area, but Michael also knew he needed to help search. Carol would not like it either, but she would understand he needed to help them search.

Michael pulled into the parking lot and waited for Donnie to get there. When Donnie arrived, he pulled up next to Michael's car. "Michael, what has been found out?" Donnie asked. "We are still looking for them," Michael told him. "I want them found before Charles wakes up so I can give him and his wife the comfort they have been taken care of," Donnie told him. "Michael, I have a feeling they will try to break into something else. It may also be one of our properties. I want one Patrol vehicle in the area from 4th and Sycamore to 9th and Oak. Also, advise our posted officers to look out for these 3," Donnie advised Michael. "Got it, I know your gut feelings, boss," Michael said. "Don't use the radio, call everyone with a landline, just in case." "Donnie, do you think it might have been one of our own"? "Call it a hunch, they took Charles' radio when they left," Donnie told him. "When did you hear that?" Michael asked. Donnie explained that he had looked at the video again and seen them take it. I just found it in the video. We need to surprise them. Michael made the calls to everyone. "Done, Donnie. Where are you going to be?" Michael asked. "In the center area so that I can get there quickly."

Donnie told him he would see him later, then headed toward the center of the search area. Michael called Donnie and said everyone was in position and waiting now. There were still a few vehicles moving around, looking. This gave the three assailants a chance to see them. Donnie knew they were being watched, and he wanted the radio to be limited to the few vehicles roaming and looking for them. All the officers were instructed to watch for unusual vehicles as well. Please pay attention to the cameras that were installed at each assigned post.

A couple of hours passed, and Donnie's phone rang. It was Michael; they had identified some individuals who resembled the three assailants. Donnie told him to make 100 percent sure it was them. Each Patrol supervisor had a second phone that officers could use. Donnie could hear him talking to the officer at the post.

Donnie knew everyone was dealing with the thought of someone being attacked and could have been killed. He understood they were jumpy. He needed to confirm it was them before they acted. He asked Michael where they were. Michael said they were at 7th and Pine. Donnie knew there was a large storage unit on that corner. "Let them enter the property and watch them", Donnie told Michael. He told Michael to move in that direction, and he was headed there as well, but to take his time until they confirmed it was them. Inform the closest patrol vehicle to move in that direction, but stay approximately a block away.

Michael asked Donnie how far he wanted him to be, and Donnie said to stay about a block away. Donnie moved to 6th and Pine and parked his vehicle. He left the vehicle and walked close to where the three were seen. He called Michael and asked if the officer on post could confirm it was them. Michael asked the officer to confirm it was them. He told Michael he could prove they were on the property. Does he see a radio on any of them? Michael asked if they had a radio. The officer said it looked like they didn't. "Okay, radio everyone where they are. I want all sides of the property to be covered. Have four patrol teams stay a block away in case they do have a radio and start to run." Michael grabbed his radio and advised all the patrol teams of what had been found, instructing teams 3, 4, 7, and 8 to stay a block away and remain mobile, just in case. Donnie got on the radio and said, "David 31, David-3, Go ahead, David-3." Lock the office doors and report what you see, including their location on the property and any visible weapons. Donnie moved to the property and heard David 31 respond, "10-4," indicating he understood. David-22, call it, I am on foot in the area. Michael responded 10-4 David-3. All units 10-33, emergency traffic only. As the additional patrol officers arrived, they exited their vehicles and assumed positions around the property. Michael arrived at a distance from the property, exited his vehicle, and joined Donnie.

Donnie, even though he was armed with a sidearm, had a riot-sized straight baton. These are usually not used here, but they are about 32 inches long and have rounded ends. They have grooves cut into one end and are typically made of solid Oak. Donnie purchased it a few years ago and had been trained on how to use it. Michael had his sidearm and a collapsible baton, the type used now. They are impact weapons and less-lethal tools that require sustained impact for maximum force.

As Donnie and Michael stood by the front entrance, Donnie radioed David-31 to request the status of the assailants. David-31 responded that they were between rows 3 and 4, checking the locks. They were also examining numbers, as if they knew there might be a specific one they wanted to break into. 10-4 David-3. He advised him to keep his eyes on them and to advise David-22 and him as they were entering the property. "David 3 to all other units, standby at your locations. I will advise further. No need to respond to this transmission." Donnie said into his radio microphone.

The storage unit had 12 rows in the same direction, their ends facing north and south. Each had 15 storage units on either side, each with a roll-up door. Each Storage unit had a 12-foot-by-20-foot interior and was

15 feet high. As they entered the property, they were near the first row. Which meant the assailants were not far away, so they needed to be careful and quiet as they entered the area. There are cameras on every corner, and several more along each row.

David-31 stated the assailants were stopped near 408, close to the center of the row. And they were on the East side of the row between rows 3 and 4. So they were two rows over from them, halfway down the unit block. Facing away from them. Donnie motioned to Michael to move towards the corner of the 3rd row and wait. Donnie radioed to David-31, "David-31, advise if they enter the unit". David-31 responded 10-4, and they have just cut the lock on the unit. Donnie responded 10-4. Donnie looked up towards the sun. It was setting, and shadows were forming. He knew the lights would be coming on soon. They had to wait until the three were inside the Storage unit and then move in to catch them. "David-31, have they entered the unit?" Donnie asked. David-31 said, "2 have, one is still outside holding a long straight object, possibly a bat". 10-4 was Donnie's response. He had to wait for the 3rd one to enter the unit. David-3, they are now all inside the unit. The bolt cutters were placed just outside the unit against the wall. "10-4", Donnie responded. He motioned for Michael to move to the East side along the row and start moving up. He was right behind him.

Donnie radioed David-31 and asked if he could see where the three were inside the unit. David-31 paused and then responded. One is on the North Side, along the wall, the one with the bat is with the third one, about the center of the unit, digging through a box they had opened, their backs to the open door. The one furthest south may be carrying a weapon under his T-shirt, possibly a gun. Donnie looked at Michael as he said 10-4 to David-31. He motioned to Michael to grab the bolt cutters and move after he did, towards the open door. Michael nodded. They moved quickly up the wall to the open door. Michael reached with his left hand and grabbed the bolt cutter, pushing it as Donnie moved around him.

Donnie had the baton secured in both hands and moved to the opening, turning towards the 1st assailant. He plunged the baton into his stomach, causing him to gasp and fall backward into the pile of boxes behind him. The other two turned towards the noise and saw Donnie. The one with the bat raised it and started towards Donnie. Donnie swiveled and struck his forearm with the bat he was holding. Donnie used full force and could hear a snapping sound as the assailant dropped the bat, screaming. He froze in place, looking over at Michael, pointing his sidearm at him. After striking the second assailant in the stomach, he dropped to his knees. Donnie turned to the third assailant; he saw him reach around behind his back. As he brought his arm around again, Donnie saw a handgun in his hand. As he started to raise the gun towards Donnie, Donnie moved in and swung his baton to strike his arm. The assailant ducked slightly, causing Donnie to strike his Jaw with the full force of his swing. He dropped the gun, and Donnie heard it thump onto the top of a box in front of the assailant. Instead of stopping, the 3rd assailant reached for the gun again with his good arm. Donnie swung at his arm, but he moved forward and was struck in the back of his skull. The third assailant fell forward, into the stack of boxes, knocking the gun to the floor. The second blow knocked him out.

With all three subdued, he radioed David-31 to contact Law Enforcement. Donnie looked at the first assailant and realized that he had voided his bladder when Donnie struck him in the stomach. A small smile came to Donnie's face. Michael was heard telling the 2 to sit in the opening under the roll-up door. Michael also told David-31 to advise Law Enforcement to have an ambulance respond as well. David-31 responded with "10-4." Donnie moved to the 3rd assailant and checked his vitals; he was breathing, with a gash on the back of his head. He was still unconscious. Donnie and Michael advised all officers that they were Code 4, which meant they were okay. Donnie then radioed the Patrol officers to return to their areas and continue to patrol, thanking them for their assistance. And cleared the 10-33. Return to regular radio traffic. The patrol units, one by one, radioed they were 10-8, back in service.

Donnie radioed David-31 to leave the video as is and allow Law Enforcement to review it. He could hear the sirens coming close. It sounded like there were four law enforcement vehicles nearby. He advised David-31 to unlock the gate so they could let them in. He radioed 10-4 and asked Donnie if he wanted him to stand by where he was. "Affirmative," Donnie responded. Donnie looked at Michael and told him it was going to be a long night, and he needed to call the owner. Michael agreed and holstered his sidearm.

Donnie saw the Law Enforcement vehicles enter the property one by one. 2 going around the opposite side and coming in behind where he was. As the officers exited their vehicles, they dealt with each assailant. Then they looked at Donnie and advised him that the detectives were also on their way. Donnie told them he figured they would be. He then heard the ambulance siren and saw its lights as it entered the property.

They began working on the three, realizing only two required attention, until they noticed that the third also needed checking. Law Enforcement stood by for the detectives. As they were working on the assailants, a second ambulance arrived just before the detectives arrived.

When they got close, they saw Donnie and the riot baton. They looked at the three assailants, then looked back towards Donnie and Michael. "Before you two start yelling at me, look at the video. It will tell you the truth of what just happened", Donnie told them. They stopped and asked him why. Donnie said, "You are going to question them and me, but this storage facility has some amazing cameras." About that time, the senior detective's phone rang. It was the Lieutenant; he told the detective to wait until he got there. He ended the call abruptly, and the detective told Donnie who had called. Donnie just looked at the detective and nodded. "I need to call my boss; is it okay if I do?" They told him he could. They wanted to hear what he said to his boss.

Donnie hit his speed dial, and his boss picked up. "It's Donnie, we found the assailants, and Law Enforcement and ambulances are here. Yeah, the same Storage I told you they would be at. The detectives are here. Their Lieutenant is coming here, too. Yes, sir, him. I will do my best. Ok, I will." Ending the call, he smiled at the Detectives. They looked annoyed that he didn't say much of anything.

About 20 minutes later, the lieutenant arrived and got out of his vehicle. He was staring at Donnie. Timothy, how are you doing this evening? The Lieutenant didn't look pleased. I instructed your detectives to review the video of what happened before you yelled at or questioned me. He turned and ordered his detectives to go to the office to see if they could obtain the video. "It's available. I have an officer in there waiting for you guys to look at it. He can show it to you before we talk any further. Lieutenant Tim didn't look happy at all. "Sorry to bug you this evening, Timothy," Donnie told him. "Shut up, Donnie, I told dispatch to contact me if this happened, you were told to let us deal with this," The Lieutenant yelled at Donnie. "Go look at it and tell me what you see on it," the lieutenant told them. "Why did you do this, Donnie? You were always running off and doing your own thing; nothing has changed, has it?" The Lieutenant stared at Donnie, waiting for a response. "You want me to answer that, Timothy?" Donnie asked. "Because it sounded like that was more of a statement to me," Donnie said.

The Lieutenant was about to respond when he saw the detectives coming back. Can we speak with you? He looked at Donnie and told them they could say whatever they needed to say in front of Donnie. From the video and the Security officer's statement, it appears that he and another individual were defending themselves and stopping the theft. They are under contract with the owners, and we have also contacted them. The one male had a baseball bat. The same one used on his employee in the hospital. He was about to hit Donnie with it when Donnie struck his arm. No intent to injure him worse. Another security officer drew his weapon to protect Donnie. The other one did have a gun; our officers found it. Donnie swung on him with that baton, but didn't aim at his head either time. This looks like self-defense based on the video we just saw." The senior detective told the Lieutenant.

"We will still need to get statements from everyone. I'm not sure this will go where it should, but we still need to conduct an investigation. Have the video sent to the office and have forensics review it. Also, take the statements from these two," the Lieutenant said to the detectives. He turned to Donnie and said, "Some things never change; you might walk away from this again." "Timothy, I remember your actions, too," Donnie said. The Lieutenant turned and walked back to his vehicle.

The detectives separated Donnie and Michael. The Senior Detective spoke with Donnie. "You still have some skills, Donnie," the detective told him. "I just practice a lot and run those scenarios in my head every day, still," Donnie replied.

After four hours, they were free to go. Donnie went to the office and asked David-31 to email him the video. He told him he would. "Donnie, can I ask you something?" Chris asked him. "Yes, Chris, ask away." "When I saw that gun, I would have drawn on him. Why didn't you draw your weapon?" Donnie stood there, looking at Chris for a couple of minutes; the pause made Chris uncomfortable. Donnie thought about it. He had had to use his weapon before. He never thought about why until now.

"Chris, there is mostly a choice when to draw and use your weapon," Donnie began. "Over the years, I have studied probably hundreds of shooting scenarios, and many, I discovered, could be avoided. There is often another way. It can come down to training. Taking a life, because I was taught that is why weapons come out, is the last thing I want to do, especially today. We always have non-lethal options available; that is why I insist that all of you be trained to use them. Did they deserve it, maybe, especially for what they did to Charles? But before I entered the Storage facility today, I chose not to take a life. If things had been different and all three of them had guns, it would have ended differently. If they had pointed a gun or fired towards Michael or me, things would have been different. I chose to use the baton, so they would have to face Charles in court and pay for what they did to him. In the end, it was their choice as to how I was going to react." Does any of that make sense to you, Chris?"

Donnie looked at Chris again, silent, reading his face. He was thinking, and Donnie would use this as training for Chris. He would later use every situation to train the officers to handle things better. As Donnie stood there, Chris looked at him. Chris saw something different in him today. He had heard the stories about Donnie from the other officers, but seeing him on the cameras doing what he did today was different.

Chris said to him, "Donnie, I have heard stories of how you handle things, but I have never seen you do things. I watched you and learned a lot today. I learned why you tell us to work out scenarios in our minds all the time. You once told me that by doing that, we could manage things better, faster, and with less harm to ourselves and others. Hearing it and seeing it are two different things. Now I do know the difference between them. I still have a lot to learn," Chris added, "I knew you could handle things and that you were fast when you reacted, but I never knew how fast until today." Are you going to show that video footage to the company in our next training?" "That is up to the owner," Donnie replied.

Donnie always reminded Chris to be ready for everything, work through scenarios as he worked, and keep his head on a swivel, always be aware of his surroundings. Train with the non-lethal tools he carries. And the weapon is the last tool he has to use.

Chris said he would. Donnie told him to have a safe rest of his shift tonight and to call for Patrol if he needed assistance. “I will, sir,” Chris replied. Donnie smiled and left the office.

When Donnie arrived at the facility's entrance, Michael was waiting for him. “Donnie,” he asked, “when and where do you want to debrief and go through our protocols?” There was always an after-action protocol that was followed, completed by a senior supervisor, usually one who had not been involved, to ensure objectivity. The officer wrote an incident report, as required, and submitted it within 24 hours, which was then reviewed. A meeting was set up with senior management when the incident was major. The primary meaning is the use of any force. They were to review everything with each officer, identify training opportunities, and ensure the officer was cleared for their next shift.

All of this was put into place by Donnie years ago. He knew that every incident was different, and everyone could learn something from each one. There are times when it is simply a matter of paying closer attention to tactics that need to be taught or changed because of bad habits.

Donnie told Michael he needed to go to the hospital and check in on Charles. Then he needed to talk to Carol. Michael told him he understood. “I will get the report done afterward. Make sure you have yours done and tell Chris he will need to provide one as well.” Donnie told Michael. “I will get it done, Donnie. One other thing, I am glad we got them for Charles.” Donnie agreed and said he would be back later.

Donnie headed to his vehicle. When he entered it, he sighed and let out a deep breath. He was wondering why he hadn’t shot them, why he let them live. But he also knew he had to let the courts figure everything out. There was gnawing in his gut about everything. Why did they choose Charles? Why did they take his radio? Why did they choose that storage unit to enter? All these things came to his mind as he sat there. There was more to this than he knew right now. Donnie radioed David-31 to landline him. 10-4 David-31 responded. His phone rang.

Donnie asked Chris to look up the name of the company that was renting the storage unit. He asked Donnie to stand by while he looked. I found it. Donnie instructed him to contact the renter and inform them of the break-in. He said he would. David-22, meet me at my vehicle. When Michael arrived, Donnie instructed him to have Chris call the renter and stand by to find out what was in the box they were going through. He said it felt like this was a targeted job; he wanted to know more.

While Donnie and Michael were talking, Donnie's phone rang. As the boss, he wanted to know what had happened. Donnie told him the three were in custody but at the hospital. His boss pressed Donnie for details. Donnie told him what happened, and the boss then asked what Law Enforcement would do. "They saw the video of the incident and said it looked like self-defense, and they were protecting their property," Donnie replied. Timothy wasn't happy about everything, but he couldn't do anything about either. I told him everything, and he accepted it." Donnie told his boss. "Okay, Donnie, as long as nothing comes back on you for any of this, I am good with everything." He said to Donnie.

"One other thing, have you heard anything about how Charles is doing?" His boss asked. "Not yet. When I clear out, I am going to the hospital to check on him. I will ask how those three are doing when I am there," Donnie chuckled as he said it. The boss laughed at that and said, "Sounds like something you would do, Donnie, but please don't." Donnie said he wouldn't, but they both knew he would anyway.

The boss ended the call, and Donnie smiled at Michael. "I know that smile, I heard what you said, even though he told you not to do it, you will anyway." They were both sitting there, smiling, as Donnie told Michael he needed to get to the hospital to check on Charles. Michael asked Donnie to let him know when he can and to say hi to Carol for him. Donnie just said OK as he started his car. Donnie radioed he was 10-8, back on duty. Michael responded 10-4, understood.

On the way to the hospital, Donnie thought about the incident and conducted his debriefing. It could have gone better, and no one needed to get hurt, but he also knew the three assailants were not going to go easily and that it could have turned out a lot worse for everyone. He was thankful it wasn't.

As Donnie was driving to the hospital, Susan texted him to call her when he could. Donnie called her after he read the text. "Donnie, I'm hearing from the Patrol staff that you were able to find those three who attacked Charles?" Donnie smiled. She wanted to know if they were arrested; usually, she would start with a bit of small talk. "Yes, we found them, and they were arrested. I am headed to the hospital right now."

He purposely left out that he was going to see Charles to gauge her response. "WHAT! Are you okay? Did someone get hurt?" Susan was firing questions at her rapidly. "We are all good. I am going to check on Charles." Donnie was smiling when he said it. "Donnie! That was mean," she responded. "The three assailants are also on their way to the hospital. All was legal. No one got shot. I used my riot baton. Michael was with me while we stopped them in another storage facility," Donnie told her.

He knew Susan was like a mama bear when it came to the staff and always wanted to know everyone was safe. She had been a dispatcher for a long time and decided to leave that and come to work for the company. Usually very stoic, but there were times when her mama bear nature would emerge. She was especially protective of Charles; he reminded her of her son. She would say he looked like her son. Susan's son was in the military and was assigned to a consulate overseas.

Donnie laughed and told Susan that when he knew anything about Charles, he would call her and let her know. "Thank you, Donnie," her tone sounding softer, "I do like that kid, and I know he and his bride are expecting a baby in a few months." Her voice sounded like a proud mama when she said that. Donnie smiled and told her he was parking his vehicle and needed to get going. They said goodbye, and he walked towards the entrance. While he was walking, he texted Carol to let her know he was at the hospital and would check on Charles. She texted back and said they had been busy with three guys from law enforcement. It looked like they had gotten into a nasty fight, kept saying something about getting jumped by some old guy with a big club. You wouldn't know anything about that, would you? Donnie knew she knew, so he texted her: "Yes, I do." I will talk with you in a bit when I come by the ER. She responded with OK and thank you.

Entering the elevator, Donnie pushed the button for Charles' floor. A hand stopped the door, and when Donnie looked to see who it was, he saw the Lieutenant step in. They looked at each other for a couple of minutes, neither saying a word. "Are you following me, Timothy?" Donnie asked. "I am here to see if your guy is awake and can talk," he responded. "Taking a special interest in this case, Timothy, that isn't like you." Donnie looked at him and smiled. He knew there was something Timothy wasn't telling him, but he would wait for that answer for the moment. The door opened, and the Lieutenant followed Donnie to the room.

They entered the room, and he saw Stacy sitting in the chair next to Charles' bed. She was holding his hand and looking at his face. She heard them come in and looked up at Donnie and the man with him. Stacy had an expression of asking Donnie who the stranger was. Donnie realized what she was doing and asked her how Charles was doing in case there were any changes in his condition. Stacy told Donnie he was about the same, breathing better, but not anything else.

Donnie turned to Timothy and said, "Lieutenant, it appears you can leave now. Charles is still unable to talk to you, and he needs his rest. I would strongly recommend that you give Charles about five more days before trying again. I have your department phone number and will give it to Stacy to call you on behalf of Charles."

The lieutenant just stood and stared at Donnie; a look of rage was beginning to appear on his face. In a low and strained voice, Timothy said, "So you are dismissing me, Donnie? You have done some stupid things in the past, but you have never done this. I outrank you and always have. You do not order me around!" Smiling, Donnie repeated what he had just said but added, "That wasn't an order, that was a command. Now leave and let Charles get his rest, Timothy. The Lieutenant looked at Donnie, then at Stacy, standing there, then he turned away and left the room. Donnie moved to the door and watched Timothy get into the elevator before saying anything else to Stacy.

Once he got into the room, he shut the door. Not trusting Timothy, Donnie wanted to tell Stacy everything and let her know it would be OK. "Stacy, we were able to find the people responsible for hurting Charles. We found them in another storage facility. They were all arrested. And will be charged," Donnie told her. Stacy looked at Donnie, tears welling in her eyes as she said, "thank you." She continued, "Did anyone else get hurt catching them?" Donnie looked at her as she wiped away the tears, looking down at Charles lying there in the bed. "Stacy," Donnie began, "there was some trouble stopping them, but they are the only ones who got hurt this time. They will be spending some time in the hospital as well, but will also be guarded by law enforcement, while here." Stacy turned her face back to Donnie. She searched for his expression to see if there was more he wanted to share with her. She remembered Carol telling her that he would find them.

Not seeing anything there, she asked him, "Did you find them? Was it you who put them into the hospital?" "Our crew found them; they had been looking for them from the time they heard about Charles. Yes, I was the one who put them here. They tried to take me and one of our Patrol officers out but failed." Stacy looked at Donnie. She heard the words but wondered why he had said them. Donnie could see the questioning look on her face, so he told her what had happened, leaving nothing out. She rose from her chair and walked towards him, putting her arms around him, like a daughter would a father. She hugged him tightly and started sobbing, thanking him. "Stacy, we take care of family." Donnie hugged her and then led her back to her chair. He told her he still needed to talk to Carol. He asked her what else she could tell him about Charles. Stacy told him that Charles had been in and out of consciousness since she arrived. He would look at her and smile, tell her he loved her, and then would fade out again. He squeezed her hand a few times as well. "That sounds promising, Stacy. I am glad you are here for him; you are the best medicine for him." Donnie said to her. He turned to leave, saying he would be back to check in with them again. "Donnie, she said, thank you again for everything. It means a lot to both of us, I hope you know that." He smiled, opened the door, and headed to the elevator.

Once inside, he texted Carol and said he was on his way to see her, hoping she had time to meet with him. She said she did, at least right now. When the elevator door opened, Carol asked how Charles was. Donnie told her what Stacy said, and Carol told Donnie they needed to make sure he got better. But it depended on Charles at this point. Donnie said he understood.

Carol then pulled him into one of the ER rooms and shut the door behind them. "OK, tell me about those three guys who came in here a couple of hours ago."

"Well, they were the three who jumped Charles, and they tried to attack Michael and me. One still had his bat with him, one had some bolt cutters, and the other tried to handle a gun. It didn't end well. The one with the stomach issues and wet pants went down first, the one with the broken arm had the bat removed from his hand and the one with the broken jaw, did have a gun for a few seconds but dropped it twice, before passing out."

Donnie paused for a minute, to let Carol ask more questions about the whole thing. Carol looked Donnie up and down to make sure he was OK. Carol asked, "what did you use since none of them were shot?"

"My riot baton is what I decided to use for this. I wanted them to stand and face Charles in court. They need to pay for what they did to him." Donnie said.

Carol looked at Donnie and nodded her approval, then she hugged him and told him she was proud of him for defending Charles and not using deadly force. Donnie smiled. He thought to himself how Carol had changed over the years, and how much she was OK with his job, which was different from before. He liked this new Carol. She looked at him and playfully slapped his arm. "I need to get back to work, Donnie," Carol told him.

On a whim, he asked her if she wanted some decent coffee. She smiled and told him it would be great. He told her that two cups would be coming right up. She looked at him and asked, "Why two cups?" He smiled and said, "One for you and one for me." "Oh, now I know why you asked me if I wanted some good coffee," she said, smiling. "There is no fooling you, young lady," Donnie said as he turned to go. I will be back in a few. Heading out to his vehicle, Donnie realized he would like to get coffee with Carol sometime.

11

THE COMFORT OF THE BADGE

As Donnie sat in the car, his phone rang. He answered it and heard James on the other end. "Is everything okay, Dad? Are you working?" James asked. "Yeah, it has been a day," Donnie answered. James responded, "Alright, anything I can do to help?" "Not with this son, I will tell you more when I get back to the house," Donnie told him. I'm fine, but I have an officer in the hospital, and now I'm going to get your mom a coffee. Does she still drink those caramel and cream coffees? It has been years since I've ordered for her, "Donnie asked James. Laughing, James told him she did and then had to add, "You are getting a coffee for mom, interesting." Donnie told him to stop, explaining it was just coffee. James couldn't resist, "Yeah, okay, Dad, it's just coffee. Isn't that how you started everything?" James started laughing. Donnie could feel his face turning red, but maintained his voice, saying, "Yes, son, just coffee." James told Donnie he would let him finish his errand and talk to him later.

Donnie got the coffee and brought it to Carol. She said thank you and took a sip. With a smile on her face, she told Donnie, "You remembered my order!" Donnie had to confess to James, explaining that he had called to ask about his order. They laughed, and Donnie told her he needed to get to the office and write his report about what had happened today. Carol said she figured and teasingly said, "This brings back memories." Smiling, Carol turned around and headed to the nurse's station to finish some paperwork. "Now that looks familiar, Donnie said jokingly. He turned around and walked to his vehicle. Carol watched him walk away and smiled.

Once in the vehicle, Donnie called the boss to report on Charles. His boss thanked him for the update and said the company would ensure that Charles and his wife were financially provided for. "Are you headed home now, Donnie?" the boss asked. "No, headed to the office to write my report and have it ready for the review committee." Okay, Donnie, I will hang up and let you take care of everything. "Good job today," he said. "Thank you," Donnie responded.

When Donnie arrived at the office, Susan was still there. He asked her why she was still at the office. She told him she wanted to wait and find out how Charles was doing. "Susan, I am sorry for not calling you," he said. "Donnie, you have had a tough day, and I completely understand. I also ordered food; it's in the kitchen." Susan then asked about Charles. "He is in and out right now, according to Stacy. Carol is going to talk to the nurses taking care of him and let me know if anything changes," Donnie told her. "Thank you for the food, Susan. I have not eaten since this morning." Donnie went into his office and sat, letting out a heavy sigh. He opened his computer and began the report.

Susan yelled from her office that he hadn't grabbed any food, and then she got up and made him a plate of the spaghetti she had ordered. When she came into his office, she looked at him and said, "You have a one-track mind, always on business, I am surprised you eat at all." He looked up and started chuckling, responding, "That's why I appreciate you so much, always taking care of me." She tried to frown at him, but ended up smiling as she turned to go back to her office. He could hear her on the phone telling the patrol staff about Charles.

Writing reports had become second nature to Donnie after years of writing them. As he began writing, he made it concise, just as he had learned. The report included the who, what, where, when, why, how, and outcome. As Donnie finished it and looked it over to ensure it was complete, Susan came in and said she had finished calling all the patrol staff and let them know about Charles. Looking up, Donnie told Susan thank you. "I am done with this. I need to send it and print a copy. Are you ready to leave now?" Donnie said to her. "Yeah, let me just clean up the things in the kitchen and then I will be," Susan said. Donnie printed the report, put it in a file, and set it on his desk. Susan finished with the kitchen and turned off the light. She and Donnie walked to their cars, said goodnight, and finally left.

Donnie was thinking about calling Carol when the phone rang. Donnie answered, and Carol told him that Charles' nurses had given her an update she wanted to share. "They are saying the swelling in his head is already beginning to go down. He is already showing signs of improvement. They said he is a tough fighter, and that will help with his recovery process." Donnie felt a wave of relief for the first time in a couple of days. "Thank you for the update. I am happy about his recovery so far. He is a tough young man. I knew that when I hired him. David told me the company will take care of them financially as well today. He will still get paid his normal wages." Donnie told Carol. "Wow, Donnie, that is better than most places would do!" Donnie agreed. He asked her how much longer she had left on her shift tonight. She asked him if he had checked his watch. It was almost 0130. He had no idea how late it was. Her shift ends at 0400. He realized it after he looked at his watch.

As Donnie spoke to Carol, he remembered those nights when they would talk all night; both were working nights and sleeping during the day. When one woke up, they would call the other and say, "Good morning." It became a game to them. A way to stay connected while they were dating. "Donnie, are you still there?" "Yes, sorry, got distracted for a second. I am heading home now. The report is done, and James called earlier, checking on me." He told her. Carol told Donnie he checks on her about every day. "We have done a good job with our son Donnie," Carol said. "Yes, we have, he is a great combination of both of us", Donnie told Carol. Carol told Donnie she would check on Stacy and Charles during her next break and asked him if he wanted her to call with an update. He told her he did. "I need to get back to my charting," she told Donnie. "Okay, I will remember your coffee order the next time," Donnie said jokingly. "Well, we will see," Carol quipped teasingly. They both laughed, and Carol said she would call later. Ending the call, Donnie was smiling at the conversation. Realizing he had missed them.

Turning into the driveway, Donnie was glad to be home. He also knew James was wanting to know what had kept him out all day. When Donnie got inside, he heard James ask if it was him, and he called out, saying it was. "I'm in the kitchen, Dad," James said. As Donnie came to the kitchen doorway, James had a cup of coffee waiting for him. Donnie told James he wanted to shower first, and then he would tell James everything. "Take your coffee, Dad," James told him. "Thank you, son," Donnie responded. Turning down the hallway, Donnie told James he would be back shortly.

After showering and sipping coffee, Donnie put on his clothes and returned to the kitchen. He looked at all the paperwork James had on the table. It looked like his background check packet. He asked James what he was working on. James told him what he already knew: it was his background check paperwork. He needed to submit 30 pages of information to the Sheriff's Department within a few days. "How far are you along in that book you got there?" Donnie asked. "I am only on page 6 but moving along. The hardest part is looking everything up for this," James responded. "I remember that part. No one keeps everything they ask for, available." Donnie smiled as he said it.

After refilling his cup, Donnie asked James if he had reached a good stopping point so he could explain why he had been out for so long. James looked up and asked him for a couple of minutes. Donnie saw that James' cup was almost empty, so he reached over and refilled it. "Thank you, Dad," James said as Donnie was sitting near him. "OK," James said as he set the paperwork aside, "I am at a stopping point. I have heard some rumors about you from some of the deputies today," James told Donnie. "Oh, what kind of rumors have you heard about me today? I hope they are juicy," Donnie joked. "Well, they involved an incident you were involved in at a storage facility today. From what I am hearing, you sent three guys to the hospital today." James said, looking at his dad.

"I did son." There is more to the story than that. When I got to the office today, Susan told me one of our guys had been attacked early this morning. He had to be taken to the hospital." Donnie continued telling James about the attack, what Law Enforcement wanted him to do, what he did, and then went into the information about the three he sent to the hospital.

James sat quietly as Donnie went through the story. when he finished, James asked him who had been attacked. Donnie told him it was Charles. James said he had spoken to him a couple of times when they were both in the office. "How is he doing?" James asked. Donnie told him, "Last I heard, he is already beginning to come out of it. Your mom is going to call after she checks on him and his wife later."

James noticed that his dad was not telling him something. Something different about him today. He knew he was tired, but something was bothering him tonight.

"Dad, is there anything else you don't want to tell me?" James asked. Donnie looked at his son. He knew he was like his mom; she could always see through him, and James was the same way.

"James, I have been thinking about today, probably more than I should. I know what I did today was necessary, but it could have easily put Michael in harm's way or worse. I was not thinking about that when I stepped up to the storage unit." Donnie looked at his son. James could see the pain in his eyes as he spoke to him just now. "Dad, Michael knows the risks. It is what he signed up for, just like you and me. We all understand that. Law Enforcement, Fire, Medical, and High-end Security risk their safety somewhere every day. Without all that, think of what the world would be like." As James finished speaking, Donnie smiled at him. "You're right, but taking unnecessary risks are not always the right thing to do. I have chased people, I have fought people, I have had to do things most won't, and you will have to as well to protect others; some will be ungrateful for it." Donnie told James. "But James, Stacy, and Michael are grateful for what you did, Dad". James told Donnie.

Changing the topic, James looked at Donnie's empty coffee cup. "Want a refill?" "Not right now, son, and thank you for understanding." Looking at his dad, James told him, "Mom understands, too. She called me before you got home to tell me everything and wanted to make sure you were okay. She also told me she was very proud of us for stepping up and doing what we have signed up to do." James put out his hand to take Donnie's cup. As he was handing it to him, he placed his hand on James's shoulder and said goodnight, then turned and headed down the hall.

James turned to wash up the coffee cups. He knew his dad would over-analyze everything once it was completed. He learned that, as he watched his dad review employee reports, it was his way of examining everything and seeing if there was another way to handle each situation in the future. He also knew his mom, and if she was calling him with an update, it meant she was concerned. He should have called her, but decided to wait. He finished what he was doing and went into the living room to watch television.

While he was watching a show, he heard a knock at the door. Curious and cautious, he went to the door, looking through the peephole, and he saw his mom standing there. When he opened the door, Carol gave him a big hug. She finished coming inside and asked where Donnie was. James told her he was in his room. She said she wanted to find out how he was doing. "Mom, you could have called me," James said. "Yes, I could have, but then I wouldn't be able to see you," she responded, looking around. James smiled at his mom; he knew the real reason she was there. He asked, "Do you want me to see if Dad is still awake?" Carol looked at him. James thought he had caught her blushing. "No, we can talk instead, waving her hand in the air," Carol responded. She moved to the couch and sat down. James joined her, and she asked him if his dad was OK. James said he was, but he was overthinking everything, as usual. She nodded her head. James could tell she was distracted. "Mom, I will be right back. I have coffee in the kitchen and creamer in the refrigerator." James rose and headed down the hall. He went to Donnie's room and knocked lightly. Donnie said, "Come in." When James went inside, he shut the door behind him. He looked at the table where Donnie was typing away and knew he was retracing his steps from that day. "Mom is here, Dad," James told him. Donnie looked up at James and asked him why. James smiled and told him to find out for himself. "Knock it off. OK, I will go and find out myself," Donnie said as he got up and went to the living room.

"Hey, why are you here, Carol. You could have called me." Donnie said as he walked into the room. "Both of you saying almost the same thing sounds like I'm not wanted," She chuckled. "How are you doing, Donnie?" "Good, Hun, just doing some after-incident processing. It helps the company figure things out." Donnie responded. "Mom, want that coffee now?" James asked, interrupting them for a minute.

Donnie and Carol knew what James was trying to do, but neither of them was angry. They were talking and joking with each other. Donnie was surprised Carol had stopped by unannounced. That was not like her, and he knew she was concerned about him, which made him smile a little. Carol knew how stubborn Donnie could be, and that he would try to hide it when he was angry or hurt. After all the years they had known each other, neither could hide those truths from the other.

They looked at each other with that knowing look, "James, that would be wonderful, thank you, son. I think your dad may need a refill as well," Carol told James. Donnie handed James his cup, and James turned and went into the kitchen. Pouring their cups and fixing his mom's, he called out to them and jokingly asked, "Do I need to go to my room for this?" They all laughed at his question. Donnie said he could be in the room. Carol told him, "Don't be silly and asked where her coffee was."

James, smiling, walked back into the living room and sat in the recliner. Watching them together made James smile. They were acting like two high school students in front of a parent. Donnie and Carol sat on the sofa. Carol then turned to Donnie and said, "I came by because I wanted to make sure you were dealing with today well. Donnie, you know I know you and how you have always attempted to keep things hidden from me, at my request, but I realized years ago that was not fair to you." I always knew when you were struggling with something, and I am here to show you I have changed and want to hear about it."

Donnie looked at Carol and saw that in her eyes, she honestly wanted to hear about it. At first, he hesitated, then he told her everything from the time Charles was attacked to their meeting at the hospital later. Carol sat there and listened. When Donnie was done, she repeated what she had told him at the hospital: that she was proud of him for not wanting to shoot them, and that she understood better why he was acting so reserved around her. She told him she was sorry for never giving him a place to release the day's frustrations. Donnie looked at her with an admiration he had hidden after they got divorced, thinking she didn't want him to tell her, but it seems things have genuinely changed. "Thank you," he said, and concluded, "That means a lot coming from you."

James was smiling at them both. Carol looked at him and asked, "What are you smiling at? Why are you acting like such a weirdo?" This made all three burst out laughing. They had not had a family conversation like this for as long as any of them could remember, and it was a nice change for all of them. Donnie sat there, looking at James, then at Carol. He knew what he had said and heard, and that taking the courage to say it was a massive step for her. He realized, in that moment, just how much she had changed. He was glad for that. Afterward, they sipped their coffee and engaged in small talk. It was nice to do so again. Donnie hoped it was the start of them being more open with each other.

Carol, looking at them, decided to tell them that when she saw the three assailants enter the ER, she had a feeling it had been Donnie who did it. She told them that the one who tried to use his gun and had been knocked out woke up in the ER, attempted to fight the staff, but Law Enforcement took care of him by having the staff restrain him. He then stopped fighting. The one with the bat, who broke his arm, complained to Law Enforcement about the beating he took and swore he did nothing wrong and said, "The old dude that attacked them will be taken care of, as soon as he gets out of the hospital." Carol told them the officers who were there said he would need to wait until he got out of prison, in a few years, to do that. And that's when he stopped saying anything and wanted a lawyer.

Carol then told them about the last assailant. He was the one hit in the stomach, did nothing but moan while holding his stomach, and kept saying he was hurting and needed some medication, which was refused by the staff. They told him he needed to be examined by a doctor, but when he refused, they told him there was nothing they could do to help him.

Carol looked over at Donnie first, then at James. She told them that the funny thing was that Law Enforcement had informed the staff they would wait until the three could be released, as they might be a flight risk, and that there were more questions they wanted to ask them. The Officers told Carol that Donnie had nothing to worry about; the video had already been sent to several officers. Hence, they knew what had happened in the storage unit, but they, too, felt it was a targeted job and wanted to find out why. The detectives had asked the officer to try to get information from them.

Donnie knew he was right in doing what he did. But now he, too, wanted to know why they had targeted that storage unit and who had hired them to do so. Carol asked Donnie if he had started to investigate the break-in. He told her he had. Donnie also told her he thought Charles had been targeted and would have been killed if law enforcement had not arrived when they did.

James sat back and listened to his parents talk. He knew his dad still had connections everywhere, both good and bad. He learned more than law enforcement did, and he did it faster. James was impressed by how fast they found the three assailants.

"Dad," James began, "have you contacted Law enforcement about your suspicions of it being a targeted job?" Donnie told him he hadn't. He also told him that it would take too long to find any information regarding the break-in.

James thought for a bit and asked him why he felt that way. "Is it because of the difference between what they can legally do and what you can legally do?" James asked Donnie. "In part, yes. I am what you can call a private citizen. I can ask the same questions, but people perceive them differently. They are oftentimes more willing to answer a private citizen's questions than Law Enforcement. Legally, we all must be careful. There are still laws controlling what can and cannot be used in court if it comes to that. Law Enforcement must prove what is referred to as probable cause to stop someone, even for a traffic violation. They must investigate crimes, gather evidence, and determine who committed the crime and when. A private investigator gathers evidence to prove something happened one way or another." Donnie said.

Donnie looked at James, then Carol. They were processing everything he had just said. Carol smiled at Donnie, knowing he was familiar with the workings of this area. However, hearing him speak about it, she admired him for it. "You should be teaching this somewhere. The knowledge you have needs to be taught to those entering law enforcement as well as security." Carol heard herself say it, then looked at Donnie to see his reaction. James told his mom, "That is what I told Dad." Carol giggled and said, "Well, we all agree!" Donnie just shook his head at the two of them. "I am not one for standing in a classroom and teaching; I believe it is better taught as they go. Most people learn by doing, making mistakes, then correcting those mistakes." Donnie said to Carol and James. They both agreed with him. He had always been that way since he and Carol met, and as far as James could remember.

Carol looked at her watch and realized how late it was getting. She told Donnie she should head home. Donnie looked and said he would walk her to her car. That caused James to smile and tilt his head towards the floor. Carol and Donnie both reached out to playfully smack him on the shoulders. Then they all laughed. Carol hugged James and told him to behave. As Donnie and Carol walked outside, Carol turned to Donnie and told him she had had a good time tonight. Donnie said he did, too, and thanked her for coming by. He went on to say she is always welcome to come by. She said OK as she got to her car. Donnie opened her door for her. She reminded him that it had been a long time since he opened her door. He responded, "It has been too long."

Starting the engine, she let the door stay open a bit longer. They looked at each other for a couple of minutes, smiled, and said goodnight. Donnie watched as she drove away. Donnie turned around and saw James in the doorway.

As Donnie went through the door, he told James to knock it off. Then he smiled and said, "It was nice of your mom to come by. It felt like the old days for our family."

12

The Faces of the Badge

Donnie shut the door behind him and heard James in the kitchen, cleaning up after the coffee break they had that evening. Donnie called out to James to ask if there was still coffee. James told him there was and asked if he wanted some more. Donnie told him he did and asked if he wanted to hear some more of his stories. James said yes and told Donnie he would bring his cup into the living room.

Sitting down in the recliner, Donnie was thinking back to when he worked in Law Enforcement as a sworn officer. He remembered the frustration of how things were constantly changing. Cell phones are out, and people are filming everything they do, especially only showing a part that would make them look like they were in the wrong, never showing what the suspect did to get them to the point of arrest. He felt frustrated as he thought about the body cams that showed no wrongdoing, at least for those who followed the rules. However, they showed and discussed everything the Law Enforcement officer did, even if it was a little wrong.

He thought of what James would face wearing a badge. The issues he will face with gang-affiliated people, hating law enforcement because they were taught to hate them by their families. It was always dangerous, but now it seems they are targets of almost everyone. Including people James personally knows. James will be facing it earlier in his career than he did, and he knew he would.

As Donnie was deep in thought, James came into the living room and handed him a fresh cup of coffee. Donnie thanked him. James sat down and took a sip of his coffee.

James, I remember a night we had a male who tried to end his own life. He used a serrated table steak knife and tried about 15 times to stab himself in the chest. Although he never got past his flesh, cuts in that area can bleed a lot. When we got there, he was sitting and leaning against a tree in the front yard. His shirt was bloody; he looked like he might be gone. The first officer who arrived moved towards him, his gun drawn, not knowing if he was faking it and waiting to stab one of us. The guy's parents were screaming at us to help their son. As we both moved towards him, we could see he was still breathing. He looked up at us, and the knife was about 6 inches away from him, in the grass. Upon finding him alive, we notified the ambulance to respond and treat the subject. He was handcuffed for everyone's safety, and we turned him over to the medical staff when they arrived. As the medical personnel worked on him, our first officer turned to speak to his parents. Asking about the subject. We found out he was in his mid-twenties; he had been drinking and was on medication for emotional issues. He had just broken up with his long-term girlfriend, and after an argument with his dad, he grabbed the knife and stabbed himself in front of his dad. He then turned and ran out the front door, sat down, and continued to stab himself. He had 21 wounds in his chest area. He had to have a solid ribcage not to put the knife deeper than flesh deep. He was transported to the hospital for treatment. He recovered and, after meeting with his doctor, started back on his meds. Later, he was released and returned to town.

Now, fast forward about six months. The same person was drinking with others and got into an argument with one of them. The suspect male grabbed a knife, a serrated table steak knife, just like the one used the first time. He stabbed the victim about 12 times in the chest. Again, the victim only suffered flesh-wound cuts on his chest. I was off that night and received a call from our dispatcher asking about the suspect. The suspect had a distinctive mark on his face. One eye had been cut, and after it healed, it appeared lower than the other. The dispatcher asked me where the suspect usually could be found. I told them, and when they hung up, I went back to bed. I still have no idea why the stabs didn't go deeper. We looked all over town for him for several weeks; the detectives couldn't locate him either. It became a cold case for our department. About 6 months later, he was in a nearby town and arrested for attempted murder.

The suspect had threatened to kill me a couple of times. He was always suitable for a warrant arrest. The court would release him, and about 90 days later, he would fail to appear again, and an FTA warrant would be issued. We would find him and arrest him again.

As Donnie was telling the story, he could see James' puzzled look on his face. Donnie stopped and told James to ask the questions he wanted. "The guy was not successful himself, and then another guy tried to do the same thing. But all he had were flesh wounds? How is that even possible?" James was shaking his head as he asked him the questions.

"The only thing we could figure out was that he had thick bones across his upper torso so that the knife couldn't get through the bone area, or he had a secret armor casing around his upper torso. We could never figure out how he didn't get more severely hurt," Donnie told James. "Dad," James began again, "he recovered from the self-inflicted wounds just to have to go back to the hospital for the same reason 6 months later?" "Yes, he did," Donnie responded, smiling at the whole thing as he remembered it. He added, "My Sergeant chalked it up to luck times 2 for the guy. Whatever the reason, he was lucky it didn't cause worse damage either time." James just shook his head, trying to figure it out.

"Dad," James began, "I know you speak other languages, and were able to pass tests and become a certified translator for the Police Department. Which meant you could take reports in various languages and testify in court cases. Was that needed when you were in Law Enforcement?" Donnie looked at James and told him he had been one of three translators, had taken more reports, and assisted both the County Sheriff's officers and the Highway Patrol.

"I remember one guy came in to report a crime, Robert-49 dispatch, I responded, and they told me to come by the office to translate. As I entered the lobby, the man was shocked to see me and asked if I spoke his language. I jokingly told him in his language I only speak English, then said Yes, I do, sir." As Donnie said this, James smiled at him. "I had to have some fun once in a while, son." Donnie ended.

"I remember a storm came through the area, and the winds were blowing hard enough to knock a large limb from a tree. When it fell, it broke a live power line that was dancing around the wet ground. We had to secure the area until the power company arrived to shut the line off and repair it." Donnie told James. "That sounds dangerous," James said. "Just another call for our officer's son," Donnie retorted.

"Did the line ever get close to you or the other officers?" James asked. "Thankfully not, we were parked far enough away, and everyone living near it stayed inside. The wind was still blowing hard, so it was better that they did. It took them about 2 hours due to the storm," Donnie told James.

"Sounds like there were always issues when you guys got storms, streets flooding, downed power lines, bad fog," James commented.

"We had our issues. One time, a strong wind blew through, stirring up the sand. The traffic lights on the interstate crossing went out one day. Highway Patrol covered the northbound lanes, and we covered the southbound lanes. As we were doing that, my partner was struck by a six-foot-wide tumbleweed in the back. While we were there, it turned to horizontal rain. Now the dirt turned to mud on us. By the time we were done, we had mud everywhere, including our weapons. It took us a while to get cleaned up. We had three more hours for our shift." As Donnie spoke, he began shaking his head, as if reliving that day.

"Law Enforcement, some high-end security, and other emergency services must be ready for anything. They work in all kinds of weather; they cannot just call in sick because it's too cold or too hot outside. That is something you will have to get used to, son," Donnie said. "I understand that it will be in all types of weather conditions, Dad," James responded.

James knew his dad was always ready to jump in if he needed anything. Since James was little, Donnie had always been there with a helping hand, encouraging and guiding him. He also knew Carol would do everything she could to protect him. He was thankful for his parents, and even though they were not together, they raised him with great love. He knew many classmates who became pawns in their parents' separations and divorces, but he was never that to his parents. James also knew, deep down, that they were concerned about his entering law enforcement for several reasons. To his mom, he was and will always be her little boy. He had seen the mama bear come out a few times growing up. It used to embarrass him when he was little, but he grew to admire her and was thankful for the times she had protected him, usually from his own dumb choices. His dad, as tough as he was, was a bit of a softie when it came to James, and he knew it. James never took advantage of that because he respected Donnie too much. He had always known his dad worked like he did to keep others safe, sometimes making himself sick in the process. But James admired him for that, and it taught him to always be there for friends and family. James respected and loved both his parents for what they taught him, and he returned the love they shared.

Listening to his dad's stories, James gained a deeper understanding of him than he had before. There was a deeper side to him that James had never seen or known before. There was pain sometimes in his words. Pain that Donnie hides from the world, especially from James. James was understanding his dad even more now.

Donnie was thinking of another story to tell James when the phone rang. When Donnie answered it, he heard Stacy's voice. It was strained, as if she had been crying. "He's awake. Charles is awake," he heard her say. "Stacy, that is great news! How is he doing beyond that?" Donnie asked her. "He said he is starving. I called the nurse in, and she got him some Jello and cookies. The Doctor was notified and will be here in the morning. He asked if you knew about his getting hurt, and I said you did. He told me he was sorry for scaring me and asked if the baby and I were OK." Stacy said with a strained voice, holding back tears. "Tell Charles I will be by in the morning to check on him. Hope he can get some good sleep now," he said. "I will tell him. Thank you for everything; it means more to me than you know. I need to get back into the room." Stacy told Donnie.

Hanging up, Donnie told James that Charles was awake, and his memory was still good. "I need to make a couple more phone calls, son. Sorry, we got interrupted," James knew that would take a weight off his dad's shoulders. "I can wait, Dad," James told him.

Donnie called his boss, and when he answered, he told him what he had just heard. His boss was happy because Charles was recovering so well. After hanging up that call, Donnie called Carol, as she had asked him to let her know if he heard anything.

Carol answered the phone when it rang. She looked at the clock, and it was 0130. She said hello with some trepidation. "Carol, sorry to be calling at this hour," Donnie told her, "Charles is awake and has his memory intact, still, according to Stacy." "That's great news for them. You told me he was a tough kid." Carol said. "I will let you get back to sleep. I just wanted to let you know," Donnie responded. "Thank you for the update. When you see them, please let them know that I will check on them tomorrow as well. They are family." Carol said to Donnie. He responded with, "I will, Hun." Donnie was smiling when he hung up the phone. He turned back to face James.

James, this one may make you smile. I was working one night when our dispatcher received a call from another department. They reported that officers were pursuing a vehicle southbound on the interstate and were requesting our assistance. My Sergeant had us block the exits into town from the interstate. We were not informed of the pursuit's purpose, but we were told to be ready.

We were given a description of the vehicle stating that a single male driver was the only occupant. After about 30 minutes, we see the suspect vehicle driving south at the speed limit. This is an active pursuit, but the driver was not speeding, as if he were trying to get away. Our local Highway Patrol took over the pursuit because it had now entered a different county. The two officers from the initial agency then pulled into town and were now on the phone with their Sergeant. As we were clearing, we heard the local HP Officers asking for clarification on the purpose of the pursuit. However, no information was provided. They continued to pursue the driver. About 30 miles south of us, the HP attempted a takedown maneuver to get the vehicle to finally pull over.

The HP Officer advised his dispatcher that the male driver was about 75 years old and had asked why they had been following him for so long. He did not understand. There was no smell of alcohol on his breath. He was having a "senior moment"; he was legitimately confused by the whole thing. Finally, the dispatcher came over the radio and told the HP officers the driver had run a stop sign. In the town from which the two initial officers came. They then asked if either of their officers would issue a ticket to the driver for rolling through a stop sign. The dispatcher hesitantly replied, "No." Now they needed to tow the man's vehicle, book him a hotel, and pay to replace all four tires and two rims. The initial officer, fresh off his Field Training Officer (FTO) time, was subsequently fired over the incident. His Sergeant knew my Sergeant and told him all of that.

James just sat there, with his mouth slightly open in disbelief. He even knew it would have been better to end the so-called pursuit. Perhaps follow the vehicle to see if the driver was driving impaired, but that was excessive.

Donnie smiled at James. There had been several new Officers who had been "over the top" as soon as they were on their own. We even had one rookie who would pull over a car, light a cigarette, and then approach the driver to talk. He would inhale and then exhale as he spoke to the driver. Unfortunately for him, he pulled over a woman who was married into the wealthiest family in town and did the same to her. He got fired.

"Wait, he did what? Why would he light a cigarette and then approach a car on a traffic stop?" James asked his dad. "He was barely 21, he thought it made him look older. Either way, he didn't last long with the department." Donnie responded.

"Some people do not belong in any form of emergency services or security. They are not equipped to handle situations when they arise. I have met people who are big and would freeze when things happen, and small people who overreact to everything, and vice versa. It is how the person processes the issue at hand that helps them perform their duties as they should and keeps everyone safe. I've heard so many so-called tough guys talk big about what they can do until they are required to do something, then they freak out. I remember working with some at-risk teens. One of them told a gruesome story about a female cousin and what she did to 2 males who had attacked her. The female I was there with was a churchgoer, and she gasped at what he was telling me. When he was done, I said, 'Okay, can we move on now?' About a year later, I ran into the guy, and he told me he realized I was different from the others who had been there trying to help the group. And then he thanked me for being honest about things." Donnie finished speaking and took a sip of his coffee.

Then Donnie continued, "There will be times when our morals and worldview are challenged. There are things that all emergency responders encounter during a shift that can cause doubts. Is this the career I want to continue in? Am I doing anything to help? The process of understanding things that seem so surreal, outside the normal daily life, can shock people to go one way or the other. Either they walk away from it, or they become numb to the garbage. Your mom is a good example. When we met, I had a 6-inch gash on my arm. It was wrapped up when I walked in, but she was required to clean it for the doctor. She unwrapped the blood-soaked wrap, cleaned it, and then assisted the doctor."

James said he remembered him talking about how they met. He remembered hearing about the cut, but he didn't recall anything about the wound. "It didn't look good, but your mom was very professional. She has witnessed a wide range of things over her years there. She is more like us than she wants to admit." Donnie chuckled as he spoke to James. He asked Donnie, "How so, Dad?" Donnie told him she is an adrenaline junky like they are. Thriving on the chaos of the ER, if not, she would have left the ER years ago.

James thought about the adrenaline junkie part; he had never considered that. He had always thought it was the mountain climbers, the race car drivers, the extreme-sport enthusiasts who were adrenaline junkies, not Emergency responders. But as he thought more about it, it made sense to him. Firefighters rush into burning buildings and respond to vehicle accidents. Ambulance crews react to these situations, working to save the lives of people they do not know, all while driving with lights and sirens to arrive quickly. He could see his dad's point.

Donnie began to tell James another story, "We got a call one night about a male caught peering into the windows of a house. Three adult females and eight children, aged 4 to 14, occupied the house. As we responded, the male left, so we searched for him. He was seen walking back to the house from about a block away. One of our officers caught him and cuffed him, placing him in his vehicle. I was at the house translating for the first officer who responded. The man was brought to the house so the women could identify him. They identified him. We booked him and wrote the reports. If you know who Charles Manson was, this guy looked like him, except one arm was smaller than the other. In other words, he was freaky. When they ran his criminal history, he had a history of peeping and attempted sexual assaults going back 12 years. When we finally got him to court, he was all cleaned up, with a haircut, and looked clean. He was found guilty in court." Donnie finished.

James looked up Charles Manson on his phone. He turned the phone around and asked Donnie if this was Manson. Donnie said, "Yes, that is him. This guy looked like that." James looked at the picture for a minute and set his phone down. "That guy looks crazy. I can see why you would say that". James said.

"Throughout all the years I have been working in Law enforcement and High-end security, the diverse types of people I have encountered have never failed to 'entertain' me. Everyone from local and state politicians, high society and low society types, kids who think their mom or dad will get them out of trouble, Real and wannabe gang members, Motorcycle gang members, and the list goes on. All of them have one thing in common: you will encounter your share of interesting people. They all have a story to tell if you listen. Some so out there they sound crazy, others sound believable, but they all have a story." Donnie told James.

James is beginning to realize there is more to law enforcement than he initially thought, and he is glad his dad is sharing stories with him. He also knows his dad will be the best sounding board when he goes into the field and starts working. He is beginning to understand better that he will see the worst of society, and few people understand the life he will have, but his dad and his mom do. Unlike many who have stars in their eyes when they enter

Law enforcement, he feels he will be better prepared for the challenges he will face because of these stories. He has been wondering how he will react as he experiences what his dad told him, and when he will numb himself to it all and see it as just another day to get through.

Donnie told James he needed a few hours of sleep before he went to see Charles and asked if he wanted to come with him to the hospital. James told him he would let him know in the morning. Donnie said that would be fine. As Donnie rose, James thanked him for sharing the stories. Some had been entertaining, and some had been eye-opening to him. Donnie told him he had shared only a few stories so far and planned to share more. James told Donnie he looked forward to hearing more about everything from him.

Donnie headed to his room to get a few hours of sleep before visiting Charles at the hospital. He could hear James washing the coffee cups and closing the cabinets. Shutting his door, Donnie lay down on the bed. Instead of falling asleep, he replayed the storage unit incident repeatedly in his mind. Making sure he did everything right. He had done this for years, after every incident. This one felt different to him. They were armed and ready to attack if they got caught. Donnie saw that as an issue. They targeted the single unit, which was also a problem. Most people who break into storage units, unless they know what is in a certain one, will randomly break in and take their chances. It might be worth gaining items to pawn or sell directly. A quick turnover, so they could do what they wanted with the money. This one was different; they were only looking into one box. Again, it felt strange and targeted. Thinking of the video of the attack on Charles, he had a gun, pepper spray, handcuffs, a taser, plus his radio. All they took was his radio. As these thoughts were running through Donnie's mind, he finally fell asleep.

Donnie heard a distant buzzing sound. It continued, and as he opened his eyes, he realized it was his alarm. After shutting it off, Donnie looked at his watch and saw that he'd slept for about five hours. He looked at his phone to see if he'd received any messages. Nothing was found. He checked his email and saw nine. Perusing through them, he saw none were pressing. Getting up, he went to the door, opened it, and could smell coffee brewing in the kitchen. James must be up. As he walked down the hall, he saw James sitting at the kitchen table, drinking coffee.

"I put a fresh pot together for us, please help yourself to a cup, Dad," James told him. "Thanks, son," Donnie said as he reached for a cup of coffee.

13

The Heart of the Badge

After eating and grabbing another cup of coffee, Donnie and James left for the hospital. The trip across town was worse than usual. They got stopped at a train crossing. While waiting, Donnie smiled as the slow train moved past them.

James looked over at his dad and asked, "Do you like to be stuck at these train crossings? Is there something funny about this?" This reminds me of another story, a tale so unbelievable, it might not even sound believable. Want to hear it?" They were both chuckling.

Donnie began, "One night, we got a call about a vehicle stuck on the tracks. The car had been struck by a train running through town. When we arrived, the vehicle had been knocked off the track but was still running. Luckily, the area where the vehicle had stopped was one where the couple of small diners and the other five businesses were closed for the night. Plus, the car was far enough away from any building that if it blew up, it wouldn't have caused a lot of damage."

Continuing, Donnie told James, "According to the train conductor, it had the front end sticking onto the tracks. When he struck the car, it moved several feet down the track and then slid to a stop. It was a four-door diesel engine car. As the first on the scene, I was tasked with checking the vehicle for any occupants. I slowly walked up to the car using my flashlight to look inside. The front end was smashed so badly that we couldn't figure out how it was still running. I looked at the battery, and it had exploded when the car was struck by the train. There were fluids everywhere on the ground around the vehicle. As I got back away and moved to a safe distance, the volunteer firefighters arrived. The fire truck with the captain was also arriving. None of them wanted to get close to the running vehicle. I was the only one who got next to it."

"After clearing the adjacent buildings, we had to wait there for another 30 minutes before the motor started to sputter and finally stopped. Then, the fire crew approached the vehicle, so slowly that a snail could have moved up to it faster. That took another 15 minutes, with fire hoses ready. They looked around it, saw no fire, and they turned the hoses to wash away the vehicle's fluids underneath the now stopped car," Donnie explained.

"After we ran the license plate of the vehicle. One of the deputies went to the house and found the owner. He and a friend were intoxicated, but in the house. They both claimed that the car had been stolen and wanted to file a report. The deputy said he looked at them both and told them it wasn't true, and that they could change their story. Realizing they had been caught in their lie, they admitted they had left the car there. They told the deputy they had tried to cross over the tracks, but the vehicle got stuck. They tried to drive it off the track, but it slid back onto it instead. They got out and left the car there. They walked to the owner's house; they passed out from drinking. The deputy relayed this through his dispatch center to our dispatcher." As Donnie was telling this part of the story to James, James began shaking his head.

"Because it involved a train and a vehicle, Highway Patrol had to be called to take the report. The deputy stayed at the owner's house. We waited almost an hour for the Highway Patrol to arrive, and he was not happy," Donnie said with a smile.

Donnie concluded, "When the Highway Patrol arrived, our other officer was cleared to leave. Because I was the first to arrive, I had to wait until he cleared me. He wanted to arrest the owner, but since we couldn't prove he was behind the wheel, there was nothing to charge him with, which made him even angrier. The train crew also had to wait until a railroad inspector arrived and checked the track rail to ensure there was no damage. He told me he would be there for about three more hours. Once he told me I could clear the accident and gave me his call for service number for my report, I left."

"Dad, that's one of the craziest stories you've told me so far," James laughed. "Son, there are a few more you may not believe still to be told," Donnie responded as they were finally pulling into the hospital parking lot to check on Charles.

They entered the hospital and went to Charles' room. When Stacy looked up, she had a big smile on her face, got up, and came towards Donnie, throwing her arms around him. Hugging him tightly, she choked back tears. "Donnie, he has been asking when you were coming to see him," Stacy said to Donnie.

Donnie hugged her back and responded, "I am here now." Donnie looked over at Charles and then at James. They were so close in age that Donnie could feel a sense of fatherly protection welling up in him toward both James and Charles. He felt his anger well up again, but as it did, Charles opened his eyes and looked at Donnie. "Donnie, I am glad you are here," Charles said with a raspy voice. Stacy turned and asked Charles if he wanted a drink of water as she moved back to his bedside.

As Donnie and James followed Stacy to Charles' bed, Charles looked at James and said he was glad to see him, too. He told Donnie Carol had been by a couple of hours ago to check on him as well. Charles smiled at Donnie and told him he felt like a member of the family now. Donnie smiled at Charles, and James told Charles he was. James reached out his hand, grabbed Charles' hand, and shook it, saying, "Well, brother, welcome to one of the craziest families you will ever know." James turned to Stacy and called her sis. Stacy giggled. Both Charles and Stacy came from single-child families, and neither had a sibling. Charles looked at Donnie and jokingly called him Grandpa as he reached for Stacy's hand, causing them all to laugh. All of this broke the tension in the room.

"How are you doing, Charles?" Donnie asked. "Other than a major headache, I'm doing okay. There is some bruising around my rib area, and my right arm is stiff, but considering the alternative, I am not bad." Charles told Donnie. Donnie turned to Stacy and asked how he was doing. Stacy looked at Donnie and told him, "He is doing better, but being stubborn. He wants out of here already." Donnie looked at Charles and told him he would listen to the Doctor and Stacy. Charles responded with a yes, sir to Donnie. James looked at Stacy and said, "Yup, he is definitely family." Causing them to laugh.

"Donnie, Stacy told me you caught the guys who attacked me. How did that go?" Donnie told him what had happened, and they were all in the hospital with Law Enforcement, waiting to be released. Charles thanked Donnie for helping them find a place. Charles reached out his hand to shake Donnie's hand.

Charles, the first thing you need to do is to heal. Once the doctor has cleared you, you can resume your work schedule if you wish. In the meantime, you will receive your regular pay, so there's no need to worry about paying the bills or making ends meet. Thank you, Charles said, that means a lot to both of us. "Don't you mean the three of you?" Donnie joked. Charles smiled, saying, "My mistake, yes, the three of us." Stacy had only met Donnie a couple of times before; she thought of him as larger than life, challenging, and demanding. She had admired him before, but now she was seeing a different side of him, a side like a dad, someone who genuinely cared. It was comforting to her to know this about Donnie.

As they were speaking, the nurse came in to check on Charles. She gave him some medication to take. Charles told Donnie and James that these were his nighttime medications. As he took them, he looked at Stacy. After swallowing them, he suggested she should go home and get some sleep. She told him she was fine and would stay. Charles looked at Donnie. Smiling, Donnie said, "I am not getting in the middle of this, but I will tell you, she isn't going anywhere." Charles just shrugged his shoulders and responded to Donnie, "Thanks for the back-up, Dad." This caused the nurse to laugh. Turning to Donnie, she told him he was a wise man; no wonder Carol loves you so much. As she walked out of the room, Donnie saw the smile on James's face. Donnie gave him the "knock it off" look. Confused, Charles looked at them both. Donnie just waved Charles off. Stacy let out a giggle at how these three were acting.

"We need to get going," Donnie told Charles and Stacy. Stacy got up and came around the bed, hugging Donnie again. "Thank you again for everything," she told Donnie. Looking at James, she said, "See you later, big brother. I always wanted a big brother." James responded, "I always wanted siblings, but those two," pointing to Donnie and Carol as if Carol were also there, "decided against it." Again, the room broke out in laughter. "We will come back later to check in with you both," Donnie told them.

He and James left the room. James was giggling a bit and looked at Donnie when they entered the elevator. "Told you, Mom still loves you." "Son, I have always loved your mom. She is the most amazing person I know. We had our issues, but maybe one day we can get past them," Donnie said, sounding a bit down to James. "It will be okay, Dad. I think things are finally working themselves out for you two," James tried to reassure Donnie.

Changing the subject, Donnie asked if James had any plans for the day. "I need to work later this afternoon, but nothing until then," James responded. “Want some breakfast?” Donnie asked. “Yeah, that sounds good to me, Dad.” He responded to the question.

When they arrived at the restaurant, James noticed a familiar car parked in the parking lot. His mom was there as well. It made James smile. “Finally work things out, Dad?” James asked. Donnie didn’t respond to the comment.

Once they were all seated, they ordered and sat waiting while drinking their coffee. The conversation was light and flowing as the server brought their food. James, always observant, couldn’t help but notice his parents were enjoying themselves. They also talked about Charles and Stacy. It was as if James were just a third wheel with one of his college buddies when they went out. James hadn’t dated much. He was focused on school and sports. He gained top honors in just about everything he did, except in the subject of dating. Not that he was awkward around girls, he just wasn’t interested in dating. James finished his food and sat back, watching Donnie and Carol as he sipped his coffee. It was fun, it made James happy to see his parents “finally working things out.”

James decided to test an idea. He looked at his dad and asked him if he wanted to share another of his stories. Carol looked at Donnie and said she would like to hear one, too. Donnie looked at them both and, without hesitation, began.

"I was working a day shift on a nice Thursday morning, it was one of those days when not much had been going on. Robert-49, I heard on the radio. Go ahead, I told dispatch. We have received a report of a "10-50" vehicle accident at the main street railroad tracks. 10-4 in route. As I responded, I had no idea what I was about to get into." Donnie paused to drink some more coffee and to watch their faces. He paused for effect. He continued, "as I was going 10-97, arriving, I saw a train stopped, pieces of a medium-sized industrial forklift all over the place. A guy was walking around and screaming. As he screamed, he also pointed at a 40-gallon propane tank, spinning in the middle of the street like a top. As our units arrived, I was advising dispatch. My Sergeant came over the radio advising us to vacate the buildings in the area. With this thing spinning, we went door to door telling everyone to leave and move out of the area. Many of the buildings had back doors, so most people went out the back. We had to get a few people out and down the street. I had parked my unit at the intersection, about half a block from the spinning tank. After clearing the buildings, my Sergeant advised that we take cover. Fire personnel had arrived. The sergeant and the fire captain were determining their next course of action. I was behind my vehicle."

Donnie looked at Carol to make sure she was okay with this story. She was sitting there, engulfed by the story's words. James sat back, waiting for his dad to finish telling the story.

Donnie told them, "While we were all there, we heard a noise. It was the tank, because the whole area was quiet. It made a hissing sound as the propane escaped from the tank's pressure. The fire department decided to let it run out. They had spoken to the driver, who had gotten stuck on the tracks. He jumped off and tried to warn the train, but it couldn't stop before it hit the forklift. He also told them he thought the tank was only a quarter full of propane and should run out soon. This time, we didn't need to call the Highway Patrol because the vehicle wasn't technically registered with the DMV. As the tank spun around, we just waited. We had Sheriff's deputies diverting traffic around the area. Finally, about 20 minutes after we had cleared everybody out, set up the perimeter, and waited, it finally stopped spinning, even though it was still hissing out propane. Three fire department personnel attempted to shut it off, but instead moved it out of the street to the gutter along the road. After another 10 minutes, the loud hissing stopped, and they checked; it was all clear, and we emerged from our cover positions. You could still smell propane. My Sergeant started to light a smoke, stopped, and decided not to. We assisted the firefighters in beginning the cleanup of the roadway. The forklift driver's boss came out with a couple of forklifts and several employees to pick up the pieces of the damaged forklift." Donnie finished, and Carol told Donnie she was glad no one got hurt. "I am too," he told her. They had been talking almost nonstop, and he realized he needed to get to the office. He asked James if he wanted to drive with him, but James said his mom would take him home if that was okay. He looked at James, and James told him he would go with Carol. Donnie told them that it was fine, grabbed the check, and headed to the front to pay. When he came back, James told him he was still drinking his coffee and asked Carol to wait a few minutes. Carol agreed that it would be fine with her. Donnie told them he would see them later.

Carol thanked him for breakfast and the invitation. Donnie left Carol and James at the table. After Donnie left, James turned to his mom and told her that he knew they still loved each other. Carol blushed at what James said. James went on to say, "If you can work things out, I will be glad for you both; you two deserve to be happy." He finished by saying he hoped they would. He also told Carol that he hadn't seen either of his parents, truly happy, in a long time.

All Carol could do was smile. She was hopeful that she and Donnie could work things out, and she apologized to James for everything she had put him through. James told his mom, "I don't blame either of you for anything. You both made a point of showing me support and love throughout my life. I am proud of you and proud to call you mom." Carol looked at James, her eyes a bit teary at what he had said to her.

"I finally realize, I enjoy your dad's stories and that my fear of losing him kept me from respecting him and his job," Carol told James. "Mom, his biggest regret is losing you; from what I've seen between you two, that was forgiven a long time ago," James said. Carol looked at James and smiled. She was glad to hear it and hoped it was true. "I suppose time will tell if that is what your dad thinks," Carol told James.

James set an added tip on the table as he and his mom got up to leave. Carol was proud of her son and everything he had accomplished. He has a fantastic future ahead of him, she thought. James noticed his mom looking at him intently and asked if everything was all right. "Everything is as it should be, James," Carol said, her amazing smile shining brightly towards James.

They got into the car, and as Carol started it, James realized, for the first time, how vital a good life partner is to someone working in Law enforcement or emergency services. Many of his instructors had discussed this in his classes. He had initially thought it was a way to warn them of the job's stress, but now he understood that a sound support system is fundamental to everyone, especially in these roles. Someone to lean on, someone who understands that there will be times when it's better just to let silence be all the conversation that's needed. A time to process the events of their shift. However, it also helps keep each other grounded and centered in the relationship, rather than letting job stress ruin it.

"Mom," James started, "I have been thinking about what I'm getting into, and I want you to know I respect your opinions." I am going to ask this question and want you to give it some time before you answer, OK?" Looking at James, Carol said, "Okay." "What are your real and honest feelings about me starting my career in law enforcement?" James asked her. Carol was thinking about him entering Law Enforcement. She had been thinking about it since he told her. "I am concerned about you and your safety, but I also know that you, like your dad, are people who will do everything you can to help others. Being your mom, I am concerned. As a nurse, I see the aftermath of the evil the world causes, but I also know you. I know who you are and how you see everything around you. You are very much like your dad. You have a way of doing things, finding the story beneath the surface, and being prepared in almost every situation. I am so very proud of you for following your heart and mind. James, I support you in whatever decision you make. Now, if this were about a girl, as your momma, I would have to approve of her." Carol finished. She and James laughed about the girl's comment. "I will remember that, Mom," James told his mom.

"Now, I am going to ask you something," Carol told James. "Why do you want to enter into Law Enforcement, son?" "I thought about it for a long time, Mom. I talked to retired and current officers. I researched statistics on career longevity and what it takes even to be considered for a position. I also knew I was drawn to law enforcement, as if it were a calling. I wish I could say the old cliché, 'I wanted to follow in my dad's footsteps,' but I'm doing it for myself. If that makes any sense," James told his mom. Carol sat for a few minutes before responding. "That makes me even prouder of your choice, James." Carol looked at him as she said it. As she pulled into the driveway to the house, stopping the car, she told him, "Let your dad know why as well. It should come from you and not me. Listen to his stories about his last 20 years. Ask him questions because he has a lot to teach about law enforcement and High-end security. He has been through more than you even know. But please tell him what you told me just now, OK, son?" She reached over and hugged James. "I will, Mom, thank you for the conversation. It does mean a lot to me." James said to Carol.

As he got out of the car, Carol sat there watching him walk into the house. She is very proud of the man he has become. She hoped that the job wouldn't change him and that he would find someone who understood the life he was entering and would stand by his side through it all. As she sat there, the phone rang. The hospital called, saying they needed her to cover a shift for someone. She told them she would be there, back to reality.

14

The Threat of the Badge

After Donnie left the diner, he called the owner and told him about Charles and his recovery. Thanked him for his willingness to cover the family by paying him his usual wages while he was out of work. He told him he had spoken to Charles about the importance of his full recovery. His boss also informed him that he had read the report on the storage unit incident. He had called a Captain at the local office, and the captain said everything was done correctly, and they were closing the case with the arrests of the three. He brought up the Lieutenant and asked him to tell Donnie that the Lieutenant would not cause any trouble. "Boss, I did everything by the book. It was clean and straightforward." Donnie said. The boss told him, "I know it was Donnie, but you know as well as I do, Timothy still has it out for you, from years ago."

Donnie chuckled at that, knowing Timothy had never forgiven him for what he did. Donnie had embarrassed Timothy in front of 20 cops when he found the suspect. They were both Sergeants; Timothy had 2 more years on the job. He thought he was better than Donnie. When Donnie broke a case, Timothy tried to take credit for it, but Donnie let him. He knew Timothy would have to explain to their captain how he had found everything and the suspect, and write a report about it. Timothy tried to accuse Donnie of setting him up. Everyone knew the truth of what happened. Donnie just sat back and watched Timothy deal with everything. It was another 2 years before Timothy got promoted because of it.

That was also around the same time Donnie decided to transition into security work and leave law enforcement. Donnie used to enjoy his job as a patrol officer, but after he was promoted to Sergeant, he began to fight department politics. Being Donnie, he quickly grew tired of it. Politics was not what he signed up for. He had discussed it with Carol at the time. It took Donnie a couple more years to make the switch.

As he pulled into the office parking lot, Donnie saw a Law enforcement vehicle parked there as well. Donnie wondered why it was there as he entered the building; he recognized it as an old friend. Frank, what brings you here today?" Donnie asked him as he walked towards him. "Is there somewhere we can talk?" Frank asked Donnie. Donnie told him yes, and they headed to Donnie's office. As they entered, Frank shut the door behind them. Donnie looked at Frank and knew there was something up. "What's up, Frank?" Donnie asked. "We just got word from 3 separate informants that you are now under contract for the three guys in the storage unit," Frank told Donnie. "OK, not the first time that has been rumored," Donnie responded. "Donnie, this was not an ordinary break-in; they targeted that unit. The company that rented the unit has information against a major international "group." The deputy chief sent me down here to tell you. We received the info from one of the informants this morning. They saw you and the family at the Diner this morning, and one of the informants, who knows you, told his handler about it. They have been tasked to watch you, Carol, and James. Additionally, that kid in the hospital and his wife. This sounds serious, Donnie." Frank sounded concerned as he spoke to Donnie. "What is the department wanting to do?" Donnie asked. "I want Charles and his wife protected as well as Carol. James and I can handle our end. "We have officers at the hospital for those three, but I'm not sure what else they are doing to protect you all," Frank told Donnie.

"Frank, who is it that has decided to take an interest in my family, and don't tell me you don't know. Either you tell me, or I will visit Anthony myself." Donnie stared at Frank. "Frank, tell me. This also puts all our employees in danger!" Donnie yelled. "I can't, you know, I can't," Frank told him. "OK, I will talk to Anthony. Thanks for telling me, Frank. You are dismissed." Donnie waved Frank off. Frank stood there for a couple of minutes, then turned and left Donnie's office.

As Frank was leaving, Donnie dialed Carol's number. When she answered, she said, "Hey, I had a great time at breakfast, James and I." Donnie cut her off, "Carol, where are you and James right now?" Carol could tell by Donnie's tone that something was going on. "I just dropped James off and am heading home," Carol told him. "Go back to the house, tell James to call me when you get there. Additionally, you may notice some law enforcement personnel in the area. Also, take the long way back to the house, making turns left and right, and watch for any vehicles that follow you." Donnie told her. "Donnie, what is going on? Why all of this? Tell me." Carol sounded a bit shaken. "Hun, I will tell you everything when I get there," Donnie explained. "I will call you when I leave here in a couple of minutes and keep you on the phone until I can explain everything, OK?" Carol said Ok but also knew something was going on.

Donnie called out to Susan and told her to lock the door behind him. An issue arose. Knowing Donnie, she didn't question and just said, 'Okay.' On his way out, he called his boss and told him what Frank had said. He told his boss he was heading home. He asked two officers from the company to monitor Charles and Stacy. He said he would. As Donnie walked to the car, he noticed a black vehicle parked across the street. He saw at least two males in it and took a mental note of them. Donnie had his weapon on and knew that if it came to it, he would handle the situation. His training taught him that.

He called the hospital and spoke with their security supervisor. He explained the situation. He told him he was sending 2 of his officers in to stay with Charles, and that they would be in that room only. He also reminded him that this was not their fight, but they could use their help. The supervisor knew Donnie and said he would do everything he could to help. They will monitor the cameras and advise him if they see anything. He thanked him, hung up, and called Carol. When she answered, he told her, “Honey, I am leaving the office now.” He watched the vehicle he saw when he came outside. As he approached the gate, he stopped to make sure the gate closed behind him. He pretended to be looking for something, turned on his turn signal, and entered the street. “Donnie, I haven’t noticed any vehicles around me. You are scaring me. What is going on? Please tell me.” She pleaded. “I will when we are home. It is best said when we are all together. I never wanted to scare you, but I need you to do just as I am saying, please.” Donnie said. “I am, just not sure why.” She told him. All I can say is that it's related to the storage unit incident, and I will provide you with what I know when I arrive. I may be a bit longer; I have a vehicle following me. I called my boss and hospital security. We have a couple of our officers going there to be with Charles and Stacy. “Donnie, this is something big, isn’t it?” Carol asked him. “It could be. I need to make some calls when I get home.” He said to Carol. “Ok, I trust you, just scared right now,” Carol said. “I am so sorry to drag you into this,” Donnie responded. “Are there any obvious cars following you?” Donnie asked. “Not that I can see.” She responded. “Good, how far from the house are you?” Donnie asked her. “About three blocks now, I wasn’t far from the house when you called,” Carol told Donnie. Okay, keep me on the phone with you until you're inside the house. I will text James and tell him to stay there, too.” Donnie told her. “OK, I will, Donnie.” She responded.

At the next stoplight, Donnie noticed the vehicle was three cars behind him. He was going to make a turn in a block to see if he was being followed.

He made the turn, pulled into a gas station, texted James to stay home, and told Carol to go back. And that he was on his way to lock the doors when she got inside the house.

The light turned green, and he made a right turn, watching the vehicle turn too. He pulled into the gas station to his right, watching his mirrors. He saw them pass and pull to a stop, across the street; he was being followed. Donnie asked Carol to stay on the line. He texted James, telling him to stay at the house since his mom was coming back. He also mentioned that something had come up with the storage unit and would explain more when he got home. James just said OK. And he would be watching outside. Donnie texted Ok. He also told him he was on his way. Again, Ok was sent by James, followed by, Just be careful, Dad, this sounds serious.

Donnie got on his radio, knowing Michael was working on Patrol, he called David-22, David-3. Go ahead, David-3, Michael responded. "David-22, I currently have a 10-37, a suspicious vehicle. Two males occupied a black SUV. I am currently ascertaining more information. I am currently traveling south on Tupelo Street, approaching Blue Ridge. I am requesting that the nearest Patrol units respond. Donnie radioed Michael to report his location and asked for additional patrol vehicles to be deployed in the area. "David-3, advise the level of response, please," Michael asked. "Normal at this time, I will advise with correction and my 10-20 as I go. All units are advised to keep radio traffic to a minimum as well." Donnie explained to everyone. "David-22-David 3." Donnie radioed. Go ahead, David-3. David-22, advise 10-19 of the situations, and I will provide further information. I am currently 10-21 with my 42. Donnie instructed him to contact the office and inform them of the situation, explaining that he was currently on the phone with his residence. Michael responded with, "Copy David-3. Further, David-22 is on route to your vicinity." "All units responding, contact 10-19 if you are. Per David-3, radio traffic is to be minimized. No need to respond." Michael turned over the radio.

Carol heard everything. She told Donnie she was worried. He asked her how close she was to the house, and she replied that it was about two blocks away. "Okay, Hun, make sure you get there and stay inside until I get home. Keep me on the line until you are in the house." Donnie told her. She agreed and told him to be careful. He said he would, which is why he called in other patrol vehicles. He asked her, "Hold on a minute, please." David-3 is passing Blue Ridge, still southbound on Tupelo. I still have one that's occupied twice, as far as I can see. "Donnie, I am pulling into the driveway. I see law enforcement in the neighborhood. What is happening? I can hear you talking on your radio to Michael and others. Are you in trouble?" Carol pleaded with Donnie. "Please get inside, honey. I will get there to explain everything as soon as I can," Donnie told her.

"David-3 passing Mountain Bluff, still southbound on Tupelo," Donnie spoke into the radio. "David-22, 97 in the area, on Dark Forest and Tupelo." Michael was heard over the radio as he arrived in the area, "David-3, where do you want me?" Michael asked. "David-22, I am heading towards you. When I pass fall in behind the other vehicle, let's set up a blocking maneuver for the vehicle and find out who they are." Donnie told Michael. "10-4 David-3," Michael responded. Donnie was two blocks away from Michael when Michael saw the black SUV and pulled in behind it. Since Michael was also in an unmarked vehicle, he didn't think the occupants realized he was behind them.

Donnie saw Michael pull onto the road behind the other vehicle. "David-22, what is the 10-20 of the other patrol vehicles?" Donnie asked. "David-3, they are parallel to your vehicle, and a block out either direction," Michael told him. "All units, I will be making a right turn into a gas station on the Southwest corner of Tupelo and Manasses. We will block this vehicle on the back side of that location." Donnie explained. All three, which included Michael, radioed out 10-4. Donnie slowed down a little at a time; the other two vehicles between him and the SUV pulled around him and passed him. That left the SUV exposed, and as Donnie slowed further, it got closer.

As Donnie got to the gas station, he made a sudden right turn and headed to the back of the station. The SUV hit the brakes, took the other entrance to the property, and headed towards the back of the station as well. Michael followed them, pulling through the parking lot, while the other two patrol vehicles positioned themselves on either side, one facing Donnie and the other facing Michael.

Once behind, Donnie stopped his vehicle and faced the SUV. As they backed up, they noticed Michael had pulled in behind them. The other two patrol vehicles pulled up alongside the SUV. All the Security officers exited their vehicles with guns pointed at the SUV. Donnie called out over the loudspeaker of his vehicle for the occupants to exit, starting with the driver. There was no movement at first. Donnie waited. Driver, open your window, turn off your engine, and remove the keys. Donnie heard the engine turn off. Driver, put both hands out of the window, holding the vehicle keys in one hand. Again, the driver complied. Donnie saw the keys. Driver, with your left hand, open the door, using the exterior door handle. Donnie watched as the driver did as he had instructed. Now, driver, exit the vehicle with your hands raised. Again, the driver did as he was told. Driver, place both of your hands behind your head and interlace your fingers. He did this as well. Driver, turn around, face towards the back of your vehicle, and walk slowly back towards me. The driver, a man in his late 20s to early 30s, turned around and followed the directions. He had a short haircut, wore average-looking clothes, and wore a button-up shirt and jeans. When the driver had moved past the front of his vehicle, Donnie told him to stop and kneel to the ground, keeping his hands where they were. After he did this, one of his officers approached the man and handcuffed him, taking him to the vehicle, patting him down. The officer called out gun, and he removed the 9mm Glock from his waistband and placed him in the back seat of that vehicle, securing the weapon.

Donnie then turned to the vehicle's passenger and issued the same command. At first, the passenger refused to comply. Donnie repeated the commands to him as well. He then complied with everything. The exact process was completed, and he, too, had a 9 mm Glock that was removed and secured.

Donnie then started with the driver's side back passenger. He had noticed him while watching the driver. This individual was much less cooperative. He refused to exit the vehicle. As Donnie repeated the command, he stared at Donnie through the vehicle's front window. After several commands, he finally complied with the request. As he was doing as Donnie told him, Law enforcement was arriving from all directions. The Third male was cuffed and was still on his knees as they arrived. Each of them had a 9 mm Glock. Each of them was a foreign national, and each had ties to the "group" that targeted Donnie, his family, and Charles' family. Donnie continued to look for a fourth subject in the vehicle. He spoke commands to exit. Law enforcement approached the vehicle and discovered he was lying on the floorboard, heavily armed and at the ready. Law enforcement officers were able to disarm him, pull him from the vehicle, and cuff him. He resisted but was still cuffed. Donnie looked around the vehicle. He noticed a radio in the vehicle that resembled Charles's. Telling law enforcement what he had seen, he put on a glove and retrieved it from the vehicle. It was, in fact, Charles' radio. He told them it was his company's radio, which they had bagged as evidence. They searched the rest of the vehicle and found other weapons and several cell phones. All were photographed and placed into evidence. Law enforcement transported each of the four back to the department for questioning.

As this was all happening, another dark vehicle pulled up behind Donnie's vehicle, and as he turned around, he noticed the vehicle's plate. It was federal officers arriving. As they exited their vehicle, Donnie thanked them for finally showing up. The Lead Officer, Agent Jaxon Burke, told Donnie he had never been so welcoming. They had worked on a case a few years ago and knew each other. Burke asked what Donnie had done to bring this much trouble on himself now. Donnie smiled and told him he should ask the idiots on the way to be questioned. Burke told Donnie to hang on, grabbed his phone, and made a call. When he ended the call, Burke told Donnie they needed to talk alone. Donnie advised his security officers to clear the area, and they could then return to patrol duty. They left, and Michael was still on scene. Donnie told Burke that Michael needed to hear this, too, because Michael had been with him at the storage unit. Burke agreed he could stay.

"Donnie, in all the years I have known you, you've always seemed to stay out of trouble, but this time you stepped into it with both feet and dragged him along with you," Burke told Donnie. "Well, I realized that when Frank came and talked to me today. Now you show up, it's like old home week all over again." Donnie jokingly said. "You have a target on your back now, Donnie, and like always, you are making jokes," Burke told him. "This is not the first time someone wanted to end me, I doubt it won't be the last time either," Donnie said. Michael looked at the two of them and realized they had known each other for a long time and had faced these situations before. He wanted to ask about it, but decided to leave it alone for now.

"Donnie, where are Carol and James right now? I sent a couple of guys over to the house. They should be there in a few minutes." Burke said to Donnie. "They are at home waiting for me." He responded to Burke. "Wait, why did you send your guys to the house?" Donnie asked. "It is a protection detail, for now. Donnie, you know how this all works. It isn't the first time for us, but it is for them." Burke said, looking at Donnie. Burke continued, "We need to meet with Frank, can we meet at your place? Carol and James need to hear about everything. I will explain everything to you then." He turned to Michael, "Where is your girlfriend?" "She is at work." He responded to Burke. "OK, we need all of you together so we can talk about all of this," Burke told them. "Donnie, your guy Charles is still in the hospital, correct?" Burke asked. "He is still there, with his wife. I have 2 of my guys there with them." Donnie said. "I sent 6 of my people there as well. Charles is a key witness to what started this whole thing. I don't think the assailants will make it out of the hospital." Burke was thinking out loud. Donnie knew he was going through his mental list of what needed to be done. "Donnie, go home. Call Frank and let him know that I need to meet with everyone. Michael, call your girlfriend and tell her you're picking her up, then go to Donnie's house. I am going to start the interviews with these four."

Burke looked at Donnie and Michael. He knew Donnie was a stubborn man who would do anything to protect those he loved or who were important to him. He had seen it the last time they were involved in a significant case. As he walked towards his car, he turned back and said to Donnie, "When you step in, you jump in with both feet!" Turning back towards his car, he yelled at them to get going.

Donnie looked at Michael, saying, "We'd better listen to the man. I will tell you all about things later. Go and get Sarah and head to my house. I need to call Frank and set a time for him to meet us. And Michael, we will all get through this."

Michael just nodded and headed to his patrol vehicle, reaching for his phone to call Sarah. He wasn't sure what he was going to tell her, but he needed to think fast. The phone rang twice, and he heard Sarah's voice. Hi, babe, I need to come and pick you up. There has been an unexpected development, and I have been asked to bring you to Donnie's house. "Michael, I am at work." Sarah reminded him. "I know, but this is an emergency. I will explain more later." Michael told her. Sarah could hear in his voice that something had happened. "OK, let me tell the boss, it isn't hectic here. I will tell them it is an emergency and hope they understand." She said to Michael. "I am on my way to pick you up. It should be a few minutes. I will call you when I get there, and please stay inside." Michael told her.

Donnie sat back in his vehicle. He grabbed his phone and realized Carol was still on the phone. "Carol, are you still there?" He asked. "Donnie, what has been happening? I have sat here listening to your voice calling people, one after the other. Are you OK?" She almost shouted at him. "I am good, Hun. I am sorry about that. Everything happened so fast. Do you remember Burke? He is here, and everyone is coming to the house for a meeting. Frank is on his way. Michael is bringing his girlfriend. I am heading home." Donnie told her. "James and I are in the house like you told us," Carol responded. Burke, from the FBI? Why is he coming over, too? This must be bad. Please arrive here as soon as possible. We need to talk about all this." Carol told Donnie. "I am on my way," Donnie said

When Donnie finally made it, Carol was almost in tears. She was scared and angry simultaneously. She had loved Donnie from the moment they met. But now it was different. She wanted him back. She tried to make up for all the time they had lost because she was so scared.

As soon as Donnie opened the door, Carol let out a sigh of relief to see him. She got up and moved towards him, hugging him. She whispered that she was scared, but she felt better with him here. James came in and looked at his dad. He knew there was something serious going on by the look on his face. "This day has been something else." He told them both. I need some coffee. Carol headed to the kitchen to pour him a cup. He had kept everything the same. She grabbed a cup and, after pouring it, she stood there staring into the cup of hot coffee.

She heard James come into the kitchen to check on her. "Mom, are you OK?" James asked as he wrapped his arm around her waist. He felt her lean into his arm. "I am now that your dad is home. How are you doing, James?" Asking him, she knew he was so much like his dad. Yet a lot like her as well. She knew he was worried as well, but would never show her how much. "I am OK I am glad Dad is home too," James said to his mom. "Let me help you, Mom. I know this is so confusing. "Uncle Frank is coming over; he never comes over. This must be bad for him to do that." James said as he reached for the coffee. "I have it, son," Carol said in that voice he knew all too well. James raised his hands and smiled at his mom. He knew she could be pretty stubborn when she wanted to be.

As Carol was walking in, they all heard a knock at the door. Donnie moved to the door and motioned Carol to the side; She moved as directed. Donnie looked through the peephole and saw it was Frank. He opened the door and let Frank in. Frank looked over to Carol. "It is good to see you," Frank said. "Frank, what is going on? Donnie won't tell me, but if you are here, I know it must be bad. How long has it been since we saw each other?" Carol said to Frank. Frank shot Donnie a look, and Donnie just shrugged. “I think it’s better to wait until everyone is here.” He said to Carol. “You too, it figures you two always tried to keep things from me. Some things never change.” Carol tried to sound angry, but they all knew she could never be angry. Hearing Frank, James poured a cup of coffee for him and walked up to him. He said, “Here is some coffee, Uncle Frank. Frank looked at James, then looked at Donnie and Carol. Frank looked at Carol and said, “Carol, it’s been a while since he was little.” Thank you, James,” Frank looked at James as he said it. Donnie, do you know when the others will arrive? Frank asked. I am not sure about Burke, but Michael should be here soon.

15

The War for the Badge

After everyone had some coffee, they moved into the living room to wait for the others to arrive. Donnie and Frank were reminiscing about their past work together. Carol would chime in with a giggle or memory.

"Donnie, do you remember the guy we stopped on the northside of town that day? He was moving around in his car like he had to go to the bathroom. You asked him why he was behaving that way. He said he heard we would beat him up. We just looked at each other and told him he could calm down." Frank asked Donnie. "That was crazy, I had never heard that from anyone else," Donnie responded.

"I remember the convenience store clerk calling about the Hells Angels showing up on a Friday afternoon. She was freaked out. When I arrived, they thought I was going to hassle them, but we ended up talking for a while. You radioed Code-4. I said I was. They were headed to their annual run-and-games weekend. They asked if I was working on Sunday, and I said yes. They said they would stop on their way through, and I said I would respond when we got the call again. They came back, and she called that day too. That was funny." Donnie said to Frank. He said he remembered.

James was sitting there listening to them talk about their days working together. He was silent as they spoke.

"Frank, do you remember that boxer we got called about on the side of the road? He was so drunk that we thought he was dead. We checked for his pulse and found he was still alive. He fought us. After he was cuffed and put in my car, he started to kick the windows. First, I sprayed him with pepper spray. We hog-tied him, and I transported him to jail. I told dispatch I needed help with him. He woke up when we were trying to clear his eyes and smacked his head on the tile of the jail bathroom. The Sergeant made me take him to the hospital. He tried to bite me, and they restrained him. But when he woke up, he was the nicest guy. He told me he started drinking and lost his shot at becoming a pro boxer. I transported him to the County jail and booked him for the attempted property destruction. But the whole ride over, he apologized for being so stupid." Donnie asked Frank. Frank told him he remembered. "The guy was something else when he was drunk," Frank said.

James asked his dad, "You guys hog-tied him?" "Yeah, Uncle Frank had a braided leather strap with a hook and a clasp on either end. We secured him with it, so he didn't kick out the window of my unit." Donnie responded to James.

Carol told them she remembered that. She had him at the hospital. "I remember watching you turning the guy's face away from you, too." She said to Donnie. "He tried to bite me," Donnie said.

There was a knock on the door. Donnie looked at Frank, and they both drew their guns as Donnie headed for the door. Donnie looked out the peephole and saw Michael and Sarah. He holstered his gun and opened the door. "Come in, Michael and Sarah," he said. Michael looked okay, but Sarah looked around and said hello to Donnie. She looked confused. We will explain everything shortly. Carol motioned for Sarah to come near. Sarah remembered Carol, so she walked over to where she was seated. "Michael, do you want coffee?" Carol asked. "That would be great, Carol." Carol looked at Sarah and asked whether she wanted any. Sarah said she would prefer water. Carol asked her to help her in the kitchen. Sarah nodded and followed her. Michael looked at Donnie and shook his head. Sarah was scared.

Sarah and Carol talked in the kitchen. “Sarah, I know this makes no sense to you right now, but it will,” Carol said. “How does this make any sense?” Sarah asked. “Trust me, it will. These men we love work in a strange career, and sometimes things happen that affect us, too. If you love Michael, he needs you right now as much as you need him,” Carol told her. For a minute, Sarah just stared at Carol. Then she asked her, “Have you dealt with this before?” Carol answered her, “Donnie has told me to be more careful when I go to work, because of things going on. Frank and Burke, the FBI agent, have dealt with this kind of thing before. My son was a baby then.” Carol told Sarah. “Here is Michael’s coffee and your water. Please take him the coffee.” Carol motioned for Sarah to bring him some coffee.

As Sarah went to the Living room, there was another knock on the door. This time, the three pulled their guns, and Donnie went to the door, looking through the peephole. He saw Burke. Holstering his gun, he opened the door. “Burke, it’s about time,” Donnie said. The other two holstered their guns as well. “Donnie, we need to talk,” Burke told him. Donnie turned to the living room and told Burke, Everyone is here, and we can talk in front of them. Burke looked at Donnie and said, "Okay."

“Donnie, how many suspects did you remove from that SUV?” Burke asked. “There were four of them. Why?” Donnie responded. “When I got to the jail and started the interviews, there were only three there. I asked and was told that one had been released. When I asked for further details, no one could explain why. Now I am trying to figure it all out.” Burke told them as he looked at Frank.

"That doesn't make any sense. They are all foreign nationals, and all of them were armed. The last one had to be pulled from the SUV and fought with law enforcement." Donnie said.

Frank grabbed his phone and made a call to the station. "Let me talk to the Desk Sergeant. Who authorized the release of any of those four individuals who were brought in today? They were being held for the FBI and were not supposed to be released." The Desk Sergeant said there was no signature and no release paperwork anywhere. "Sergeant, I want answers. Review the camera footage to find out. Call me back when you find it." Yes, sir, the Sergeant told him.

Burke and Donnie looked at each other. Then at Frank. "You know what this could mean, don't you?" Donnie stared at them both.

The room fell silent, and Donnie looked at Carol. She looked at Donnie, questioning, and had a look of concern on her face. Michael looked at Donnie, and he realized what this could mean as well. Sarah wrapped her arm around Michael's arm. James had figured it out as he observed Donnie and the others.

"Let's wait and find out before we start that witch hunt," Frank said. Burke shot him a look, slowly nodded, and turned to the rest of the room.

"It's time to explain to everyone what's going on," He started. We should probably grab the kitchen chairs and have a seat. Donnie, do I smell coffee?" Burke asked. Carol looked at Burke and said, "When you show up, it can't be good. No offense, Burke, but the last time ended ugly." James heard her words and stopped, turning to Donnie, "So this has happened before?" He asked his dad. Donnie nodded to him a yes.

James began grabbing chairs from the kitchen and bringing them in. Carol went to get the coffee pot and refilled the coffee cups. As she gave Burke his coffee, she looked at him. Then, turning to Donnie, she whispered, "I hope this ends better than the last time."

Once everyone was settled, Burke began. Several years ago, I was called in to assist with an investigation. That is where I met those 2, pointing at Donnie and Frank. There was a third one involved, too, Timothy. They had stumbled across an international drug ring on the south side of town, and after arresting the main player, they were targeted by them. But of course, the three musketeers didn't think they needed to lie low. It took an order from the Chief to finally get them to stand down. Donnie and Frank looked at each other and smiled. "We didn't need to, at the time," Donnie said, and Frank nodded. Burke put his hand up and looked at Donnie. Carol said, "You three thought you were all bulletproof, but I knew better." "Donnie here and Timothy were Sargent's, and Frank was a Lieutenant. We conducted the investigation, and it ultimately became an international matter. We were finally able to shut down most of the organization. Burke paused.

"Except for one guy, he disappeared. That one was very high up on the ladder and had help from another government," Burke looked at everyone. They were looking at Donnie and Frank, and it was beginning to dawn on them that they were in trouble.

"Donnie, when I told you today that when you step in, you do it with both feet, I meant it." Burke looked at Donnie. He continued, "Michael, those three thugs you and Donnie took down were paid by our 'friend' to steal documents from that Storage unit and get them to one of those guys in the SUV. They were stealing Documents that the Joseph Group had on the Organization. We were in the process of getting a Federal Subpoena for those documents; no one was supposed to know about any of that." They attacked Charles that day to get his radio so that they could monitor your company's movements. He was targeted because he was in the three storage units that the Joseph group had rented. That was the second one they had been through."

"Thanks for the heads up, Burke. If we had known, I could have kept Charles safe." Donnie said. Burke turned to Donnie and said, "I was about to let you and Frank know, then I heard about the attack. I never trusted Timothy; there has always been something about him that I never trusted." Yeah, he is a weasel," Donnie said. Frank and Carol chuckled at that.

"Anyway," Burke continued, "when you stopped them, and our friend found out it was you, he decided to put a contract out on you and Michael. But it doesn't stop there. He is pursuing everyone connected to you. Family as well. They have never done that before. When you three went to the diner, luckily, one of our three informants knew Donnie and let us know about everything."

"I have about 30 agents in the area to watch them. I have also asked Frank and Anthony for officers. We will stop this before it goes any further. But in the meantime, we will have protection details on all of you."

"And I have 50 officers that may or may not be targeted as well. This will not end well for these idiots." Donnie said, looking directly at Burke. "I will not let this family of ours get hurt in any way. I want photos of all the suspects you have, and I will distribute them among our officers; they have a right to be protected as well." Burke looked at Donnie and knew nothing he could say would change his mind. "I will give you what I can, Donnie," Burke said.

"By the way, who is it that is pulling the strings on all of this?" Donnie asked. I know you know who it is, Burke. We have known each other for a very long time, and you owe me that." Donnie said. "He goes by Roger, that is all we know thus far. Remember, he was the one who got away, that first time. He still harbors resentment towards you and Frank for what happened in the past. This gave him an excuse to target you again." Burke told Donnie.

James finally spoke up. "Dad or Uncle Frank, care to share with everyone what happened back then?"

"Go ahead, Donnie, you found that guy," Frank said.

"We were working a drug-dealing case. There were 22 suspects, but we didn't know that one of them was higher up in the organization. He was the shot caller for all the others. They had been targeting young kids to mule the drugs for them. We caught five kids, aged 12 to 14. They were so scared that they told us about the place where they got the drugs. We raided the place and took nine people into custody that night. The tenth slipped away. We went looking for him. The next day, he opened another pick-up point. We surrounded it, again, and he ran. Timothy thought that if he could find the guy, he would get promoted. Well, I found him hiding in a shed behind a neighboring house. He didn't want to come out. I went in and removed him. Timothy wanted to claim my arrest. I informed the Chief and Frank that I had found him. I didn't care who took the credit, I just wanted to get him off the streets." Donnie paused and looked at Frank. They smiled at each other.

Donnie continued, "Timothy tried to get me to give him details, but I refused. He then wrote a report that made no sense. The Chief and Frank called him in about the report, and he had to tell them I was the arresting officer. I was called in and told to write the report, but I had already written it for them. When I left the office, Timothy confronted me and began accusing me of setting him up. There were several officers, including Frank, standing around listening to it all. Timothy told me he was going to get me fired. We have had issues ever since. We were able to pick up eight more suspects; the others disappeared."

Frank added, "Timothy didn't get promoted for another 2 years. Donnie was offered the promotion but declined it. By the time Timothy was promoted, Donnie left the department and went into security." Burke added, looking at Donnie, "I would rather have you as the Lieutenant than that idiot." That made Carol laugh. She remembered Timothy and how ego-driven he had always been. She also remembered how he targeted Donnie afterward.

Frank brought up the guy in the impound yard. “Donnie, do you remember the guy Timothy found in the impound yard that day? He ran him, and he had $40,000 in warrants, mainly felonies. That guy took off and ran into a residential area. We were working that day too. We had the Sheriff’s department and Highway Patrol respond to help. It took almost 2 hours to find him. You were standing there in the intersection and stopped him. HP rushed in to assist with cuffing him. Timothy cut his hand, and he was whining about it. He asked you to book the guy. But the Deputy took him for us.”

“I remember, he stunk, and I was glad the deputy took him. That was the highest dollar value of warrants I ever saw. $40,000 was an insane amount,” Donnie said.

James spoke up, “The guy had 40 K in warrants, and Timothy didn’t stop him? How is that even possible?”

“That is an excellent question, son,” Donnie responded.

“He is an idiot and slow to react. He has always been that way,” Frank said.

James had to ask, “How did he ever get promoted?” Frank said, “When your nose is buried so deep into the upper management, it is going to happen. He has made a career of 'right place, right time’. They are seeing that it was a huge mistake.” Frank finished.

It was at that point that Frank received a call from the desk sergeant. “Go ahead, Sergeant”, Frank said. On the other end of the phone, the Sergeant told him that the only person seen near each suspect's door was the Lieutenant.

It appears he opened the door to one of the suspects and let him out of the building. “Wait, the Lieutenant let the suspect go?” “It appears that way. I have the video cued up for you to look at, Captain.” The Sergeant said to Frank. Frank looked at Donnie and Burke. "I will be down to the station shortly, Sergeant," Frank said. When he hung up the phone, the room was silent. Burke told him he was going to go with him to look at the video. "I thought you would," Frank said.

Burke looked at Donnie and said, "Timothy must hate you." Stay here, we have agents all around the area. I want you all to stay put, at least for the night. I will be back in a while, after we sort this out." Burke told them.

As they left, Donnie realized everyone must be hungry. He went to the kitchen to figure out what they could eat. There wasn't enough for everyone. He called Burke and told him he needed to place an order for some pizza. Burke told him to get a combo for him. Donnie placed the order and said he would keep the receipt and have the FBI reimburse them for it. Donnie went back to the living room and told everyone he had ordered pizza and sodas.

Sarah asked him why this was all happening. He looked at Michael but responded to her question. "Sarah, Michael, and I stopped three guys in a storage unit the other evening. Those three were hired by this "group" to steal some paperwork the company had on the "group." Now they are angry at us, but taking it out on our family." Sarah nodded at Donnie. She turned to Michael and said, "I knew your job could be dangerous, but I never knew how much. We need to end this." Carol looked at Donnie; he looked concerned yet determined to resolve this whole thing. "Donnie, we will get through this as a family," Carol told him. She continued, "We need to figure out the sleeping situation. I can sleep on the couch; you can sleep in the recliner, she told Donnie. Michael and Sarah can take your bed." James told his mom he could take the couch, but she insisted she would take it. "If anything happens tonight, I want Sarah protected. Since your room is across the hall from your dad's, I will take the couch." She concluded. James looked at his mom and said, "Yes, ma'am." He knew not to argue with her. Donnie sat there and smiled. He knew Carol and how she handled things when needed. It allowed him to plan the night. How they would care for everyone if something were to happen?

About 45 minutes later, there was a knock on the door. Donnie got up, and he and Michael pulled their sidearms. Donnie looked through the peephole and saw the pizza delivery person standing there. He had ordered six pizzas and seven sodas. When he opened the door, Michael came in behind him as a cover officer, just in case.

Sarah had never seen Michael doing his job. She just sat there and watched everything unfold before her. She had no experience in security or law enforcement. But she was amazed at how natural Michael and Donnie made it look.

She turned to Carol after Donnie shut the door, asking, "Has Donnie always been involved in this kind of work?" Carol looked at her and responded, "I met him in the ER when he came in with a nasty cut on his arm from a bar fight; he and another officer were trying to break up. That was my first time seeing Donnie, so to answer your question, yes." Carol smiled at Sarah. She was a young and sheltered woman. Carol envied her a little.

When the pizza was brought in, everyone realized they were hungry. Carol got up to help Donnie. Sarah came in to help, also. The pizzas were set on the table along with plates. The sodas were still cold, so they poured without ice. Everyone ate, and there were still three left, including the pizza Burke had requested.

As they were finishing, Donnie's phone rang. It was his boss. Donnie went into the other room, and Carol followed him. The boss told Donnie he had heard about everything and asked what was being done about it. Donnie told him about what Frank and Burke were doing. He told him about Timothy and what he had done. His boss paused for a second, "I knew he was self-serving, but this will end him." Donnie agreed. He informed his boss, who was at the house, about the perimeter safety plan.

The boss told him to be careful. Donnie reminded his boss that 49 other people are also in danger from all this and told him they needed to be protected. Not just the ones at his house. "And that includes you, too," Donnie told him. His boss chuckled and said he was aware and had taken the necessary precautions. Donnie knew that he had armed himself and set up "items of defense outside". Donnie just told him he understood. They hung up, and as Donnie was walking back to the living room, there was a knock at the door.

Donnie and Michael moved to the door. Donnie looked through the peephole. He did not recognize the guy standing outside. He yelled through the door, asking what he wanted. He told him he had been sent to speak with him. Donnie noticed a slight accent. He asked him to repeat himself. He hesitated and then repeated himself. "Who sent you?" Donnie asked, pausing before he responded. Donnie reached for the door handle. Motioning to Michael to get everyone out of the living room and head into the kitchen, just in case. Michael moved quickly and took cover in the kitchen. Donnie turned the handle quickly, punching the security screen out towards the guy on the porch. As he stumbled backwards, Donnie lunged towards him and tossed him to the ground. He placed his gun against his neck and shoulder area.

He asked him again who had sent him, but he couldn't say who. Donnie called Michael and said he needed to cover Donnie. Michael was right there, followed by James. James had his dad's other gun in his hand and was covering them both. Donnie searched the male, found a .45 caliber pistol in his waistband, which he removed. Cuffing him, he brought him inside. He set him in the entryway and shut the door. Then he started asking him questions. The man claimed not to understand him. He rolled him over and found a wallet. Within the wallet, he found an ID from another country. He showed it to both Michael and James. Donnie told James to call the Department and ask them to send someone here whom he knew.

Donnie also told James to stand back with his mom and Sarah. As James was on the phone, he heard a thud from the entryway. James told the dispatcher what had happened, and she immediately dispatched four units. The FBI was scanning the channel and sent three more.

Donnie was now ready to end anyone he didn't know. He had Michael call Frank. While he watched the guy. Michael put Frank on speaker. "You people are no help, Frank. I have one 10-15 in my entryway!" Donnie told Frank. "Either handle this, or I will go looking for them, for you". Donnie told Frank. "Can I talk now?" Frank asked. "Go ahead," Donnie told him. We have two officers down, about three blocks from your place. They were ambushed. At least four others are moving around your area, according to the dashcam. I know how you do things, Donnie. We are almost there." Frank told him.

Donnie looked at Michael. Michael recognized the look and moved to the kitchen. Michael moved Carol, Sarah, and James to the living room. He had James cover the windows on the far side of the living room. They turned most of the lights off, leaving only the ones in the kitchen on. Michael looked at Sarah, and she looked scared. Carol had her arms around her to help her feel a little better. She looked at James and saw his father in him, and she knew he would make an amazing cop.

The responding officers were aware of Donnie, and they knew he would be armed. They didn't draw their weapons as they exited their vehicles. There was a lot of noise, but they also heard the shot. It took one of their own, and she was down on the front lawn. The senior officer radioed their dispatch advising shots fired, and one down. Donnie opened the door, yelled for them to take cover, and moved to the porch wall. Michael moved around and turned the light off for his safety. This drew other officers into the area. Donnie yelled for them to radio the area where the shot came. The senior officer followed the instructions. Radio the captain and advise him to enter from another direction, hold your officers off as well. Frank was on the phone; Michael grabbed it as he moved back to his position and told him what had happened. Frank said he had heard the transmission, and he and Burke were almost there.

Another shot rang out; it struck the wall next to Donnie. He knew the area the shooter was in. He yelled out that the one shooter was southwest of the house: Tell your dispatcher, officer. There was a third shot, this time it struck the Cruiser, near the senior officer, as he was on the radio. They all heard a fourth shot, but nothing struck near any of them. They heard over the radio that the shooter had been neutralized; it was Frank. Then, a minute later, there are at least three more in the area; stay on alert.

Donnie saw Frank's unmarked vehicle pull up to the curb. The officers were tending to the female officer; it seemed she was going to make it. As Frank and Burke exited the vehicle, their guns out, they moved towards the house. Burke asked Donnie if the guy he had cuffed was still alive. Donnie told him he was sleeping right now. As Frank and Burke entered the porch area, Burke laughed. He knew Donnie well and had great respect for him. He also knew Donnie would bend the rules but never break them. Where is he Burke asked. Donnie told him just as he stepped inside the door.

Donnie yelled out to the officers, asking if they could move the fallen officer. She said yes. Donnie told them to bring her into the house. He turned to Frank and asked him to inform Carol that a wounded officer was on the way. As Frank entered, he yelled to Carol, who quickly got up and moved toward the door. They got her to her feet and moved her to the front door. Another shot hit the wall from the Southeast. Donnie told them to move. He said to Burke he would be right back. Donnie grabbed one of the officers and told him to follow him. They went to the Southeast and heard another shot wiz over their heads. Donnie raised his gun and fired two rounds towards where the bullet came from. About 20 feet in front of them, they heard a scream and heard someone hit the pavement. When they reached the spot, there was a male face down. They saw the blood and went to check him for a pulse. He had expired. Donnie turned to the officer and told him to advise that a second assailant was neutralized. As Donnie checked for any identification, the Officer radioed that the assailant was neutralized. The Dispatcher reported that the second assailant was down. When Donnie looked at the assailant and his ID, he realized it was the driver of the SUV he had stopped and cleared. That also meant Timothy had given them his address. Donnie told the officer he should probably stay with the body. Donnie headed back to the house. The dispatcher was staging the medical staff and ambulances a few blocks away, accompanied by a Law Enforcement escort.

As Donnie was almost to the porch, he heard gunfire from the back of the house. He went that way, advising the other officers in front to stand by and be ready to move toward the house if needed.

As Donnie turned the back corner of the house, he saw muzzle flashes on the other side of his fence. He heard something hit the fence. Then the gunfire stopped. When he got to the fence, he heard a voice say, Third assailant neutralized. Then the voice said, "Tell Burke, Jamesson got this one." Donnie knew the name. He called out, as a test, asking about his daughter. Jamesson told him she was good, just started 5th grade, and was driving him up the wall. That was the age and gender of Jamesson's daughter, but he couldn't be too careful. As he backed away, he said, " Thanks for taking the third one down." Jamesson called over, "Donnie, it really is me. We got you taken care of. How is James?" Donnie relaxed a little, "he is good. He is all grown." I will be over by the front door in a bit. I will have to say hi to him; it's been what, 12 years since I saw him?" Jamesson said. "Yeah, come on up. We have a house full, but you are always welcome." Donnie told him.

Donnie headed back to the front of the house. When he got to the door, he saw the blood from the officer, and he knew Carol was doing everything she could to take care of her. When he entered the house, another shot rang out. It came from the North, right in front of the house. Donnie turned around and looked. He stood in the dark shadow by the door. Donnie saw another flash from a gun about 100 yards from where he was standing. He fired two shots. Frank, Burke, Michael, and James all turned toward Donnie. A third shot hit above his head and splintered the doorway. As he aimed to fire, he heard five shots coming from the direction of the muzzle flashes. He heard a scream, and then it was silent. The fourth assailant, who had been neutralized, was heard over the radio. Frank came across the radio asking if it looked all clear. The officers advised that everything appeared to be clear. Frank informed the dispatcher to send medical personnel into the area and had officers secure the four assailants.

Donnie turned to see Carol working on the officer, and Sarah helping. James was smiling to see his dad safe. Michael was still guarding the back of the house. Donnie called over to Michael and told him to holster his weapon. As Donnie looked at Carol, the medical staff arrived and went to the officer. They spoke with Carol and then took the gurney in. They loaded the female officer into the ambulance and took her to the hospital. The senior medic thanked Carol for working on the female officer. Carol was covered in blood, and so was the sofa. She went to the kitchen to grab some clean towels. Donnie sent James to get some bath towels and a bucket. While Sarah was in the kitchen, Carol came in to help her. Once they returned to the couch, they began cleaning the sofa. When James returned with the bath towels, he began drying the cushions that Carol had washed.

While Carol was working on the couch, Donnie, Frank, and Burke met about this whole thing. There were law enforcement officers outside the house now. They discussed the one Donnie recognized as the SUV's driver. That proved that Timothy was deeply involved. It was also determined that this "Group" would not stop for a while. There were three officers in the hospital, and four assailants in the Morgue. The entire neighborhood was scared now. "What is the FBI doing about this 'Group'?" Donnie asked. "We still haven't found the connection between the 'Group' and Roger. I'm not sure how much Interpol has on them. What I do know is that we now have seven different foreign nationals who have tried to collect on the contract, which we believe was paid for by Roger. We have also flushed out Timothy and are looking for him. Those 3 in the hospital. And we have stopped five more trying to get in to kill them." Burke looked at Donnie, knowing he was planning something. He looked at Frank and saw that he was trying to hide that he knew. "You two had better hold off on what you are thinking," Burke said.

Donnie got up and went into the living room. He walked up to Carol, saying, "Hun, please go and take a shower. I have some robes and T-shirts you can wear tonight. Carol leaned into Donnie and said, "Thank you." Carol looked at Sarah and thanked her. She then went down the hall to Donnie's room, pulled a robe from the closet, and went to his dresser, opening a couple of drawers to find a T-shirt and a pair of sweats she could tie. She smiled. Donnie had never changed anything, she thought, after the shower. Carol went back to the living room. She told Sarah she should take a shower, too. Michael told her it might help her relax. "Donnie, can

Sarah use your stuff as well?" Carol asked. "Of course," Donnie responded. Carol took Sarah down the hall, and they got her the things she needed. Sarah finished her shower and came out looking like a kid wearing her dad's clothes. Michael met her when she came into the living room and wrapped his arms around her. They stood there, Sarah told Michael, "I have never experienced anything like this, but I now know why you do what you do." Michael looked into Sarah's eyes and saw her search his. "We are in this together now, if all that didn't scare you away, nothing will. Thank you for being you." Michael told Sarah.

Carol got up, took Sarah's clothes, combined them with hers, and placed them in the washer. That way, they can have clean clothes.

16

The Impact of the Badge

After Sarah took her shower, James went to take his. Even though the water was a bit cold, he stood under it and thought about everything the family had just been through. He watched his dad and everything he had done. He knew Donnie had shot two people, killing them. He had returned to the house to keep the family safe. James and Michael had done their part to keep the family safe. They were working as a unit. James understood the responsibilities he was getting into better. It was necessary to understand that law enforcement must work as a team, where each officer understands their partner and mirrors the other's actions.

After James showered, he returned to the living room, where everyone was gathered. He smelled coffee and could hear them talking. When he entered the room, Frank looked at him and told him he had done an excellent job today. "I have known for years that you would one day enter law enforcement," Frank told him. "Thanks, Uncle Frank," James responded. Then Burke spoke up, saying he was impressed with James today. He asked Donnie, "How much have you trained James?" "Not much yet, except how to handle a gun. But he has been through his pre-academy classes already." Donnie responded.

Carol looked at James and smiled. "He is his father's son. They are both wired to do what they do naturally." Carol had a proud tone in her voice. "Thanks, Mom," James told her.

He walked into the kitchen and grabbed a cup of coffee. He heard someone coming in, and he turned to see his dad. "Son, I am proud of you for everything you did today," Donnie told James. "I didn't do much," James responded. "You did what you were asked, keeping your mom safe was a huge weight off of my shoulders, so I could do what I needed to do," Donnie told him. James took a sip of coffee and looked at his dad.

They walked back into the living room, and Burke looked at Donnie. "We need to debrief about everything. I need to file a report with the office tonight." Burke said.

"Donnie, let's start with the one at the door," Burke told him. Donnie started, "He knocked on the door. I asked him a couple of questions to ensure he was someone I could trust to let into the house. He had an accent, something foreign. I repeated the questions to listen again. He also couldn't give me the names of those who sent him. That was when I knew I needed to take control of him. I opened the door and pulled him in. I then put him on the floor and cuffed him. When I searched him, I found the gun. I asked him who sent him, and that is when he kicked me. I defended myself from the kick." Donnie concluded.

Frank and Burke both smiled. They knew Donnie had knocked him out. However, that was not included in any of the reports. Donnie was justified in his actions.

"Ok, let's move on," Burke said. "The one you went after in the Southeast." "He shot at me from his location. The second shot, I watched the muzzle flash. I called out to an officer to come with me. As we approached, he fired again, and it went over our heads. I fired two rounds, and they struck him. He was dead when we got to him. I also realized he was the driver of the SUV. I told the officer he should stay with the subject. I returned to the house." Donnie told Burke.

"Now, the fourth shooter," Burke said. "He was due south, basically right across the street. He fired into the house. He struck a wall and the door frame with a second round. I returned fire, but I did not strike him. I heard several shots, about 5, and heard the radio state he had been neutralized." Donnie concluded.

"That is also what I remember of everything," Burke said.

"Next, how is everyone doing?" Burke looked at the rest of them. Carol said she had called the hospital to check on the female officer, who would be alright. She is out of surgery, and they got everything. Burke smiled at Carol; he asked her again how she was doing. "As good as can be expected, Burke," she told him. He said he understood. Sarah, how are you doing? He looked at her as he asked. "As good as can be expected, since this was the first time I have experienced anything like this," Sarah told Burke. "James, what about you?" "I'm good," James said to Burke. "Stoic like your parents," Burke responded. "Michael. How about you?" He asked. "I'm good, this isn't the first time," Michael said. "Donnie, I am not going to ask."

"I need to tell this now. There is more to come, and we need to make sure everyone gets through this. These people will come for you until they are either all dead or you are." Burke told them. "That's a nice way to sugarcoat it, Burke," Carol said to him. "Carol, you know I don't sugarcoat things, never have," Burke responded.

"We need to try to get some sleep. I know some of us will have dreams about tonight, and that's okay. It is part of the process. We are all here to keep each other safe and get through this." Donnie said. "I will take the first watch. In four hours, Michael will take watch. Frank, are you staying here tonight?" Donnie concluded. "Yes, I am Donnie, and I will take first watch. You need to get some sleep. Burke and I will be here and take care of the family." Frank told Donnie. "Everyone needs some sleep," Frank told them all.

James, Michael, and Sarah got up. They felt like a dad was telling them to go to bed. Once they were in the bedrooms, Frank spoke to Donnie. "Timothy is on the run. He left the area, and we are looking for him. He emptied his bank accounts and left." "I figured he would," Donnie responded. "We did find information in his house that connects him to payments from this Roger. He has been on their payroll for about 10 years now. He was mainly tasked with watching you. The night you stopped the theft, he reported to his "boss" about it." Frank told Donnie.

"I knew something was up. I knew they had targeted that one unit." Donnie told Frank. "Now that Timothy has been identified, he is of no use to this Roger guy. They may take care of the 'Loose end'. He is now a liability." Donnie told Frank. "We can only hope," Carol said. The three of them looked at her. Donnie looked at her and said, "Carol?" "Well, he was part of the people who are targeting this family, and he should pay for it!" She told them. She continued, "That officer could have been killed. Any one of us could be in the hospital or the morgue. They need to be stopped."

There was a moment when they just sat and drank some coffee. Then Burke said, "Carol, you are correct; they all need to be stopped, but I also need some witnesses. I have four suspects who aren't talking. Timothy is such a weasel; he will speak to save his skin," Burke commented. "They will be killed if they talk," Donnie said. Everyone agreed.

"Donnie, I watched you today," Frank said, "you have never lost your edge." That made Donnie laugh. It has always been training." Donnie said. "It's more than that; you have a gift for fishing out everything," Burke said. "You always have, almost like a sixth sense." He added. "I am just me. You both know that, but thank you." Donnie said. "Donnie, I have always known you were good at doing what you do; today proved it even more to me," Carol added. "And I am proud of you, but you better not get hurt, or

I will hurt you worse." She said with a chuckle. They all laughed. Donnie looked at her, "Yes, ma'am," he said with a smile.

We need to let these two get some sleep. Front or back?" Frank asked Burke. "Back, closer to the coffee," Burke responded.

Donnie got up and got some bedding for Carol. They put it on the couch, and when they were done, they hugged each other. Donnie whispered in her ear, "I am sorry about this." She looked at him and told him, "We're in this together, and we'll get out of this together." She hugged him tighter. Carol lay down and was asleep in a few minutes. Donnie went into the kitchen and poured some more coffee. Burke looked at him. He asked, "Are you guys back together?" From the other room, they heard, "We are working on it, Burke." They both laughed. They heard Frank laughing from the front of the house. "There is your answer," Donnie said. He went back into the living room and sat in his recliner. He took a couple of sips of coffee, set his coffee on his table, leaned back, and fell asleep.

While Burke and Frank stood watch, Donnie slept, but it wasn't peaceful. He kept replaying the night in his mind. He would usually do this when he was awake, but it came to him as a dream. He saw the muzzle flashes and then saw himself fire. He saw the driver's face each time. A few hours later, he woke up. He couldn't help but think he knew the driver from somewhere. As he thought about it, he remembered him from the diner. When he went to pay the bill, he was sitting at the counter. He even smiled at Donnie, and Donnie said hello. The driver had been in the same place as his family had been. Donnie got up and rewarmed his coffee. He looked at Frank and told him he had seen the driver at the diner. Frank looked at him and asked him if he was sure. "Yes, I am. Can you get the video from the diner and let me see it to identify anyone else?" Donnie asked Frank. "I will get the warrant, and we can look through it," Frank told Donnie. Burke came in because he heard the conversation. "Donnie, can you identify the driver as being at the diner?" he asked. Again, Donnie said yes, and I will bet you both, there were others in there as well.

Frank called Anthony and told him what Donnie said. He instructed Frank to retrieve the video and review it. Hanging up the phone, he told Donnie he needed to take care of the warrant, and he would be back later. Just then, they heard a shot coming from the North. Michael and James ran into the kitchen, waking Carol. She got up and looked around. Donnie and Michael moved to the front door as Sarah came out of the room and down the hall.

Just then, Burke's phone rang. One of his agents told him they had neutralized another male subject who had pulled a gun on them. He was another foreign national. Burke said OK and hung up the phone. He turned to Donnie and said Get ready. Donnie opened the door and took a cover position. Michael was on the other side. Frank instructed James to go to the window, stay where he could see, but remain covered. Donnie looked at Carol; she knew to grab Sarah and find a hiding place. Frank remained in the kitchen, and Burke went to the hallway. As this was happening, another shot was heard, and a bullet struck the wall facing the door. Donnie tried to see where it came from. Another shot was heard, a window broke, and another bullet hit the wall opposite James. Burke called his agents and advised Jamesson of the situation. Frank called the dispatch center and told them. He also suggested that the responding officers come in without lights and sirens and be ready. Burke heard glass breaking from the direction of Donnie's bedroom. Wheeling around, he heard a thud as well. There was someone inside the house. Frank heard it too. He looked at Burke, then saw Donnie exit through the front door. Another shot was heard from that direction. Burke motioned to James to reposition. He did and covered Burke. Donnie was outside, and Michael moved to the porch, watching for the shooter that way. Burke heard another thud coming from the bedroom, followed by what sounded like fighting. He then heard another thud.

Donnie yelled All clear. Burke opened the door and saw Donnie standing over a male lying on the floor. "They are not going to get to the family." He told Burke. Burke cuffed the male as Donnie went back to the front door. He saw Michael on the porch. "Do you see the shooter?" Donnie asked. Only a quick movement across the street and to the east. Donnie looked that way. He saw movement as well. He turned to Frank and motioned for him to come to where he was. He pointed to the location and asked Frank to advise the responding officers. Frank called the dispatcher and relayed the area to her. She informed the responding officers. Within a couple of minutes, they arrived about a block away. They heard yelling and then two shots. An officer called Frank to tell him they had stopped the shooter.

While this was happening, another shot whizzed into the wall from the west side of the house. This time, when the glass broke, a piece cut James's face. Carol saw the blood start to roll down his cheek. James turned to the window in time to see a man moving towards the house. He fired, striking the male in the chest, causing him to drop to the ground. Donnie looked at James. He knew he would need to help him manage the shooting. James wiped the blood off his cheek and onto his jeans. Donnie knew it was adrenaline that was assisting James with the situation. James looked at his mom and told her he was OK. He looked at his dad and said There may be more. Donnie went to James to look at his face. Turning to Carol, he said he needed a bandage. She got up and grabbed what she had. Telling him to sit down, she cleaned up the glass and bandaged him. She then smiled at him and said, "Girls like scars." James looked at her and laughed.

Burke and Frank looked at Donnie with a reassuring expression. Donnie looked back at them and nodded. Frank's phone rang, and the dispatcher asked about their status. Frank informed her that one was injured, three were down, and one was in custody. He asked medical personnel to respond and send a couple of units to the house. While she was calling in the requested personnel, she heard an all clear for the site commander. She advised Frank of the "all clear."

They holstered their weapons. A couple of agents came to the front door to speak to Burke. They told him the latest and urged him to move everyone to a safer location. He said he would talk to the family. Burke now knew the assailants would not give up. He did need to move the family, especially since James had been injured.

He called Donnie and Frank over to speak to them. They should move out of the neighborhood, and they both agreed. Burke looked at Donnie and said he had a place they could go to. But it was a bit out of town. Donnie asked him where, and he told him it was out on Chicago Road. It is a farm. Donnie knew the area; he thought it was a good idea. He turned to Carol and the family; Michael had gone to hold Sarah. James was sitting with Carol. He looked at them all and told them they needed to move to a different place. We need to get out of the neighborhood. Burke had a place out on Chicago Road for them. They asked when they were leaving. Burke said he would need to get the vehicles ready soon.

Carol asked Burke if there were clothes there. She said she liked wearing Donnie's clothes, but she and Sarah needed clothes, and they were sure Michael would need some, too. Burke told her they would get everyone's clothes. He asked the ladies to give their sizes for everything, so they were okay with the clothes.

Carol and Sarah wrote everything down and handed it to Burke. He made a call and had a female agent pick up the list and complete the necessary shopping. She spoke with both Carol and Sarah before she left. In the meantime, James and Michael looked through his clothes to see if anything would fit him. Donnie went and prepared his clothes. By the time the female agent returned, everyone had gathered all the necessary items. Frank and Burke knew there were more clothes at the safe house.

When the FBI's SUVs arrived, a wall of officers and agents stood between the door and the vehicles. Everyone quickly got into the vehicles. Law enforcement vehicles escorted the SUVs, with agents following. These vehicles were equipped with bulletproof glass and solid tires so they could not be blown out. The FBI drivers had been instructed not to stop for any reason. The drive was about 30 minutes from Donnie's house to the farm.

As they approached the farm, Donnie noticed snipers on the roof of the house and the barn. He also noticed roving agents with dogs along the perimeter. Donnie looked back at Carol. She and James had sat behind him. She was looking around and nudged James as they entered the farm. Carol looked at Donnie and smiled. He knew it was a forced smile, but she was doing her best to get through everything. He hoped Stacy was still holding up.

As the vehicles pulled up, He saw four agents exit the house and fan out. They were equipped with rifles and held them at the ready as the family, Frank, and Burke left the vehicles. The drivers stayed seated. They all entered the house. And after the doors were closed, the SUVs drove to the barn and parked.

Once inside, Burke told them about the house. It was a 7-bedroom two-story building with reinforced walls and thick window glass. He informed them that the three doors were also heavy and solid core. The house featured fire-retardant specialty paint and shingles on the roof, all situated on 6 acres of land. That way, anyone approaching would be visible before they reached the house.

Donnie told Burke it would do for the time being. He was already thinking about what he would need to do if someone attacked him. "Let's get settled in and maybe wash up," Donnie suggested to Carol. "Sounds like a good plan," Carol responded.

Carol, James, Sarah, and Michael went upstairs and found a room. The rooms had a bed and a dresser. They all placed their belongings in the rooms and returned to the living room.

Donnie and Burke were talking about the situation. "We need to figure out how to end this once and for all. You and I both know they will come here and start up again. This time with more gunmen," Donnie said to Burke. Burke responded, "We have a plan in place. That's why all the agents are here." "You better be right, because this is my family who is at risk now," Donnie said. "Donnie, you trust me, don't you?" Burke asked. "I just want to keep the family safe. Plus, we need to find Timothy," Donnie responded. "I think Timothy will come out of hiding when he thinks he can come for you, Donnie," Burke said.

When the others came into the living room, Carol asked Burke what the plan was to end everything. Burke looked at Donnie and smiled. "Something's never changed; we have a plan in place. We are certain they will try to get everyone while you are here. Normally, a safe house is low-key, but we have made this a prime target. That's why we chose this location," Burke told Carol. "In other words, we are bait," Michael stated. "Unfortunately, yes," Burke responded. "Great," Sarah quipped. Frank came into the room from a downstairs bedroom. "What did I miss?" he asked. "Only that Burke has decided we make good bait, Uncle Frank," James said. "Well, alright," Frank said.

Burke looked at everyone and told them the kitchen had everything they needed, including a fully stocked Pantry, refrigerator, and freezer. Donnie asked about coffee. "Yes, Donnie, there are several containers of coffee and tea.

"Also, we will have three more joining us in a while. They need to be here as well." Burke told everyone. "Oh?" Donnie asked. "Charles, his wife, and her mom will be here soon," Burke responded. "It's about time," Donnie replied.

Just then, Burke got a message from the agents out front. They had arrived. The door opened, and they stepped in. Everyone was happy to see them. Carol went up, hugged Stacy, and her mom. Charles looked better, as if completely healed. Donnie and Michael approached him and shook his hand. James came from the kitchen and said, "It's good to see you guys." Charles, you look a lot better than the last time I saw you.

Charles said he was feeling much better, but still had a lingering headache. James and Charles gave each other a fist pump. Charles looked around the room and asked Burke why they had been brought to the farm.

"Charles, we need to keep you all safe as well. There was no good way to keep you all safe unless you were here." Burke told him. "You were targeted by the 'group' the day you were attacked, and now they want to shut you up. We need you here with everyone else." Burke finished. Stacy looked at Burke and asked him what he meant by that. "Your husband was the first one to be attacked by a group of international terrorists and drug dealers. He had a radio that they could clone. That radio relayed the locations of other officers in the company. They paid those three who attacked Charles to steal information that a company had that would destroy the "group," and Interpol wanted to put an end to their drug trade. This group has existed for several years. Since Donnie, Frank, and Timothy were all working together." Burke told her.

Stacy looked at Donnie. "I know Donnie, but who are the other two?" Frank raised his hand and said, "I'm Frank." She said hello. Donnie told her Timothy had switched sides and was working for the "group" and law enforcement until he was found out. Now he is running from everybody.

Stacy looked at Donnie and shook her head in disbelief. "I don't understand," she said.

Burke told her what had happened. That there was a contract on each of them. Because this "group" doesn't care, they pay to have people eliminate anyone they see as a threat, and their families.

Stacy looked at Charles. "Did you know any of this?" She asked him. "This is the first time I have heard of any of this. But it makes more sense why I was attacked." Charles told her.

"Stacy," Donnie said, "we have been finding out more and more. This place is an FBI safe house, and you should be here with us, so we can keep you all safe." He finished telling her.

Carol looked at Stacy and told her, "Donnie, Frank, and Burke will not let anything happen to you guys and that baby. We are family, sweetie."

After Carol said that, she looked at Donnie and changed the subject. "Are we eating cafeteria style or family style?" Everyone stopped what they were doing and looked around. It also made them all realize they were hungry. Donnie smiled and realized what Carol was doing.

Since no one answered, she looked at Burke and asked how big the table could extend for seating. 'I don't know, Carol,' Burke said, 'but I'm sure we'll find out.' Burke looked at Donnie and told him they should go find out. Donnie laughed and followed him into the dining room.

James looked around and asked who wanted coffee. He got up and walked into the kitchen to start the coffee. Charles went in with James. He knew Stacy preferred tea.

Sarah headed in to see what they had to eat. She knew Michael would heat a frozen pizza. She wanted something better than that. Michael got up and went with her.

Carol looked at Stacy and asked her if she wanted to help cook for the whole group. Stacy smiled. My mom and I will help you, Carol. Sarah told Carol she would help, too. Frank stood there and asked who needed help.

As everyone got busy with their tasks, the conversation became more lighthearted and enjoyable. They started joking and teasing each other, creating a more family-like atmosphere. The food came together, and the table can seat 16 people. Frank, Michael, Donnie, and Burke set the table.

James and Charles found the sodas, then the glasses, and finally the coffee cups. They all got busy preparing everything.

When everything was ready, they all sat down and enjoyed the meal, talking and laughing. After the past couple of days, it was needed to relax, enjoy the company, and have a home-cooked meal. After everything was cleaned up and put away, they all went to the living room and sat, talking and enjoying coffee, sodas, or water. As the night progressed, Burke received updates about what was happening outside. He would look at Donnie and nod when things were good outside.

Eventually, everyone started talking about going to sleep. Donnie, Frank, and Burke told them they would be up for a bit. Carol walked over to Donnie and told him she needed to get some sleep. She hugged him and went up to her room, followed soon after by Sarah and Michael. Charles and Stacy headed to their ground-floor room. That left the three still up with James.

Frank laughed at a thought. James asked, "Uncle Frank, what is so funny?" "I was thinking of the time your dad was out with me. We found the group we had been looking for, and one of them was suspected of intimidating a witness with threats. He also stole a ten-dollar speaker from the witness's garage. They didn't know your dad spoke the language they were speaking. The one suspect was telling each of them to take the blame for the theft. Finally, your dad told me what was being said. We arrested the one guy." Frank paused for a minute.

After cuffing him and placing him in the vehicle, he started begging us not to take him to jail. He was almost crying. Donnie, what else was he telling you?"

"He gave himself up. Told me he would tell me where the speaker was if I let him go. He begged me not to take him to jail. He was always trying to be such a tough guy. Not now, he was like a little kid who got caught by a parent doing something wrong." Donnie told them.

“The next day, I spoke with the district attorney about the case. He was only going to charge him with petty theft. I told him he had a sheet full of charges from his juvenile years. He looked at it and said he would charge him with a felony burglary.”

“When he finally went to court, he started acting up in the courtroom in front of the wrong judge. He started throwing his arms back and forth as I was testifying against him on the stand”, Donnie said. “The judge told his attorney to get him under control. He wouldn’t stop. The judge had the bailiff remove him to the jury box. As he walked, he showed an even bigger disrespectful attitude. As he sat down, he flung his chair back, making a loud clanking sound. The judge then told the bailiff to remove him from the courtroom. Before he left, he looked at the defendant and told him the following:” You are being held in contempt of my court. It is November, and 2 weeks before Thanksgiving, and I have up to 90 days to bring you back into this court. I am setting your court date for the contempt of court charge on January 5th. I hope you enjoy celebrating Thanksgiving, Christmas, and New Year's in the County Jail.” Donnie finished, and he and Frank were laughing at the story.

James looked at them, then at Burke, who was smiling and nodding. He then turned to his dad and asked, “All that over a 10-dollar speaker?” “He threatened the mom of a teenage girl; the theft from her garage was a threat to the family. He figured he would get away with this, too. He was also a suspect in a shooting. He was a piece of work.” Donnie said. “Yes, he was,” Frank said.

“What happened to him at trial?” James asked. “He got convicted for intimidation of a witness, burglary, and contempt of court. He served two years in state prison for that,” Donnie told James. “That is crazy. Just because he thought he was tougher than he was.” James stated to them.

Well, it's getting late, and it's been a busy last 36 hours. I am going to bed too. Night, everyone,” James said as he started up the stairs.

Now that it was just the 3 of them, Burke told them what would probably happen in the next couple of days. "According to our informants, we are hearing that they are getting about 30 or more gunmen to attack the farm. We are ready for them, but I wanted to let you two know in advance. I am sure it will be at night. Our cameras are equipped with night vision, and the agents also wear night-vision goggles. In the barn, a team of agents is monitoring the cameras and will alert us if anyone attempts anything. I am sure some will get through everything and get to the house. The basement is very secure, which is why we need the family to be there. Donnie, I know you and Michael can use sniper rifles. They are upstairs in the east and west bedrooms under the beds, in a case." Burke looked at Donnie; he knew Donnie was ready to do whatever he needed to keep everyone safe. "Donnie, you will draw fire from them, which will enable our agents to take them out. I have about 50 agents on the property and another 20 about 10 minutes away." Burke told both Donnie and Frank.

He turned to Frank and told him, "We will stay downstairs in case they can get in, to defend the family." Frank nodded. "I don't believe they will, but just in case," Burke said.

"No one hurts the family, Burke," Donnie told him. "Agreed," Frank said. "I know Donnie," Burke said.

"We need to try and get some sleep," Burke asked Donnie. "Where are you going to sleep?" "In the recliner," Donnie stated.

Burke and Frank got up and walked down the hall to their rooms. Donnie moved to the recliner and covered himself with the throw blanket, resting it on the back. Donnie fell asleep as soon as he closed his eyes.

17

The Escalation of the Badge

Burke's phone rang, waking him up. It was one of the agents in the barn. He told Burke that several vehicles were surrounding the farm, with people exiting them. They appear to be wearing all-black clothing and are heavily armed. "OK, advise everyone while I get the family ready." He told the agent on the phone.

He got up, grabbed his pistol and rifle, and went to knock on Frank's door. Opening it, he told Frank, "Here they come." He then went into the living room and woke Donnie, saying, "They are here." Donnie stood up and cocked his pistol. "We need to get everyone to the basement." He said to Donnie. "I will go and get them up and moving," Donnie told him as he moved towards the stairs.

Once upstairs, he went into Carol's room. Gently nudging her, he told her, "Carol, I need you to wake up and get everyone to the basement." As she looked up at him, she got up. She moved to James' room first and woke him. He got up and headed down the stairs, gun in hand. She then went to Michael's and Sarah's room. She woke Sarah first, "Sarah, we need to get up and move to the basement." Sarah looked at Carol, and it took her a minute to understand. Sarah nudged Michael, "Honey, get up, we need to go to the basement."

That is when Donnie walked into the room. Sarah, I need Michael up here. You go with Carol, please. We'll see you both in a bit." Sarah hugged Michael and kissed him. "Be safe please," she told him. He got up and looked at Donnie. Donnie waited until they left the room. "Burke is going to have us up here with sniper rifles. We will be under attack shortly. We will be a second level of shooters." Donnie told him. Michael nodded, but he asked Donnie, "With what? All I have is my pistol." "There are rifles under the beds," Donnie said.

They looked under the beds, found the cases, and opened them. They retrieved the scopes and went to the east and west windows. Looking out, they noticed the scopes were night-vision. Michael called back and said he saw movement. "I have it on my side as well," Donnie called back. While Michael was watching, he heard a shot ring out.

While Donnie and Michael were getting set, Frank and Burke were getting the rest of the family into the basement. James and Charles argued with them, but Frank looked at James and told him they needed him with the others to protect them. James responded, "Frank, I am not 10 years old, and I know you are telling me I am not ready." Frank looked at James and told him, "James, if anything happens to you, how am I going to tell your mom and dad I didn't keep you safe? We do need you and Charles in the basement, in case these idiots get in there. You are both armed and trained. Do you trust your dad and me?" "You know I do," James responded. "Then get down there and keep us safe, too," Frank told James. James shrugged and went into the basement, locking the door behind him.

Burke and Frank looked at each other. "I heard a shot from the east." Frank said to Burke, "I heard it too. Here we go. This place had better be everything they told me it is. If not, I will get everyone killed." Burke said. "I am going to call in the other agents. How many officers do you have available and waiting?" He asked Frank. Anthony told me we have 30 officers about 2 miles out, which will give us almost 80 agents and officers." Frank told Burke. "OK, that should get us through," Burke said.

Frank's phone rang. It was Timothy. "Are you ready to die?" He asked Frank. "Are you ready, Tim?" Frank asked him. Timothy started laughing. He told Frank they were all going to die. "Tim, you always were a drama king. Come and knock on the door; let's finish all of this. Just you and me," Frank said to Timothy. "No, this is between me and Donnie. He is hiding behind all of you, and none of you see it." Timothy told Frank.

While Timothy was taunting Frank, Donnie was on the phone with his boss. "Hey, will you make sure all of our people stay out of what is coming? I know there is talk about helping, but they need to be kept safe." "Donnie, just get through everything; we'll see you on the other side of all this. I know you are doing what you need to do." His boss told him. "Anthony called me and told me that there was an international contract out on you, your family, and Michael. Also, Susan is here at the house, and we are keeping safe." He told Donnie. "OK, well, I need to hang up. Just keep everyone out of the way and let us take care of everything." Donnie said as a bullet whizzed past his head. "I have to go, boss." Hanging up the phone, he turned to Michael and told him to be careful.

Donnie then called Burke. "Am I able to shoot back at them yet?" He asked. "I am not going to sit here much longer and not fire," Donnie told him. "Use your best judgment," Burke responded. "How many are you two seeing? We lowered the shutters down here. Also, your buddy called Frank and taunted him." Burke told Donnie. "Funny, he didn't call me," Donnie responded. "There are at least 15 on the east side of the house. What are your people telling you they see?" "The last report I got is that there are about 40 on the property, all heavily armed and heading towards the house," Burke told Donnie. "Okay, that will give me an idea. Keep the family safe." Donnie told Burke. "We are, just like old times," Burke responded to Donnie. "10-4, here we go again." Donnie joked.

They are almost to the creek on the east side. That is about three-quarters of a mile? Donnie asked Burke. "Give or take," he responded. I will start shooting at about half a mile. Let your people know." Donnie told Burke. "Michael, where are they on the west side?" "Approximately the same distance," Michael said. "Burke, we are close on the west as well," Donnie said to Burke. "Copy that, I will advise my people. I will have them start firing on your signal." Burke said, hanging up. He then called his command center and relayed the information. "Understood, the agent in charge told Burke. Sir, she asked, "Why are you giving him the command?" Burke chuckled because he is the one man in all of this, I trust, to make the right call. Most of the people in this building are like family to him, so there is that, too. Advise the other agents." Burke said. "Yes, sir," she responded.

Burke heard a shot coming from upstairs. He wanted to see what was happening, but the blinds were down, and this close, they would be visible through the windows. If they had remembered to bring radios into the house, it would be easier. He called the command center and asked for an update. When the agent answered, she told Burke that one was down. "I don't suppose there are more radios there, are there?" Burke asked. "There are, but you are under fire as well, sir," She responded. "Hold on." He said to the agent.

Yelling up to Donnie, "I need to get a radio from the barn, can you two cover me?" "Michael can," Donnie replied. "Burke, tell me when. Also, tell your guys up top." "Copy that," Burke told her. "Advise the agents up top as well," Burke instructed her. "Yes sir," She responded.

Burke turned to Frank and ensured he was close enough to close the door behind him. It was about 400 feet to the barn, and the lights outside had also been shut off. So, he had the dark on his side. As he was about to open the door, a series of knocks on it signaled the emergency signal they had devised. There were four agents outside with six radios. When he opened the door, they handed them to him and turned back towards the barn. Shots were heard from upstairs. They looked and saw a group of attackers there, three of whom were on the ground. The others were turning away. The four agents rushed them, disarmed them, and then took them to the barn.

Burke used the radio to thank the agents who brought the radios and his command center agent in charge. He called up to Donnie and said he had radios now. Michael told Donnie he would get them. Donnie said OK as he fired another shot, dropping another attacker. Michael grabbed them from Burke, ran back upstairs, and brought one to Donnie before returning to his window. Looking out, he fired another shot, dropping another attacker.

"We have 7, between the 2 of us down," Donnie advised Burke. The agents on the roof had taken down another eight. At that moment, there were several bullets aimed at the roof. He heard someone yell, and one of the agents radioed that there was one down, and another had been hit. They were targeting the agents. Donnie looked for the shooters and fired, taking one out. The second one threw something at the house. When it exploded, it was a flash grenade. It blinded Donnie's scope for a minute. Shots came into Michael's side of the house. One bullet struck his right upper arm. Donnie heard him yell, but he didn't go down. Donnie went to him. Michael said it was just a scratch, and Donnie needed to go back to the other side. Michael rose, firing two rounds that took down two of the shooters. He then grabbed a pillow, removed the pillowcase, tore it, and wrapped his arm. Several more shots struck around the window, but nothing hit him.

Donnie went back, fired and dropped another shooter, reloaded, and fired, hitting another shooter. He went down. Donnie radioed and asked where the other shooters were. The command center agent advised him that they were engaged with the other officers to the south. Several were neutralized, but three agents had also been hit. As she was speaking, she told him to stand by. "Be advised, two large vehicles are entering the property from the North at high speed. They are heading directly for the house. Donnie came back on the radio and told Frank that they were planning to either make a run at the house or blow up the vehicles by it. Burke instructed the agents on the roof to remove the vehicles before they got too close. One of the SUVs emerged from the barn and drove towards the vehicles to block them. There was another agent in the SUV, and he opened fire with a roof-mounted 50-caliber gun. He shot into the engine area and then across the windshield. One of the vehicles did explode, as it was struck by the bullets, confirming they had explosives. The agents took out the second from the roof. They blew it up with a rocket-propelled grenade (RPG). The vehicles were stopped about a hundred yards from the house.

The agent with the .50 caliber turned it towards the West side of the house and opened fire. There were eight shooters still moving towards the house; the 50 caliber took down 6. The other two turned and moved to the south side of the house. The agent then turned his gun to the east, saw several shooters there, and then opened fire on them, eliminating 8 of them. The other five moved towards the south side of the house. They were stopped by six agents who came out of the barn. 2 of them fired on the agents and were shot instantly. The other three were taken into custody. The two from the east side left the house and headed south towards the others.

The agents who were in that area had released their security dogs to chase the shooters attacking from the south. The Belgian Malinois dogs are highly protective and well-trained; they have taken down several shooters. The agents came up behind the dogs, shot another six shots, neutralizing more of the shooters. The shooters shot two dogs and 4 of the agents. None of the dogs or agents sustained life-threatening injuries.

After a couple of hours of this fight, it came to an end. The remaining shooters escaped on foot. As the sun rose, they could see the results of the battle. Both the backup agents and law enforcement were advised of the direction they went and what the shooters were wearing. Additionally, they were armed and should be approached with caution.

The command agent radioed for a status on all the officers, and they responded one by one. One of the agents who was shot on the roof didn't make it. When that was completed, she contacted Burke and advised him that all was clear, but there was a mess outside, and she urged him to keep the family inside. She also suggested having all the wounded brought to the barn, as medical staff were standing by to treat them.

Donnie heard all clear and went and walked Michael to the barn. As he was walking, a bullet struck the dirt near him. He turned, saw the shooter, pulled his pistol, and fired, striking the shooter and eliminating him. As he turned back and finished walking Michael to the barn, he radioed Burke and told him not to let the family out yet, until they secure the area. Burke said he copied. He then went in to speak to the Command agent.

Do you have enough agents on-site to secure the area, or should local law enforcement be responsible? She looked at him for a minute. You are a former military and law enforcement professional, aren't you? I am. He told her he was Donnie as he stuck his hand out to her. Hello, I am finally meeting you. My name is Agent Pamela Jenkins. We will need help securing the scene. Several of our officers were shot. And we need to retrieve Samuel's remains from the roof area.

Donnie radioed Burke, instructing him to have Frank call in his officers to help secure the scene and warn them not to screw anything up. They could respond with haste, but there was no need for sirens. Probably 8 of his officers should be enough. Agent Jenkins nodded as he gave the number. Burke said OK and looked at Frank, who was already on the phone.

Burke came out onto the porch and looked around. He could see bodies everywhere. The SUV was parked by the north entrance, with the two blown-up vehicles nearby. The responding officers would have to park and walk around the vehicles to help secure the scene. Donnie joined Burke on the porch. He knew he needed to get everyone out of the basement. He also knew Sarah would want to check on Michael. What he didn't know was if she was up to seeing the bodies they still needed to check and cover.

As they stood there, law enforcement vehicles began to arrive. Donnie called Frank, and the units were in route. Frank stepped out and asked them how much longer they were going to keep everyone in the basement." Let's get at least the bodies along the way to the barn checked and covered," Donnie told them. "Burke, did you guys remember to bring sheets, blankets, or body bags?" Frank asked. "We have body bags in the barn," Burke told Frank.

Frank stepped off the porch and met the officers, directing them to the bodies between the house and the barn as a priority. He sent one of the officers to the barn to get the body bags. As he opened the door, Michael met him on his way out. He had a bandage and a wrap on his arm. He walked to where Donnie and Burke were. "Did you keep everyone in the basement?" He asked Donnie. "I did, because of the bodies, and you weren't out yet. Didn't want to give Sarah more to deal with.

Michael walked inside, announcing his presence as he opened the basement door. He saw James and Charles with their guns pointed up towards the door. It is all clear, and you can all come up here now. Sarah walked past the two guys and came up to hug Michael. She stopped when she saw the wrap on his right arm. "What happened, Michael?" She asked him. "I got a scratch." He responded with a little nervous chuckle. "Michael!" He heard the voice from behind Sarah, "Don't tell her stories." Carol scolded him. "Yes, ma'am." He said to Carol. "Honey, I got shot, but it only grazed me," Michael told Sarah. "Michael, are you sure?" Sarah responded. Carol looked at it and asked to see it. Michael nodded. Carol unwrapped it and saw the stitches. "Sarah, he will have a scar, but he will be okay." Carol turned to Michael so that Sarah could see. She rewrapped it and went in search of Donnie.

James and Charles arrived, followed by Stacy and her mom. Carol stepped outside and saw the cars at the entrance. She walked up and looked at Donnie. "Nothing happened to me, Hun," Donnie said. "I just needed to check. I know how you are." She told Donnie. "Burke, are there more injured? Carol asked. "Yeah, in the barn." He responded. "Agent Jenkins, we have an ER nurse coming over to help with the wounded." "Copy," Jenkins responded.

Donnie walked with Carol to the barn. "Michael got hit today," Donnie told Carol. "I saw the wound." She responded. "I need to end all this. Too many people are getting hurt to keep us safe." Donnie told her. "Donnie, that is their job; it's Michael's job as well," Carol said. "Sweetheart, I can end this, and no one else will have to get hurt for me. I have an idea that will also draw Timothy out." Donnie said. He knew she wouldn't want to hear that, but he needed to end the attacks.

Carol stopped walking, turned to Donnie, looked into his eyes, saying, "Whatever you are planning, you'd better come back to me. I have loved you since the day we met. I made you work for it, and I was wrong, and I realize that now. Donnie, I want to spend the rest of my life making things up to you, if you will have me." She wrapped her arms around him and held him tight. "I don't want to waste time, not with you anymore." She looked into his eyes. She saw the pain he was feeling because others were getting hurt and even killed because of him. "None of this is your fault. They brought this to us. We need it to end, I agree, but you'd better come home to James and me." Carol concluded. She reached in and kissed him. She turned and opened the barn door. "Do what you feel is right, I trust you." Carol closed the door behind her.

Donnie stood there for a few minutes, having decided what he needed to do to draw them all out. He needed to know who Roger was and to put an end to Timothy's freedom run. They needed to pay for Samuel's death and the injury to several agents and Michael. It was time. Donnie turned and walked back to where Burke and Frank were. He needed to tell them what he knew he needed to do to stop all of this.

As he approached the other 2, Michael, James, and Charles stepped out onto the porch as well. Donnie knew they would all tell him he couldn't do what he was planning. He will talk to Burke and Frank later. As he stepped onto the porch, the first ambulance arrived. There would be several to come and transport the agents who were shot. The K-9 officers were already being transported to the vet with their handlers. The FBI medical staff was still treating two of the agents. There would be others to transport Samuel and the deceased shooters to the morgue. There was still a lot of cleanup to do. They all agreed this was only the first attack on the farm. Donnie decided to tell Burke and Frank his plan later; for now, they needed to find out who these people were and what those in the barn-holding cells knew about the one paying them, the one called Roger.

Sarah, Stacy, and her mom had made coffee and brought everyone a cup. They also found some snacks. I asked the guys if they wanted anything to eat, and they told me maybe later. Frank said, "Ladies, thank you. Sarah hugged Michael. Stacy kissed Charles and told him she knew they were making plans. She told the others to go inside and decide what to do next.

The clean-up was underway once the wounded agents were taken to the hospital. Burke reminded the others that there are still three other witnesses. The locals who attacked Charles. They were now inside holding cells at the county jail, under guard by FBI agents.

All of the deceased shooters were checked for ID, and photos taken. The FBI contacted Interpol to identify and locate Roger. They were international, mainly from Europe. Interpol was beginning to send Burke the names of the shooters. The ones he had received information on were identified as mercenaries. Interpol also cleared several off their wanted list. Burke was told they were getting closer to identifying Roger.

Donnie knew that when James heard what he planned to do, James would insist on going to protect him. Donnie wanted James far away from the area, but he also knew James would get there anyway. Carol would be upset, but would go along with it only if he didn't get hurt. Burke and Frank would try to talk him out of it. Michael and Charles would likely react similarly to James.

Donnie's biggest concern is that they will return to the farm and use larger weapons, such as grenade launchers, RPGs, and other high-caliber firearms.

Carol came back from helping the medical staff and went upstairs to shower. The rest of the family went back inside and started looking for something to eat. Donnie used the shower downstairs, and when he was done, he went in and poured himself another cup of coffee. He decided to wait for Carol to finish showering before he ate.

After Donnie poured the coffee, he went into the living room and sat in the recliner. He could hear everyone talking and enjoying each other's company. He was deep in thought when he felt a hand softly touching his shoulder. He looked up and saw Carol studying him. He smiled at her. She still knew Donnie and knew how he could be. "What are you thinking about?" Carol asked him. "Everything that is happening now is because of what we did years ago, and they still blame us for everything that happened," Donnie told her. "None of this is your fault, Donnie. It is all on them." Carol said. Donnie just shrugged his shoulders.

18

The Burden of the Badge

After the talk, Donnie and Carol went into the kitchen to get some food. Everyone else looked at them because of everything that had happened; they weren't even thinking about food. But because of the death around them, they were still in a bit of shock. Michael and James joined them in the kitchen, and they all sat down to eat at the table. After eating, they went in and talked with the others.

There was a lot of clean-up outside. The FBI agents placed Samuel in a body bag and carried him to a waiting ambulance, not allowing any other remains to be placed inside with him. They told the ambulance driver to transport him to the morgue. A couple of them rode with him to the Morgue.

The shooters were photographed and searched for any identification. Most had none, but they also did fingerprints of each so they could search for them in the database. Several were identified quickly through international databases. Most were mercenaries, and many had served in various militaries. Following the death of one of their agents, Agent Jenkins reached out to international organizations and began to identify a pattern. There was a link to the organization that Roger headed. It helped the FBI to link several of the shooters to Roger and his organization.

Donnie poured a cup of coffee for himself and Carol after eating. When he brought it to her, he told her he wanted to step out onto the porch. She told him she would go with him. As they stepped out, they watched as the coroner personnel were placing the shooters into body bags. A realization came over Donnie as he watched them. He turned to Carol and said, "Babe, this won't end until they either face Frank and me or we take them completely out. I cannot endanger you and James anymore." Carol, taking a sip of coffee, stared forward for a few minutes, thinking of what Donnie had said. She knew he was right, but she didn't want to lose him, especially now that they were beginning to come back together. "Donnie," she started, "James and I need you. I know you are doing this for us. Why not let Burke handle everything?" Donnie looked at Carol; he could see concern and a touch of fear in her eyes. He knew he was the target of all of this, and they were using Carol, James, and the others to get to him. He needed to protect them all. "Donnie, I know you are planning something. Something I will hate. But I also know you will do what you think is best for James and me." Carol reached over and took Donnie's hand in hers as she spoke. Donnie held her hand securely and took a drink of his coffee while looking at everything that was going on around the farmhouse.

"I need to keep you, James, and the others safe. These people are targeting all of you because of what I did." He told her. "I cannot let that happen. It would kill me if anything happened to any of you because of me. They only understand violence." Donnie turned to her as he spoke, looking into her eyes. He asked, "Do you understand that, Hun?" "I understand. You had better come back to James and me. We need you." She said to him. "I will do my best, babe," Donnie told her.

They heard footsteps behind them. Turning, they saw James coming out to join them. He had heard a little of what was being said. He still had the bandage on his face from the glass hitting him at the house. "Dad, I will not let you do anything that will get you killed," James told his dad. "Son, I must take care of this. I will not let you or your mom be hurt because of this group. They are targeting you both to get to me; now it's time to take the fight to them. I will have plenty of backup from Frank and Burke. We will end this. But they need to think I am alone. This has gotten people killed, and you hurt." He told James and Carol. "What do you have planned?" James asked. "I need to talk to Burke and Frank. We will plan it out and then end this insanity," Donnie told them.

When he finished speaking to them, everyone slowly joined them to see what was happening outside the farmhouse. Carol and Donnie stood there holding hands. There were whispers of questions and answers as they watched everything. Agent Jenkins came over from the barn and asked Donnie where Burke was. "He may be sleeping," Donnie responded. Jenkins told him she needed to talk with Donnie and Burke because she had some information she urgently needed to share with them. James told them he would find out what Burke was doing. He turned and headed into the house. "James," Donnie called out, "get Frank too." Everyone looked at Jenkins, and she realized this was going to be a group conversation. Let's all go inside and wait for them.

Waiting in the living room, they were all a bit nervous to hear the news Jenkins had to tell them. After a bit, Burke and Frank came into the living room, and Agent Jenkins began to share the information she needed to tell them. She had been able to link 15 of the deceased shooters to Roger. We are still looking for his name so we can connect everything to it. What we do know about Roger is that he is not in Europe or the Middle East. Interpol has determined that much. It sounds like they have taken an interest in this case after today. Donnie, they know your name now, too.

"Is that a good thing or a bad thing?" Donnie asked Agent Jenkins. "Donnie, it's a good thing. They have become more interested in helping you protect everyone here. They understand the backstory and see it as a

David and Goliath kind of story now," She responded. "Oh great, which one am I?" Donnie asked with a chuckle. "You tell us, wise guy," Jenkins quipped. "The scrawny kid with the slingshot," Donnie said. "You are correct, and you win the prize! An entire international agency working to find and arrest your biggest fan." Jenkins told him. Carol shot a look at Donnie. "Does that make Timothy Saul?" She asked, smiling. Everyone sat silently for a minute, then started laughing. Donnie said, "Well, maybe it does."

After the laughter slowed down, Donnie looked at Burke, Frank, and Jenkins. He told them he had an idea that might flush out the remaining shooters, including Timothy. Frank stopped Burke and told everyone he had received a call from Timothy, as the shooters were moving towards the house. He told everyone that Timothy said he would take care of Donnie once and for all. The others looked at Frank. I have the number on my phone. Jenkins wrote down the number and radioed the barn, instructing the agents to locate the phone, then turned back to Donnie. "I have not known you long, Donnie, but from what I heard about you, this is probably going to be dangerous." "Pam, you have no idea with him," Carol said. Several in the room muttered under their breath. James looked at Donnie and said, "Just make it home, Dad." "Well, let's hear this new plan you have, Donnie," Jenkins asked.

Donnie looked at Charles. "When those three attacked you, they took your radio so it could be cloned. They wanted the company's radio frequency. They came after you because they were already searching for the storage place that had the information they were paid to steal. They have our radio frequency. I discovered that when we pulled over the SUV behind the gas station. They had one of our radios in it." Donnie paused, "When Michael and I interrupted their theft, Timothy advised Roger of what we did. This all goes back to the drug bust Timothy and I participated in years ago. Fill in the blanks for me, Burke," Donnie said.

"Roger was in charge of the drug trade in the area, and when you found the guy, who was Roger's younger brother, he went into hiding, thinking he was next. After he took off, Interpol conducted a raid on the top players of the Poseidon syndicate in Greece. Because the brother and Roger had different fathers, it's still difficult to track down Roger. I understand Interpol had several leads, but none were him." Burke looked at Donnie and said, "Both feet, Donnie."

"That is the backstory," Donnie commented, and continued. "The Joseph Group has ties with several organizations. Most are legal, but a few aren't. They were associated with Poseidon. The paperwork that the three were sent to steal included offshore accounts and Swiss bank numbers. There was still a significant amount of money available from Poseidon. Burke finally obtained the warrants he needed to uncover all this. Michael, you stopped them from getting the money. Charles, you were never supposed to be attacked. It was a wrong place, wrong time situation." Donnie stopped for a minute to let everything sink in.

Burke looked around and said, "I am still wondering why they put all that paperwork in the storage unit. I would have thought it would be safer to keep it in a secure location, such as a vault. Seems stupid to me. But I suppose if you have dirty money floating around, you should hide it."

Donnie spoke up again, "That leads me to what my plan is. There is an old warehouse on the other side of town, off Old Mill Road. I know they are monitoring our radios. With the help of Burke and Frank, approximately 150 armed agents and police officers will hide around the warehouse. I will radio that I am checking the inside of the property. Michael and a couple of other agents will be up in the rafters' area. There is only one road into the warehouse. I will be the bait. I will not let anyone else in our family get hurt. I will be heavily armed as well." Donnie paused and looked at Carol. He knew she would not like the plan. He knew James wouldn't either, but it seemed like the only way. "I also was told by Frank that Timothy is close; he called him right before the attack this morning. After what he told Frank, I believe this will also flush him out." Donnie paused for a minute.

James said, "Burke and Uncle Frank, you better get my dad and Michael back in one piece." Carol and Sarah echoed the statement with a nod. "That is our plan, everyone. This is more of a catch-and-capture operation. I don't like Donnie being used as bait, but it is the only way to stop this," Burke told them.

Just then, the Jenkins telephone rang. It was the barn. After taking notes on the call, she looked at everyone. "We have a real name for Roger now, and Andropalos is his last name. Interpol has tracked him to Canada, specifically to the area around Manitoba, where he is believed to be hiding in the forest. He entered Canada about six months ago. They have thirty agents and about fifty Mounties headed his way now. Let's hope he is still there. His organization's name is Chronos. It means time in Greek. I am sure he decided on that because he was waiting for this." She concluded.

Donnie looked at Burke and said, "It's time to take Chronos down, but this time, there can be no one left to run another syndicate."

"It's all up to Interpol; there are seven other locations they are active in, all of which will be taken down as soon as Andropolos is stopped," Jenkins said.

Everyone sat in silence for a few minutes. Sarah whispered to Michael, "You better come back to me, mister." Michael leaned over and kissed her forehead. "I will make sure I do."

Charles asked if he would be going along on the operation. Donnie looked at Burke and Frank to answer that. Charles, you can ride with me, Frank told him.

Stacy looked at Charles and started to say something, but he interrupted her, looking into her eyes, and said, "I know if I get hurt, you will hurt me worse when I get better, yes, ma'am," and hugged her. That sent the group into laughter.

Carol caught Donnie looking at her. She knew what he was thinking and understood that he felt this was the only way to end everything, hoping to catch Timothy in the process. She also knew Timothy would never go quietly. She smiled at him and gave him a knowing nod. One that told him, even though she didn't like the idea, she understood. Donnie smiled back at her.

The room got quiet again. They sat there, thinking about what was to come. They all hoped this would finally bring everything to an end and allow them to return home.

Donnie looked at his coffee cup and stood up. "I need some more coffee," he said, and asked who wanted some more. Several stood up with him and followed him into the kitchen. Carol came up behind him and hugged him.

After he poured his coffee, he turned to Carol and asked her if she wanted to step outside with him. She nodded and grabbed his hand, walking with him. Once they were outside, Donnie turned to Carol and told her, "This situation has put every one of you in danger. Timothy wants to kill me. I have to stop him before he does, I hope you understand that, Hun." Carol responded, "Donnie, I screwed up years ago when I walked away from you. I want to have years with you; that idiot Timothy needs to be stopped. I know what he wants, but I also know you, and I know you will keep us safe. Just come back to me. I have years to make up to you if you will allow me." Donnie took her into his arms; I will have to think about that. Then he laughed and said he never blamed her for leaving. He knew he had over-shared that night about the shooting in the hotel. Yes, I will allow you." Donnie pulled her close and hugged her. Carol hugged him back. "Donnie, I have had years to understand the job you do. I still don't want that knock on the door, but I have loved you almost from the beginning, and I still do." Carol told him. Donnie leaned and kissed her forehead. Carol smiled as he did.

Burke sent James to get his dad. Jenkins had just received a call from the barn and had more information. James went out to the porch, paused, and smiled at his parents. "It's about time you two," James told them. "Burke needs you in here, Dad." Donnie and Carol smiled at James as they walked past him into the living room.

"What is going on, Pam?" Donnie asked. "As of 20 minutes ago, Interpol has Andropolos in custody. He did fight and was shot, but he was taken to the hospital. Now they are going to raid the seven other locations." Jenkins told them. Donnie asked her, "How sure are you of the information?" "I am 95 percent sure of it." She responded to him. But just in case there are 2 of our agents up there, including Jamesson. He flew up today and was with them when they raided the house. We have permission from Interpol to have them stay close, also." Jenkins said. "Okay, part one down. We need to get going on the plan before we lose the opportunity." Donnie told Burke and Jenkins. Frank said he needed to notify Anthony and have the officers ready. Jenkins said she would call her agents and tell them it's a go. "Michael, are you ready?" Donnie asked. "I am Donnie," Michael responded.

19

THE RECKONING OF THE BADGE

Within 15 minutes of the calls, once they had everything ready, Donnie directed Michael and the agents to the best line of sight for a shot, if needed. They moved into the positions. Burke and Jenkins were positioning their agents outside. They had left the dogs at the farm. Frank and Charles were with the law enforcement personnel as they moved into position. They decided to use phones to let Donnie know they were set. When everyone was set, they informed Donnie. Donnie had handed James a radio. When Donnie knew everyone was in place, he went back to his car and picked up the radio. He keyed the mic and said, "David-25, David-3." James responded, "Go ahead, David-3." "David-25, I am at the warehouse on Old Mill Road, doing a check. I will be 10-6 for a while, will advise when I go 10-8." Donnie said. "Copy David 3, at the warehouse on Old Mill Road, 10-6, with a check, will advise when 10-8," James responded. Donnie stood there for a minute. James had already mastered radio traffic. Donnie reached into the vehicle and picked up his flashlight. He then entered the warehouse. Jenkins had a spotter and James, about a mile away, watching traffic. Donnie didn't know how long it would take. He went in and sat in the old office.

Timothy had a radio tuned to the Security channel. He had heard the traffic and called the rest of the shooters to head to the warehouse, where he would meet them. He also told them Donnie would be his. They were going in case it was a setup.

Timothy pulled up to the road, where he was met by most of the shooters. He directed them left and right. They moved up beside the road in the grass. Timothy moved slowly along the side of the driveway in, as he watched them.

The spotter called Jenkins and told her that most of the shooters and Timothy were moving towards the warehouse from the road, moving up the driveway area. The others were on the south side, moving towards several agents. She told the spotter to let her know when the ones on the road were halfway up the driveway. She then called the agents on the south side, where shooters were moving towards them. She called Frank about the situation. Additionally, she called Donnie and informed him.

Donnie got up, pointed his flashlight at Michael, and signaled him to get ready. He waved back at Donnie to let him know he had seen the signal. The agents did the same. From there, Donnie began acting as if he were checking the warehouse.

The agents on the south side shifted further out to let the 15 shooters through towards the warehouse. That way, they would not give away the trap that has been set. No gunfire until it was necessary. Burke and Jenkins wanted them alive, so they could stand trial for the crimes they had committed. It will be up to the shooters, though.

On the North side, moving up the road, the 20 shooters and Timothy may or may not know that Interpol had arrested their boss yet, or even care. Some of the mercenaries were known to finish the job; they were hired killers who would do as they pleased. For them, killing is like a dog trained to fight; they would not stop until the opponent was defeated. Based on the photos of those they had in custody, their history is like a K9 trained to fight and kill.

Burke and Jenkins have assembled four teams of 10 agents, all former military personnel trained in commando tactics. They were further trained to home in on a target and shoot only as a last resort. If fired on, they would respond. They were equipped with a military-style rifle, a .45-caliber pistol, flash grenades, and a knife, all of which they were trained to use.

The law enforcement team consisted of SWAT and street officers. All were ordered to wait until Frank told them to fire unless they were fired upon. Three of them were some of the officers who responded when the female officer was shot. Frank knew they wanted to act against the shooters, seeking revenge. But he trusted them to obey orders as well.

The plan devised by Donnie, Burke, Jenkins, and Frank was to position them near the warehouse. Let Timothy enter to search for Donnie. They planned to have 7 to 10 shooters follow him and bring them in once they were inside, to close the trap from the outside. Michael and the agents inside with Donnie had suppressors on their rifles. They would eliminate the additional shooters before they located Donnie.

They all knew things could go in any direction, and they understood this would be a dangerous plan. Donnie had insisted on taking this course of action. He told them he needed to protect the family and end the violence. They knew he would take care of things himself if they didn't help him.

They were all watching and listening to the movement of the shooters, ready to stop them. Donnie was inside, running scenarios through his mind, planning for everything he could think of, as he had always done. This was personal, but he also had to remind himself that he would need to approach it like any other assignment he had been given. He needed to think clinically, meaning he would manage it as if he were working if he didn't know the main character in all this. After years of working in law enforcement and security, he had trained himself to think that way.

Part of the plan was to protect the family at the farm. Jenkins had assigned an agent she trusted to the protection detail. Highly trained in hostage situations and incursions into hostile situations. She trusted him with her life and knew he would protect the family. Carol was concerned, but also knew Donnie would do everything he could to stay safe. James was with the spotter, who would keep him safe. Sarah and Stacy were worried because the reality of the job appeared right in front of them. They talked about the men they had chosen to be with. They seemed to thrive in the chaos of the job. Although they were not in law enforcement, their job had become increasingly similar to it than they had thought. Sarah told them she had not fully understood the nature of Michael's job until she had seen him at the house. Stacy said she understood Charles loved his job. He had applied for law enforcement but wasn't hired a couple of times, so he then applied for security. He had told her that the training Donnie insisted on had trained him better. He had thought about reapplying for law enforcement, but also knew Donnie would take care of him and their growing family.

Carol listened to these young women and realized she had lost so much when she divorced Donnie. She should have stood by him and allowed him to discuss his work concerns with her. They did anyway when they talked on the phone, but it wasn't the same as how Sarah and Stacy were living. She put those thoughts aside and told them they were always welcome to call her if they needed to talk. They smiled and exchanged numbers.

Stacy's mom was glad there was a woman who understood this type of life, because she knew she didn't. Carol told them they were all family and always would be. They all smiled and then started talking about Stacy and the baby, anything to keep their minds off everything that was happening.

At the warehouse, Michael signaled to Donnie that Timothy had entered the warehouse, bringing seven shooters with him. The shooters were fanning out left and right. Donnie signaled to Michael that he understood. He signaled Michael to wait to take the shooters down. Donnie continued to act as if he were searching the warehouse. As he did, he looked up to

Michael as he signaled the movement of Timothy and the squad of shooters with him. Michael signaled for Donnie to stop where he was. The next signal he gave Donnie was that there was a shooter in front and to the right of him. Donnie signaled for Michael to take the shot. Michael was able to neutralize the shooter. Donnie moved him under a shelving unit and grabbed his rifle.

Donnie stood still for a few minutes to make sure he was clear to move. One of the agents signaled that there were three more on the far left of Donnie. Donnie signaled to hold. Donnie then moved away from the shooters, knowing that Michael had covered him.

During that time, Timothy was searching for Donnie to end the feud once and for all. Timothy had hated Donnie for so long that it was all he thought about. Since they worked together, Timothy had made his life miserable. Donnie had created problems for Timothy, embarrassed him, and cost him his promotion. Timothy hated Donnie for having ruined his life. Timothy knew Donnie needed to pay for the humiliation he had caused him. He was going to kill Donnie, finally, and cause his family to live some of the pain he had been forced to live for so many years. This was personal to Timothy.

The agent signaled to Donnie that there were two shooters to his right. Donnie signaled them to neutralize them. Donnie heard two thuds as they hit the ground. He moved around and cleared the area. He took the mags from their rifles and covered them with a nearby tarp. Donnie continued to move around, knowing there were still four shooters and Timothy in the warehouse.

Donnie looked up at Michael, signaled him for a location on the other shooters, and Timothy. Michael signaled, and two were behind him; the other two shooters were on the other side of the warehouse. Timothy was now in the center of the warehouse. Donnie knew that Timothy would not stop until either one of them was killed. Donnie told Michael to neutralize the two shooters on the other side of the warehouse. Timothy was too close to the ones behind him to take care of them now.

Donnie needed the seven shooters to be removed so he could face Timothy alone. Otherwise, he would be fighting several shooters at once while dealing with Timothy. Donnie moved to the far side of the warehouse, away from the last two shooters, so that he could draw Timothy to him. When he reached the other side, he signaled Michael to take down the other two shooters. The agents did. That left Timothy to face Donnie alone.

Donnie made some noise to attract Timothy's attention. As Timothy moved towards Donnie, Donnie called out to him. "When are you going to stop this nonsense, Timothy?" Donnie shouted. Timothy fired a shot towards Donnie, but it missed him. "I suppose you are still just as stupid as you always were, Timothy," Donnie yelled. Timothy yelled back, "You have this coming, Donnie. You ruined my life, and you deserve to die for that." Donnie could see Timothy now. He yelled out, "What happened to you? You used to be at least a decent person, for the most part. Why did you decide to betray your oath and your department?" Timothy yelled back as he walked towards Donnie, "You have no room to talk. You betrayed me and everything we swore to uphold. I am just following in the steps of the great Donald LaDue."

Timothy fired another shot at Donnie. This ricocheted off the wall behind him. "Timothy, do you remember that time we stopped the drunk driver, and you suggested he hop on one foot? He had failed all the field sobriety tests. He was told what? To hop up seven, turn around, and hop back 10. He kept falling in the grass next to him. That was a fun night. Do you remember that?" Donnie asked him. "Yeah, but that was a long time ago," Timothy responded.

When Burke heard the shots from inside, he ordered everyone to advance on the shooters outside. As the agents and law enforcement appeared in the open, the shooters opened fire, striking two law enforcement officers.

The Agents and officers opened fire, hitting several of the shooters. As soon as the shooters realized they were surrounded, they set their guns down and put their hands behind their heads. A couple tried to run, but they were stopped at gunpoint by a few agents.

"It sounds like there is a gunfight outside. Seems neither of us can be trusted. Donnie said to Timothy. By the way, the seven that came in with you can't help you now. Do you remember when you recognized that address where an assault happened because it was your dad's boss's? When we arrived, it was like walking into a 1960s movie set. He was beaten badly, as I remember. It was so bad that he didn't make it. Timothy, I remember you were scared for him that night. Do you remember that?" Donnie asked him, "Yeah, I remember. My old man was worried about losing his job." Timothy said as he walked closer to where Donnie had been. While Timothy was talking, Donnie had moved.

As Donnie and Timothy were about to face each other, there was another attack at the farm.

This time, six shooters attacked the barn to try to free the eight in the holding cells. As they moved up towards the barn, there was a shot that rang out from the upper section of the barn. One shooter dropped. The other five opened fire and tried to shoot their way into the barn. As they moved closer, twelve agents appeared from the barn and returned their fire. Three more dropped quickly. The other two kept coming, and four of the agents were hit with bullets. One more shooter went down. The fifth shooter looked at the agents and smiled. He lifted his gun. They fired, and he dropped to the ground.

When the shooting started, Carol and the others looked at each other, turning to go to the basement, they stopped and remembered there were guns upstairs. Carol and Stacy headed upstairs to get them. When they came down, there was a pause in the shooting. The agent with them had grabbed Sarah and was holding her in front of him. She was shaking and crying. His gun was pointed at her head. Carol and Stacy stopped, looking at the agent and Sarah. Just then, Sarah dropped to a knee and flipped the gun-holding agent over her shoulder to the floor; his gun fell out of his hand. Carol moved forward, kicking the gun away. Sarah grabbed his cuffs and cuffed him. Carol and Stacy looked at Sarah in amazement. She looked at them and said she was a black belt in Brazilian Jiu-Jitsu. They all smiled and looked at the handcuffed agent. Carol remembered Donnie always carried another handcuff key in his belt. She then searched the agent and found his cuff key, removing it. Stacy called over to the barn and told them what had happened. They sent three agents to remove the agent and hold him until Burke and Jenkins returned.

"Donnie, here is one for you. Do you remember the baby boy that Jones was doing CPR on when we arrived? He had him laid out on the back of his patrol car. The Ambulance crew called us back later and said the kid didn't make it. We charged the family with neglect. Do you remember that?" Timothy said to Donnie. As Donnie responded, Timothy realized Donnie had moved and was now behind him. Timothy turned around, saw Donnie, and raised his gun to fire. Donnie fired two shots, hitting Timothy in the chest. As Timothy fell to the floor, he fired a shot, striking Donnie in the leg. Donnie went down too. Lying there, Timothy and Donnie stared at each other. Timothy looked at Donnie and told him he hated him for everything he had done. He also admitted he was caught by Andropolis and forced to work for him.

The agents in the rafters had advised Burke that Timothy and Donnie were down and needed immediate medical attention.

Donnie looked at Timothy and told him, "You always tried to take credit for everyone else's work. You got caught by Frank. This all falls on you, Timothy, not me. Besides Timothy, your boss is in custody now."

Michael and the agents climbed down from their positions, and by the time they reached Timothy and Donnie, Timothy had stopped breathing.

They removed his gun and advised the medical staff to respond, saying he was not breathing. He had been shot in the chest twice and would need medical attention immediately. Michael went to Donnie and told him he had better not die, because he was not going to face Carol with that news. Michael applied pressure to the wound to help stop the bleeding. "I got hit in the leg, not my heart," Donnie told Michael.

The agents inside went to check the seven shooters for signs of life. They also checked for documentation and took a photo of their faces. None were alive. The images were sent to the barn computer for facial recognition. Two of them were quickly identified as wanted by Interpol for crimes.

Burke and Frank were taking care of those outside, and zip-tie cuffs were used on each person they captured during the search for documents. One of them had photos of Carol and James. The others were checked for identification and had their faces photographed, which were then uploaded to the barn computer.

As the various medical crews arrived, James called Carol. "Mom, Dad was shot, but he will be okay. Medical is here, and they are working on him." "Wait, what?" Carol responded, but she didn't fully comprehend what James had said. "Dad was shot in the leg. Medical is here, and they are triaging him now. They will be taking him to the hospital in a couple of minutes. If he goes." James told his mom. Carol looked around the room at the ladies with her. "Anything else happen to anyone?" Carol asked James. "Nothing, everyone else is OK, Mom," James responded. "OK, and what about Timothy?" She asked him. "Dad took care of him; he is leaving in a body bag. He was the one who shot Dad," James told his mom. The looks on the faces around her told her she needed to talk to them. "OK, son, are you going with your dad to the hospital?" "If he goes, I will," James said. "He'd better go! He knows what will happen if he doesn't! They can work on a gunshot victim and an assault victim!" Carol said to James. "I will tell him that for you. Mom, how are all of you?" We are all good. I will explain things once we know about your father, that stubborn man." Carol told James. "OK, I will pass on the information to everyone. I have to go, they are bringing dad out now," James told his mom. "Call me with the news on your dad," Carol told James. "I will, Mom," James responded, then ended the call.

As Carol ended the call, she stood with her eyes closed for a few minutes. Her thoughts raced as she thought about the last few years and how she wanted to make up to Donnie and James. She didn't want to lose the opportunity to heal the family after the divorce. She was worried Donnie may not be able to walk again, and that terrified her. She knew it would change Donnie. But she knew the Doctors at the hospital and knew they would do everything they could to save Donnie's leg.

She composed herself and turned to the others standing with her. "Everyone is safe. Donnie got shot. He'd better go to the hospital!" She told them.

Sarah asked Carol if she was going to the hospital to see Donnie. "I don't even know if he is going; I need to wait and find out first." She said. The others looked at her in disbelief. Why wouldn't he go? She read their faces. "You should know by now he can be very stubborn. I am not there to force the issue with him, so I have to wait to find out how bad it is first and if he needs to go." Carol told them. "If he doesn't, I will take him myself and probably just kick him out of the car as I slow down." They all laughed at that.

Then, to change the subject, Carol asked if anyone was hungry, got up, and headed to the kitchen.

20

THE HEALING OF THE BADGE

As Donnie was being wheeled out of the warehouse, he stopped the medical staff, who were approaching James. "I am fine, it didn't do much damage to my leg. I will be fine. Let me guess, you called your mom already." Donnie said to James. "Of course I did, Dad, you got shot. Now, are you going to the hospital with them or with Mom?" James asked. Donnie looked at James, then looked at the medical staff. He smiled and said, "It would be safer to go with these people than with your mom." They both laughed. "James, I will call your mom," Donnie told James. James nodded. At that time, Michael, Charles, Frank, and Burke approached them. "You just had to cause stress for all of us, didn't you, Donnie?" Frank said to him.

"I was shot in the leg, nowhere else," Donnie said. "Yeah, because if it had been your head, it would have just bounced off that rock-hard part of you," Burke said. Everyone laughed because they knew it was true. The Medic looked at everyone and told them they needed to get him to the hospital. "We will have someone drive Carol over to the hospital. After I figure out what happened at the farm." Jenkins said. Donnie put his hand up. "What happened at the farm, Pam?" Donnie asked. "I am still not sure yet. I will find out and let everyone know." She responded. She turned and walked to a waiting car to drive back to the farm to investigate. As the car pulled onto the road, Jenkins called the farm. "You need to tell me what happened, and do not leave one thing out." She told the lead she had left at the farm. "The agent was assigned to stand with the remaining members of the family. When the shooters attacked the barn, we engaged them. Our people dropped all five. Two of our people were hit; they are being treated now." "OK, that was done correctly. What happened in the house? That is what I am asking about." Jenkins almost yelled into the phone.

"The agent turned his gun on Sarah. He held her and had his gun to her head. She has a black belt in Jiu-Jitsu and flipped him, causing him to drop the gun. They cuffed him and called us." The agent told Jenkins. "I am on my way and want to know everything about this 'Agent'. Everything! This was on our watch and should have never happened." Jenkins said. She disconnected the call. She turned to the driver, "We need to get this taken care of, speed up, I want to be there quickly."

At the farm, the family was talking about everything that had happened. Stacy looked at Carol and thanked her, not realizing they had a secret weapon. Everyone laughed, and Stacy just nodded. They were finishing their meal, and the coffee was brewing. They were beginning to relax and feel that things might be returning to normal now that everyone had been either arrested or neutralized. They were talking when there was a knock at the door. They looked at each other, and the tension grew again. Carol got up and asked who it was. "It's Pam, Agent Jenkins." The voice from the other side said. Carol opened the door slowly. Pam was standing about a foot away from the door, looking at Carol. "Can I come in, Carol?" Carol opened the door so Jenkins could come in and then shut it.

"Is everyone okay after today?" Jenkins asked. Carol told her to ask the rest of them; they are in the kitchen. They walked into the kitchen. They were seated at the table. Sarah asked Pam if she wanted coffee. "Yes, please, Sarah, thank you." She told Sarah. "I will get right to it. We are looking into this "agent". It would appear he slipped in, and we didn't vet him properly.

This falls on us, but I will make sure it never happens again. Burke and I had discussed what we needed to do to make sure of that." Jenkins told them. "It cannot, we have to trust all of you," Carol told Jenkins. The others nodded as Carol spoke. "How was Donnie doing?" Carol asked. "Donnie was being Donnie. He was joking and trying to make light of everything. Would you beat him?" Jenkins asked. "Yes, I would, that stubborn man never listens," Carol said with a smile. "I can see he is. But most men are." Jenkins said. "I need to get over to the barn and figure out why this happened to you all. It will be taken care of. We are sending a driver, whom I trust, to take you to the hospital." She told Carol.

Sarah told Jenkins they were all going. This family does things together. "I figured," Jenkins smiled as she said this. She had learned this group was bonded to one another. Jenkins turned and walked over to the barn.

Burke, Frank, Michael, and Charles were getting ready to leave for the hospital. They had things well in hand at the warehouse. The shooters were all loaded into a bus. The Ambulances had the ones who needed attention. Donnie was on his way to the hospital with James. Law enforcement was sweeping the area for anyone else who might have been left unaccounted for. The agents were examining the scene to set up evidence collection.

"I had no idea this would be this big when we started all of this," Burke said to the others. "It just needs to come to an end," Frank said. "I remember what you told Donnie behind the gas station, Burke. You're right; he uses both feet to step into things," Michael said to Burke. "Michael, it was the same the first time. He changed things for himself and all of us. But that is Donnie, he never gives up until he gets everyone involved." Burke told him. "That is the thing about him and what made him such a good cop. I'll let Donnie tell the stories, but he's what all law enforcement needs to be: never takes things at face value and makes sure the victims never get victimized again," Frank told Michael and Charles. "That is Donnie in a nutshell," Burke said.

As they turned to go to the cars, an agent radioed Burke. "You may want to come to their vehicles. We found something," The agent said. Burke looked at Frank, shaking his head in disapproval. "What now?" he said under his breath. "You guys go to the hospital, and I will meet you there," Burke told Frank. "OK, let me know what you find. I need to let Anthony know." Frank told Burke. "I will," Burke said.

Frank, Michael, and Charles left for the hospital, knowing he would be in surgery by the time they arrived. They discussed some of the things Donnie and Frank had done when they were cops together.

"I remember riding with Donnie when we got a call to a house for a noise complaint. When we arrived, we spoke with the neighbor who had called about their neighbor's noise issue. We knocked on the door several times. The homeowner would not answer. We went around the back to try to get the owner's attention. When we flashed a flashlight at her, she froze and left the room where the TV was so loud we could hear it. A couple of minutes later, our dispatcher notified us that the owner was on the phone, saying there were burglars outside her window. The dispatcher tried to tell her the Police were outside. The woman was so hard of hearing that our dispatcher had to shout at her. It took us about 35 minutes to finally get the owner to open the door. When she opened the door, we also had to yell at her to hear us. We explained why we were there and that she needed to turn the TV down." Frank paused for a minute.

Michael and Charles were smiling and giggling a bit. Michael asked Frank what happened. "She filed a complaint against us for scaring her with our flashlights at the department. The Chief called us in and laughed with us about it, telling us to stop scaring 80-year-old ladies," Frank told them. All of them were laughing at that. "Over the next several months, we received calls to that same house for the same issue. The neighbor eventually moved to another house so he and his wife could sleep at night." Frank finished telling them.

After Jenkins talked with the family at the farm, she went to the barn to question the "agent." There was a knock on the door of the farmhouse. All of the women looked at each other. Carol called over to the barn to speak to Jenkins. She and Sarah had their guns in their hands, just in case. When Jenkins answered the phone, Carol asked her why someone was knocking on the door. She told Carol she would send one of her agents over to check. They both forgot that the driver was supposed to pick them up. Carol looked out the window and saw the agent come from the barn. When the agent arrived, he realized it was the driver. He knocked at the door as well. Carol looked out and realized there was an SUV parked out front. Feeling embarrassed, she opened the door and apologized to them. They told her it was okay, they understood. They also asked Carol to please set her gun down. Carol looked down at her hand and placed it on the table by the door. "After everything that had happened over the past few days, I am a bit on edge right now. I am normally not like this." She explained to the agents. They both looked at Carol and the others and told them it was normal.

The women grabbed their few things and went out, climbing into the SUV. The driver asked them what music they wanted to listen to. They told him they preferred none right now. On the ride over, they sat quietly. Stacy fell asleep. Another FBI car followed them as a cover car.

When they arrived at the hospital, the family were told to wait in the car for a minute. The FBI agent exited, followed by the cover car agents. They checked the area and made sure it was safe. One of the cover car agents radioed saying it was clear. The SUV driver returned to the vehicle and told them they could exit, but they chose to stay with the SUV driver. Carol just nodded as they all walked into the hospital.

Several of the staff saw Carol, and a couple walked towards her. One of the agents stepped in between the staff members and Carol. Carol said it was Ok, she knew them. The agent said, "Yes, ma'am," and stepped aside. They informed her that Donnie was in surgery and that the others were already there. Carol hugged them and thanked them. They all went to the elevator, rode it to the third floor, and walked towards the surgery waiting room. The Nurse there also knew Carol. She saw the agents and waited behind the desk. "He is still in surgery, Carol. Frank and the guys are in the waiting room." She told Carol. Carol thanked her and walked towards the waiting room.

Once inside, the couples moved towards each other and hugged. Frank walked over to Carol and told her that Donnie was joking and being his usual self as he went into surgery. He even told the doctor they needed to stop meeting like this. Laughing, the doctor told Donnie he agreed. "Frank, how bad is it?" Carol asked him. "Mom, Dad will be OK. He has to be." Carol turned and hugged James as he approached. James told her his dad had been awake and asking questions as the medic worked on him. He refused the painkiller the medic wanted to give him and asked if he had talked to her again. James looked at his mom; she looked tired and worried. That made him feel she knew something he didn't.

"I need to talk to Julie at the desk and find out if I can see his chart," Carol said to them. An agent started to follow her, but she turned towards him and gave him a look that stopped him in his tracks. James went with her anyway. The Agent followed at a slight distance behind.

Carol and Julie spoke for a couple of minutes. Julie handed Carol Donnie's chart. As she read it, she went back to the second page. It said the bullet had missed his Femoral artery, but there was significant damage to his quad muscles, and the bullet had chipped the bone. Carol shook her head and handed the chart back to Julie. She knew the doctor working on him was the best the hospital had to offer. She looked at James and said, "he will be laid up for a while. He will not be happy about that. It looks like we will have to hire someone to repair the house. I will stay there to ensure your father does what he needs to do." James saw the determined expression on his mom's face. It made him smile. He couldn't help it. She looked at him and asked, "What's funny about this, James?" "Mom, the expression on your face. I've seen that look so many times. One that tells me, don't even ask, do what I told you."

The surgery took several hours. Finally, the doctor emerged from surgery. He looked worn out. He saw Carol walking towards him. "Carol, it took a while to get everything fixed. He will be laid up for a while. But he will recover if he gives himself time, and we all know Donnie." He said to her and James. "Oh, he will give it time," Carol told the doctor. The doctor looked at James. "Are you James?" He asked. "I am, doctor," James responded. The last time I saw you, you were a lot smaller." He said to James. "I get that a lot anymore," James responded. "When will he be able to see us?" Carol asked. "He will be in recovery for a while. The surgery, I am sure, took a lot out of him. Maybe about two or so hours." The doctor responded to her question. "I will be back in a while to check on him. I told the nurses to let me know if anything changes with him." The doctor told them. Turning to leave, he stopped and turned back to Carol, "Donnie will be fine, Carol." Carol nodded and said, "I know he will be."

As Carol and James walked back to the waiting room, Burke turned the corner and walked towards them. "Come into the waiting room, and I will let everyone know what is going on," Carol told him. Once they were in the room, Carol informed them of the doctor's statement. They all just stood there. She turned to Michael and asked him to call their boss; she needed to talk to him. She told him.

After he punched in the number, he handed the phone to Carol. When the boss answered, she told him what was happening with Donnie. He informed her that Michael had already called him and thanked her for the update. He also asked her to tell Donnie he needs to get better. She told him she would. Ending the call, she gave the phone back to Michael. "I need some coffee," Carol said to no one in particular.

James told her he would go and get one for her. Burke looked at James and told him he would send one of the agents to get it. Turning to one of the agents, he instructed him to take everyone's order and get coffee; the FBI would cover the cost. After taking their order, he left to get them the coffee.

Burke turned to the family, asking each of them how they were holding up. Everyone replied that they were okay. They also asked if things were calming down now that everything seemed to be in order. "We are making sure that everyone can go home," Burke told them. He also apologized for the wait. "Frank, can you come outside with me?" Burke asked. Frank nodded and went with Burke.

Once out of the waiting room, Burke said to Frank, "When I got to the vehicles, we found several explosives in one of them. We still haven't discovered what they planned on using them for." "Oh, isn't that lovely?" Frank responded. "Have we taken care of everyone now?" "They," pointing towards the waiting room, "need to be able to get back to some sort of normalcy," Frank said to Burke. "We may need a couple more days to determine that," Burke responded. "Jenkins has agents searching everything she can think of to make sure we can let the family get back to their homes." Burke further said to Frank. "I will have the department look into things," Frank said. He stepped away from Burke and called Anthony about everything that had happened today.

Frank explained everything to Anthony. Anthony said he would order the detectives to drop their cases for now and look into everything. Frank ended the call and told Burke what Anthony had said. "We need to tell them what is going on," Burke told Frank. They headed back to the waiting room.

"Can I get everyone's attention?" Burke began. "Jenkins and law enforcement are checking on any leads we still have about Chronos and if they have assailants still in the area. We believe we have all of them either in a holding facility or the morgue, but we want to confirm this before we say that everything has been taken care of. I know this has been the worst experience for some of you, but you have all been amazing throughout all of this." Burke told them. "Frank, is there anything you want to add?" Burke asked. Frank shook his head, indicating that he didn't. "Carol, do you have any updates on Donnie you want to share?" Carol also shook her head. "Guess I am done too," Burke concluded. Everyone sat in silence. They were all tired. All of them were thinking about the situation, occasionally looking at each other.

The agent returned with the coffee for everyone. They thanked him for getting it. Sitting back down, they fell silent again. Burke turned to the group and asked if anyone wanted a ride back to the farm. They all told him not until they knew Donnie was okay. Carol smiled at them and thanked them. James, sitting next to his mom, took her hand. He knew she was worried about his dad.

The doctor entered the waiting room, surveying the occupants. He turned to Carol and said, "Donnie was asking for you and James. They got up and followed the doctor to Donnie's room. Carol had been concerned about how everything would go with the surgery, but also knew Donnie was strong. When she entered the room, she had a clinical approach to everything she saw. He was still on oxygen and had IVs in both arms, connected to the heart monitoring machine. She asked the doctor about the IV drips. He smiled and said she could read his chart. He knew what she was doing.

Donnie looked at Carol and James as they entered the room. He smiled, but was still a bit groggy from the anesthesia they had given him. His throat hurt, but all he could have for a short time was ice. He opened his hands to take hold of their hands. He looked at both of them, thankful they were there.

James was worried about his dad. Donnie had always seemed bigger than life to James growing up. His hero and his dad. He knew that Donnie worked in a dangerous career, but he always knew he would come home every night. As he grew older, he realized that Donnie was more than just his dad; he was the person James wanted to be like. He had wanted to follow in his footsteps. Seeing him in a hospital bed, the reality of the career James had chosen hit him. He realized that it could be him lying there.

Donnie struggled to talk. But he told them that everything had finally stopped and apologized to them both for getting shot. He told them he would be up and around in no time and that the doctor told him he would need physical therapy. He told them he might get a bit angry from time to time, but he wanted them both to know he didn't want to take it out on them. He looked at James and told him he was proud of him and that he should constantly remember that things are never routine in law enforcement. And to continually watch his six. Then he looked at Carol and told her he was hungry for a burger, fries, and a chocolate shake. Then he smiled and said he loved them.

Carol looked down at Donnie and told him, "Not to worry, I am going to be your nurse while you are recovering." Donnie smiled and said, "Yes, ma'am." James smiled and shook his head, telling them he was still in the room. "Donnie, there is a whole room of people who want to see you," Carol said to him. "Can we wait for a while until the medicine wears off?" Donnie asked. "Take my card and go eat somewhere that has hamburgers, fries, and a shake," Donnie told them. "Burke is here, maybe he will pay for the food for all of us," James told Donnie. "Just tell him what I want to eat, son," Donnie said to James. "OK, Donnie, we will go and get something to eat, and I will tell everyone you want to get some rest. We will find your order somewhere as well." Carol said. "OK, thank you, Hun." He told Carol.

Carol and James hugged Donnie. Carol looked at Donnie's chart and saw that the doctor had to repair his quadriceps muscles, believing the bone would heal with time, making a bone graft unnecessary. She looked at Donnie, smiled, and they left the room, entering the waiting area, where everyone was smiling. "Donnie is doing well, but wants to rest a bit more. He said he wants some food." Carol told them. Burke agreed it was time to eat something. I will cover it. Where do you want to eat?" They all decided on a restaurant and headed there in the SUVs. Burke had called ahead to request a special section they could use, so they could still feel safe and relaxed. The restaurant provided them with a separate banquet room, distinct from the rest of the establishment. When they arrived, the agents ensured that everyone got inside okay.

During dinner, Burke told the group he had never seen a better group of people in the years he had been with the FBI. They are stronger than most people he has met. He told them he knew Donnie appreciated every one of them standing with him, and they are a family. Carol looked at Burke and said, "That includes you, mister." Everyone agreed. Burke smiled and thanked them. But he reminded them every time he was around that something had happened. Carol told him that it was okay. Everyone giggled at that.

When they returned to the hospital, they went to Donnie's room. He was awake and sitting up. Stubborn to the core, Carol thought. At first, the Nurse on duty protested that there were too many, but Carol looked at her, and she said, "Okay." When they were in, James handed his dad the burger, fries, and shake. Donnie took them and ate some fries.

"This group around you reminds me of that time you were dealing with that group of teens," Frank told Donnie. "That was interesting for sure," Donnie said to Frank. They looked at Donnie, waiting to hear the story. Burke had heard bits and pieces, but not all of it. Frank looked at Donnie and said, "They want to hear about everything." "You set me up, Frank," Donnie said. Frank smiled at Donnie.

Frank and I were on patrol when I discovered a group of about 15 teens had broken into a private meeting location. After I radioed Frank, I pulled up about a half block away. The building was a private meeting location, and I knew none of them belonged to the group. I waited for Frank, but before he could arrive, they had started exiting the building. I exited my vehicle and walked towards them. I told them I needed all their names. A couple of the males in the group got mouthy. I turned to them first and told them I needed an identification card. They told me they didn't have one. I asked them their names as Frank was showing up. I got all their names, and Frank stood by, watching the group for me. After they left the area, we checked the property. Other than some trash, they left everything looking OK. We had the dispatcher contact the person of record. They told the dispatcher they would contact the department if they found anything wrong the next day.

"Are you saying we are a bunch of teenage gang bangers, Frank?" Michael asked, laughing. "No, although looking at this group, you could be." Frank quipped back at Michael. They all laughed at that.

"I want to tell all of you how much I appreciate you all. It means a lot to me to have you here." Donnie told them. "And no, it's not the medication talking," he added, looking around the room. "We are family, always will be." He finished. They all smiled at him. Carol said, "Yes, we are all family now. Charles, never upset Stacy; she will hurt you." He looked at Carol and smiled, "I know, she has some skills, she told me what she did, and your reaction." Stacy swiped at Charles.

Donnie looked at Stacy and asked her, "What happened?" "Carol, should I tell them?" Stacy asked. "Go ahead, they will hear about it sooner or later," Carol said.

"Waiting for you guys to come back, the FBI agent, who was not an FBI agent, took me hostage. When Carol and Sarah came back downstairs with their guns, because of the attack on the barn, I dropped him with my Jujitsu. I have a black belt. He wasn't going to hurt the baby. Carol and I handcuffed him, then Carol called Pamela." Stacy told everyone.

There was silence after she finished telling them. Donnie told Stacy she did a great job. Looking at Carol, he asked, "You didn't tell me they attacked the compound, too." "You had other things going on. The shooters were taken care of. Stacy took care of the fake FBI agent, and all was good." Carol told Donnie. James piped in and said, "I knew, but wanted to wait to tell you, until after the surgery, because we all know what you would have tried to do." Everyone agreed it would be better if Donnie were to find out after the surgery.

Donnie looked at Burke. In a lowered voice, asking him, "How did that happen? I thought everyone on that detail was vetted." "Donnie, he was, he checked out," Burke told him. "What about those agents out in the hall? Are they vetted?" Donnie asked, his tone laced with anger. "Donnie, we handled it," Carol told him. It will be Ok; we are safe." Carol told him. "I need you to calm down because of the surgery." He looked at Carol, "This family needs to be safe." Donnie said. "We are honey, I promise," Carol told him. She reached over and put her hand on his shoulder.

21

The Promise of the Badge

Burke told them Donnie needed some rest; they should go back to the farm. He had the SUVs out by the entrance. We could all use some rest, he told them. "I'm staying here with Donnie," Carol told Burke. "I figured you would," Burke said. I'll leave two agents that I trust here with you. "Carol, you know the staff here. If there's someone you're concerned about, let them know; they'll check on them." "I will, Burke," Carol said.

As they filed out, they all told Donnie they were glad he would be back to normal soon. "I am going to stay too," James said. "Son, you need to get some sleep; we will be okay," Carol told him. He decided he should do what she told him. He left with the rest.

When they were alone, Donnie looked at Carol. He had always thought she was a strong woman, but he was seeing a different side of her. He watched her pull the chair closer to him, and he smiled at her as she sat down. "What are you smiling at?" She asked him. He told her he was happy she stayed behind. She smiled back at him. He reached out his hand to her, and they sat there holding hands with smiles on their faces. They let the quiet encircle them. It was finally peaceful. Donnie drifted off to sleep. Carol sat and admired him. Even when he was so beat up, he still wanted to take care of everyone.

She thought back to the day they met. It seemed to her their life had revolved around the hospital. As she was the one wanting them to be together, she thought about that night she had walked away from him. She realized she had allowed her fear to overpower her love for him. But now with him lying in this bed, she wanted to make up for lost time. She sat and watched him sleep.

The rest of the family arrived at the farm. They filed into the house; they sat down for a while. James thought of his dad, his hero, who was hurting and wanted to be there to help him. Then he realized that repairs were needed on the house. He looked at Frank and said, "I need to fix the damage on the house before Dad gets released from the hospital. Windows are broken, and the bullet holes need to be repaired." "James, I am one step ahead of you. I called a contractor friend of mine; he has already been working on the house. He is close to being done. He also installed cameras around the house; all you need to do is upload the signal to the laptop in the house. I know you will add the program to your phone." Frank told James. "Thank you, Uncle Frank. I know that will mean a lot to my parents. Frank just nodded and smiled.

Jenkins called Burke and told him she had information about the fake agent she needed to share. He told her she could come over and talk to everyone. She agreed and walked to the farmhouse. When she came in, she walked to the living room. As she walked, she began. "After a bit more digging, we discovered he is a Canadian national with ties to Chronos. He was recruited by Andropalos and paid a large sum of money to kill the three ladies. He never expected you, Stacy."

"Pam, how did we not catch that before?" Burke asked her. "Somehow, he obtained some deep-cover papers. We have done the same thing." Pam responded. "I notified Interpol, and they are looking into his known associates. We are doing the same thing." She told the group. "This needs to be done quickly," Burke said. "We have identified four subjects so far. The

RCMP are picking them up." She told Burke. "Good, they are working with us on this at least," Burke said. Jenkins nodded yes.

There was silence amongst the family. They were all so tired of this, and they wanted it to end. It seemed it may never end for Sarah, but she also knew no matter what, she would stand by Michael. Stacy looked at Charles and took his hand in hers, telling him it would soon be over. He nodded at her. Frank looked around at everyone and said, "There is nothing we can do for now; we should all try to get some sleep." Like preteens, they started moving to their rooms. James stood up and moved towards Jenkins, putting his hand on her shoulder, he thanked her for all of her hard work in keeping the family safe. Jenkins smiled at him and said she was doing her job.

When the family left the room, Burke, Frank, and Jenkins looked at each other. Burke asked her whether she thought more would be found. She told Burke it seemed like the 5 of them had made a pact to become part of Chronos. But there was no longer a Chronos. It ended with the arrests.

"Nothing about this situation has been normal, so we shall see," Burke said. Frank and Jenkins agreed. "Pamela, you should get some sleep yourself. There is another bedroom on this floor." Burke told her. She told him she would take him up on that. "It's back there," pointing to the other end of the first floor. She walked that way, and they heard the door shut behind her. "Will this ever end?" Burke said. "It has to; they need to get back to something normal," Frank said. "I spoke with my higher-ups, and because Interpol got involved with this case, I have been instructed to monitor the family for the next two years," Burke told Frank. "You need to let Donnie know. If he finds out another way, he will not like it," Frank told Burke. "Yeah, I am just figuring out how to tell him," Burke responded. They looked at each other and knew it would not be an easy conversation.

22

The Justice of the Badge

After napping, they met again in the kitchen. They were pouring coffee when James received a phone call. They all looked at him as he answered. It was Carol who told him to let everyone know that Donnie was undergoing physical therapy at the moment, yelling at the guy for making him start to stretch. James laughed and told everyone. They laughed, and Frank asked if Donnie had threatened the poor guy. James asked Carol, laughing, she told him it had only happened six times in twenty minutes. James told Frank, and everyone laughed again. Michael commented, "That guy is braver than I am." Carol said she needed to get going, but she wanted to let everyone know how much fun she was having. When the call ended, people were still laughing at the idea of Donnie starting the physical therapy, and a couple said they knew why a male was called in to do it.

About that time, Frank's phone rang. It was Anthony, and he told Frank that Donnie's boss, David, had been shot. It seemed like a random attack, but they were looking into it, and there were no other leads. "Ok, I will tell everyone," Frank responded. Anthony told Frank he would tell Donnie himself. Ending the call, he looked up, and everyone was staring at him. He told them what Anthony said. There was silence in the room. Michael and Charles looked at each other. Everyone looked around, speechless.

When law enforcement arrived at David's house, they found three males outside, deceased. They called for backup and waited for them to arrive. When the other four units arrived, they approached the house. Searching through the house, they found Susan locked in a bedroom, crying. Susan told them there had been shots coming from outside the house about fifteen minutes ago. David told her to lock herself in the bedroom. She said she then heard shouting coming from the living room and then several shots. Then there was silence, but she was too scared to come out. The law enforcement officers talking to Susan heard the other officers over their earpieces that they had a male subject with multiple gunshot wounds on the living room floor, who appeared to be deceased. There was no pulse, but medical personnel were dispatched to the scene.

When medical personnel arrived, they confirmed that David was deceased. They called for the coroner to remove him for an autopsy. The other medical crews were with the three males in the yard. They confirmed that all three were deceased. However, they noticed a difference with the males. Two were dressed differently. They stopped and covered each other. They notified law enforcement and then called the FBI. They had been advised to do so after everything involving Donnie and the family. The law enforcement officers guarded the three until the FBI arrived. Burke received that call and sent agents immediately. He also notified the agents, including Donnie and Carol, to watch closely for anyone trying to approach them. Updated them on the situation and instructed them not to mention David to anyone. They responded that they understood.

Law enforcement was present in the house with Susan. She was shaken by everything and finally able to speak to them in more detail. She gave them some idea of what they may have looked like. All appeared to be WMAs dressed in black and looked like they had military or police training. She told them she heard them speaking a different language. They took her statement and asked her if she knew where the cameras were relayed to. She told them she didn't. Susan was told detectives would want to speak to her when they arrived.

Burke sent Jenkins to the shooting scene. She called, telling him one of the shooters was killed and that he was a foreign national. She took his photo and sent it in. They got an almost instant match. He was identified as a Greek national, affiliated with Chronos, and a member of a hit squad. They had at least nine confirmed kills according to Interpol. There were four other subjects associated with the one they found. She said she saw the computer with the recorded video on it and was bringing it back to confirm their identities. "They need to find them before something else happens," Frank told Burke.

While they were talking, Anthony was on his way to see Donnie. He knew the news of David's death would hit Donnie hard, as the two had been working together for over 12 years and had become friends. Donnie had transformed David's company within two years, helping the employees and growing it into what it was now. Few privately owned security companies have gained the respect of local and state law enforcement like Donnie had fostered between the company and law enforcement. He worked hard to transform the company's dynamic into one that others have tried to emulate to compete. Always doing what he needs to do to show the employees how a leader should lead.

Anthony arrived at the hospital, where he sat in his car before heading to the door. He entered the hospital; he saw a couple of FBI agents in the lobby. They're easy to spot; the earpieces give them away. He was thankful that the agency was still around; the family deserved protection, especially after what had happened today.

Entering the elevator, Anthony wondered how Donnie would take the news. He needed to heal, and this might set that back some. The doors opened, and he stepped out, heading to the room. As he turned the corner, one of the FBI agents approached him. He had his law enforcement badge ready to show them. Frank had briefed him on the details. The agent looked at the badge but also asked for a photo ID. Anthony told the agent he needed to reach into his coat pocket. The agent told him to retrieve it. Anthony presented it to the agent, who checked it, then handed it back to Anthony and said, "Thank you, Deputy Chief, the room is down the hall to the right." Anthony thanked him. He told the agent it was essential to make sure Donnie and Carol were kept safe.

As Anthony entered the room, Donnie and Carol were talking. Donnie looked up and greeted Anthony with, "Well, look who's here." "Hey, Donnie. Carol, it's good to see you. This is a two-fold visit, Donnie," Anthony said, approaching them. Donnie looked at Anthony and then at Carol. Carol reached and grabbed Donnie's hand, squeezing it.

"That doesn't sound good. What happened?" Donnie asked. He studied Anthony's face. He looked stressed. Donnie waited to hear the news that was about to be delivered. "Donnie, there was an attack at David's house about 2 hours ago. There was a hit squad sent to kill him. He was shot and died from the wounds he sustained." Carol said, "Oh no. How is Susan?" Susan is Okay. She was locked inside one of the bedrooms and hid from them, Anthony stated." "At least she is OK," Carol said. "Donnie, I'm sorry, I know David was more than your boss; he was also your friend." Donnie had gone into his clinical mode. He wanted answers. He asked Anthony, "Are there still suspects at large? Do I need to worry about the family? Is Carol safe here with me, or should she go to the farm?" Donnie paused for Anthony to respond before he continued with the questions. Anthony let him speak, and he had known Donnie for a long time. "There are four more suspects, the FBI has leads, and there was a video of them that they are looking at to confirm their identities. The farm is locked down. There are at least 12 agents here, and Burke is sending 10 more. The agents already have photos of the other four, but this feels more like he was targeted specifically for some reason."

Anthony looked at both of them as he finished. Donnie sat for a minute. "Are they linked to any group?" Donnie asked. "They are Chronos. At least the one that was shot was confirmed to be, through facial recognition." Anthony told him. Speaking more to himself, Donnie asked, "Is this ever going to end?" "Agent Jenkins has some of the best computer operators I have ever heard of working on it. She contacted Interpol about the other four. They are working on it too. The one that was shot was confirmed to be a Greek national, the same as Andropolis. Interpol has him in custody, and I was told they are pressing him for the names." Anthony responded.

Donnie looked at Carol. "Sweetheart, I'm sorry I dragged you and James into this mess, not to mention everyone else." "You have always done your job. You were doing your job when you were a cop and busted that guy, and you were doing your job when you and Michael stopped those guys in the storage unit. I have never blamed you for doing your job. I won't start now." Carol told him, and he raised his hand to her mouth, kissing it. "We will get through this together," Carol added. Donnie smiled, his mind racing and getting agitated because he wanted to be out hunting them. "Donnie, this time you need to let us deal with them," Anthony told him.

Anthony's phone rang. He answered it. It was Frank. Anthony told him to hold on. Anthony pushed the speaker on his phone and told Frank to continue. "They have been identified; I asked Jenkins to forward it to our dispatch center to distribute to all the officers. Four SUVs left the farm a brief time ago to inspect a house associated with them. They're not getting away. We will have them soon." Frank told them. "You and Burke better get them sooner rather than later," Donnie told him.

"I need to contact Dispatch to make sure they received the photos and are sending them to our officers," Frank told Anthony. "OK, Frank, keep Donnie informed. I will go back to the station to follow up and send updates. "Donnie, everyone is hunting these assailants down. We will not stop until we have them in custody or the morgue." Anthony said. "Anthony,

I want them alive so they can stand trial. David deserves that." Donnie stated. "I understand, Donnie; I'd better get going. This was something I knew you needed to hear in person and not over the phone." Anthony said. "Thank you, Anthony. It means a lot," Donnie stated. As Anthony was leaving, Carol approached him to thank him for coming in person. "He and David were two peas in a pod. Thought the same about the people they employed and served." Anthony said he had good memories of David. He told her, "I hope the business can stay open. Once the dust settles and they lay David to rest, there are still 51 families to think about." Carol looked at Anthony and thanked him again.

Walking back to Donnie, she noticed him staring at his hands. He was deep in thought. "You OK?" she asked. "We have to figure out how to keep everyone employed. I am stuck in this bed; I need to be in the office to figure this out. We have enough for payroll. If the probate attorney allows it, I can sign for the direct deposits. Without David, the company could close. I could apply for a loan to buy it, but everything has to wait until probate is completed. That could take up to six months. Having to listen to some attorney, second-guessing every penny being spent." Donnie sounded frustrated. Carol understood, and she smiled at him. "We will get through this. I can go and get what's needed from the office if Susan knows where to look." She giggled, "She has been running the business for years." Donnie looked at her and agreed. "I'll call Susan," Donnie said. "No, give me your phone, I will call her, you need to gather your thoughts," Carol told him. "And we need his laptop. He kept everything on it." Donnie said. Carol reached over and kissed his forehead. Donnie looked at her as she pulled away. He drew her towards him and kissed her lips. It was a quick kiss, and he was afraid she would smack him. She pulled away, looked at him, smiled, and leaned in to kiss him. As they were kissing, there was a knock at the door; the nurse came in. Carol sat next to Donnie on his bed. The nurse just smiled and apologized for interrupting them. They all laughed at that.

James called his mom to ask how his dad was doing. He is getting better every minute. She smiled at Donnie. “Here, let me put you on speaker,” she told James. “Go ahead, James, your dad can hear you, too.” She held the phone towards Donnie. “Dad, I asked how you were doing,” James said. “Like your mom said, getting better every minute. How are things at the farm, son?” Donnie asked. “Getting better; we're doing well. Uncle Frank, Burke, and Pamela are making sure of it. I feel like I am being babysat.” James told them. They laughed. “Well, deal with it until everything is cleared up.” Carol quipped. “Yes, ma’am,” James responded, trying to sound like a kid. That made Carol and Donnie giggle and look at each other.

“I wanted to check in on you since it takes a military maneuver to go anywhere right now,” James said. “James, this is what we need to do to keep everyone safe. I thought we had everything under control until I heard about David. I don’t like it either, but we need to follow Burke and Frank's instructions until we get the okay. It is like being in combat, waiting for the shelling to stop. It’s one thing to deal with local gang bangers; it’s another thing to deal with what we are.” Donnie told James.

“That makes sense. I know you have dealt with both. I was venting,” James said. “I know it isn’t easy, but it is for the best now. There has been enough violence pointed at us. I hope it stops soon so we can get the house repaired and move back in. I need to heal, and it seems like the nurse isn’t going to take no for an answer.” He laughed at the last part, looked at Carol, who looked right at him, and said, “You have that correct, sir!” That made them all laugh. “OK, Dad, I get it,” James told Donnie. “Son, the nurse just came in. I need to go. I'll call you later and check in,” Donnie told him. “Ok, we’ll talk more then,” James said. They all said goodbye, ending the call.

The Nurse told Donnie that she had never seen as much determination in her patients as she saw in him. She then turned to Carol and told her she may need to hold him back a bit. "You don't know that man; holding back will be impossible. I have tried that before, but it never worked. He has a stubborn streak miles long." Carol told the nurse, grinning at Donnie. "I am not that bad, Hun." Donnie defended himself. "Worse, actually, mister." Carol laughed as she said it, causing Donnie to join in the laughter. The nurse just smiled. Finished up what she was doing. She turned to them and said, "Sounds like you two have some fun times together. I love hearing couples joke about their great relationship, just like you do. I will be back in a couple of hours to check on you after you eat. Carol, I told the staff to bring you a tray of food too." She turned, exiting the room.

Burke and Frank were talking with Jenkins when James entered the room. They turned towards him and stopped talking. "Sorry to interrupt, I can leave if you need privacy," James told them. "It's ok, James; we were just talking about everything that happened today. I received a call from David's corporate attorney seeking your dad. He told me he needs to speak to him about something." Frank said. "We're deciding on when it would be safe to let you all get home again," Frank added. "I was talking to my parents about that on the phone. They said we need to stay here until you decide. I know everyone wants to get home, and I'm sure that includes you." James said, looking at them. "You are your parents' kid, James; you sound like your dad more and more," Burke said. James smiled, "That apple didn't fall far from the tree. Thank you for saying that, Burke." James stated.

Jenkins looked at James; she realized the same thing had occurred to her. During this situation, James stood his ground, defended his family, and never gave up. He was going to be an outstanding police officer. She thought he would make a great FBI agent because he has a lot of talent.

Agent Pamela Jenkins, in her mid-30s, had to fight for her spot. The FBI was still a male-dominated agency. But she had proven herself time and again. Finally, she was assigned to Burke's team. She was promoted because Burke saw in her what she now sees in James. She owed Burke, but she also knew he didn't make promotion recommendations for anyone without first proving to him that they could manage it.

"Uncle Frank, any word of the other four assailants?" Frank turned to Jenkins and asked her to tell him what she found. "The four are still in town. They are in a rundown house on the Northside of town. We have agents and Law Enforcement in the area watching them. We are working on a way to arrest all four of them. Your dad said he preferred that. With that in mind, we're working to honor his wishes if we can. But from what we have learned from our background investigation and what Interpol has told us, this group will fight and die if they get cornered." Jenkins looked at James as she spoke, trying to gauge his thoughts. "What do you think we should do, James?"

The question caught James off guard a bit. Looking at them, he said, "I know my dad thinks David deserves justice, but after everything we have all been through, it's time to end this and let everyone return to a somewhat normal life. I know some here will never live as they did before. We have learned to be more guarded and less trusting. But if it were up to me, I would move forward with the plan to take them all alive, while also being prepared to handle the situation as it dictates. Just my opinion." James concluded.

The three looked at each other and then back at James. "It is as if you were listening to our conversation," Jenkins said. We all agreed we need to act and not let them get away with it. All this needs to come to an end." Jenkins told James. "I will let you get back to planning." Turning to leave, Jenkins said, "Thank you for the honesty." James turned around, smiled, and continued out of the room.

After James left, they continued to plan for the assault on the house. They agreed it should be tonight, after dark. They had photos of the house and knew there were two doors. Looking at the pictures, they determined that seven windows needed to be covered. They planned who would make the assault, and they agreed that the FBI should. Local Law enforcement is covering the windows and doors. Not knowing what to expect, they decided flash bombs would be best after breaching the doors. Jenkins suggested tear gas also. They agreed. Jenkins told them she had handpicked the team. She said she would have spotters around to make sure no one slipped by. Burke told her he trusted her judgment and let them get some sleep. Frank said he would call Anthony and advise him of the plan.

Once the planning was completed, they sat back, silent for a while. It had been a rough one this time. Burke, deep in thought, fell asleep. Frank smiled, realizing he was tired, and soon he fell asleep.

They awoke to the sound of their phones going off. Answering his, Burke heard Jenkins say they were ready to leave. Frank answered, and Anthony told him to stay at the farm to keep the family safe, as he would be on the scene for the assault. Anthony and Jenkins were in constant contact throughout the day, coordinating all activities. The last thing anyone wanted was to alert the assailants of the planned assault.

Burke told Jenkins he would observe, leaving Frank at the farm to be with the family. Frank, feeling a bit left out, agreed begrudgingly. He knew the family needed to be protected. This should be the last time they need to feel the fear of being killed. Burke told Frank to be on alert. Frank told Burke not to get hurt. They laughed, shook hands, and Burke left with the assault team.

Frank heard James and Michael in the kitchen. Realizing he was hungry, he joined them. As he entered, James handed him a cup of coffee. Thanking James, he took a sip. "Are the others awake?" He asked. "I'm not sure. Do you need them?" Michael said. "I need to talk with them about what is about to happen." He told Michael. James and Michael looked at each other and headed up to wake them up. Frank, standing in the kitchen, sipped on the coffee.

Once everyone was downstairs, they headed to the living room to hear what Frank had to say. "In approximately 90 minutes, the FBI will be entering the house where the other four assailants are. We plan on taking them alive, but they aren't known for giving up easily. Jenkins is in the barn, monitoring the situation, advising us as she can. Law enforcement will assist them with the breach of the residence. We want to take them into custody. Again, they're known not to want to be taken into custody and will fight." Frank told everyone.

While Frank was talking, the FBI and law enforcement were preparing for the breach. They knew, as they prepared, that the suspects were known to fight and not allow themselves to be taken into custody. As they mounted their body cams, they knew Jenkins was covering them. They had the house layout and had prepared everything except the suspect's response. They knew the suspects were trained and heavily armed. The flash bombs will stun them; they will use tear gas to affect their eyes.

The eight agents were trained to respond within 15 minutes of the breach. Quickly restrain and then remove. They had completed twenty-five assignments as a team over the past three years. They know what they are doing and can read each other without words. Trained to the level of experts, yet they always know something can and will eventually go wrong. This might be the one time. As they prepared, each member checked their communications. Checking in with Agent Jenkins as they did. They are ready for whatever they encounter inside.

The team leader, Travis Jacobs, is a ten-year veteran of the FBI counter-terrorist units, with a military background. Jacobs was always the first to arrive and the last to leave on all operations. He knew his team well. Knew their families and took great care of them on their way home. He remembers one time when he had to tell a family that their son was not coming home. He remained stoic throughout the notification. Later, he broke down. From that day, Jacobs vowed never to have to do that again.

Jacobs looked at his teammates, and he remembered the beginning of bringing them together. He sat down with each one, making the team one he knew he could trust. They were hand-picked, including the two female members, Jessica Hernandez and Cheryl Jackson. Both members graduated first in their respective training classes. Hernandez had been with the FBI for 6 years, serving on the team for 4 of those. Jackson, two years after Hernandez had been picked for the team. Both were tough and capable of doing the job. He knew he could trust them never to give up. Jacobs, whose radio call sign was Lincoln 1, admired them all. They were dedicated to their work and were willing to go above and beyond. Hernandez led the second squad into eight breaches so far. Jackson was his second in, right behind him.

Jacobs met Donnie once and quickly realized they were a lot alike. They took care of their team members, always trying to avoid letting anyone down. They were both blunt and to the point. They both believed in leading from the front. If someone took a hit, it should be them. Neither thought they were better than the team, but they knew they were responsible for the team.

As the team was suiting up, Jacobs went to each member to make sure everything was set correctly. He spoke with each one, verifying they were in the right space to do their job and not distracted by anything. Afterward, he went off by himself, running the plan through his mind, ensuring it was ingrained entirely so nothing went wrong.

Jenkins keyed her comm and told the team they had 15 minutes to breach. Told them to watch their six and get home safe. The members acknowledged her transmission. Jacobs called the team together and reviewed the planned breach in detail. He made sure they were ready. They walked the block to the residence; he wanted them ready. They started their walk to the house. There was silence between them, each one prepared to do what they needed to do to accomplish the task at hand.

They split up, four going to the back and four to the front. Their weapons were up and pointed at the house, always ready for what may come. Jacobs and his unit went to the front, while Hernandez and her unit went to the back. "Lincoln 5, advise when in place," Jenkins radioed. "Copy," Hernandez responded. As they approached, Jenkins radioed the spotters she had placed to cover Jacobs' people, clearing the four sides as the team came. All clear, they continued forward. The front had a raised porch with four steps up to it. The house had a basement with egress windows on two sides.

Hernandez approached the back door, taking in the three steps leading up to it, which were a tight fit, but she knew there would be enough room to swing the breaching hammer and let all four in. Once in place, she keyed her comms. Lincoln 5 in place, came over the radio. "Copy, Lincoln 1 in place," Jacobs responded. Jenkins advised, "Clear to breach."

Both team leaders nodded, and the member with the breach hammer swung back, hitting the door in front of them and busting it open on impact. Lincoln 1 and two others tossed a flash bomb into their door, followed by a tear gas canister.

The teams entered, with two members to the left and two to the right. Hand signals were now being used. The sweep of the residence was done step by step. Looking around and listening for noise, voices, or anything that might indicate where the suspects are.

As Hernandez entered the door, she heard a door slam to her right. She signaled the two agents, Lincoln 7 and 8, on the right by touching her ear and pointing down the hall. They nodded and moved in that direction. Setting up on both sides of the door, listening and waiting before entering. Lincoln 7 had a flash bomb ready. Lincoln 8 tried the doorknob, as he did, a shot penetrated the door and lodged in the hallway wall. They knew at least one suspect was inside. As he turned the knob and pushed the door open, another shot was fired. Lincoln 7 tossed the flash bomb in, pausing until the flash exploded. As they entered, a male stood there, a rifle pointed at them. They fired, striking him, and he fell. The agents looked around the room, finding no one else, and cautiously approached the suspect. They removed the weapon and checked for booby traps, but found nothing. He was deceased. They still secured his hands and moved back to the door. One suspect down, Lincoln 7 reported over the radio. Looking to the left and right, they entered the hall again. They saw another door as they approached the first door. Setting up left and right, Lincoln 8 tried the knob. It was locked. Pulling a tool from his belt, he pried the door open. Lincoln 7 peered in. There were three females in the room, tied up and appearing to have been beaten. He radioed, Lincoln 1, three hostages found. "Copy, secure them". Lincoln 5 continues on the sweep for the suspects." "Copy Lincoln 1," Hernandez continued in the section of the house where she and her second, Lincoln 6, was back and to her right. He heard a noise coming from behind a door to his left. He stopped, and Hernandez saw it, stopping where she was. Lincoln 6 put his hand to his ear and pointed at the door. She moved to the door, just to the right of it, and he moved to the left. They paused, hearing what sounded like a shotgun being racked. Six reached for the doorknob as Hernandez grabbed a flash bomb. Waiting for him to turn the knob and push the door open. As he turned the knob, there was a shot, and the center of the door exploded outward; some of the splinters struck six in his vest, lodging there. He pushed the door open, and Hernandez tossed the flash bomb into the room. Shielding themselves as it went off, Hernandez entered first with six right behind. She went left; he went right as another blast from the shotgun tore into the wall above her head. She fired at the suspect, striking him in the chest. He yelled and fell to the floor. Six moved closer towards the suspect, Hernandez right beside. The room's window was open, so the blast had been weakened. There was no one else in the room. They moved the shotgun and zip-tied the suspect. She keyed her comm, saying, "One down, deceased and secured."

Travis's team had not yet entered the hallway on his side of the house, as they had to clear several closets, and the room was full of garbage, making it an easy hiding place. As they turned into the hallway, Travis noticed someone standing at the end of it. "Cover, subject at the end of the hall." He yelled to the team. As Lincoln 3 was moving towards cover, a shot rang out, and the bullet struck him. He fell with a thud. Travis spun out into the hallway, firing at the shooter, striking him in the head. He fell back against the wall and slumped to the ground. Lincoln 4 moved to Lincoln 3 and checked him. He had been shot just to the side of his body armor in the side of his chest. Lincoln 4 moved him and radioed one down, chest hit. Travis looked back, signaling Lincoln 4 to stay with him. He advised Hernandez and her second to move towards his position. As she responded, he and Jackson moved up the hallway, facing each other. They approached a door on Jackson's side of the hallway.

While they were moving up the hall, Jenkins, seeing the wound in her feed, had medical ready to move in when it was all clear. She advised them that there were other victims and that they needed additional medical crews.

Travis moved to the left of the door as Jackson stayed where she was. He tried the doorknob. As he slowly turned the knob, he heard movement inside. Jackson had her flash bomb ready as he opened the door, and she tossed it in. They waited for the explosion, then entered the room. Travis, on the left, and Jackson, on the right, saw a figure near the window. He raised his gun and fired, just as two bullets struck his chest. He fell to the floor, and Travis and Cheryl Jackson approached him. He looked at Jackson and smiled. It was as if he wanted to die. Travis told him he was the last and that Chronos was gone. He looked at Travis and mumbled something as he passed. They removed the gun from his hand and secured his hands.

There was another door further down the hallway. Travis and Jackson moved towards that door as Hernandez and Lincoln 6 arrived. Jackson was on the left this time and tried the door. As she turned the knob and opened it, Travis entered the room, with Jackson right behind. They found a female in the room; she was tied to the bed and appeared to have cuts on her legs, abdomen, and face. As they searched the room, she tried to scream, but her mouth was gagged. Finding no one else, they approached her. Jackson removed the gag, and the woman started thanking them.

Travis advised Hernandez that they were clear. He told her to check out the basement. "Copy Lincoln one." She and Lincoln 6 moved the kitchen and slowly opened the basement door. Making their way down the staircase, they saw crates and stacks of boxes. They searched the basement, and they found no one. Hernandez advised that they were clear.

Travis radioed to Jenkins, "Bravo one, Lincoln one." "Lincoln one," Jenkins responded. "Bravo one, the building's secure, four suspects are down, need medical to respond immediately, one officer down with a gunshot," Travis advised Jenkins. "The medical crews are a block away, advising them to proceed in," Jenkins advised him. "Copy Bravo one." Travis continued, "We also need support for the four captives located within the building; all need medical care." "Copy Lincoln one, sending additional services to your 10-20. Is there more required at the scene?" Jenkins requested. "Affirmative, we have located items in the basement and need assistance retrieving them. There is a large quantity of weapons and ammo." Travis told Jenkins. "Copy Lincoln one, additional personnel will be sent to your location," Jenkins advised him. "Copy Bravo one, we will secure the property until cleared." He stated to Jenkins.

Travis stepped outside, waiting for the ambulance for Lincoln 4; Lincoln 3 was still with him. Travis heard the siren and then saw the lights. Lincoln units, the first ambulance is arriving, get ready for transport by the medical team." Travis spoke to his team. "Copy Lincoln one," was heard over the comms.

Travis spoke to his team, "Be advised, additional resources will arrive to help the hostages. Maintain cover for them to reassure them we have help arriving soon." "Copy Lincoln one," Hernandez said. "Copy Lincoln one," Jackson said.

In the distance, Travis heard three more ambulance sirens. The other FBI agents had moved in, covering the area to protect the outside. The local law enforcement officers are working crowd control, keeping the neighbors away. The local news media were beginning to swarm the area. They had been placed in a controlled area to prevent them from entering.

Travis looked around; it had been a night he'd remember for a long time. He knew Lincoln 4 would recover, but he was angry that he had been shot. Travis tried to remember that the suspects were known not to give up. Still, he had tried to keep everyone safe, despite the danger of what they did for the FBI.

The first ambulance team was bringing a gurney up the sidewalk to take their team member to the hospital. He hoped the family was worth the risk his team took with their lives. "Bravo one, Lincoln one." "Lincoln one." She responded. "Bravo one, we could use some water and food. Can we get something?" Travis told Jenkins. "Lincoln one, speak to the officers on site, they will take care of everything." "10-4 Bravo one, thank you." He spoke.

Jenkins had one of her people contact Frank and ask him to come to the barn. When Frank arrived, she told him the four suspects had been neutralized and one of the team members was shot, but was en route to the hospital. They looked at the fake Agent. Frank asked Jenkins to clear the room. She complied.

They walked towards the prisoner and told him he had five minutes to say whether others were coming. They stood there waiting. He looked at them as Jenkins unlocked the door to his cell. He told them there weren't any more. Frank told him, "If you are lying, you won't make it to trial, I promise." He looked at Jenkins as if he were waiting for her to tell him he couldn't do that. Jenkins told him, "You'd better rethink your answer." "I swear, I don't know of any others coming for them." "We can always have the woman who took you down, some hired idiots attacked her husband. She has a reason to make sure you're telling the truth." Frank told him. "I'm telling the truth!" he yelled at them, asking them not to let her near him. Jenkins relocked the cell.

They looked at each other, and Frank said to the fake agent, "It better be true, you're expendable. If anyone else comes after the family, I will hold you personally accountable." "I understand, please believe I'm telling the truth." He pleaded with them. Frank and Jenkins looked at each other and then at the fake agent. "You'd better hope you are telling us the truth. I will be waiting and watching. If anything happens to any of them, I will know where to find you. Rumors in any prison can be hazardous to one's health." Frank told him.

As he and Jenkins turned to walk away, they glanced back, and Jenkins smiled as she watched the Fake agent start pacing the enclosure where it was being held.

23

The Legacy of the Badge

After the ambulance team had stabilized Lincoln 3 and moved him, they placed him in the ambulance for transport. Lincoln 4 asked permission to ride with him. Travis okayed him to go. They started for the hospital. As they were pulling away, the first of the three other ambulances arrived, and as the crew exited, Travis led them to the woman they had found on the bed. They had covered her to help her understand that they were there to assist her slowly. She had some water, and Jackson had stayed with her.

Jackson had found out the woman's name. She advised Jenkins of her name, and she was a missing person from another area. She told Jenkins she had been attacked by the suspects about 4 weeks ago and brought there with three other women to be abused by the suspects. She hoped they were still OK. Jackson told her they had found them, and now they would all be safe. She said her name was Tracy. Jackson passed that info on to Jenkins, who confirmed her name.

As the Medics were about to remove Tracy, she grabbed Jackson's arm. She expressed her gratitude to them for their help. Jackson told her she was glad she could. Moving Tracy out of the house, the Medic's made sure they protected her from the onlookers. Entering the ambulance, they got her secured and left for the hospital.

The other women were then moved from the closet to the kitchen area, given water, and Hernandez asked their names. No one was sure how they would react to the male members. After getting their names, they were all confirmed as reported missing. She had them stay in the kitchen because the four suspects were still in the other rooms of the house. There was also blood from Lincoln 3 in the living room. Hernandez asked Travis if it would be better for the medics to come to the back door. He agreed it would be better for the three female hostages.

As the other two ambulances arrived, Travis had them go to the back door of the residence. As the medics entered the kitchen, Hernandez reassured the female hostages that it was OK. They had been beaten and were dehydrated. The medics ensured the females were okay with them before they had them walk to the gurneys. Everyone agreed they had been traumatized enough already. They looked to Hernandez for assurance. She told them she would check on them later at the hospital.

Once the hostages were taken to the hospital, Travis advised Jenkins. "Bravo 1 Lincoln 1." He spoke over his comms. "Lincoln 1, go ahead," Jenkins responded. "Bravo 1, we can have the other vehicles come in now to remove the suspects," Travis told Jenkins. "Lincoln 1, copy, sending them your way," Jenkins advised. "10-4," Travis responded.

Within a few minutes, the vans arrived to remove the suspects, moving them to the morgue. Travis met them at the door with the body bags. He showed them where the suspects were. They placed each one in a bag and carried it out of the house. Finally, the basement can be cleared. "Bravo 1, Lincoln 1," Travis called Jenkins. "Go ahead," Jenkins responded. "We are ready for the basement clearing now." He told Jenkins." "Lincoln 1, I will advise the clean-up crew and have them proceed to your 10-20," Jenkins responded. Burke had made his way to the house. He was standing with Travis as he directed the process of clearing the house after the breach. "I am impressed by your process for the removal of the people and the items.

I need to have you teach other teams." Burke told Travis. "Thank you, sir, it works best for me and the team," Travis responded. "I heard you had a team member shot, sorry to hear that," Burke told him. "He will recover, and we will be back to full strength soon enough. It is time we go on our downtime after this." Travis said.

Travis looked at Burke. He looked tired. "How is Donnie doing?" Travis asked. "He will recover. The physical therapist will have the worst part of everything." Burke responded. "I heard about everything he and the family have done since this all began. They sound similar to a Sert team." Travis said with a smile. "They almost are," Burke responded. Jackson stepped out on the porch with them. Burke told her hello. She said hello. "I need some air. After we clear here, I am going to see Tracy later to check on her." Jackson told Travis. He told her he thought that would be a good idea. "Have you found anything that will help find out why they decided to fight or who paid them?" Travis asked Jackson. "This place is bare bones. Not much of anything here. We went into the basement, and they were ready for a war. Rifles and Pistols, more ammo than I have seen since the academy, smoke bombs, grenades, even a couple of rocket launchers." Jackson told them. Burke and Travis looked at Jackson, shaking their heads in disbelief.

"Lincoln 1, Lincoln 5." Hernandez radioed Travis. "Go ahead," Travis responded. "The three I have will be moving in a couple of minutes," Hernandez advised. "10-4, Lincoln 5," Travis replied. "Bravo 1, Lincoln 1," Travis radioed out. "Lincoln 1, go ahead." "Bravo 1, we will be ready for the remaining cleaning crew in approximately 15 minutes." He told Jenkins. "Lincoln 1 confirming 15 minutes for the crew," Jenkins said. "Affirmative," he responded. "Lincoln 1, I will advise them," Jenkins told him.

Burke asked Travis if they had identified any of the four inside. Travis said he hadn't heard, but he had been a bit busy. Burke smiled and agreed he had been. "I went through and took the photos, then sent them over to the barn," Jackson told Burke. "Thank you, " he told her. "I am sure they will get the IDs soon." He looked at Travis and could see he was still thinking through everything. He knew he would debrief the team this evening. "I wonder how Matt is doing?" Jackson asked. "Haven't heard from Marcus yet."

Everyone had names, but they were rarely used in public to protect themselves and their families. Lincoln 4; Marcus told them he would tell Travis when he knew about Lincoln 3.

Something came to Travis' mind as he was standing there. He had replayed when Matt got shot. He excused himself and went back inside. He looked around the area where Lincoln 3 had been. There was a sofa and a table. Just beyond that, there was an old chair where Lincoln 4 had pulled him to. He then stood where he had been when the suspect fired from the end of the hall. He pulled a red pointer light from his lower pocket and went to the end of the hall. He stood about where the suspect had been standing, pointing down the hall. "Lincoln 2 come into the building." Jackson stepped in, Burke following. Cheryl,"Stand between the sofa and the table for me." Travis told her. As she moved there, he told her to stop. He had his pointer in place. OK, move two more steps towards the chair. As she moved, his pointer was right beside her. "Stop there," he called out. She stopped. When he looked down the hall, he saw Burke. "Burke, will you move to the wall, then turn around and pop your head around the corner. "I knew it, he was targeting me, but he hit Matt instead," Travis said out loud. Jackson and Burke looked at him and realized why he had brought them in to stand where they did. "Travis, it wasn't your fault," Jackson told him.

Burke walked towards Travis, and he knew what he was feeling; it had happened to him. "I remember when I was on a team, one of our guys got hit. He was in the wrong place at the "right time." "I felt guilty for a long time." He told Travis. Travis looked at Burke, knowing he was feeling guilty for getting Lincoln 3 shot three times; it should have been him. "How did you get past it?" Travis asked. "He and I talked about it. We realized it could have been either one of us in the situation. He never blamed me for it." Burke told him. Travis nodded that he understood. "I will talk with him when I can," Travis said. Burke looked at Travis, knowing the guilt he was feeling over this, and said, "All you can do is talk with him, and I bet you he won't blame you."

As the vans arrived, Travis, Jackson, and Burke moved to the porch. They knew it would take a while to clear the basement. "Lincoln 5, the vans are here. Is it better if they come back to clear the basement?" "It would be better if they did Lincoln 1," Hernandez told him. He directed the agent in charge to go and speak with Hernandez. She had seen the basement and knew more about it than he did. The agent went towards the back of the house and met with Hernandez. He was stunned by the number of items to remove and agreed it would be best to move them to the back. He also called for more vans to assist in the removal. Hernandez radioed Travis, "They agree it is better to offload to the back of the dwelling." Travis heard the sarcasm in her voice. "Copy Lincoln 5," Travis responded. He looked at Jackson and Burke, "She thinks the agent techs are dumb." Jackson started laughing, knowing Hernandez as well as she did. Burke told them they had everything well under control. "When you finish, I would like you all to come to the farm and meet the family," Burke said. But first, he needed to go to the hospital, he explained. "We have five people to see first," Travis concluded. "I understand, great job today. Tell your team they have my admiration for staying so professional today." Burke told them. He turned to leave. "We will, Burke, and thank you," Travis told him.

Burke walked away and headed to the farm. He called Donnie on the way. As Donnie picked up the phone, Burke started talking. "Donnie, I have some news for you and Carol. The last four suspects have been neutralized. The team tried everything they could to take them alive, but they were shot at. I believe David would understand." Burke said. "I figured it would end that way. I wanted them to stand trial but also remember you saying they wouldn't allow themselves to be taken alive." Donnie told Burke. "At least it seems to be finished now," Burke said. The team leader remembers meeting you." He told Donnie. "Oh? What's his name?" "Travis Jacobs is his name," Burke responded. "I don't remember him, maybe if I saw him," Donnie said. "He has a team member, Matt something, in there for a gunshot," Burke said. "Not another injury because of all this?" Donnie sounded upset. "Not your fault, Donnie," Burke told him. Carol grabbed Donnie's hand and told him Burke is right. Chronos brought this on, and they are responsible. "Listen to Carol, Travis may stop by when he is at the hospital to see you," Burke told him.

Donnie looked at Carol and told her he would do his best to remember that. He also knew several were injured and a couple had been killed because of the situation. He was angry because he was laid up in the hospital, and everyone's life had been disrupted because of Timothy and Roger. He felt it was not their fault but his. Donnie didn't care what the reason was; he was too angry to worry about it.

While Travis and his team stood watch over the final cleanup, he knew the crew needed to get some rest. The cleanup finally finished after three hours. They inventoried the entire cache of items and realized there were more weapons, ammo, and grenades than they initially thought. With the amount they had, they could have started a war. The weapons were the same weapons they had been using against the family. This had to be the primary supply location for everything. Travis notified Jenkins of the total amount. She responded, telling him Thank you for everything you and the crew have done.

As Burke left the property, instead of returning to the farm, he drove to the hospital to inform Donnie about everything. He also wanted to check on him. Driving across town, he called Frank to update him. Frank answered with a hello. Burke told him, "I am clear of the property and heading to the hospital to check on Donnie." Frank responded, "I have received some updates since the breach. I am still wondering who is taking the cases of the hostages?"

Burke hadn't thought of who was going to look into the situation, with everything happening so fast. "The FBI can take it on; we have plenty of agents in the area. The hostages might feel more comfortable with a female agent and have taken to Hernandez and Jackson." Burke told Frank. "Whatever we decide, I need to let Anthony know. If you have the resources to help them in place, that might be best." Frank said. "We will take the cases," Burke responded. "I will call Anthony and tell him when we are finished here. How is the team and your agent who was shot?" Frank asked. "He is the other reason I am going to the hospital. I need to let Travis know. I know Matt from a few years ago; he is as tough as Donnie is." Burke told Frank. "That's good, he needs to be a fighter to get back to his strength." "We will have our psychologist check on the team, it is standard after each operation. But with him getting shot, she will look a bit deeper." Burke said. "Understandable," Frank said

There was a brief silence, then Burke asked Frank, "Did you think, years ago, with Donnie's arrest, we would be here?" "I never thought we would face what we have had to face. Donnie has always done his job, but with all this, who knew?" Frank responded. "None of us knew this would happen," Burke responded. "Let me know about Donnie. I will update Anthony on him as well. "Copy that," Burke replied. They ended the call.

As Burke pulled into the hospital parking lot, he noticed the agents' vehicles parked around the lot. He then called Jenkins, and as she answered, he told her he was at the hospital to check on Donnie and Matt. "Pam, I know Donnie is going to ask this: Where are we with determining the threat level on the family now?" "As far as we can determine, the threat has been neutralized. The level is down to almost zero." Jenkins responded to

Burke. "That is good, after everything they have been through, I want it to be zero, but I will take almost zero now. I will tell Donnie and Carol. Have you heard from Marcus or Travis about Matt yet?" Burke asked. "Nothing yet on Matt, Travis just cleared the property. Hernandez and Jackson are heading to the hospital to check in with the female victims and Matt as well. The whole team will probably come in for Matt," Jenkins told Burke. "I am sure they will. Better get in there, I will let you know how everyone is when I get back." Burke told her.

As Burke headed in, an agent approached him. "Any word on Lincoln 3? We heard he got shot." He asked Burke. Burke looked at the agent and asked him for his Identification. Puzzled, he handed it to Burke. Looking it over, he asked the agent how he knew about the agent being shot. Their team was notified by Agent Jenkins to be on alert because of the shooting. Hold on, He stepped away from the agent and called Jenkins. When she answered, "Jenkins, did you advise the detail at the hospital to be on alert because of the shooting?" "I did notify them, yes. Why do you ask?" Jenkins asked. "One of the agents just asked about Matt's status. After everything, I wanted to check." Burke responded. "I felt they needed to know, but never told them to check on him," Jenkins told Burke. "It would not be anything, normally, but I wanted to check." "Understood," Jenkins responded. Ending the call, Burke walked back to the agent; Burke told him, "I suggest you make sure you are doing what you were told to do." "Yes sir." The agent said to Burke.

As he went into the hospital, Burke turned back to the agent. "Hey, I will let you know when I know." "Thank you, sir," he responded. He turned and entered the hospital. When he got into the room, Donnie and Carol were talking. "Did I interrupt you two?" Burke jokingly asked. Looking at Carol, he asked her how Donnie was doing. "Do you know this stubborn man?" Carol asked. "Why are you asking my nurse? Isn't that privileged information?" Donnie told Burke. It helped ease the tension in the room.

Donnie knew the breach didn't go the way he had wanted. "They are going to release him in a couple of more days. That is, if he doesn't hurt the physical therapist first." Carol told Burke. "James and I need to fix the house, after those two attacks we went through," Donnie told them both. "That has been taken care of for you, Donnie; Frank took care of it," Burke told him. "Wait, Frank had the house repaired? Why did he do that?" Donnie asked, not accusingly, but thankfully. "I heard him tell James the other night. You will have to ask Frank that." Burke said. Donnie looked at Carol in disbelief. She looked at him, knowing they had friends, but never imagined Frank would do that for them. "I will call him later to thank him," Donnie told Burke.

"Ok, Burke, give me the news you came here to give me." Donnie turned the topic of conversation. "We breached the property. The four suspects are all dead. They were true to their reputation and fought the insertion team. One of the team members was shot. He is here in the hospital. The team found four female hostages in the property and a large cache of weapons, ammo, and more. The four females are here in the hospital for exams. All four were reported missing by friends and family. At least the women will be safe now, and the weapons and other items have been removed from the streets." Burke finished telling them the overview.

"How bad is the agent?" Donnie asked. "I don't know yet. I need to find his teammate and find out. When I do, I will let you know, and he may still be in surgery." Burke explained. "Yes, let me know. I owe him a visit too." Donnie said. Carol reached over and squeezed Donnie's hand; she heard the angst in his voice as he spoke. Looking at him, she told him the agent would pull through. "I understand he is a lot like you, Donnie. His team leader remembers meeting you." Burke said. "What is his name?" Donnie asked. Burke smiled and said, "You will meet him again; he and the team have cleared the property and are coming here." Burke told them. "Also, the bureau is taking the kidnapping case; we have more resources still here to help Frank out with," Burke added.

Donnie looked at Carol and asked if the Doctor would let him use a wheelchair to see the Agent. Carol said she would get up and head to speak to Julie at the nurse's station.

"OK, Burke, tell me what else is going on with getting the family off the farm," Donnie asked. "Burke smiled; he told Donnie he had called before coming in because he knew he was going to ask. Jenkins told him the threat was near zero now." Burke responded. "When will it be zero?" Donnie asked. There was anger in his voice that Burke picked up on. He knew Donnie was feeling responsible for all of this. "Donnie, we are still checking with the national and international databases, and nothing is coming up. Jenkins told me she wants it at zero as well, but we cannot always find that, no matter how we try." Burke told him. "I have the feeling something is off, and there may still be a threat," Donnie said. "I know your feelings; we will look deeper for you, Donnie." Responded Burke.

Carol opened the door and felt the tension in the room. "What were you two talking about?" She asked. Burke looked at Donnie. "We were talking about when everyone can go home from the farm," Donnie told her. "Oh, and?" She said. "We need to look into a few more things, Carol," Burke said. "Always do, Burke. Will this ever end for us? Our lives have been flipped upside down. All because Donnie did his job." Carol said with some disgust in her voice. Burke looked at Donnie and then at Carol. "It has done that. People have lost their lives. Some are in this hospital recovering from it. Things will be better, and we all hope it will be soon. I cannot let anyone else get hurt or worse because of all this. I swore an oath to protect, and you are my family, too." Burke told Carol. "Burke, I'm sorry this is a lot to deal with. I don't mean to sound like I am blaming you. These people brought this to us; they need to end this." Carol said. "We are checking everything to make sure you are all safe again," Burke said to them both.

Donnie, sitting silent, listening to them. Looking at Burke, Donnie began speaking, "All I have tried to do is protect my family and the families of others. It is time this ends, and we can all go home and pick up the pieces of our lives. Charles and Stacy are expecting a baby. James is preparing for the academy. Michael and Sarah are just starting. Stacy's mom wants to go home and become a grandma. Your people have friends and family to get back to. I need to heal and keep the business open, now that David is gone. I haven't heard from Susan yet. There are enough who have given their lives for this. We will all deal with the aftermath in our own way. Those innocent women who were victimized will suffer because of them. It needs to end for everyone."

Donnie spoke with determination; he was frustrated lying there in the hospital. He felt responsible for getting people killed or injured. He thought that it was entirely up to him. A heavy burden for him to carry. He will work to make sure it doesn't happen again to any of them. Carol, looking at Donnie, knew it all weighed him down. She knew he was feeling responsible for it. "Donnie LaDue, none of this is your fault. It belongs to Roger, and all he did was make you the one responsible. He is guilty of everything. I hope they do the worst they can to him and the others they arrested." Carol's tone turned to an anger she had growing within her heart.

As Carol was speaking, there was an unexpected knock on the door. They all looked towards the door. Burke reached for his weapon out of habit. Donnie saw to it. Carol moved towards Donnie. Donnie said to the person knocking to come in. When he appeared in the doorway, Donnie knew him. It was Jeremiah Thacher, the corporate attorney.

Donnie felt a bit of dread overtake him. "Mr. LaDue, I am Jeremiah Thacher. I was David Samson's corporate attorney. Sorry to bother you, but I need to give you some important papers. Mr. Samson gave me a directive over a year ago. He stated in writing that, if anything were to happen to him, he wanted to legally transfer ownership of the company to you. I hope you are well enough to sign these documents transferring ownership to you." Shocked, Donnie stared at the attorney. He then looked at Carol, and she, too, was standing there in disbelief. Mr. Thacher turned to Burke; I am assuming you are Agent Burke?" "I am," he stuttered in response. "Would you be willing to be a witness to the signing?" He asked Burke. Looking at Donnie, he muttered, "If Donnie wants me to." "Mr. Thacher, I want to read the paperwork before I sign it. Is there anything you'd like to share with me about the transfer? I will need to obtain a business license and look into the legal aspects of everything. I know you were the corporate attorney; I would still like to retain you. Are you willing to continue that partnership?" Donnie said to Mr. Thacher. "Mr. LaDue, the business license and other legal issues will be taken care of by me. I will continue with the company." The attorney said to Donnie. "I will leave the paperwork with you, and I will come back tomorrow to follow up with you." Handing the paperwork to Donnie, Thacher turned and left the room.

Sitting there, looking at the paperwork, Donnie shook his head. He looked at Carol. "What is going on? Did David have a feeling something was going to happen to him?" Donnie said to Carol. Carol could only look at Donnie, processing everything that had just happened. Burke was smiling. He knew Donnie had earned the opportunity to own the business. He would do a great job if he could separate the owner from the security work. He knew Donnie was more of an "in the trenches" kind of boss. Donnie looked at Burke, "Why are you smiling?" He asked him. "You have earned it, Donnie," Burke said. "Carol agrees with me," Burke added. Carol reached over and turned Donnie's face to her, looking into his eyes. She told him, "I do agree with Burke, Donnie."

"Let me look over the paperwork, and I will decide about this," Donnie told them. This was completely unexpected, and Donnie was trying to make sense of everything. He set the paperwork aside for a bit. "Let me know how your agent is doing. Tell him thank you for protecting the family, and I am sorry he took a bullet for me." Donnie said to Burke. "I thank you for taking a bullet for me," Burke told Donnie. "We found paperwork in Timothy's vehicle with a handwritten 'hit list'; it included me and Frank," Burke explained to Donnie. Donnie shook his head and looked at the bed. "This went way too far. Let's hope it is finally over." Donnie said.

I should go and check on Matt. I think he's out of surgery and recovering. I need to speak to Marcus to debrief him. Burke said he would stop by and let them know how he's doing. Turning towards the door, Burke told Donnie he deserved the company. Burke told Donnie, "It was what David wanted; he trusted you."

As Burke approached the operating room, he heard someone talking and recognized a familiar voice. Travis was there, and he assumed the team was too. As he passed the door, he saw the team. He turned in, and Travis approached him. "Matt is out of surgery. The Doctor told us he will recover, but it may take some time. The bullet severely damaged nothing. He won't be able to lift weights for a while, but he'll be fine. Burke nodded. "Is he taking visitors yet?" Burke asked. "The doctor told us we needed to wait until tomorrow," Travis told him. "Okay, I wanted to check with him." He turned to Hernandez and Jackson. "How are the hostages?" He asked. "They are doing as well as expected," Jackson responded. "Okay, I was over speaking to Donnie LaDue. He wanted me to tell Matt thank you. I think you should all see him. He feels responsible for all this." Burke told them. Travis said they would go with Burke. Looking around, he saw Marcus. "How are you holding up?" He asked him. "I am better now that I know Matt will pull through," Marcus responded.

Everyone, but Marcus, headed over to meet Donnie. When they got to his room, Burke went in first and told Donnie that people wanted to talk to him. Donnie told him they could come in. Burke opened the door and invited them in. Travis looked at Donnie and told him they had met a few years ago when Travis was working a case in the area. Donnie said he remembered him. Travis introduced the rest of the team to Donnie. Donnie thanked them for everything they had done to ensure the four suspects never hurt another person. David would want to say, "Thank you." Travis told him they were doing their job. Donnie looked at Burke, "Does he remind you of anyone?" Burke looked at Donnie and smiled. "Yes, he does." Burke chuckled when he said it.

"Travis," Donnie began, "I want to tell you and your team that I am sorry to put you all into the situation that got one of your team members shot. I never thought it would ever come to this." Burke looked at Travis and said, "This is from a man who spent time in the military and over two decades in law enforcement and security. I have known him for years, and he is just like all of you," pointing at the team. "He would rather take the lead in everything than see someone he works with get hurt." Burke looked at the team and watched as they all shifted their attention to Donnie. "Donnie, I remember that about you when we met. You offered to take the lead on the investigation we were doing because of the people we were dealing with." Donnie nodded. "I knew about the group and what they were doing. You showed up and wanted to do things that could harm you or your people, or worse. You finally listened to me." Donnie told Burke. Burke just smiled. "A brick wall calling out another brick wall." He told Donnie.

Carol looked at both of them. She knew they admired each other because their work was almost identical. "Knock it off you two. Not in front of the kids," she pointed at the team and laughed. This made them all laugh. "Carol is right; I have seen it myself. Donnie taught me, and Burke taught me almost the same things, just a bit differently," Travis told the team.

"Donnie has forgotten more about doing the job than most people will ever learn," Burke said. Travis nodded in agreement with Burke's comment.

"I am right here, everybody, I can hear all the nonsense you are spewing," Donnie told them. Carol looked at Donnie with "that look." "Donnie, you have never sought attention, but it is now being discussed in front of you. The nurses are aware of everything you do. Yes, they talk about you, too," Carol told him. "Oh, great, that makes it all better," Donnie said. "Julie has even told me a few things," Carol retorted.

"Now this contract. It is a bit overwhelming. If I ever put this in a book, no one would believe it. Life is crazier than fiction." Donnie had grabbed the contract and shook it as he spoke. "Can I look it over? I was a law major in college." Travis told him. Pausing, Donnie then handed it to Travis. Looking it over, Travis smiled. "There is nothing in here that should stop you from signing it. Right here, you are also receiving the bank accounts that David set up over the past 25 years. Did you see the amounts in each of them, Donnie?" Donnie reached out to retrieve the paperwork. When he looked at the figures, his eyes widened. "There are things the company can do with that. I had no idea he had that set aside." Donnie said. "I didn't see any restrictions on the money in there. I would ask your attorney if he can see anything." Travis told Donnie.

Donnie showed it to Carol. "I am going to make you a partner in the business, and we can run the company together," Donnie told Carol. She looked at Donnie and knew he was serious. She knew once Donnie made up his mind, there was no going back. Something she both admired and hated about him was his stubbornness. "OK, we will co-own the company." She told Donnie. "I will talk with Mr. Samson tomorrow when he comes by. He will need to clarify some things and rewrite it to include you." Donnie told Carol. "Thank you, Travis," Donnie said to him. "Donnie, you deserve this. All the years and the positive changes you made in the company over the years, you earned it," Burke told him.

Donnie looked around the room at the faces of each person, ending with Carol, who had always encouraged him. She had supported him since the beginning. She had been his rock, his lie detector. He admired her, adored her, loved her from the start. "Ok, everyone, I will accept the company. Burke, all I have ever done is work for the people, working for David. We occasionally disagreed, as I saw a need to do more for our people. He didn't always see my point, but as I let him think through it, he would later agree." That thought brought a smile to Donnie's face. "Now it's up to you and me to work through everything," Donnie said, looking at Carol. "I need you to be my truth detector still." He told her. "I always have been, weirdo." She said playfully. Giggles could be heard. Smiling Donnie told them she had called him a weirdo from the beginning. "She has always thought I was a weirdo." He said, smiling.

Burke turned to the team, "It's time for us to go back to the farm. Jenkins needs to debrief you on today's breach. Marcus should stay here." As Burke was speaking, Travis' phone started ringing. It was Marcus answering. He heard Marcus tell him, "Matt is in recovery. The doctor said he will be good. He recovered from the surgery better than he expected. I will update you as soon as I know."

"That is great news. I need you at the farm as soon as possible. Jenkins wants to figure out what happened today. We're leaving in a couple of minutes," Travis told Marcus. "Copy that, boss," Marcus responded.

Ending the call, Travis shared the news with the team. They all made their comments. Travis then told them it was time to drive to the farm. Turning to Donnie, he said, "I'll come back and check in on you." "I'd like to speak with your Agent when he can," Donnie replied to Travis. "I think that's a good idea, Donnie," Travis answered. I will have Marcus come to see you and give you Matt's room number. Those two are like twins, so be prepared to deal with their antics. I wouldn't trade any of this team for anyone else. We are family like you, and your people are to you." Travis said.

"Travis, I appreciate you and all of you. We'll have to get together when there's time," Donnie told him. "I agree," the team nodded. "I'll see you then," Travis told Donnie.

Carol was sitting and watching everyone. She felt like it was a reunion, as if they had all known each other for a long time. It felt peaceful and familiar. Looking at them, Carol began, "I want to tell each of you, I cannot thank you enough for what you have done. It's amazing how strangers can come in and change a life. The shared experiences of all this now bind us together. I want you all to know you have a place to stay anytime you need it. Burke, please give them all our address. We are family. Please, never forget that." Her voice faded off as she spoke. Her thoughts were turning back to the time she met Donnie. Looking at him, her look was telling him she was serious, and he knew she meant it. She was also making sure he agreed with her. Donnie smiled and turned to the team, "Just don't expect Christmas gifts every year." Donnie said.

Carol got up and went to each team member, hugging them and telling each one, "Thank you." Travis was last. "Take care of them; they are your responsibility, and they look to you to get them all home safely." Turning to the team, she said, "Take care of him; he is like that guy over there." She pointed at Donnie. "Both of them will do what it takes to get you each home safely, no matter what it takes. I didn't always understand that, but I do now."

Carol's eyes began to tear up, knowing she had a second chance to show Donnie how much she had always loved him. She also now understood why she feared losing him for so long; he would give his life to protect those he cares about. He has always been that kind of man. She knew who he was, and it scared her at first, but now it is the meaning of his love for her and others. Travis held her for a minute longer, feeling her emotions welling up. He looked at her, he whispered, "My mom was just like you. She knew who my dad and I were. We give everything for those we care about. Thank you,

Carol, for being you." "You can call me Mom; I feel like you're one of my sons, Travis. Make it back home to us." "Ok, Mom." He told her.

Separating, they looked at each other. She turned to the group and apologized for the tears, wiping them away as she stood there. "Get to the farm and take a shower!" As they laughed, each told her, "Yes, ma'am." As they left, they all said they looked forward to Christmas this year. That made Carol smile as she turned to Donnie, "We need to be healthy too, mister." He nodded, smiling at her.

After they left, Donnie told Carol he needed to get the paperwork signed. We will help the company grow again and ensure that everyone remains employed. As he was speaking, there was a knock at the door. "Come in," Donnie said. As the door opened, he saw Susan standing there. She looked worn out, and He asked her if she was OK. Susan nodded and told him she was glad he had made it. "Donnie, do you think everything is over now?" She asked him. "According to Burke and Pam, it seems to be." He responded. "What is going to happen to the company now?" Susan asked him. But as she did, Donnie noticed there was something off about her tone of voice. He passed it off as fear, but there was something different in the tone. "It appears that David left it to me," Donnie said. "That sounds good. When did he set that up?" She asked. "Apparently over a year ago." He said. Her expression was one of deep thought and concern, as if she were confused. "We will make it work; I am adding Carol to the ownership." He told Susan. Looking at Carol, she said, "That was a good idea." Susan's face didn't look happy, though, they both noticed. "I will go to the office and get things for you both. I should get going." She told them. Turning to leave, she asked about David's funeral. "We will get that figured out," Donnie said. "Okay, boss." Was her reply as she left the room. As she walked down the hall, her expression changed. She had a look of determination on her face. Anger was forming within her. After all that had happened, she was still ready to do what she needed to do. No matter the cost now. It was up to her.

Donnie and Carol looked at each other. They both had questions. "She is probably just processing everything," Carol said. Donnie nodded. He felt uneasy, as if something were off, but maybe that was the reason; she was processing everything.

"Can you see if they can get that wheelchair?" Donnie asked Carol. As she left the room, Donnie was thinking about the way Susan had acted. She seemed to be faking. He needed to find out why. He picked up the papers and re-read through them.

He reached for his phone as Carol came into the room. He dialed the phone. Mr. Thacher, I have decided to sign the paperwork once Carol is added to the ownership. I need to see everything. The financials, the bank accounts. I need to review them as soon as possible. We also need to figure out David's funeral arrangements. He deserves to be at peace. Also, are you still the corporate attorney?" "Yes, sir, I am, and I will bring the documents to you later today," Thacher said. "Thank you, we need to get busy getting everything in order," Donnie told him. "Sir, I have heard many stories from Mr. Samson about you; it would seem they are all true," Thatcher told him. "I may be worse than what you have heard, Mr. Thatcher," Donnie said with a smile. Can you have everything ready by 4 pm today?" "Yes sir." He told Donnie. "I will have everything prepared. We will need a witness to the signing." "I will have someone here." He told Thatcher. "Ok, sir." He responded.

Donnie looked at Carol and the wheelchair. "This thing just needs to be temporary. I hate it already," he said. Carol laughed. "I knew that," She said. "That was Mr. Thatcher; I told him we are signing the paperwork, and what we need to look over as we get going. Also, we need to get everything prepared for David's funeral." Donnie said. Working himself over to the edge of the bed, he groaned as he lowered his shot leg. It hurt, but he was going to get out of this room. "Stubborn to the core, mister!" Carol told him. "Always have been love." He retorted. She smiled, saying, "I have known all that from the day we met." Once he was in the chair, she leaned forward, hugging his shoulders. "You need a bath, mister."

Wheeling him through the door, she asked, "Where to?" "Let's go outside," the FBI agent replied. The agent followed them out, one of them on the radio advising the other agents that they were coming out. Julie told Carol she would call the Doctor and inform him where they were; he was on rounds and wanted to talk to Donnie.

Once outside, Donnie saw the six agents moving around to cover them. He looked at Carol, and he was smiling for the first time in what seemed like a long time. The sunrise was appearing, and a crispness filled the air. He felt so alive. He realized the hospital's sterility had made him cranky. He didn't dare tell Carol; he knew how she would respond. As he took in the cool morning air, his phone rang.

"Dad, how are you doing?" James asked him as he answered. "I am finally outside of that room. Your mom is wheeling me around." Donnie responded. "I heard a rumor about you two now owning the company," James told him. Putting it on speaker, he responded. "For once, a rumor about me is true." He told James. "That is great for you both," James replied. "The attorney is bringing over the paperwork later for us to sign. I want you here when we do. Can you make that happen, and will you tell Frank I want him to be the witness on the signing?" Donnie told him. "I will tell Uncle Frank, Dad. How are you doing?" James asked. "I will have your mom answer that," Donnie said. "Your father is being your father." She said. They all laughed. "Also, I hear you have adopted another eight kids," James playfully told them. "Have you met them?" Carol asked. I have, and Travis calls me the baby. He also told me he was looking forward to my graduation from the academy. They are all planning to be there." Donnie looked at Carol; they smiled at each other. "Sounds like you'd better get through it then." Donnie poked at him with a smile. "I got this Dad." He responded. "You sound like your mom," Donnie said. Carol playfully smacked his shoulder. "The doctor is going to meet with us this morning. Afterward, we will let you know what he says." Donnie told James. "Sounds good. Enjoy your freedom. Remember, your nurse is going to make you get better. Are you ready for that, Dad?" James asked. "Young man!" Carol playfully said to James. "I am, I can't think of a better nurse for me. She will try to hold me back, but we all know how that will work." Donnie said, preparing to get smacked again. "I will let you guys go. I know you still have some ground rules to figure out. Good luck with all that." James said. As they ended the call, Donnie looked at Carol and asked, "Are we going to fight over this?" You know better than that; you never win a fight." She said with a smile. "Yes, I know," he said. They both giggled.

As the sun was coming up, the doctor found them outside. He looked at Donnie and told him he had some news about his progress. He told him he was healing better than expected. He needed to continue with the physical therapy for at least 6 months. That way, he could have full use of the leg. Donnie stopped him. "Could? You said I could use my leg fully. You know what I don't, you?" "Donnie, I have known who you are for years. I also know what you do for a living. You should get full use, but I also need to tell you it may never be one hundred percent again." The doctor looked at him as he spoke. He was as blunt and to the point as Donnie was. "Well, Donnie started, it's time to change that. I will get it back completely." The doctor looked at Donnie, smiled, and said, "I have no doubt you will." Looking at Carol, you were right, he is stubborn." "That he is," she said. He looked back at Donnie and said he needed to get on with his rounds. "Donnie, I will look over everything, and I think you can be released tomorrow. Talk with you later." He left and went back inside.

Donnie looked at Carol. "It seems I have been the conversation piece with a lot of the staff over the years." He said. "As many times as you have been in here, both for yourself and for others, yes, they have talked about you over the years. But most of the time, it has been that they admire you." She told him. "You have been the face of the company; you have been a leader who showed others how to lead. I have always been proud of you and have told everyone that, even after the divorce," She concluded. Donnie studied her face; he saw both pride and sadness there. He loved her for that. "I believe you. You have always been my support and strength. Thank you for that love." Donnie said. "Weirdo," Was her response, and she started pushing him along the sidewalk.

When they returned to the hospital room, Julie was waiting for him. She told him he could shower for the first time. The wound was healing well, and the doctor said if he was careful, he could shower. "Here is a fresh gown for you. There is just one stipulation: you have to use the bench in the shower." Carol told Julie he would. He had no choice. They both laughed at him as he tried to protest. "Yes, ma'am," was all he could say. That made them laugh again. Carol looked at him and said, "Get to it, mister. Julie and I will be here if anything happens." He rolled himself to the bathroom and shut the door. The two of them looked at each other and started laughing again. "I heard that!" he said. Carol took the gown and placed it near the door for him, then went back to talk with Julie.

"He is a stubborn man for sure," Julie told her. "That is one of the things I adore about him, though," Carol said. Julie looked at her. They had known each other for several years now. She had heard about Donnie, seen him a few times, but never had the opportunity to spend much time around him. He was who she thought he was. Julie asked about the FBI and why they had been around. As Carol explained things, Julie felt both relieved and nervous. She had seen law enforcement stay in the hospital, but not the FBI. "This should be over soon," Carol told her. "You act like this is just a normal day in your life. Federal officers standing watch over you two." Julie told her. "This had been building for several years. This is the end of it now." Carol told her. Julie looked puzzled. "Donnie has always just done his job. He busted a guy years ago, which led to an international situation. That guy's brother decided Donnie needed to pay. Donnie stopped a theft in a storage unit that led back to the brother. He figured it was time to repay Donnie for his brother's arrest years ago. The FBI agent Burke has known us since the first arrest. He heard about everything that happened and decided to help. Then those same people killed Donnie's boss. It has been a hectic 2 weeks for all of us." Carol told Julie. "I cannot imagine what you have all been through. I would be a total wreck." Julie responded. Carol smiled and said, "I was in the beginning, but I knew Donnie would never let us get hurt. That is who he is." They heard the shower shut off. They heard Donnie fussing about the leg. As the door opened, he wheeled himself back to the bed. "That was harder than I thought it would be," Donnie told them. "I need to look at your leg and replace the bandages with fresh ones," Julie told him. "Let me get back in the bed first, please," Donnie said. He looked at Carol, and she told him he could do it himself. "Thanks, nurse, I see how this is going to be. Getting up, he placed some weight on the leg and straightened it. He then stepped the two steps to the bed, swung around, and sat down. Carol smiled. "If you are going to heal, Mister, you need to want it." She told him. Julie removed the bandages and examined the wound; it was still a bit damp. She decided to leave it open for a bit before covering it again. After Julie left, Carol examined the wound. It was healing nicely. Donnie had always healed quickly. He may not need the covering much longer, except when he is around other people, Carol thought. When Julie came back in, she looked at the wound and turned to Carol. She asked, "What do you think of the area? Should it be covered?" Julie knew Carol had taken a look at it. Carol smiled and said she wasn't the nurse in charge, but to her, it would be best to leave it open so it could heal faster. Julie smiled and said she agreed. They left it open for now. "Donnie, just don't tear the stitches," Julie told him.

As she was leaving, she told them she was off in a couple of hours, but the doctor would be in to look at it. And talk with them about when Donnie can go home. Carol looked at Donnie and told him he would probably be released in the next couple of days. He told Carol he was ready to leave now. She just smiled and nodded. "He can be so stubborn," she thought to herself.

After they ate, the doctor came by. He looked at Donnie's leg and liked the progress of his healing. Then he asked him to stand on it. You want me to stand on it?" Donnie asked. "Yes, Donnie, stand on that leg." The doctor told him. As Donnie moved to the edge of the bed, he grimaced as he rose and put weight on it. Carol could tell he was in pain, but held her opinion, knowing the doctor was only gauging how much longer he needed to heal fully. She knew it was a good sign that he could stand on the leg so soon after the surgery. This was only the fourth day after surgery, and he was already able to put some weight on it.

The doctor told Donnie he could sit back on the bed again. "That is a good sign, Donnie. I know that hurts, but I also know you will push yourself to get better. I was hoping you could work with the physical therapist for another four weeks, and we will review your progress then. For now, I will release you into the care of your nurses, starting tomorrow. One more night to see how that test makes you feel." The doctor told them. "Call for a ride for tomorrow, and we'll get the paperwork prepared for discharge," He concluded.

After the doctor left, Donnie confessed that standing on it was worse than when he got shot. Carol looked at him and told him to suck it up. He will be back to full strength sooner than they all think. "I know how you are, Donnie, but I want you completely healthy too." She said. "I need to be at the office and start getting everything taken care of," Donnie said. "Donnie, we will have everything brought over, or I will pick it up and bring it to you," Carol told him. "Now we need to be cleared to go home." He told her.

As Donnie lay back, his leg was throbbing. It hurt, but he wanted to see how much pain he could manage before asking for medication for the pain. He knew he needed to be completely healed and return as close to 100 percent as possible. He knew Carol would insist on it.

He reached for her hand, and as he held it, he looked at her, thankful she was there with him. He had missed her more than he realized. All the years apart had faded away for him. She was an amazing woman, and he realized how much he adored her. He had never blamed her for leaving. He understood why. He was overwhelmed by the emotional attachment he still had for her. "What are you thinking?" She asked him. "Just how lucky I am to have you here with me." He responded.

As he was saying this, there was a knock on the door. He asked who it was. A male voice said it was Marcus. Donnie told him to come in. As Marcus entered, he explained who he was and that Matt was finally awake and was asking to speak to Donnie. Donnie looked at Marcus and saw James standing before him for just a second. Donnie told Marcus he would like to meet Matt. Carol went and got the wheelchair for him. They followed Marcus to Matt's room. As they entered, Matt smiled at them.

Marcus introduced everyone. Donnie looked at Matt and asked how he knew him. Matt said he remembered hearing Donnie's name and that he had been shot and was probably still in the hospital. Donnie wheeled himself closer to Matt and extended his hand. As they shook hands, Donnie told him thank you and that he was sorry he had been shot to protect him and the family. Matt looked at Donnie and told him he would be up and moving in no time. The doctors had said that because of the amount of upper body muscle Matt had, the bullet hadn't hit any vital organs. That his body armor slowed the bullet enough not to injure him worse. "I have a broken rib, and the muscle needs to heal," Matt told Donnie. "How are you doing?" Matt asked. "I stood for the doctor; I can get out of here tomorrow," Donnie said. "I hope to leave in a couple more days," Matt said. Marcus told Donnie, "I hear this guy is a lot like you, stubborn and eager to get back to work." "Not another one." Carol jokingly said. "That is a good way to be," Donnie commented. "I will see you guys at the farm soon, then." Donnie smiled as he said it. "We should let you get some rest. I will tell you both what I told your team: we are now family. You are always welcome at our house." Donnie said. Matt looked at Donnie. "From what I have heard about you two, I am honored. What do I call you now, Mom and Dad?" Donnie smiled and said that was fine by him. Carol agreed. Burke told them that Matt no longer had parents. They had passed away when he was young. The team had been his only family for the past couple of years. "When you get to the farm, I will introduce you to your other siblings," Carol told him. "I look forward to meeting them," Matt said. "We should let you rest for now," Carol told Matt. As she turned the wheelchair around, Matt told Donnie he would take a bullet if it meant keeping the family safe. Donnie stopped the wheelchair and spun it around. He looked at Matt and said, "It won't come to that, we have all ended the problem." Matt nodded. Donnie and Carol then left the room.

Matt looked at Marcus. "That man can be scary. It was like he was staring into the back of my skull." "I have heard he can be quite intimidating. The team said he and Travis are a lot alike. Leading from the front and making sure everyone gets home safely." They sat in silence for a bit. Marcus turned the TV on and found cartoons to watch. As Matt watched, he thought about what Donnie said. "We have ended the problem," kept echoing in his mind. "At least for now," Matt thought.

When they returned to Donnie's room, he called James and said the attorney would arrive around 4 pm. He also asked if Frank was coming. "Dad, we will be there. Burke may ride along; he needs to talk with the other two agents there." James said.

At about 3:34 pm, there was a knock at the door. Donnie asked, "Who is it? "James, Frank, and Burke." He heard James on the other side of the door. He told them to come in. Once inside, James came to his parents and hugged his mom. He turned to his dad, looking him in the face before asking how he was doing. "I'm ready to get out of here," Donnie told him. "But I stood on my own feet today," Donnie added. Donnie looked at James, and James turned to his mom, seeking confirmation. Carol laughed and told James, "Yes, son, he is telling you the truth." Frank and Burke smiled as Donnie looked at James. "Oh, I see how it is. You two need to stop that." He said

At almost 4 pm, there was a knock at the door, and they heard a voice say, "It's Mr. Thacher." "Come on in", Donnie said to him. As he entered, he had a folder in his hand. It included the new document for the change of ownership, the records Donnie had requested, and one more document. As Thatcher approached Donnie, he handed the folder to Donnie. He looked and saw the others. Agent Burke, Captain, and this must be James. He named each of them. "I am Jeremiah Thatcher, the company attorney. Mr. LaDue needs at least one non-relative to witness these documents. I will ask both Mr. Burke and the Captain to be witnesses to Mr. LaDue's signature. Are you willing to be witnesses?" They both told him they were. "Very well, Mr. LaDue, as you can see, I have rewritten the paperwork to reflect the addition, and as Carol, I took the liberty to use LaDue as her last name." Looking at Donnie and Carol as he made this statement. They both said yes, that's correct. "There are four areas I need both of you to sign the document. Each has a line with your names printed below. Feel free to review it. Included is my fee schedule as well, which will need your initials." Thatcher said to them.

Donnie reviewed the paperwork, signed where he found his name, and initialed it near the fee schedule, then passed it to Carol to review. As Carol looked over everything, she noticed the fee schedule. She looked at Donnie, and it seemed like an expensive fee. He nodded to her. She went ahead and signed it, initialing where needed. Thatcher then turned to Frank and Burke, handing them his pen, and they signed it as witnesses. "Thank you all, Mr. LaDue. I will make four copies of this. One for each of you and Mrs. LaDue, one for the court, and one for your company. Are you going to change the name of the company or keep it as The Keepers Security Services?" Thatcher asked. "We will let you know, Mr. Thatcher," they replied. "Very well, sir, I will leave you now." He then left the room.

Donnie watched the door close and looked at the paperwork in front of him. It was surreal to him. What made David prepare for something like this? He moved the contract to the side and looked at the account forms Thatcher had left. The numbers are at the bottom of each page. The total came to a number Donnie never thought he would see. Adding the amounts up on his phone, he realized several million dollars were staring back at him. Shock took over his mind. How did David set aside that much money? He wanted to know but also knew it would be figured out later.

Everyone in the room was staring at Donnie as he looked over everything. He looked up at them and began, "Carol, we're going to need to make some changes in the company. We can talk later. I need your input about my ideas." Carol smiled and told him they had time to do that.

Looking at Frank and Burke, he said, "You two have worked hard to keep this family safe. Your people have gone through a great deal to protect us. Thank you for that. We are more than friends, we are brothers. Please share a message with your people. Tell them I am humbled by their sacrifices and willingness to help our family." They just looked at Donnie and told him they would pass the message on.

"James," he began, "I have watched you grow into the man you are today. I am proud of you and how far you have come. As you start your career, know that we will all be here for you and walk with you through the ups and downs. These two care about you as much as Mom and I do. Plus, all these new siblings you have now will stand with you. Son, I love you and haven't told you that enough." Donnie looked at James as he said it.

"I am blessed beyond anything I deserve to have all of you walking with me in this life. Thank you each for that." Donnie said.

The room was silent for a few minutes. Carol reached over and felt Donnie's forehead. "What are you doing, love?" Donnie asked. "Checking to see if you have a fever." She responded. Looking at her, he smiled. "I know I've become all mushy, but I'm serious. This change for us has caused me to realize I will never be the same. We will never be the same."

Burke looked at Frank and then back at Donnie. "In all the years I have known you, I have seen you as a leader like no other. You have always put other people first. Those you worked with and those you were called to help. You have the power to change people's lives. Now you can." As Burke finished, he looked at Frank, who was nodding. "Donnie, you deserve this opportunity. You have earned it." Frank told him.

"Burke, will you go get with your guys and let me know how Matt is doing?" He said to him.

"Frank, can I ask you to go back to the farm and make sure everyone is good?" He asked.

They told him they would, and both left the room. Donnie then turned to James and Carol and told them the total he had calculated. Both of them stared at him as he told them the amount. Shocked, Carol asked him if he had added it correctly. He smiled, handed her the papers, and asked her to verify the calculations. He never imagined he would have access to over $8 million. The company could use upgrades. He can now make those upgrades.

As Carol added everything up, she understood the shocked look on Donnie's face when he saw the number. "Your numbers are correct, Hun." She handed the papers back to Donnie.

"James, please understand," Dannie said. "You have a lot of influential people watching you now. Law enforcement knew you as my son; now they see you as you. You have earned the change. I am proud of the way you have stepped up to take charge of your own life. Everyone will be there at your graduation from the academy. They will be there to honor you." Donnie smiled and put his hand on his son's shoulder. "No pressure, bud." He turned to Carol, "We have some work ahead of us."

She looked at him, "First, we need to get you healed and back to one hundred percent healthy. James agreed with her.

"Okay, you two, quit ganging up on me," Donnie joked.

"Donald James LaDue!" Carol grabbed his hand as she said it.

"Yes, ma'am," was all he could say.

James laughed and said, "Big tough guy, bested by my mom."

"She scares me more than a big, angry, bad guy with a gun!" Donnie said. They laughed.

www.ingramcontent.com/pod-product-compliance
Lightning Source LLC
LaVergne TN
LVHW010639110826
845149LV00014B/2891

* 9 7 9 8 9 9 5 1 7 0 9 4 5 *